TEEN TITANS GO!

VOLUME 1

PARTY, PARTY!

Sholly Fisch Amy Wolfram
Merrill Hagan Ricardo Sanchez
Writers

Jorge Corona Ben Bates
Lea Hernandez Chris Gugliotti
Artists

Jeremy Lawson Ben Bates
Lea Hernandez Chris Gugliotti
Colorists

Wes Abbott
Letterer

Dan Hipp
Cover Artist

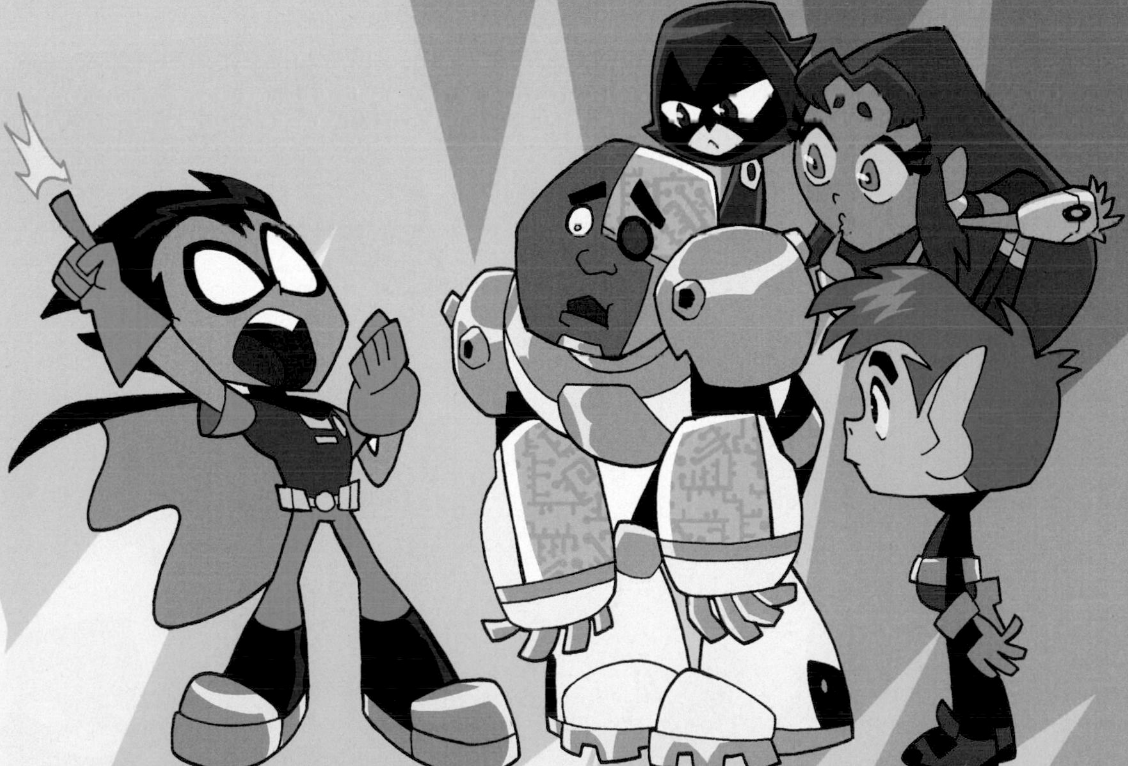

ALEX ANTONE Editor – Original Series   JEB WOODARD Group Editor – Collected Editions
PAUL SANTOS Editor – Collected Edition   STEVE COOK Design Director – Books   SARABETH KETT Publication Design

BOB HARRAS Senior VP – Editor-in-Chief, DC Comics
PAT McCALLUM Executive Editor, DC Comics

DIANE NELSON President   DAN DiDIO Publisher   JIM LEE Publisher
GEOFF JOHNS President & Chief Creative Officer
AMIT DESAI Executive VP – Business & Marketing Strategy, Direct to Consumer & Global Franchise Management
SAM ADES Senior VP & General Manager, Digital Services   BOBBIE CHASE VP & Executive Editor, Young Reader & Talent Development
MARK CHIARELLO Senior VP – Art, Design & Collected Editions   JOHN CUNNINGHAM Senior VP – Sales & Trade Marketing
ANNE DePIES Senior VP – Business Strategy, Finance & Administration   DON FALLETTI VP – Manufacturing Operations
LAWRENCE GANEM VP – Editorial Administration & Talent Relations   ALISON GILL Senior VP – Manufacturing & Operations
HANK KANALZ Senior VP – Editorial Strategy & Administration   JAY KOGAN VP – Legal Affairs   JACK MAHAN VP – Business Affairs
NICK J. NAPOLITANO VP – Manufacturing Administration   EDDIE SCANNELL VP – Consumer Marketing
COURTNEY SIMMONS Senior VP – Publicity & Communications
JIM (SKI) SOKOLOWSKI VP – Comic Book Specialty Sales & Trade Marketing
NANCY SPEARS VP – Mass, Book, Digital Sales & Trade Marketing   MICHELE R. WELLS VP – Content Strategy

TEEN TITANS GO! VOLUME 1: PARTY, PARTY!

DC Comics, 2900 W. Alameda Avenue, Burbank, CA 91505
Printed by LSC Communications, Kendallville, IN, USA. 2/23/18. Fourth Printing.
ISBN: 978-1-4012-5242-7

Library of Congress Cataloging-in-Publication Data

Fisch, Sholly.
Teen Titans go!. Volume 1, Party, party! / Sholly Fisch, Lea Hernandez.
pages cm
Summary: "Based on the hit TV show, feast your eyes on this all-new, all-ages comic book series! Join Robin, Starfire, Beast Boy, and Raven as they display their unique brand of hijinks, mayhem and justice! But giant pizza monsters are not the only dastardly and delicious villains on the menu... so dig in, Titans! Collects TEEN TITANS GO! #1-6"-- Provided by publisher.
ISBN 978-1-4012-5242-7 (paperback)
1. Graphic novels. I. Hernandez, Lea, illustrator. II. Title. III. Title: Party, party!
PZ7.7.F57Te 2015
741.5'973--dc23
2014049015

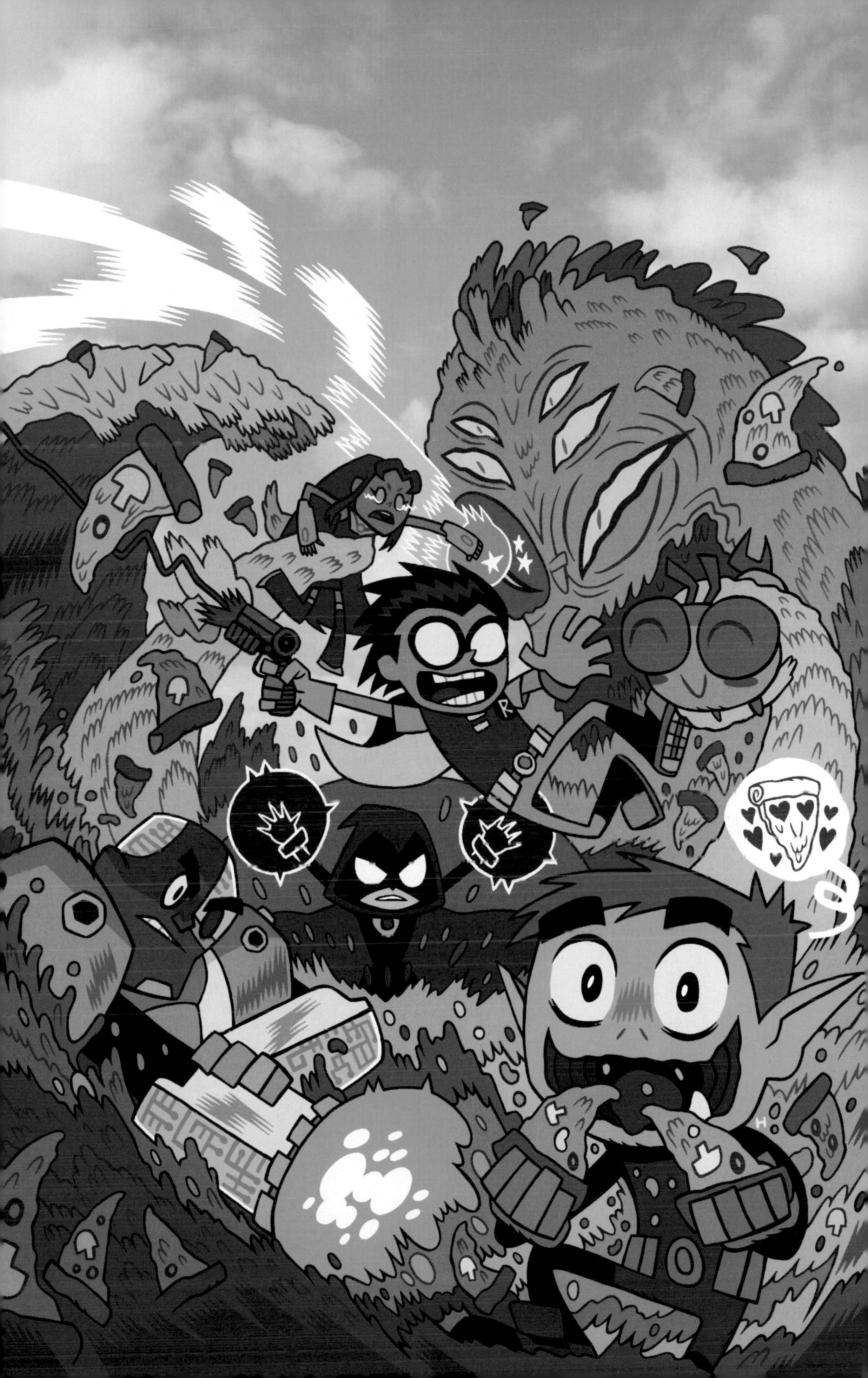

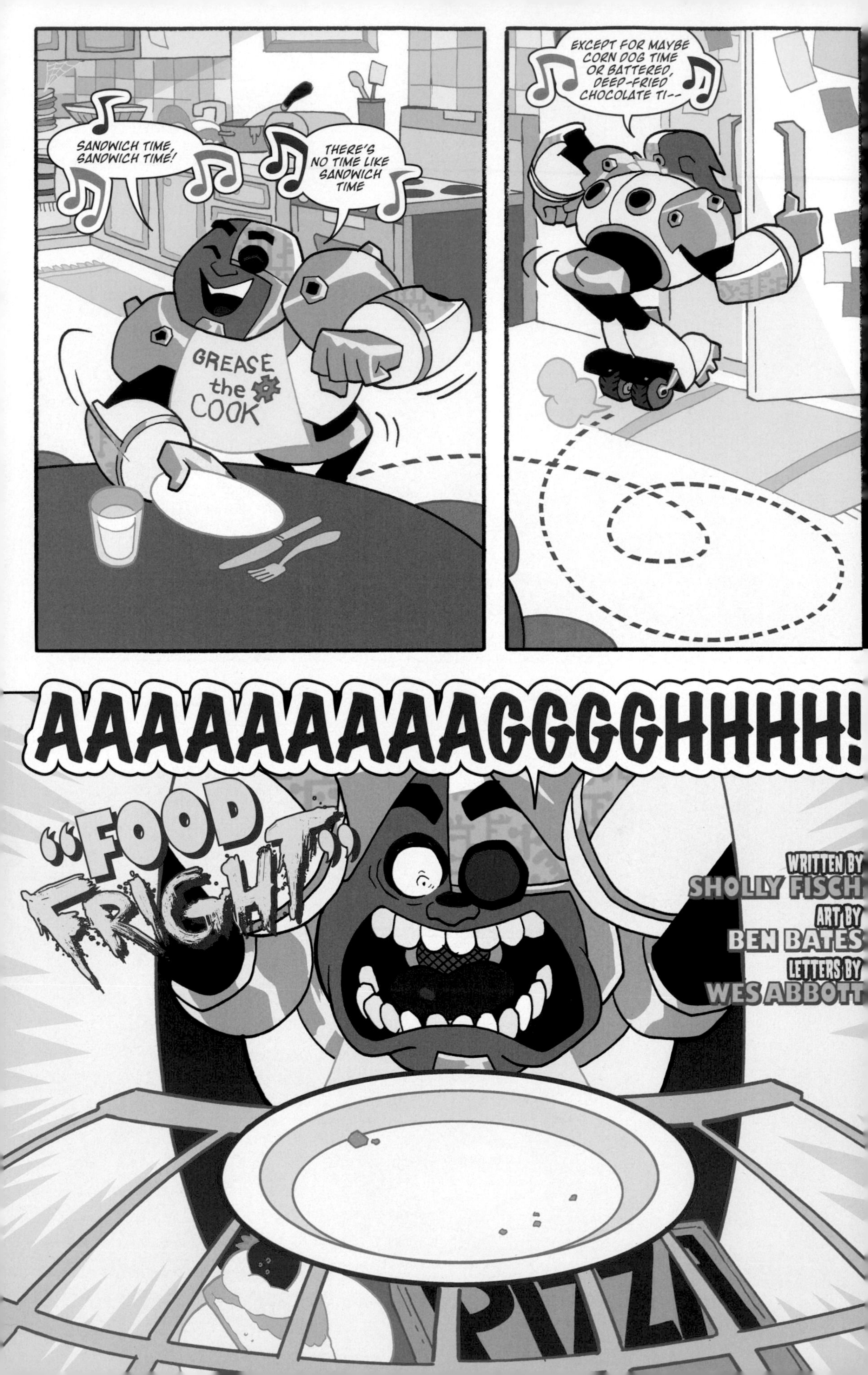

SANDWICH TIME, SANDWICH TIME!
THERE'S NO TIME LIKE SANDWICH TIME
GREASE the COOK
EXCEPT FOR MAYBE CORN DOG TIME OR BATTERED, DEEP-FRIED CHOCOLATE TI--
AAAAAAAAAAAGGGGHHHH!
"FOOD FRIGHT"
WRITTEN BY SHOLLY FISCH
ART BY BEN BATES
LETTERS BY WES ABBOTT
PIZZA

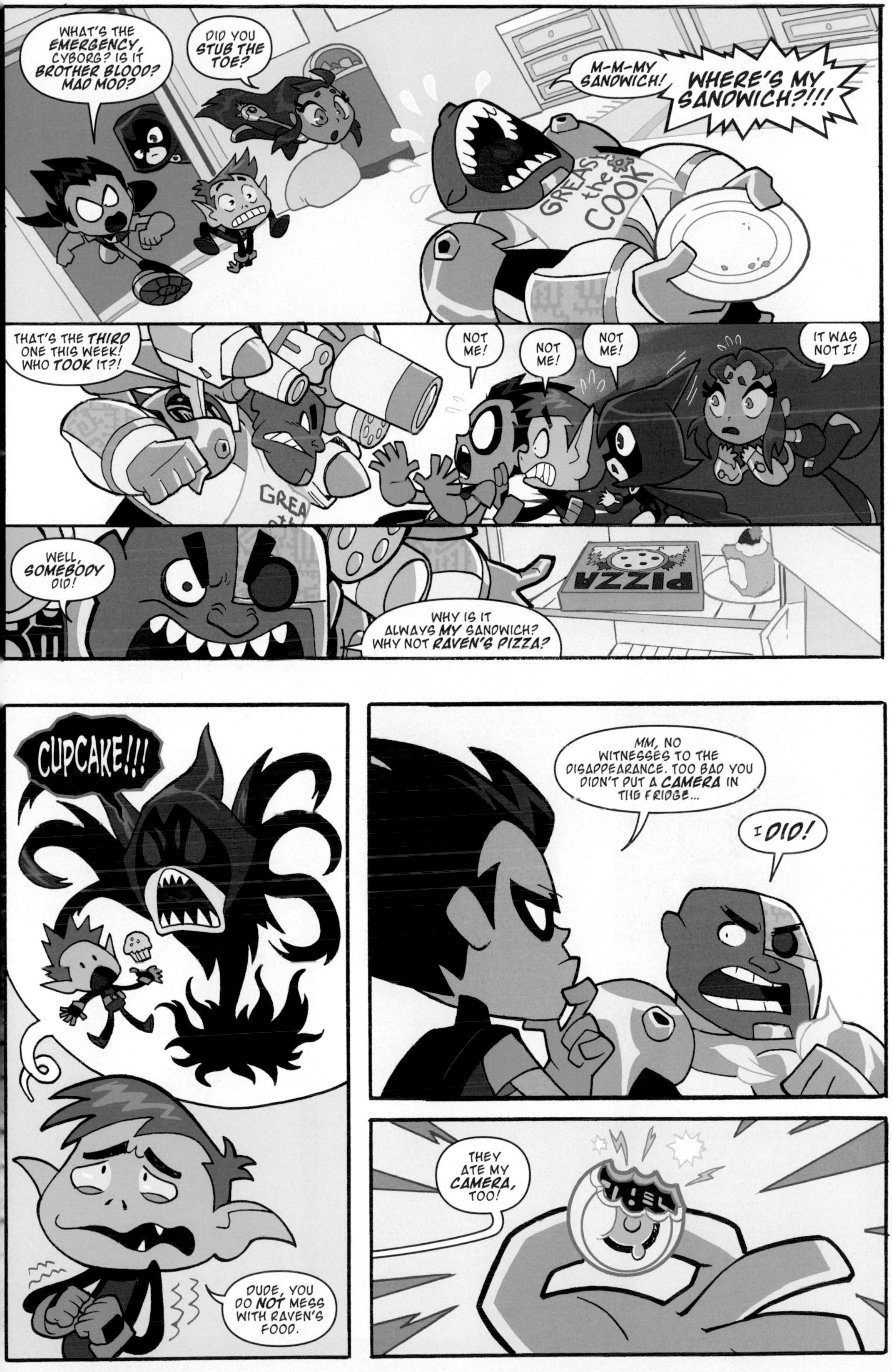
WHAT'S THE EMERGENCY, CYBORG? IS IT BROTHER BLOOD? MAD MOD?
DID YOU STUB THE TOE?
M-M-MY SANDWICH!
WHERE'S MY SANDWICH?!!!
GREASE the COOK
THAT'S THE THIRD ONE THIS WEEK! WHO TOOK IT?!
NOT ME!
NOT ME!
NOT ME!
IT WAS NOT I!
WELL, SOMEBODY DID!
WHY IS IT ALWAYS MY SANDWICH? WHY NOT RAVEN'S PIZZA?
PIZZA
CUPCAKE!!!
DUDE, YOU DO NOT MESS WITH RAVEN'S FOOD.
MM, NO WITNESSES TO THE DISAPPEARANCE. TOO BAD YOU DIDN'T PUT A CAMERA IN THE FRIDGE...
I DID!
THEY ATE MY CAMERA, TOO!

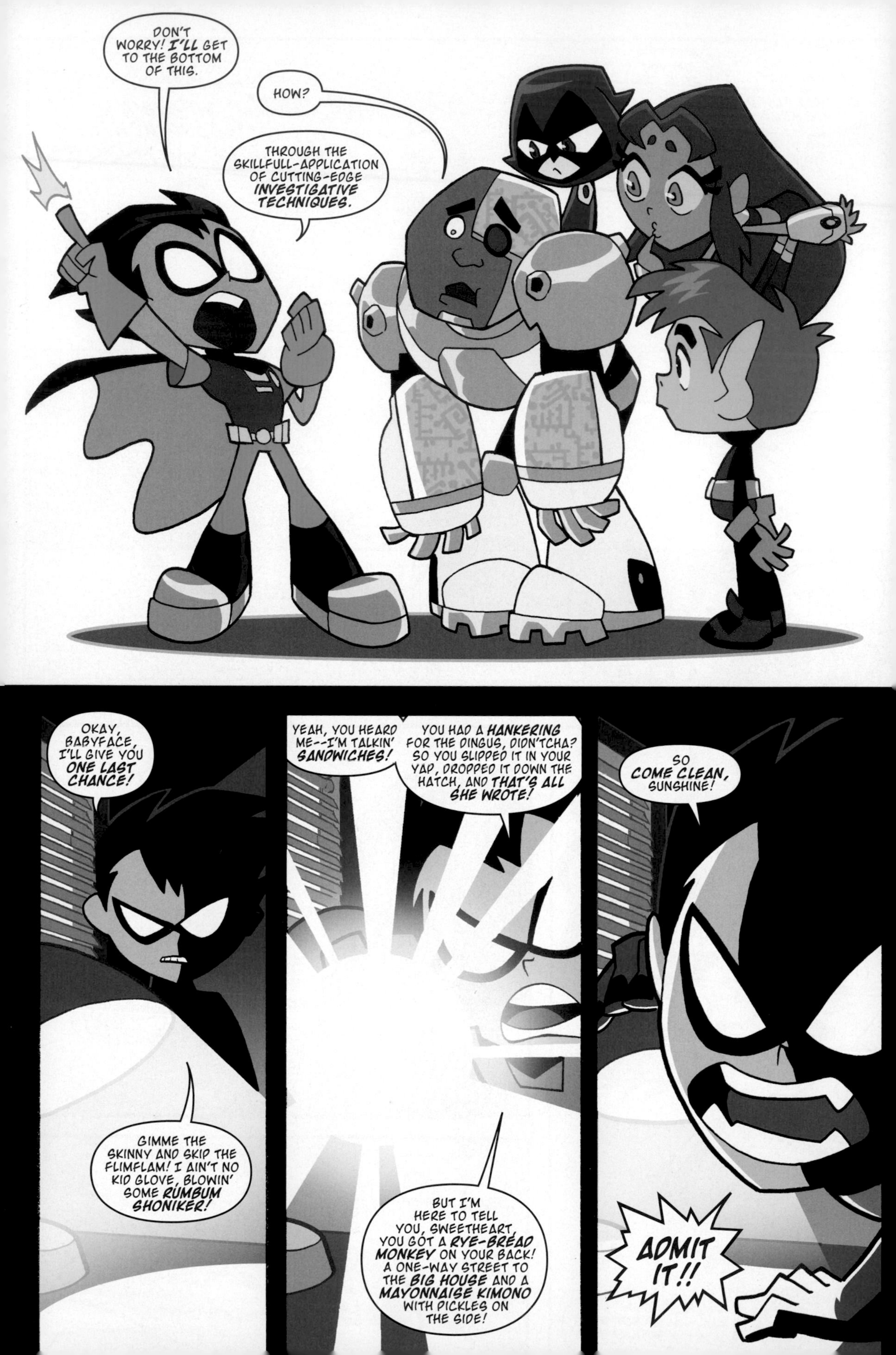
DON'T WORRY! I'LL GET TO THE BOTTOM OF THIS.
HOW?
THROUGH THE SKILLFULL-APPLICATION OF CUTTING-EDGE INVESTIGATIVE TECHNIQUES.
OKAY, BABYFACE, I'LL GIVE YOU ONE LAST CHANCE!
GIMME THE SKINNY AND SKIP THE FLIMFLAM! I AIN'T NO KID GLOVE, BLOWIN' SOME RUMBUM SHONIKER!
YEAH, YOU HEARD ME--I'M TALKIN' SANDWICHES!
YOU HAD A HANKERING FOR THE DINGUS, DIDN'TCHA? SO YOU SLIPPED IT IN YOUR YAP, DROPPED IT DOWN THE HATCH, AND THAT'S ALL SHE WROTE!
BUT I'M HERE TO TELL YOU, SWEETHEART, YOU GOT A RYE-BREAD MONKEY ON YOUR BACK! A ONE-WAY STREET TO THE BIG HOUSE AND A MAYONNAISE KIMONO WITH PICKLES ON THE SIDE!
SO COME CLEAN, SUNSHINE!
ADMIT IT!!

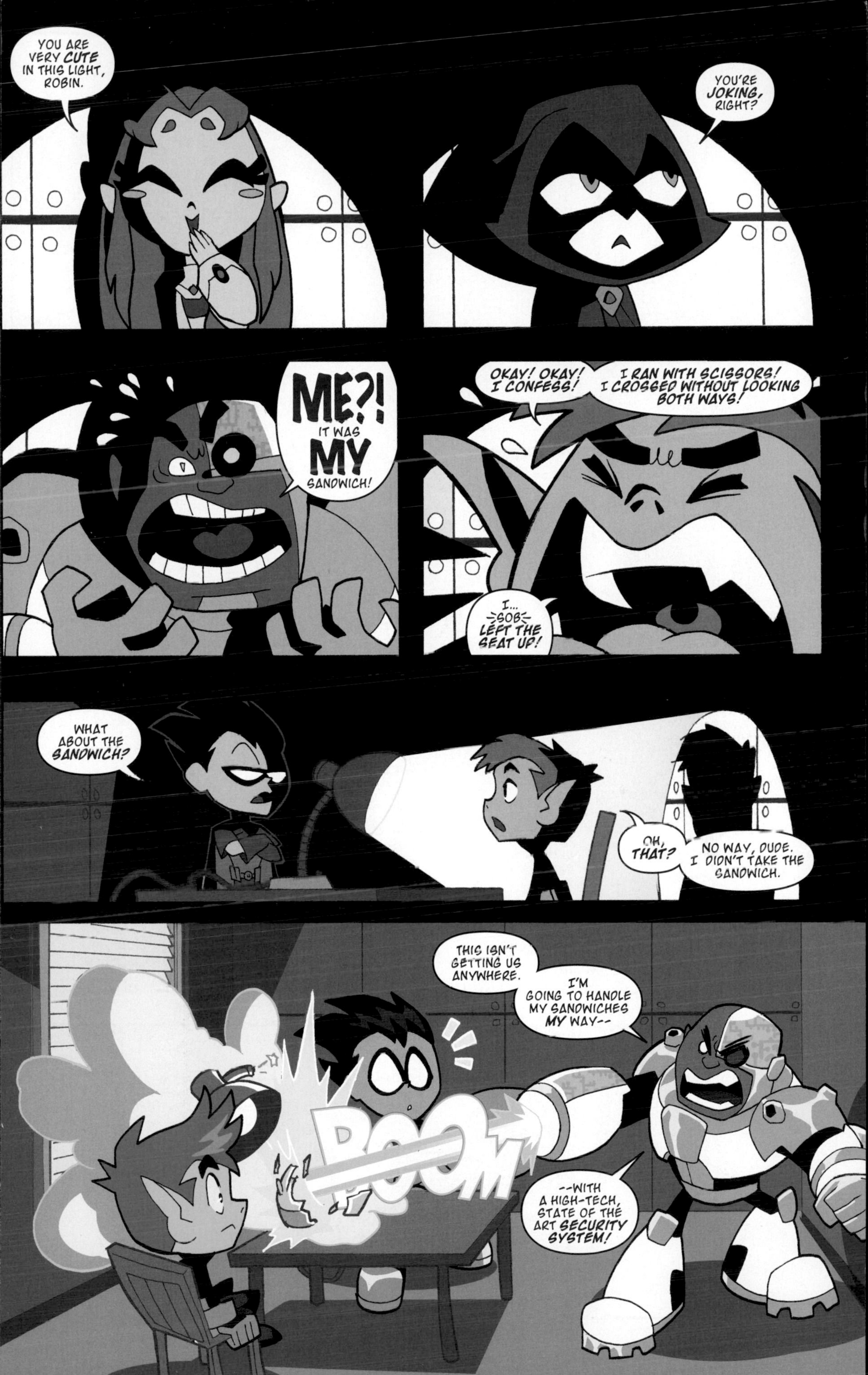
YOU ARE VERY CUTE IN THIS LIGHT, ROBIN.
YOU'RE JOKING, RIGHT?
ME?! IT WAS MY SANDWICH!
OKAY! OKAY! I CONFESS!
I RAN WITH SCISSORS! I CROSSED WITHOUT LOOKING BOTH WAYS!
I... SOB LEFT THE SEAT UP!
WHAT ABOUT THE SANDWICH?
OH, THAT?
NO WAY, DUDE. I DIDN'T TAKE THE SANDWICH.
THIS ISN'T GETTING US ANYWHERE.
I'M GOING TO HANDLE MY SANDWICHES MY WAY--
BOOM
--WITH A HIGH-TECH, STATE OF THE ART SECURITY SYSTEM!

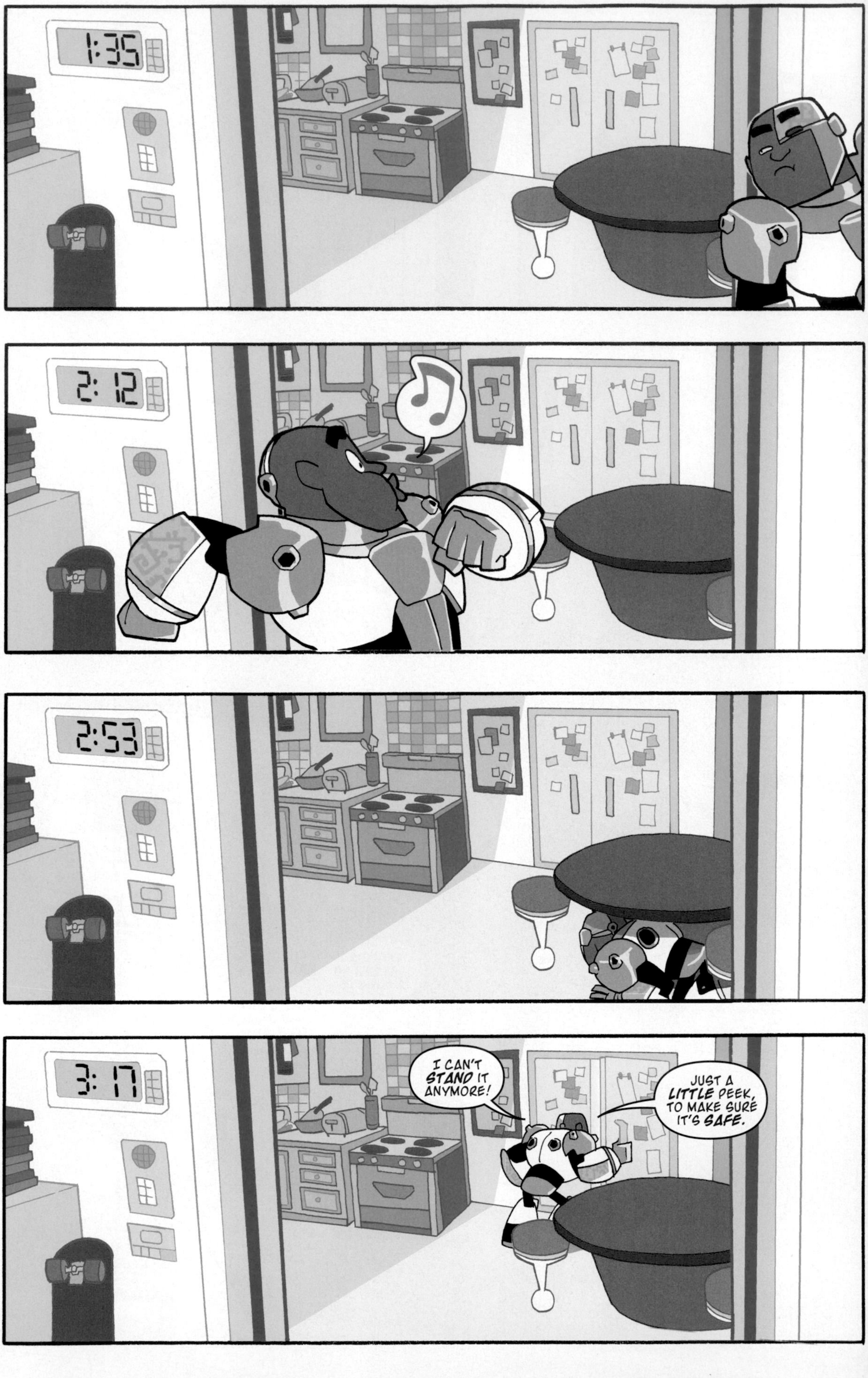
1:35
2:12
2:53
3:17
I CAN'T STAND IT ANYMORE!
JUST A LITTLE PEEK, TO MAKE SURE IT'S SAFE.

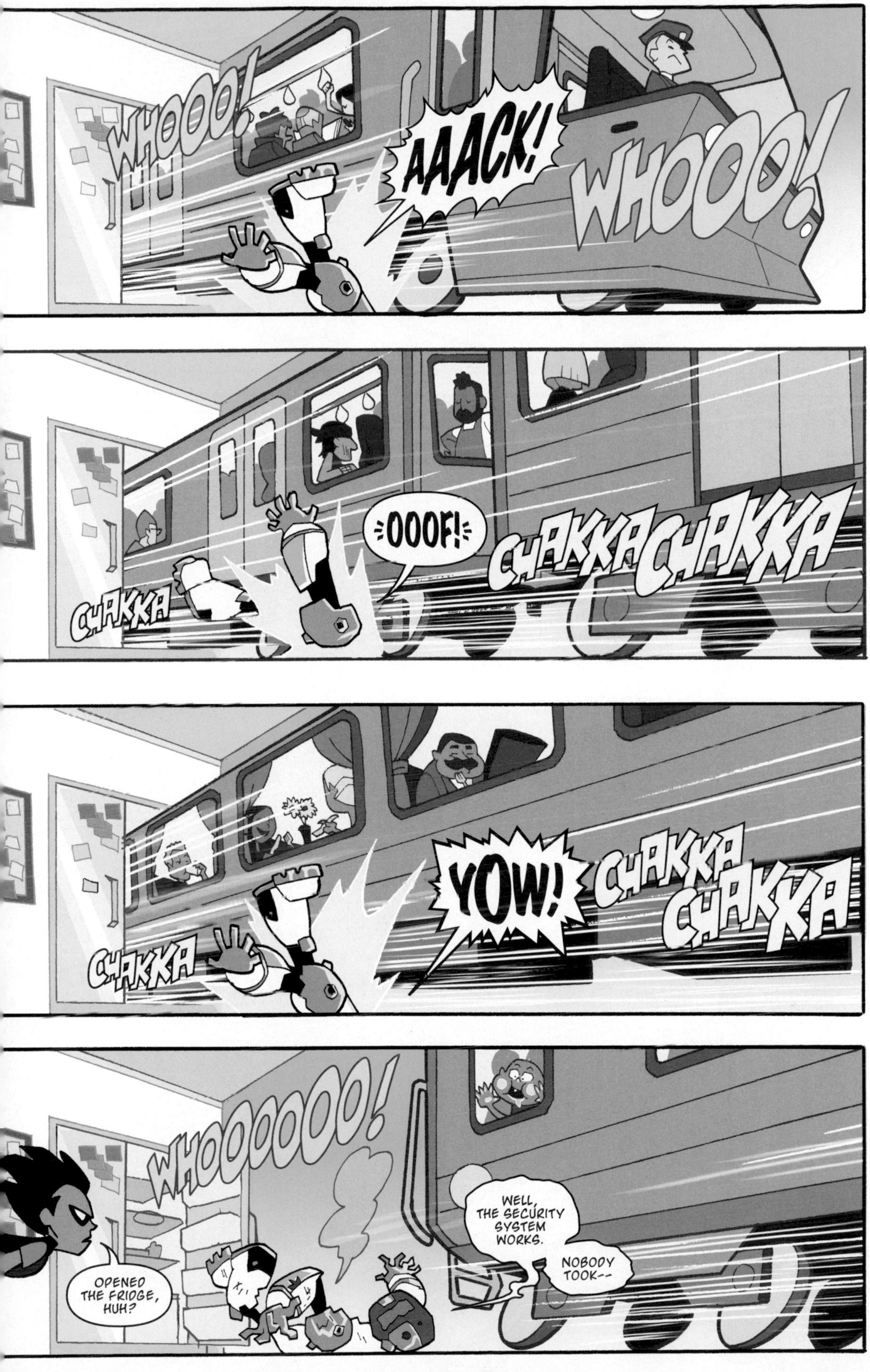
WHOOO!
AAACK!
WHOOO!
OOOF!
CHAKKA
CHAKKA CHAKKA
YOW!
CHAKKA
CHAKKA
CHAKKA
WHOOOOOO!
OPENED THE FRIDGE, HUH?
WELL, THE SECURITY SYSTEM WORKS.
NOBODY TOOK--

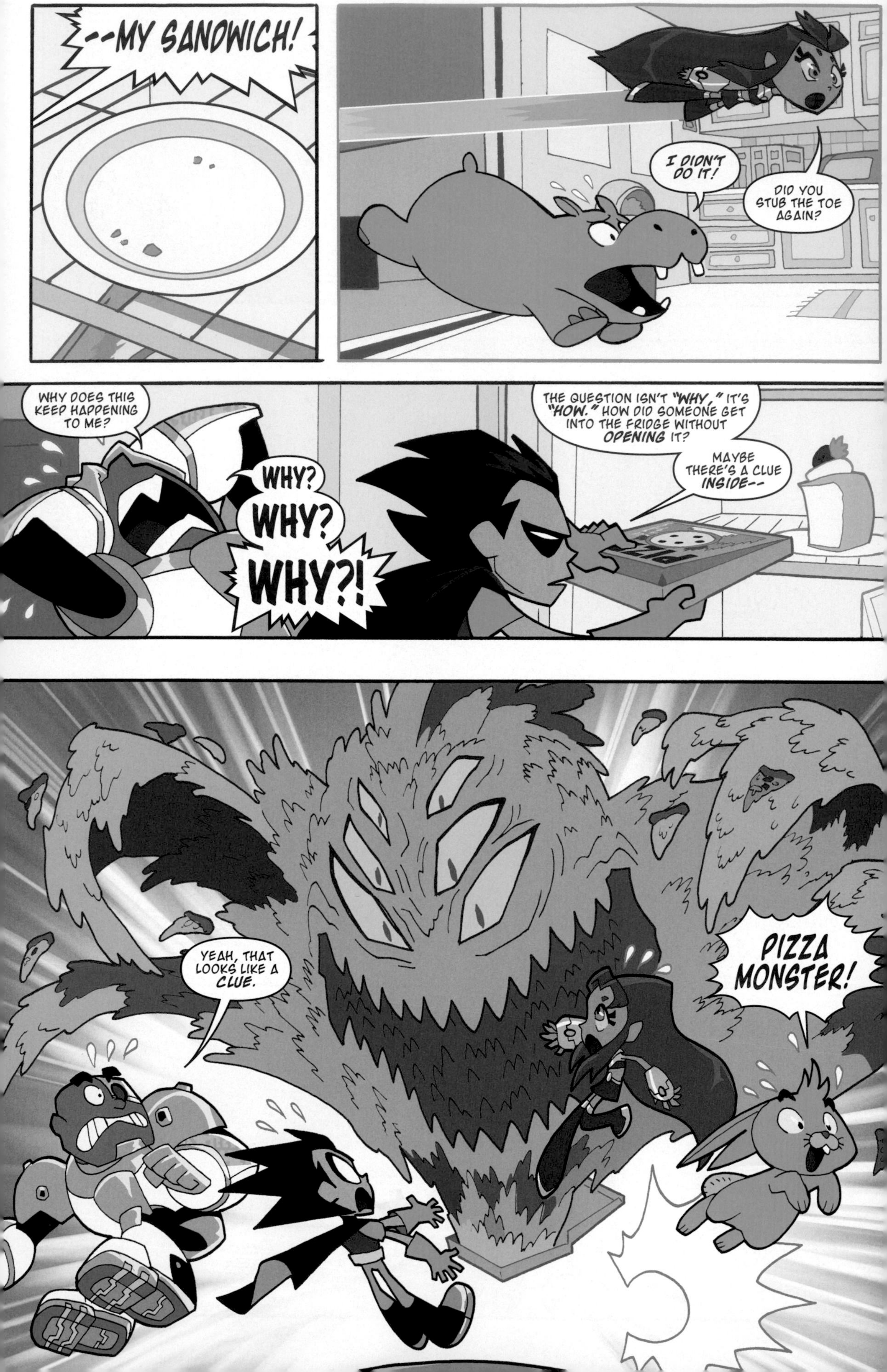
--MY SANDWICH!
I DIDN'T DO IT!
DID YOU STUB THE TOE AGAIN?
WHY DOES THIS KEEP HAPPENING TO ME?
WHY?
WHY?
WHY?!
THE QUESTION ISN'T "WHY," IT'S "HOW." HOW DID SOMEONE GET INTO THE FRIDGE WITHOUT OPENING IT?
MAYBE THERE'S A CLUE INSIDE--
YEAH, THAT LOOKS LIKE A CLUE.
PIZZA MONSTER!

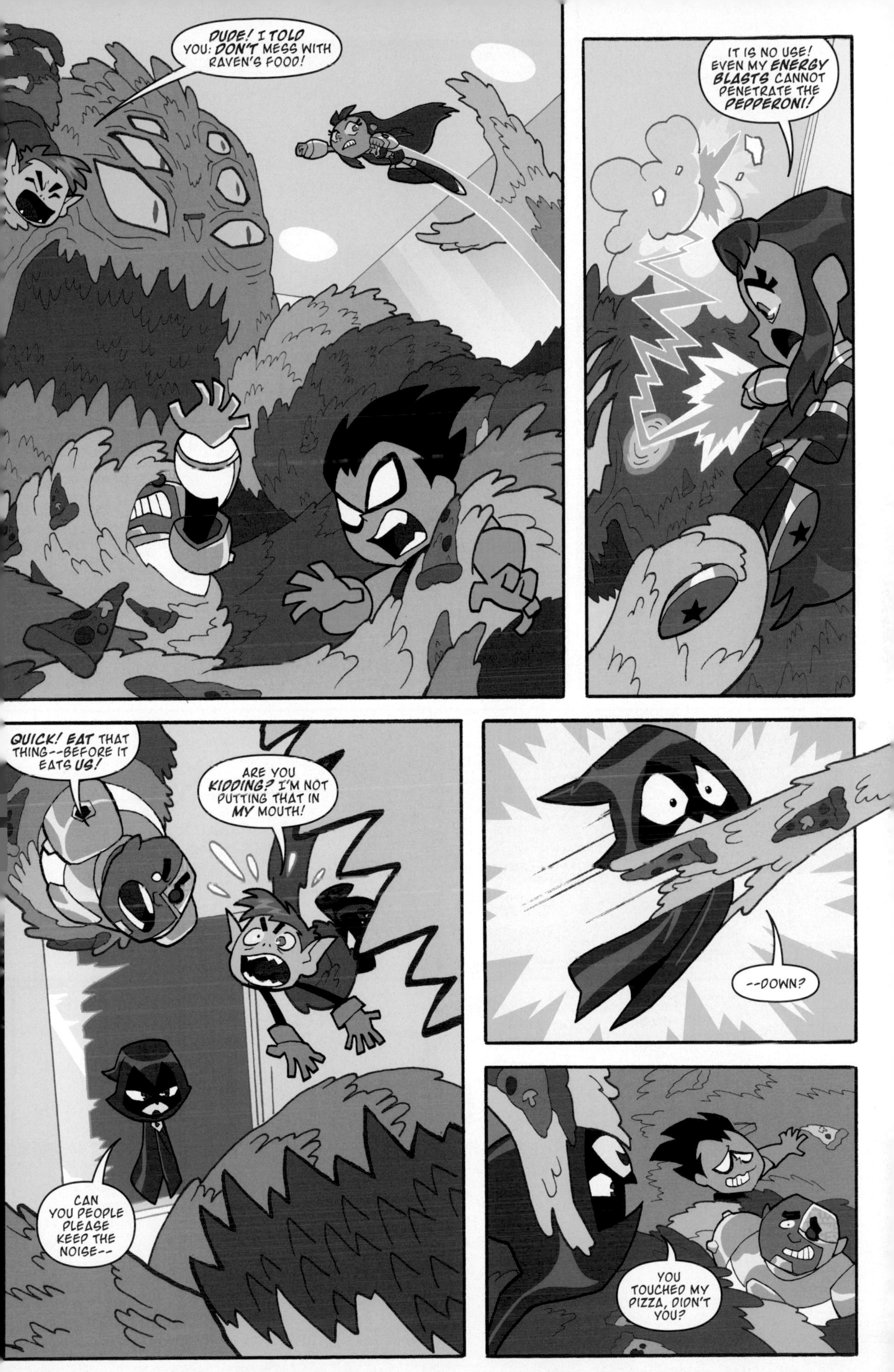
DUDE! I TOLD YOU: DON'T MESS WITH RAVEN'S FOOD!
IT IS NO USE! EVEN MY ENERGY BLASTS CANNOT PENETRATE THE PEPPERONI!
QUICK! EAT THAT THING--BEFORE IT EATS US!
ARE YOU KIDDING? I'M NOT PUTTING THAT IN MY MOUTH!
CAN YOU PEOPLE PLEASE KEEP THE NOISE--
--DOWN?
YOU TOUCHED MY PIZZA, DIDN'T YOU?

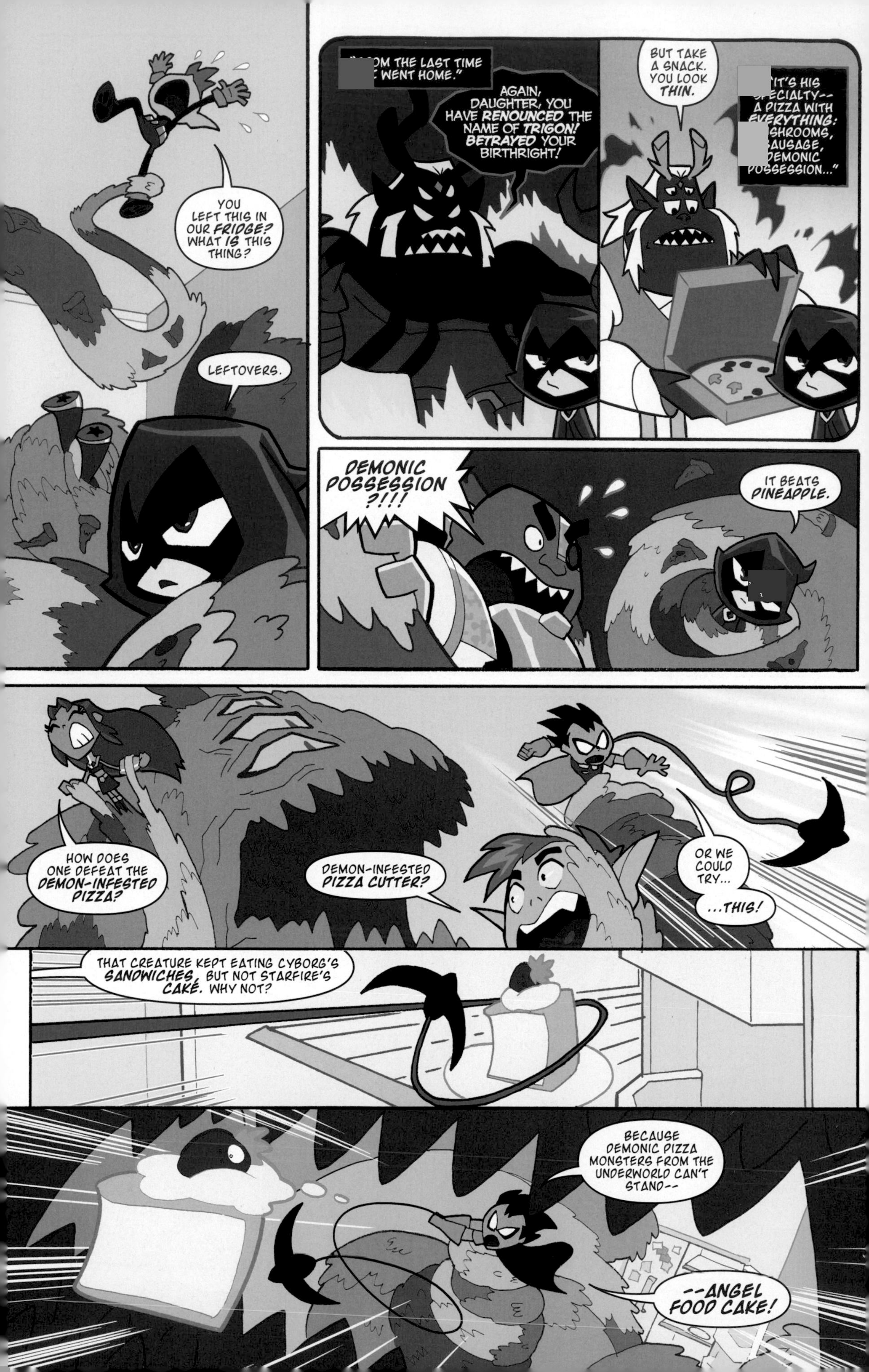
YOU LEFT THIS IN OUR FRIDGE? WHAT IS THIS THING?
LEFTOVERS.
“[redacted]OM THE LAST TIME [redacted] WENT HOME.”
AGAIN, DAUGHTER, YOU HAVE RENOUNCED THE NAME OF TRIGON! BETRAYED YOUR BIRTHRIGHT!
BUT TAKE A SNACK. YOU LOOK THIN.
[redacted]IT'S HIS SPECIALTY-- A PIZZA WITH EVERYTHING: [redacted]SHROOMS, SAUSAGE, DEMONIC POSSESSION...”
DEMONIC POSSESSION ?!!!
IT BEATS PINEAPPLE.
HOW DOES ONE DEFEAT THE DEMON-INFESTED PIZZA?
DEMON-INFESTED PIZZA CUTTER?
OR WE COULD TRY...
...THIS!
THAT CREATURE KEPT EATING CYBORG'S SANDWICHES, BUT NOT STARFIRE'S CAKE. WHY NOT?
BECAUSE DEMONIC PIZZA MONSTERS FROM THE UNDERWORLD CAN'T STAND--
--ANGEL FOOD CAKE!

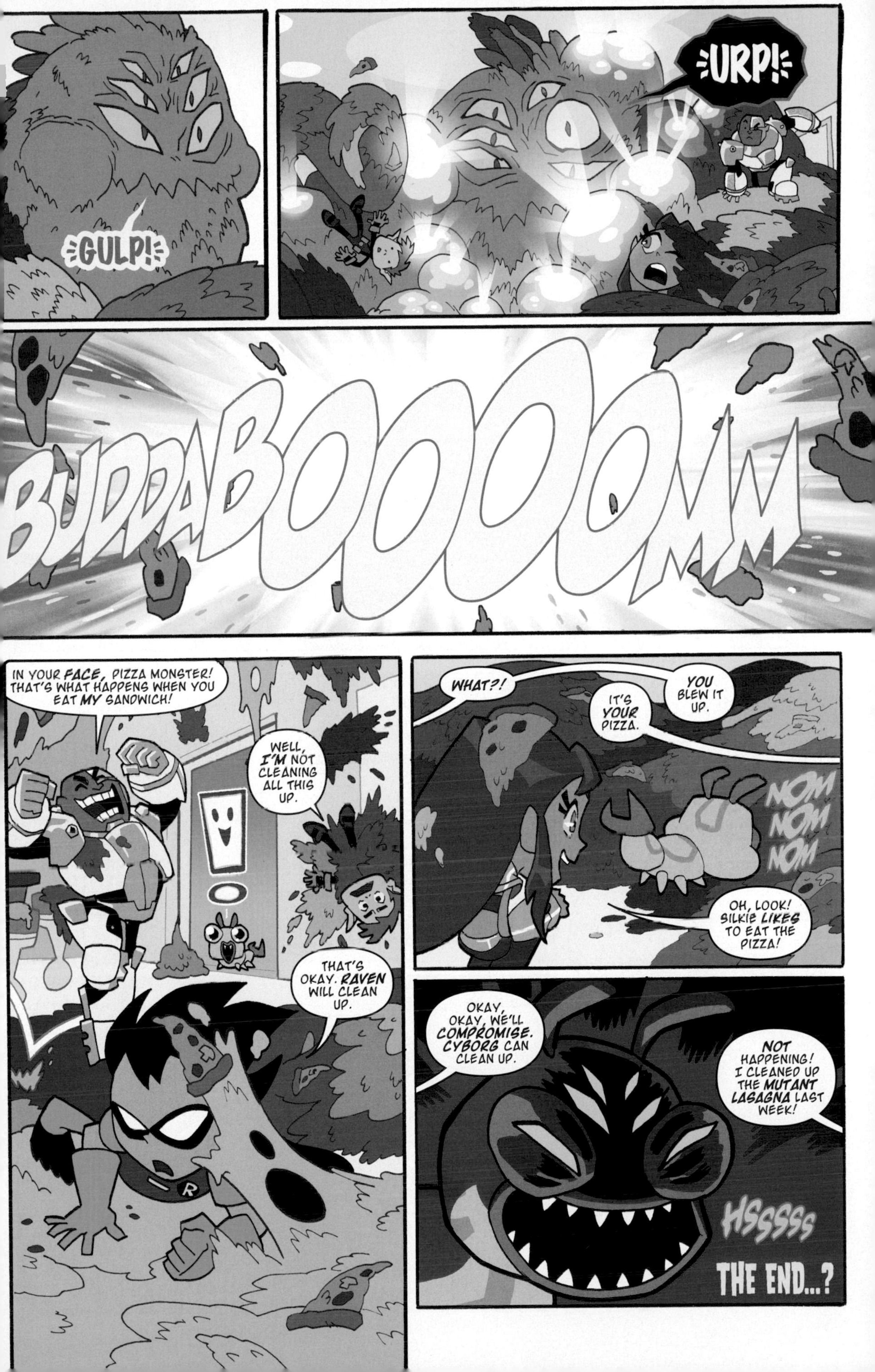
GULP!
URP!
BUDDABOOOOOMM
IN YOUR FACE, PIZZA MONSTER! THAT'S WHAT HAPPENS WHEN YOU EAT MY SANDWICH!
WELL, I'M NOT CLEANING ALL THIS UP.
THAT'S OKAY. RAVEN WILL CLEAN UP.
WHAT?!
IT'S YOUR PIZZA.
YOU BLEW IT UP.
NOM NOM NOM
OH, LOOK! SILKIE LIKES TO EAT THE PIZZA!
OKAY, OKAY, WE'LL COMPROMISE. CYBORG CAN CLEAN UP.
NOT HAPPENING! I CLEANED UP THE MUTANT LASAGNA LAST WEEK!
HSSSSS
THE END...?

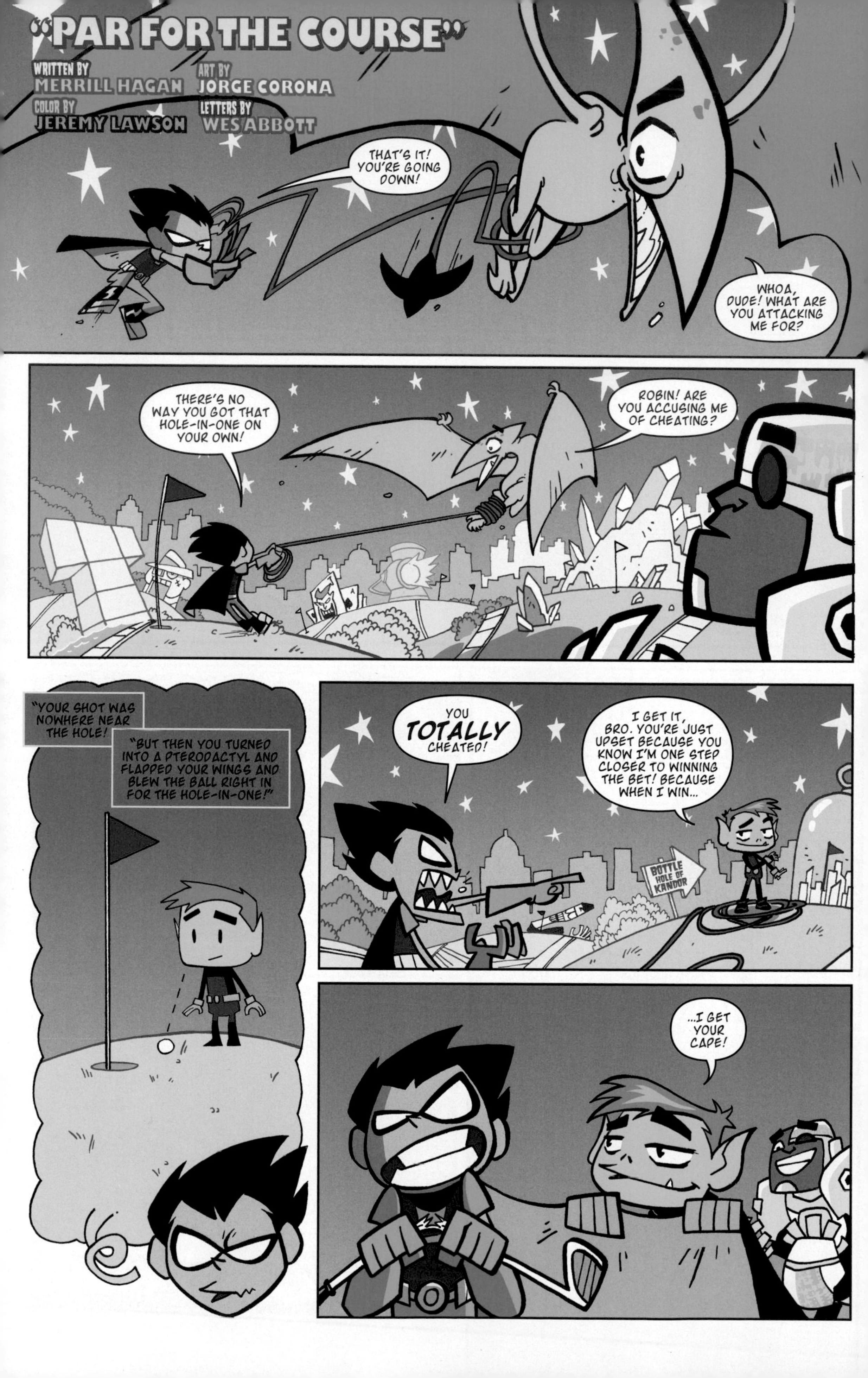
"PAR FOR THE COURSE"
WRITTEN BY MERRILL HAGAN
ART BY JORGE CORONA
COLOR BY JEREMY LAWSON
LETTERS BY WES ABBOTT
THAT'S IT! YOU'RE GOING DOWN!
WHOA, DUDE! WHAT ARE YOU ATTACKING ME FOR?
THERE'S NO WAY YOU GOT THAT HOLE-IN-ONE ON YOUR OWN!
ROBIN! ARE YOU ACCUSING ME OF CHEATING?
"YOUR SHOT WAS NOWHERE NEAR THE HOLE!
"BUT THEN YOU TURNED INTO A PTERODACTYL AND FLAPPED YOUR WINGS AND BLEW THE BALL RIGHT IN FOR THE HOLE-IN-ONE!"
YOU TOTALLY CHEATED!
I GET IT, BRO. YOU'RE JUST UPSET BECAUSE YOU KNOW I'M ONE STEP CLOSER TO WINNING THE BET! BECAUSE WHEN I WIN...
BOTTLE HOLE OF KANDOR
...I GET YOUR CAPE!

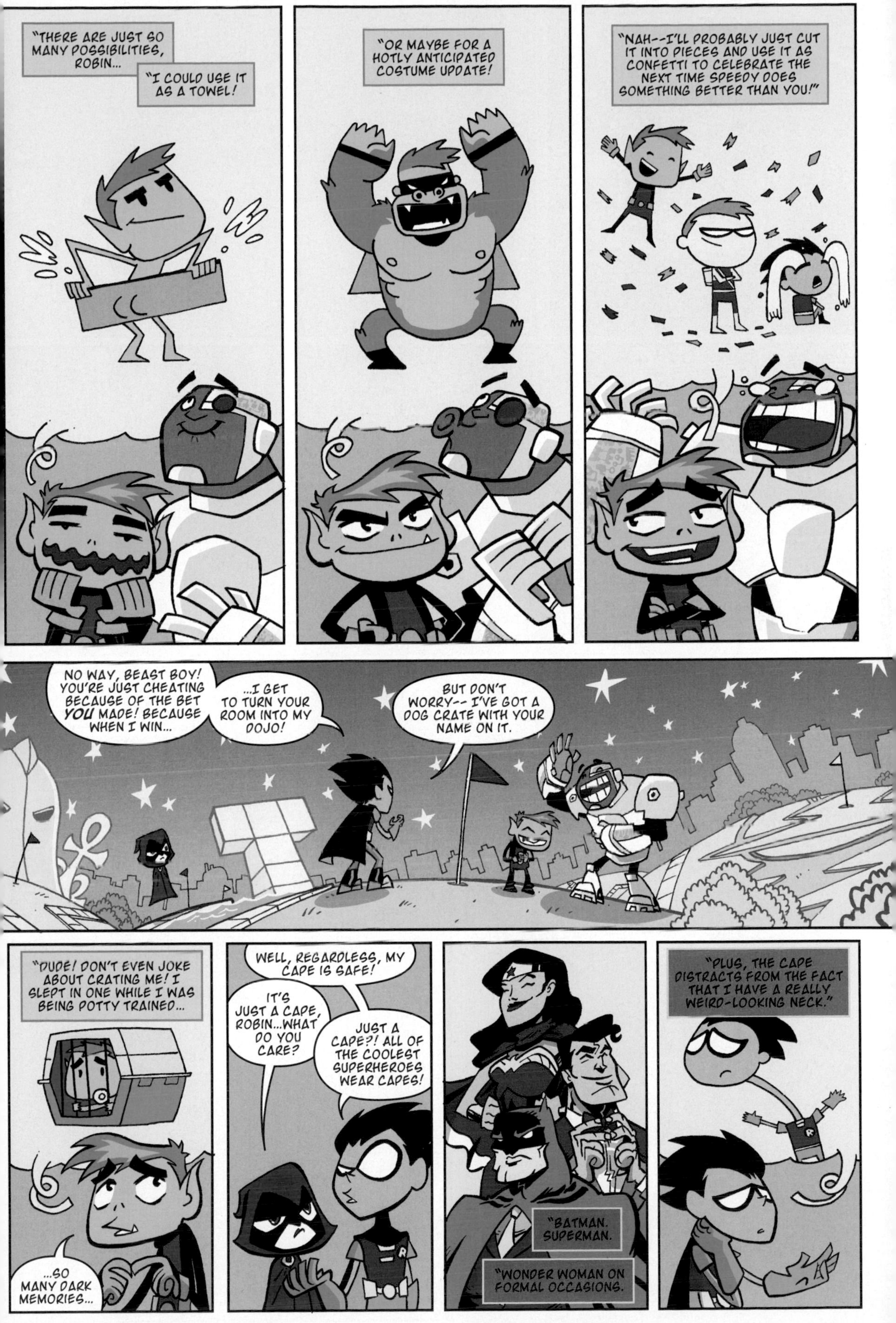
"THERE ARE JUST SO MANY POSSIBILITIES, ROBIN...
"I COULD USE IT AS A TOWEL!
"OR MAYBE FOR A HOTLY ANTICIPATED COSTUME UPDATE!
"NAH--I'LL PROBABLY JUST CUT IT INTO PIECES AND USE IT AS CONFETTI TO CELEBRATE THE NEXT TIME SPEEDY DOES SOMETHING BETTER THAN YOU!"
NO WAY, BEAST BOY! YOU'RE JUST CHEATING BECAUSE OF THE BET YOU MADE! BECAUSE WHEN I WIN...
...I GET TO TURN YOUR ROOM INTO MY DOJO!
BUT DON'T WORRY-- I'VE GOT A DOG CRATE WITH YOUR NAME ON IT.
"DUDE! DON'T EVEN JOKE ABOUT CRATING ME! I SLEPT IN ONE WHILE I WAS BEING POTTY TRAINED...
...SO MANY DARK MEMORIES...
WELL, REGARDLESS, MY CAPE IS SAFE!
IT'S JUST A CAPE, ROBIN...WHAT DO YOU CARE?
JUST A CAPE?! ALL OF THE COOLEST SUPERHEROES WEAR CAPES!
"BATMAN. SUPERMAN.
"WONDER WOMAN ON FORMAL OCCASIONS.
"PLUS, THE CAPE DISTRACTS FROM THE FACT THAT I HAVE A REALLY WEIRD-LOOKING NECK."

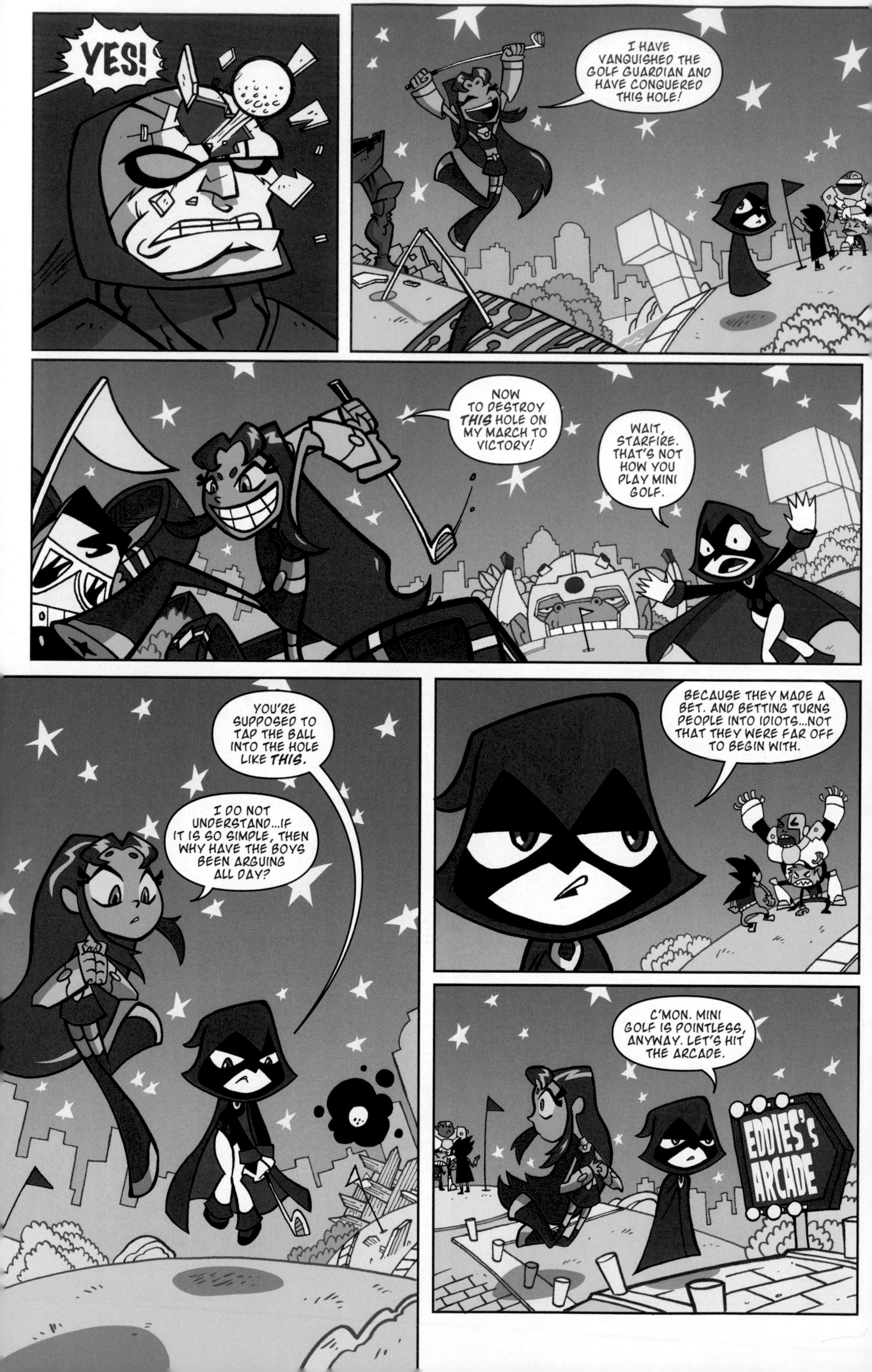
YES!
I HAVE VANQUISHED THE GOLF GUARDIAN AND HAVE CONQUERED THIS HOLE!
NOW TO DESTROY *THIS* HOLE ON MY MARCH TO VICTORY!
WAIT, STARFIRE. THAT'S NOT HOW YOU PLAY MINI GOLF.
YOU'RE SUPPOSED TO TAP THE BALL INTO THE HOLE LIKE *THIS*.
I DO NOT UNDERSTAND...IF IT IS SO SIMPLE, THEN WHY HAVE THE BOYS BEEN ARGUING ALL DAY?
BECAUSE THEY MADE A BET. AND BETTING TURNS PEOPLE INTO IDIOTS...NOT THAT THEY WERE FAR OFF TO BEGIN WITH.
C'MON. MINI GOLF IS POINTLESS, ANYWAY. LET'S HIT THE ARCADE.
EDDIES's ARCADE

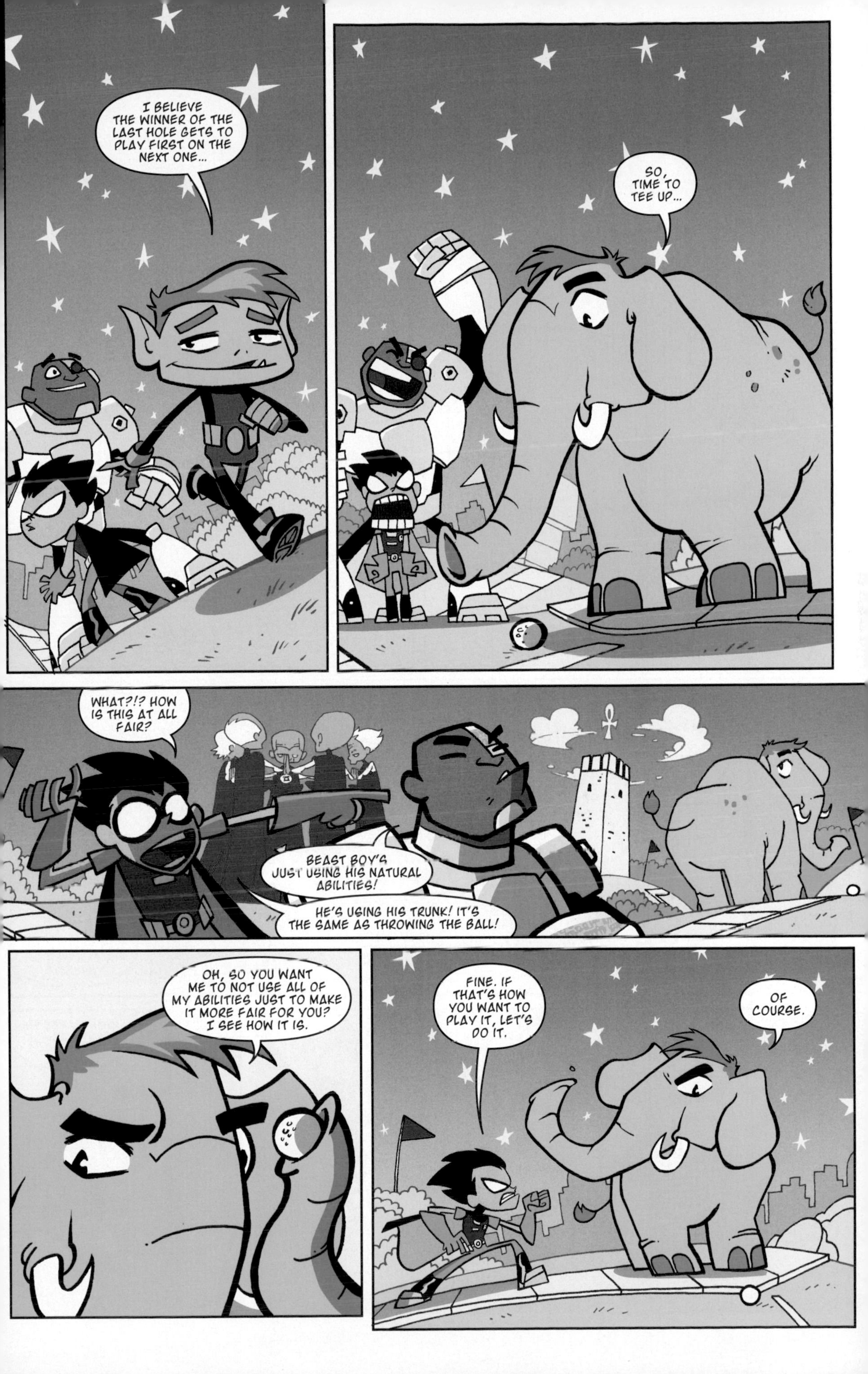
I BELIEVE THE WINNER OF THE LAST HOLE GETS TO PLAY FIRST ON THE NEXT ONE...
SO, TIME TO TEE UP...
WHAT?!? HOW IS THIS AT ALL FAIR?
BEAST BOY'S JUST USING HIS NATURAL ABILITIES!
HE'S USING HIS TRUNK! IT'S THE SAME AS THROWING THE BALL!
OH, SO YOU WANT ME TO NOT USE ALL OF MY ABILITIES JUST TO MAKE IT MORE FAIR FOR YOU? I SEE HOW IT IS.
FINE. IF THAT'S HOW YOU WANT TO PLAY IT, LET'S DO IT.
OF COURSE.

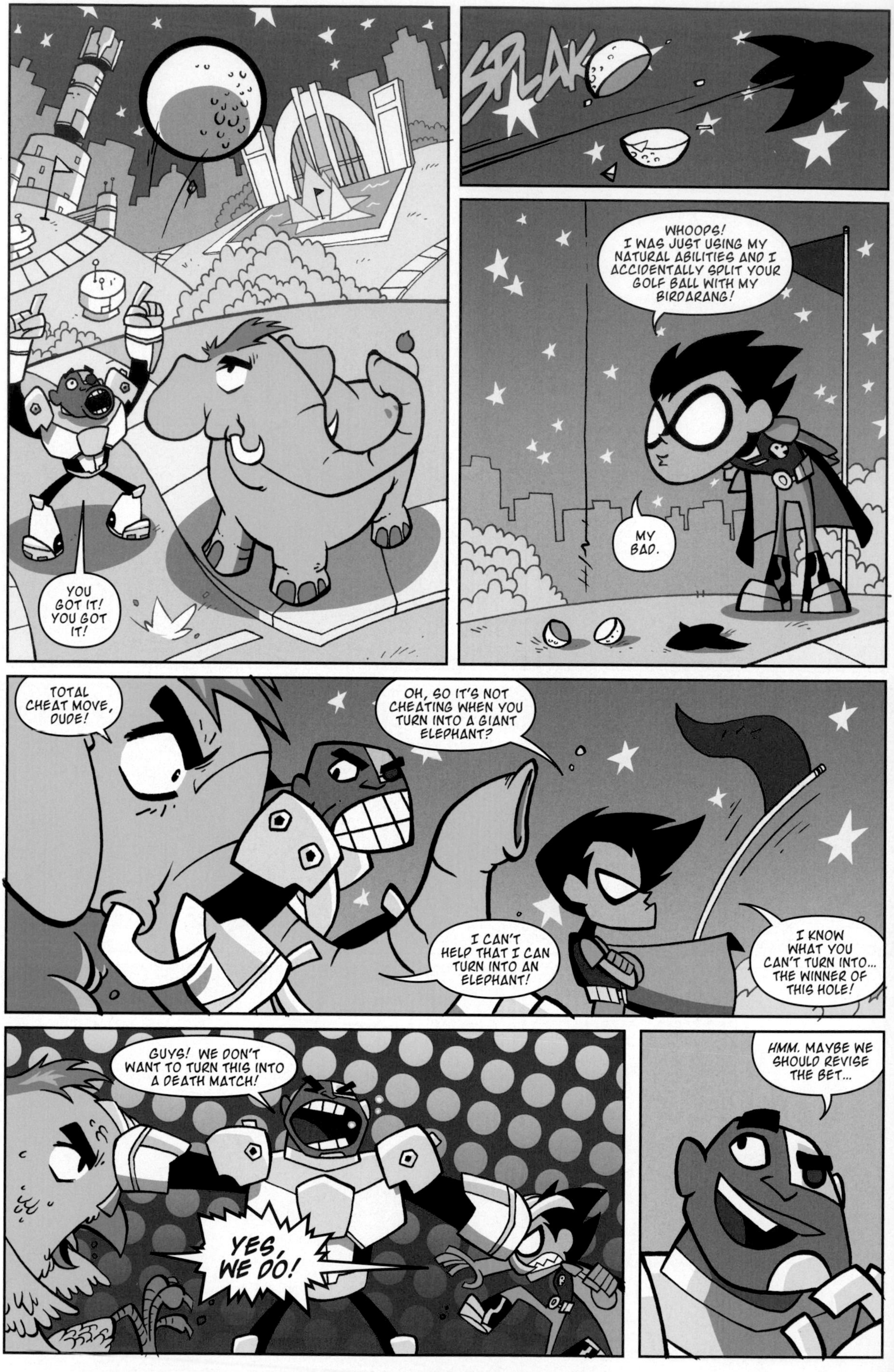

YOU GOT IT! YOU GOT IT!
SPLAK
WHOOPS! I WAS JUST USING MY NATURAL ABILITIES AND I ACCIDENTALLY SPLIT YOUR GOLF BALL WITH MY BIRDARANG!
MY BAD.
TOTAL CHEAT MOVE, DUDE!
OH, SO IT'S NOT CHEATING WHEN YOU TURN INTO A GIANT ELEPHANT?
I CAN'T HELP THAT I CAN TURN INTO AN ELEPHANT!
I KNOW WHAT YOU CAN'T TURN INTO... THE WINNER OF THIS HOLE!
GUYS! WE DON'T WANT TO TURN THIS INTO A DEATH MATCH!
YES, WE DO!
HMM. MAYBE WE SHOULD REVISE THE BET...

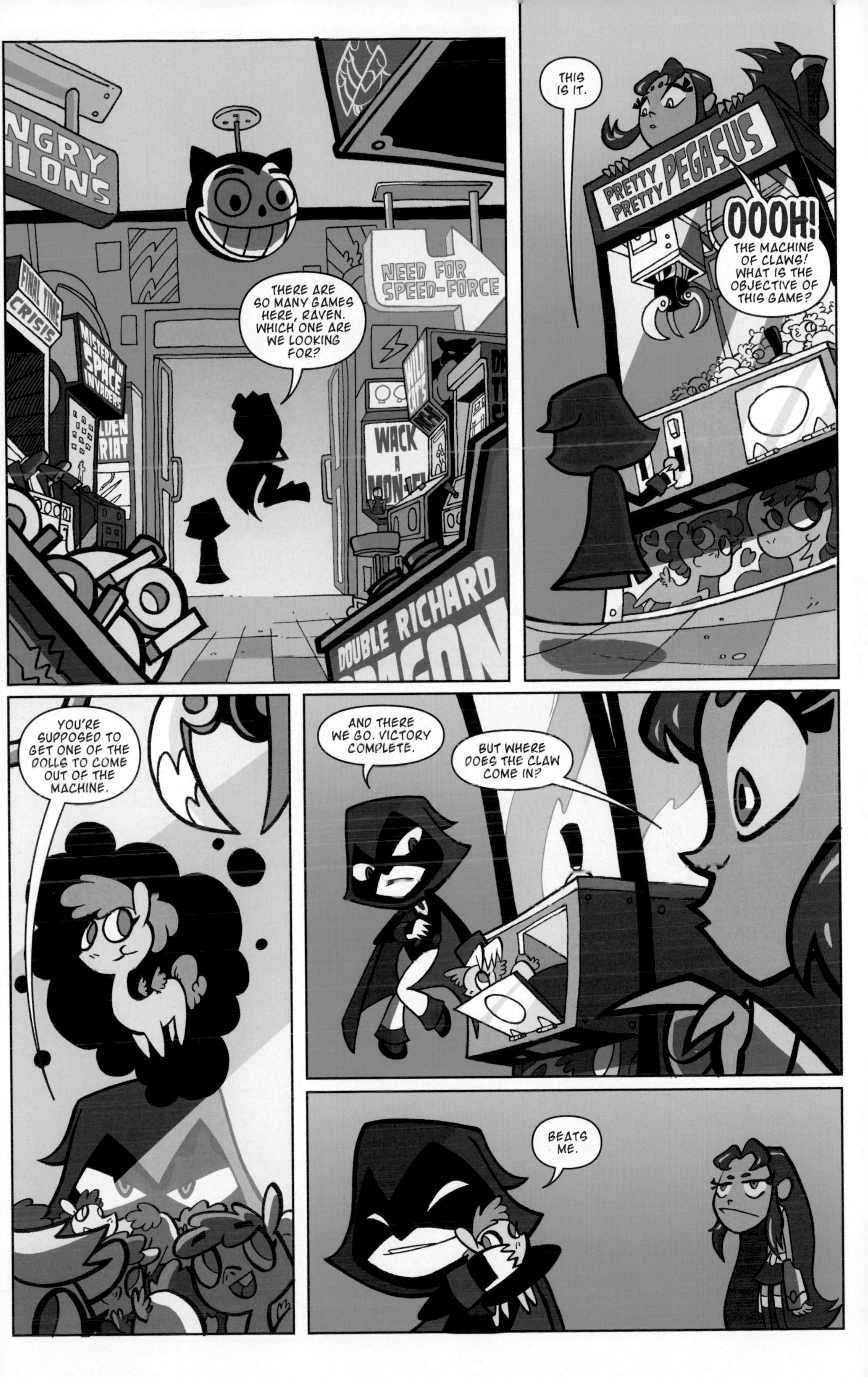
NGRY
LONS
FINAL TIME
CRISIS
MISTERY IN SPACE INVADERS
NEED FOR SPEED-FORCE
WACK A MON-
DOUBLE RICHARD
THERE ARE SO MANY GAMES HERE, RAVEN. WHICH ONE ARE WE LOOKING FOR?
THIS IS IT.
PRETTY PRETTY PEGASUS
OOOH!
THE MACHINE OF CLAWS! WHAT IS THE OBJECTIVE OF THIS GAME?
YOU'RE SUPPOSED TO GET ONE OF THE DOLLS TO COME OUT OF THE MACHINE.
AND THERE WE GO. VICTORY COMPLETE.
BUT WHERE DOES THE CLAW COME IN?
BEATS ME.

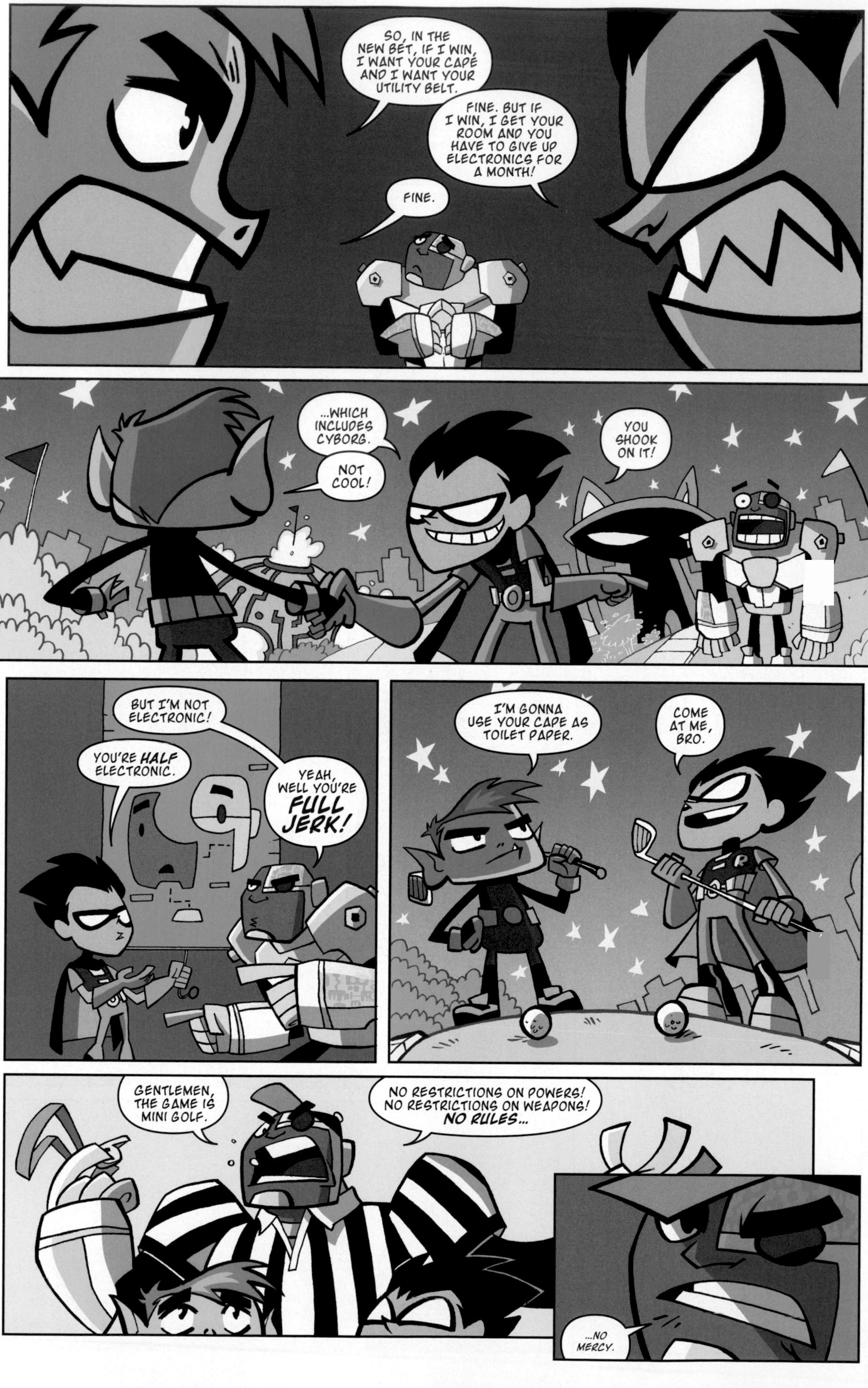
SO, IN THE NEW BET, IF I WIN, I WANT YOUR CAPE AND I WANT YOUR UTILITY BELT.
FINE. BUT IF I WIN, I GET YOUR ROOM AND YOU HAVE TO GIVE UP ELECTRONICS FOR A MONTH!
FINE.
...WHICH INCLUDES CYBORG.
NOT COOL!
YOU SHOOK ON IT!
BUT I'M NOT ELECTRONIC!
YOU'RE HALF ELECTRONIC.
YEAH, WELL YOU'RE FULL JERK!
I'M GONNA USE YOUR CAPE AS TOILET PAPER.
COME AT ME, BRO.
GENTLEMEN, THE GAME IS MINI GOLF.
NO RESTRICTIONS ON POWERS! NO RESTRICTIONS ON WEAPONS! NO RULES...
...NO MERCY.

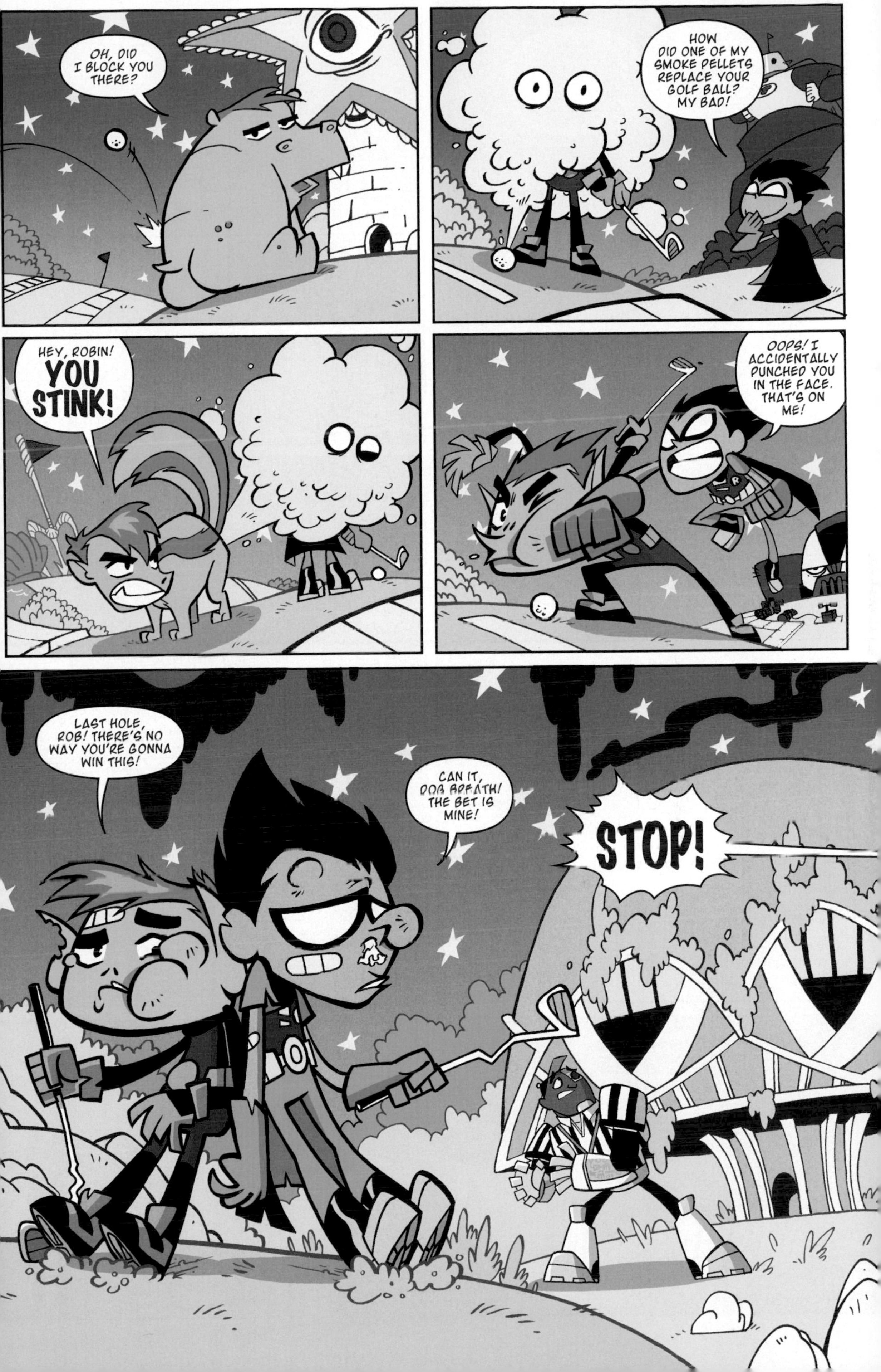
OH, DID I BLOCK YOU THERE?
HOW DID ONE OF MY SMOKE PELLETS REPLACE YOUR GOLF BALL? MY BAD!
HEY, ROBIN! YOU STINK!
OOPS! I ACCIDENTALLY PUNCHED YOU IN THE FACE. THAT'S ON ME!
LAST HOLE, ROB! THERE'S NO WAY YOU'RE GONNA WIN THIS!
CAN IT, DOG BREATH! THE BET IS MINE!
STOP!

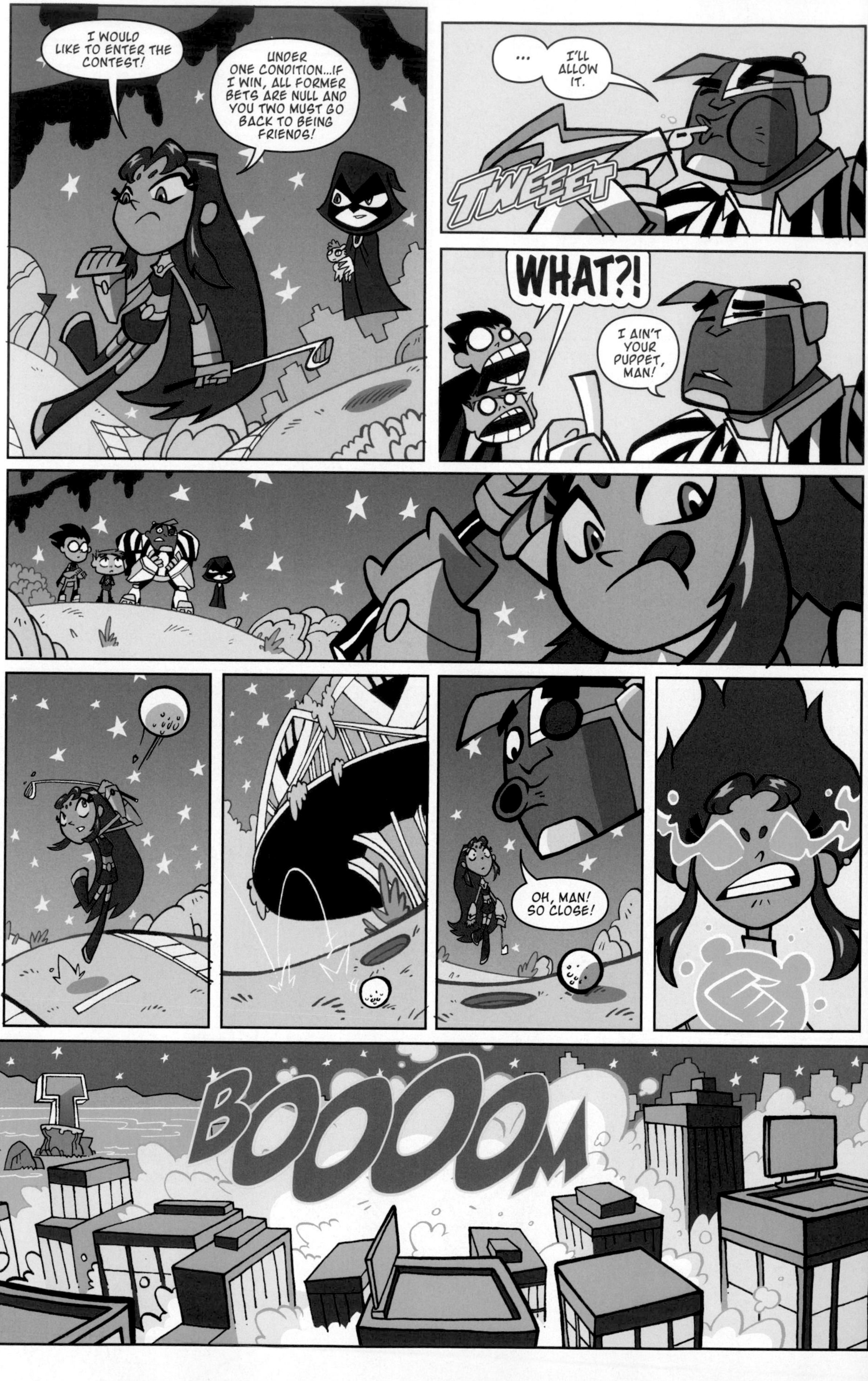
I WOULD LIKE TO ENTER THE CONTEST!
UNDER ONE CONDITION...IF I WIN, ALL FORMER BETS ARE NULL AND YOU TWO MUST GO BACK TO BEING FRIENDS!
...
I'LL ALLOW IT.
TWEEET
WHAT?!
I AIN'T YOUR PUPPET, MAN!
OH, MAN! SO CLOSE!
BOOOOM

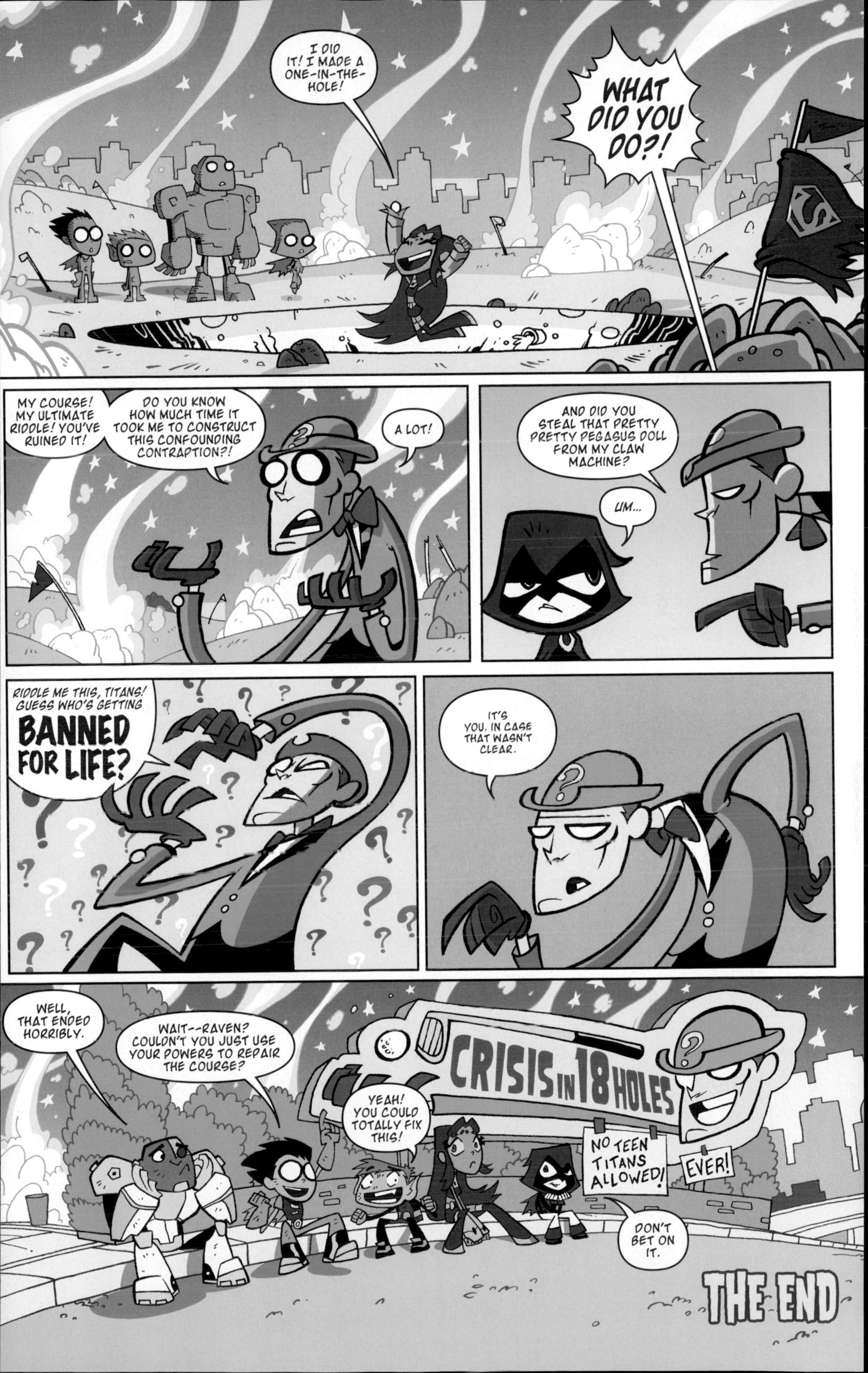
I DID IT! I MADE A ONE-IN-THE-HOLE!
WHAT DID YOU DO?!
MY COURSE! MY ULTIMATE RIDDLE! YOU'VE RUINED IT!
DO YOU KNOW HOW MUCH TIME IT TOOK ME TO CONSTRUCT THIS CONFOUNDING CONTRAPTION?!
A LOT!
AND DID YOU STEAL THAT PRETTY PRETTY PEGASUS DOLL FROM MY CLAW MACHINE?
UM...
RIDDLE ME THIS, TITANS! GUESS WHO'S GETTING BANNED FOR LIFE?
IT'S YOU. IN CASE THAT WASN'T CLEAR.
WELL, THAT ENDED HORRIBLY.
WAIT--RAVEN? COULDN'T YOU JUST USE YOUR POWERS TO REPAIR THE COURSE?
CRISIS IN 18 HOLES
YEAH! YOU COULD TOTALLY FIX THIS!
NO TEEN TITANS ALLOWED!
EVER!
DON'T BET ON IT.
THE END

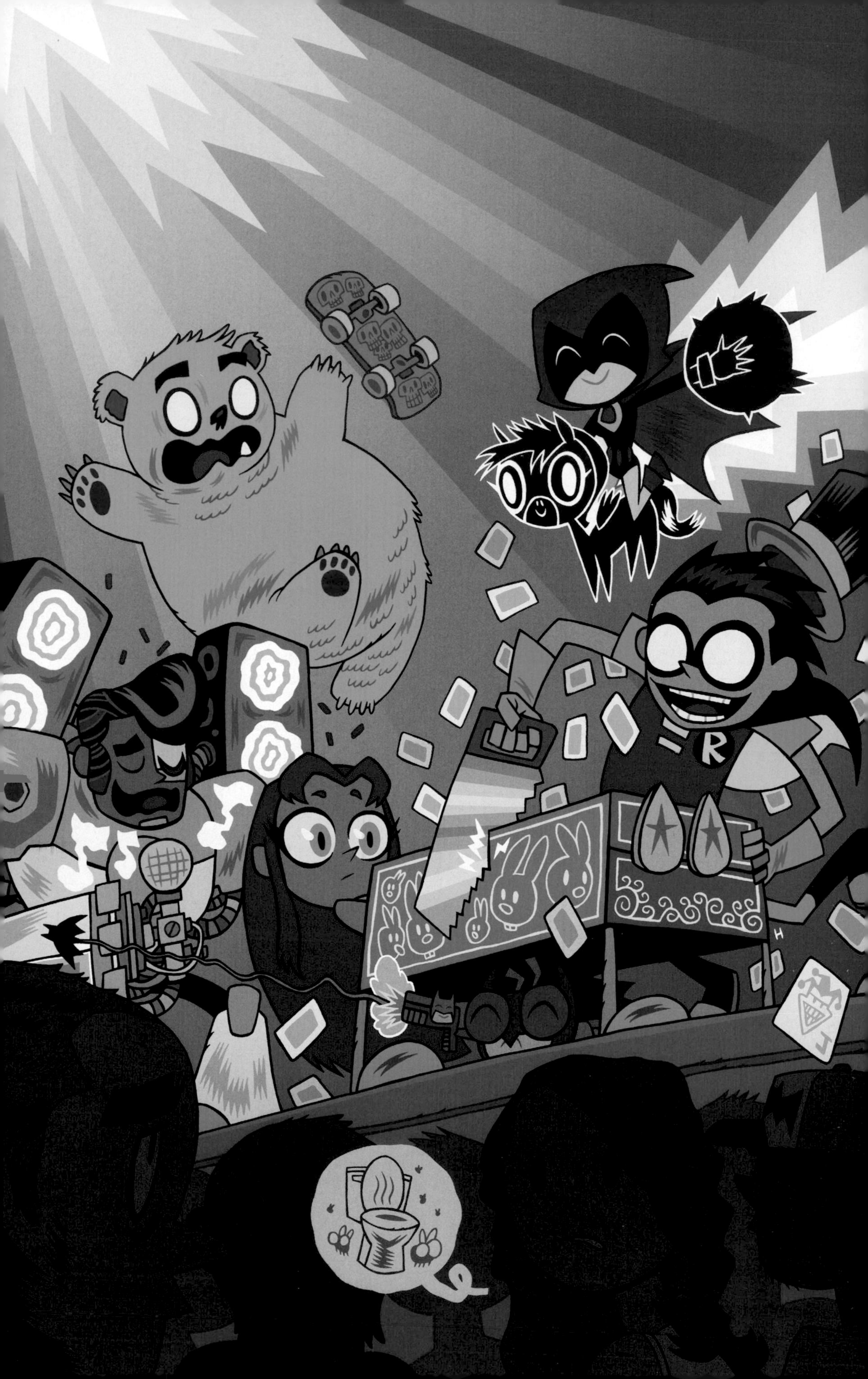

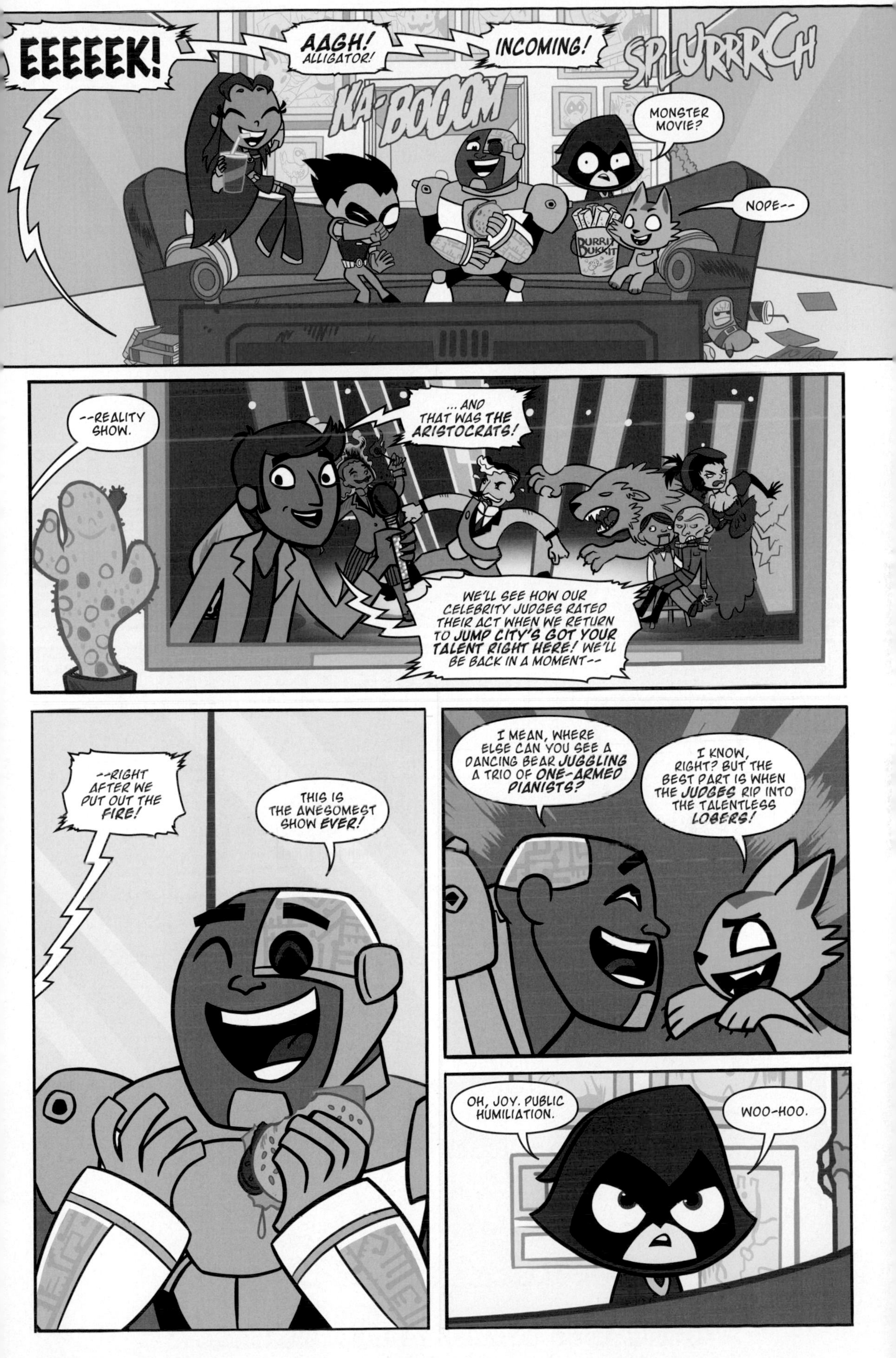
EEEEEK!
AAGH! ALLIGATOR!
INCOMING!
SPLURRRCH
KA-BOOOM
MONSTER MOVIE?
NOPE--
BURRITO BUKKIT
--REALITY SHOW.
...AND THAT WAS THE ARISTOCRATS!
WE'LL SEE HOW OUR CELEBRITY JUDGES RATED THEIR ACT WHEN WE RETURN TO JUMP CITY'S GOT YOUR TALENT RIGHT HERE! WE'LL BE BACK IN A MOMENT--
--RIGHT AFTER WE PUT OUT THE FIRE!
THIS IS THE AWESOMEST SHOW EVER!
I MEAN, WHERE ELSE CAN YOU SEE A DANCING BEAR JUGGLING A TRIO OF ONE-ARMED PIANISTS?
I KNOW, RIGHT? BUT THE BEST PART IS WHEN THE JUDGES RIP INTO THE TALENTLESS LOSERS!
OH, JOY. PUBLIC HUMILIATION.
WOO-HOO.

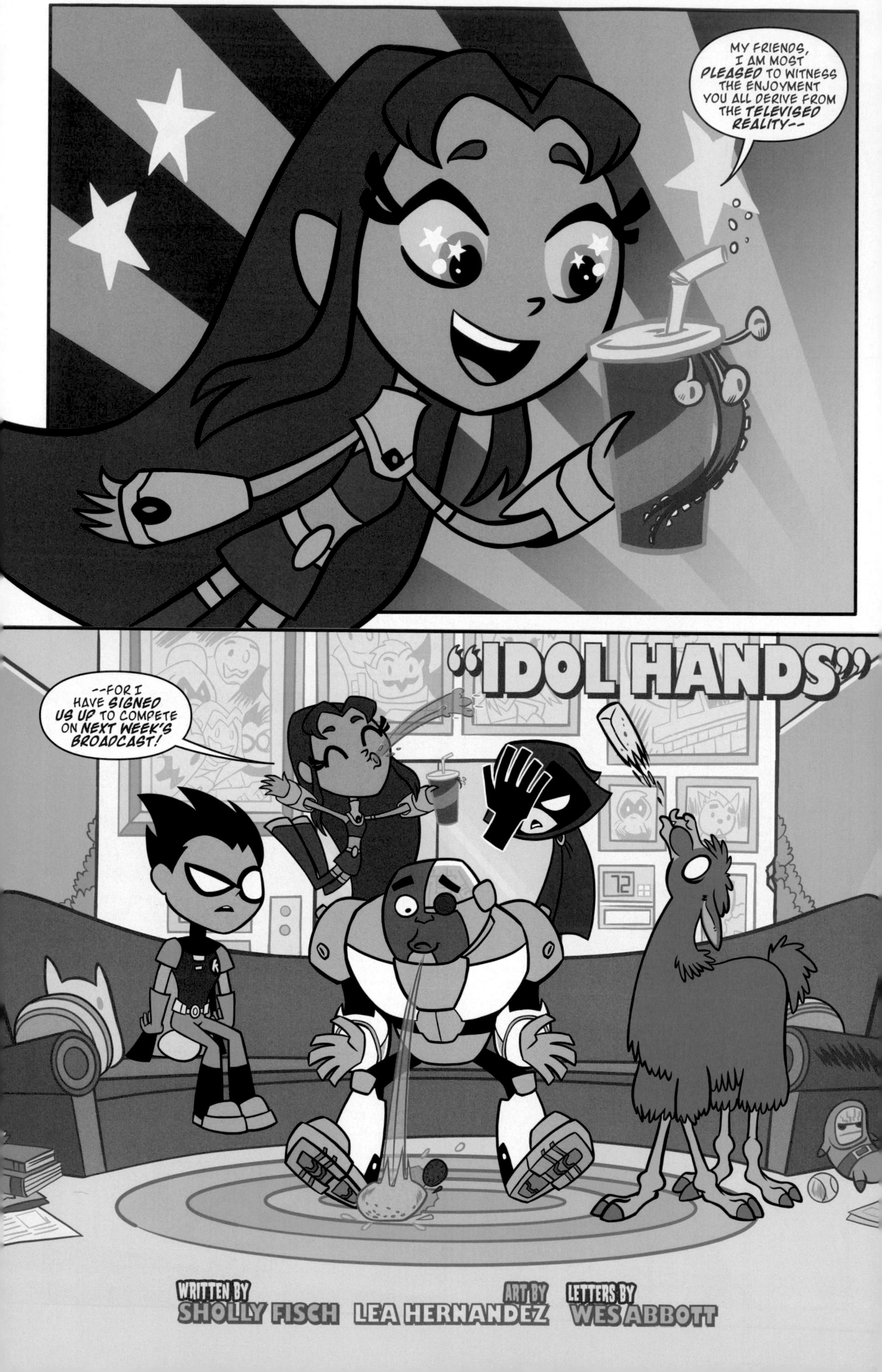
MY FRIENDS, I AM MOST PLEASED TO WITNESS THE ENJOYMENT YOU ALL DERIVE FROM THE TELEVISED REALITY--
"IDOL HANDS"
--FOR I HAVE SIGNED US UP TO COMPETE ON NEXT WEEK'S BROADCAST!
72
WRITTEN BY SHOLLY FISCH
ART BY LEA HERNANDEZ
LETTERS BY WES ABBOTT

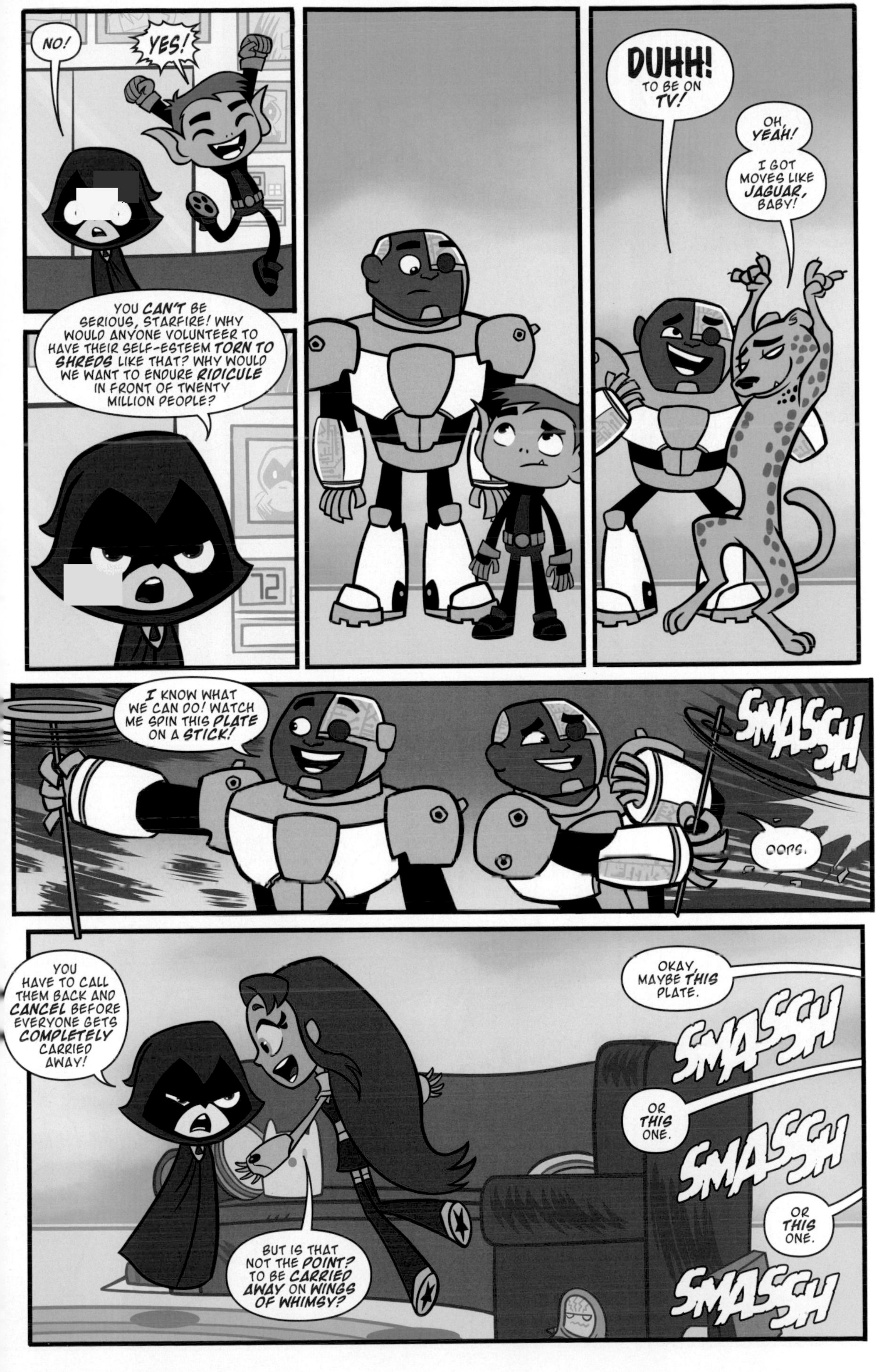
NO!
YES!
YOU CAN'T BE SERIOUS, STARFIRE! WHY WOULD ANYONE VOLUNTEER TO HAVE THEIR SELF-ESTEEM TORN TO SHREDS LIKE THAT? WHY WOULD WE WANT TO ENDURE RIDICULE IN FRONT OF TWENTY MILLION PEOPLE?
DUHH! TO BE ON TV!
OH, YEAH!
I GOT MOVES LIKE JAGUAR, BABY!
I KNOW WHAT WE CAN DO! WATCH ME SPIN THIS PLATE ON A STICK!
SMASCH
OOPS.
YOU HAVE TO CALL THEM BACK AND CANCEL BEFORE EVERYONE GETS COMPLETELY CARRIED AWAY!
BUT IS THAT NOT THE POINT? TO BE CARRIED AWAY ON WINGS OF WHIMSY?
OKAY, MAYBE THIS PLATE.
SMASCH
OR THIS ONE.
SMASCH
OR THIS ONE.
SMASCH

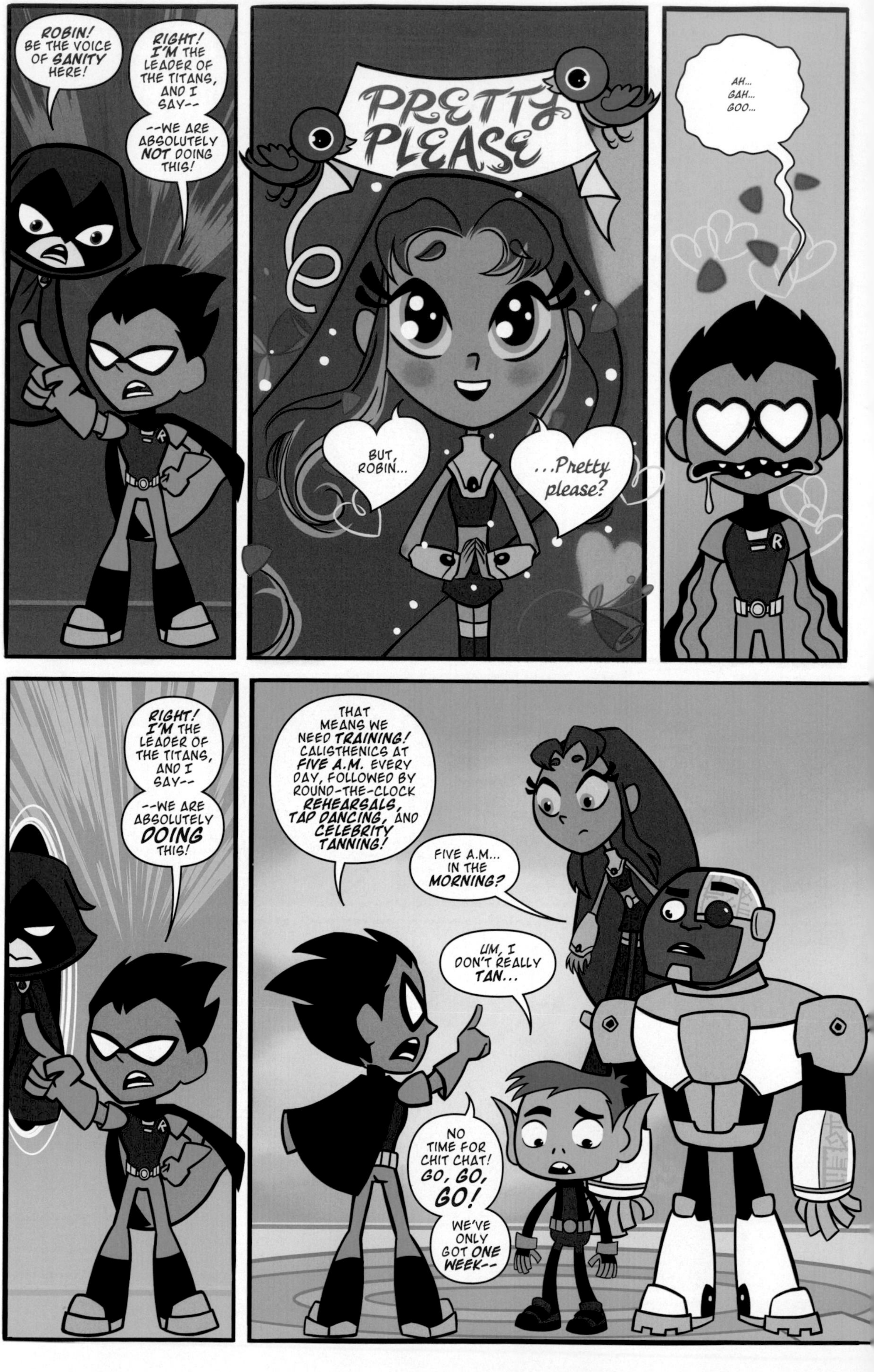
ROBIN! BE THE VOICE OF SANITY HERE!
RIGHT! I'M THE LEADER OF THE TITANS, AND I SAY--
--WE ARE ABSOLUTELY NOT DOING THIS!
PRETTY PLEASE
BUT, ROBIN...
...Pretty please?
AH... GAH... GOO...
RIGHT! I'M THE LEADER OF THE TITANS, AND I SAY--
--WE ARE ABSOLUTELY DOING THIS!
THAT MEANS WE NEED TRAINING! CALISTHENICS AT FIVE A.M. EVERY DAY, FOLLOWED BY ROUND-THE-CLOCK REHEARSALS, TAP DANCING, AND CELEBRITY TANNING!
FIVE A.M... IN THE MORNING?
UM, I DON'T REALLY TAN...
NO TIME FOR CHIT CHAT! GO, GO, GO!
WE'VE ONLY GOT ONE WEEK--

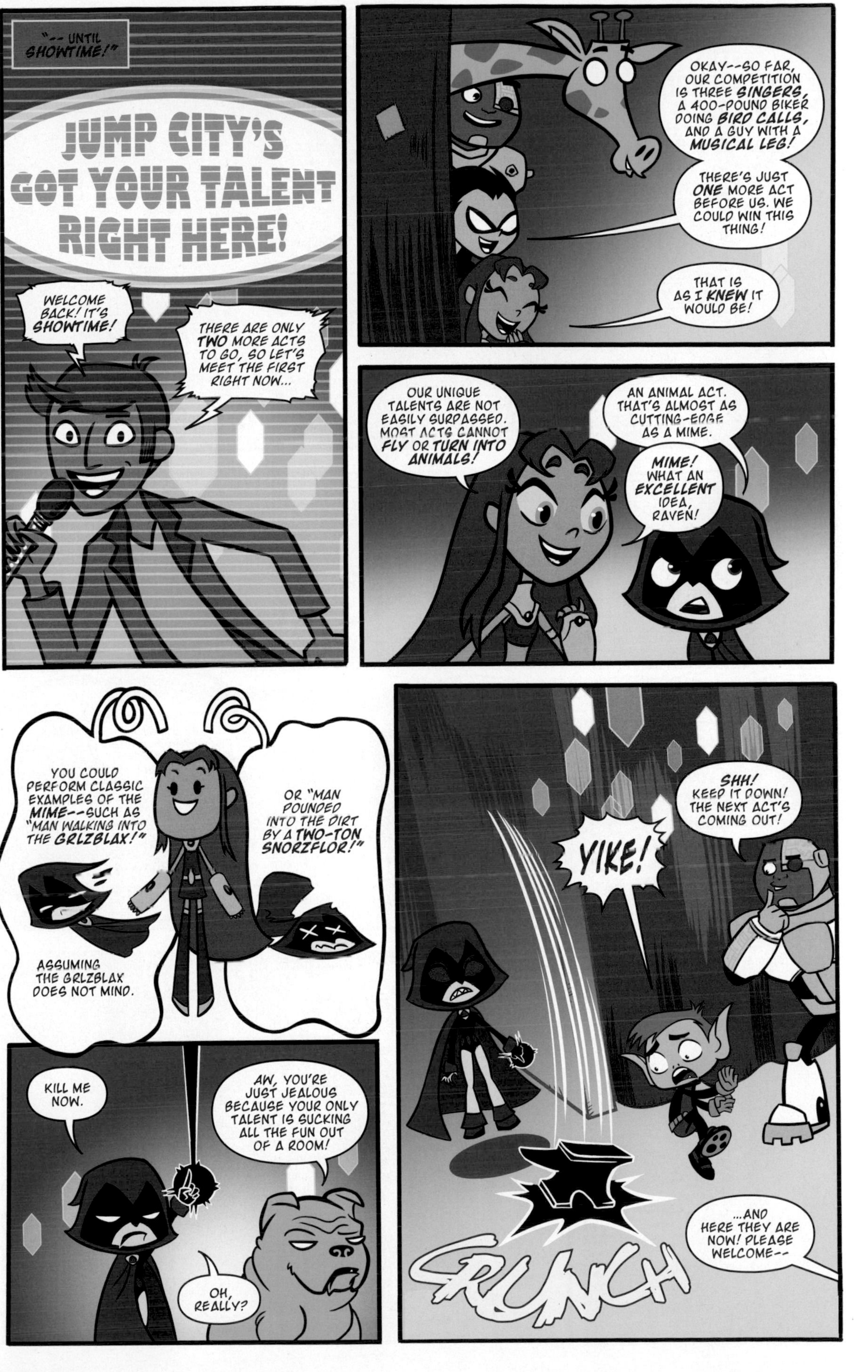
"-- UNTIL SHOWTIME!"
JUMP CITY'S GOT YOUR TALENT RIGHT HERE!
WELCOME BACK! IT'S SHOWTIME!
THERE ARE ONLY TWO MORE ACTS TO GO, SO LET'S MEET THE FIRST RIGHT NOW...
OKAY--SO FAR, OUR COMPETITION IS THREE SINGERS, A 400-POUND BIKER DOING BIRD CALLS, AND A GUY WITH A MUSICAL LEG!
THERE'S JUST ONE MORE ACT BEFORE US. WE COULD WIN THIS THING!
THAT IS AS I KNEW IT WOULD BE!
OUR UNIQUE TALENTS ARE NOT EASILY SURPASSED. MOST ACTS CANNOT FLY OR TURN INTO ANIMALS!
AN ANIMAL ACT. THAT'S ALMOST AS CUTTING-EDGE AS A MIME.
MIME! WHAT AN EXCELLENT IDEA, RAVEN!
YOU COULD PERFORM CLASSIC EXAMPLES OF THE MIME--SUCH AS "MAN WALKING INTO THE GRLZBLAX!"
OR "MAN POUNDED INTO THE DIRT BY A TWO-TON SNORZFLOR!"
ASSUMING THE GRLZBLAX DOES NOT MIND.
KILL ME NOW.
AW, YOU'RE JUST JEALOUS BECAUSE YOUR ONLY TALENT IS SUCKING ALL THE FUN OUT OF A ROOM!
OH, REALLY?
SHH! KEEP IT DOWN! THE NEXT ACT'S COMING OUT!
YIKE!
GRUNCH
...AND HERE THEY ARE NOW! PLEASE WELCOME--

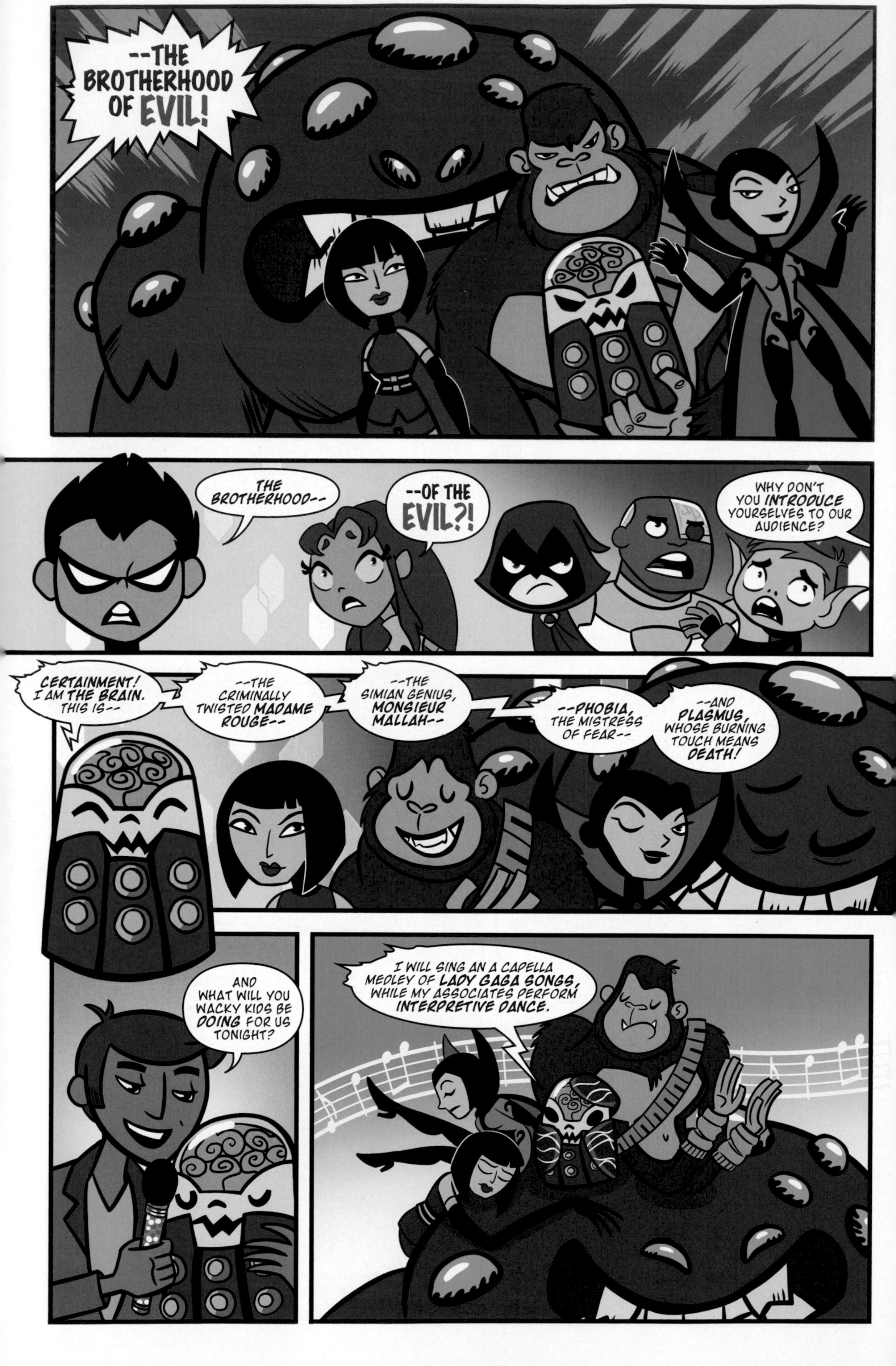
--THE BROTHERHOOD OF EVIL!
THE BROTHERHOOD--
--OF THE EVIL?!
WHY DON'T YOU INTRODUCE YOURSELVES TO OUR AUDIENCE?
CERTAINMENT! I AM THE BRAIN. THIS IS--
--THE CRIMINALLY TWISTED MADAME ROUGE--
--THE SIMIAN GENIUS, MONSIEUR MALLAH--
--PHOBIA, THE MISTRESS OF FEAR--
--AND PLASMUS, WHOSE BURNING TOUCH MEANS DEATH!
AND WHAT WILL YOU WACKY KIDS BE DOING FOR US TONIGHT?
I WILL SING AN A CAPELLA MEDLEY OF LADY GAGA SONGS, WHILE MY ASSOCIATES PERFORM INTERPRETIVE DANCE.

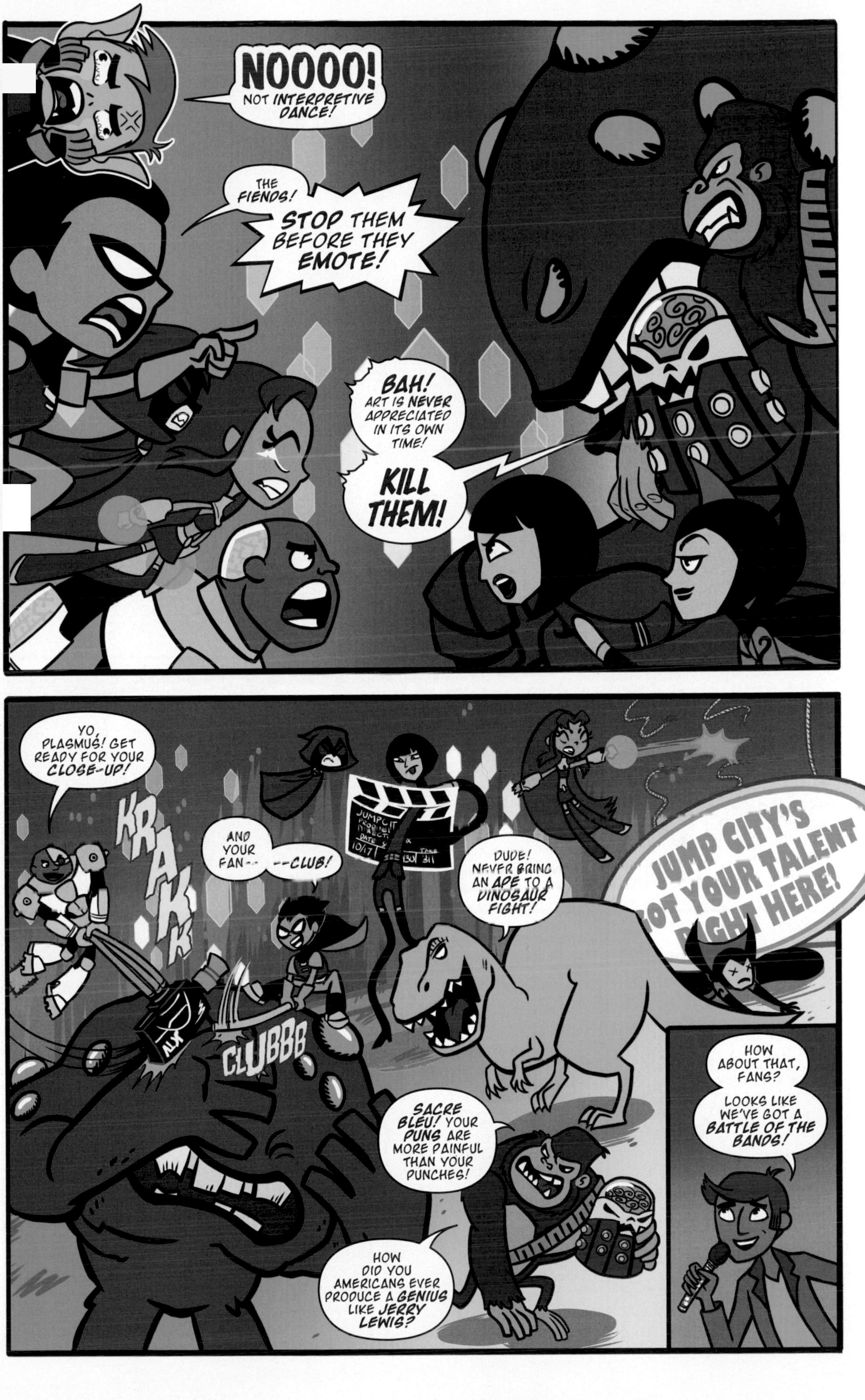
NOOOO! NOT INTERPRETIVE DANCE!
THE FIENDS!
STOP THEM BEFORE THEY EMOTE!
BAH! ART IS NEVER APPRECIATED IN ITS OWN TIME!
KILL THEM!
YO, PLASMUS! GET READY FOR YOUR CLOSE-UP!
KRAKK
AND YOUR FAN--
--CLUB!
CLUBBB
DUDE! NEVER BRING AN APE TO A DINOSAUR FIGHT!
JUMP CITY'S
OT YOUR TALENT
IGHT HERE!
SACRE BLEU! YOUR PUNS ARE MORE PAINFUL THAN YOUR PUNCHES!
HOW DID YOU AMERICANS EVER PRODUCE A GENIUS LIKE JERRY LEWIS?
HOW ABOUT THAT, FANS?
LOOKS LIKE WE'VE GOT A BATTLE OF THE BANDS!

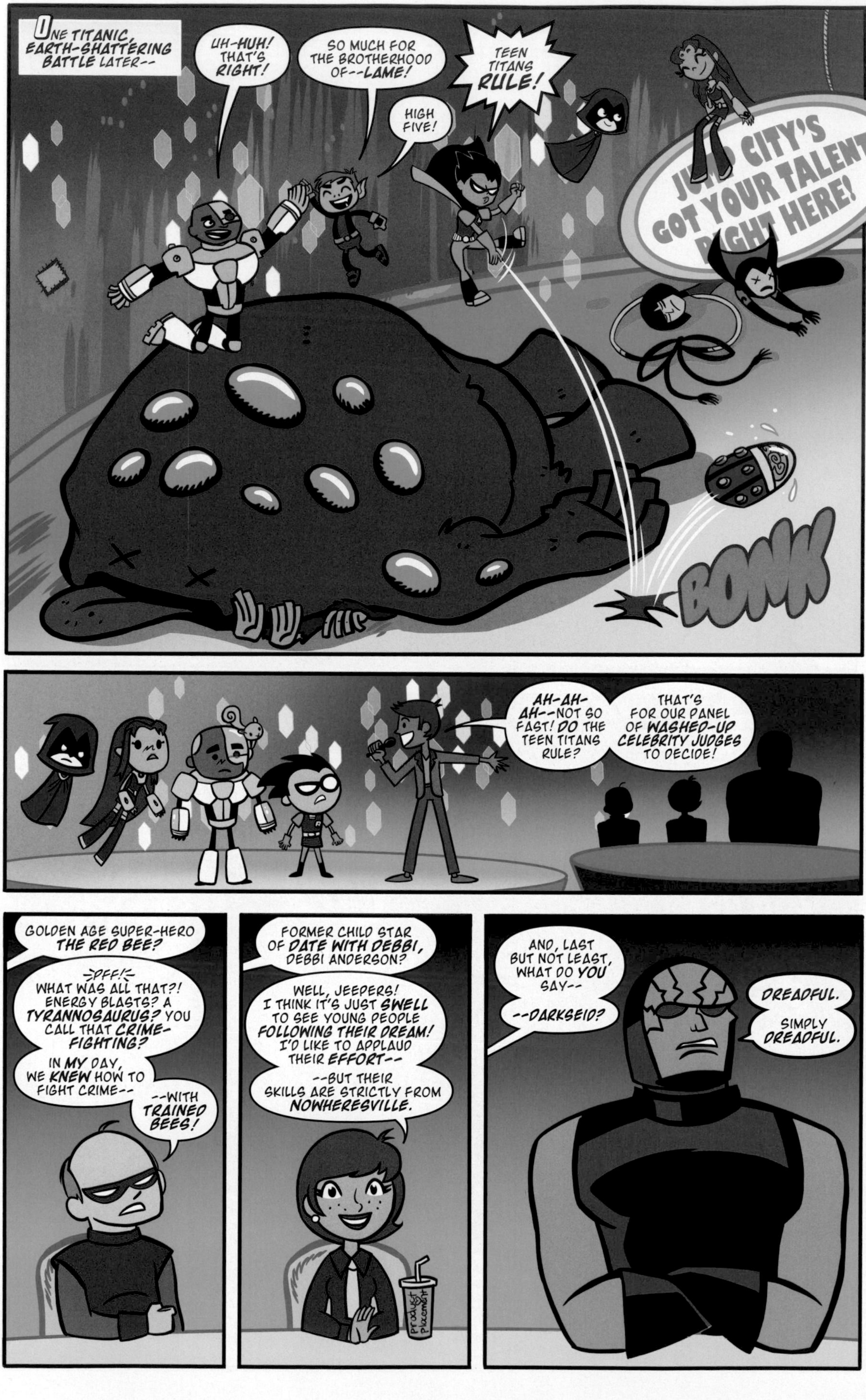

ONE TITANIC, EARTH-SHATTERING BATTLE LATER--
UH-HUH! THAT'S RIGHT!
SO MUCH FOR THE BROTHERHOOD OF--LAME!
HIGH FIVE!
TEEN TITANS RULE!
CITY'S
GOT YOUR TALENT
HERE!
BONK
AH-AH-AH--NOT SO FAST! DO THE TEEN TITANS RULE?
THAT'S FOR OUR PANEL OF WASHED-UP CELEBRITY JUDGES TO DECIDE!
GOLDEN AGE SUPER-HERO THE RED BEE?
PFF!
WHAT WAS ALL THAT?! ENERGY BLASTS? A TYRANNOSAURUS? YOU CALL THAT CRIME-FIGHTING?
IN MY DAY, WE KNEW HOW TO FIGHT CRIME--
--WITH TRAINED BEES!
FORMER CHILD STAR OF DATE WITH DEBBI, DEBBI ANDERSON?
WELL, JEEPERS! I THINK IT'S JUST SWELL TO SEE YOUNG PEOPLE FOLLOWING THEIR DREAM! I'D LIKE TO APPLAUD THEIR EFFORT--
--BUT THEIR SKILLS ARE STRICTLY FROM NOWHERESVILLE.
product placement
AND, LAST BUT NOT LEAST, WHAT DO YOU SAY--
--DARKSEID?
DREADFUL.
SIMPLY DREADFUL.

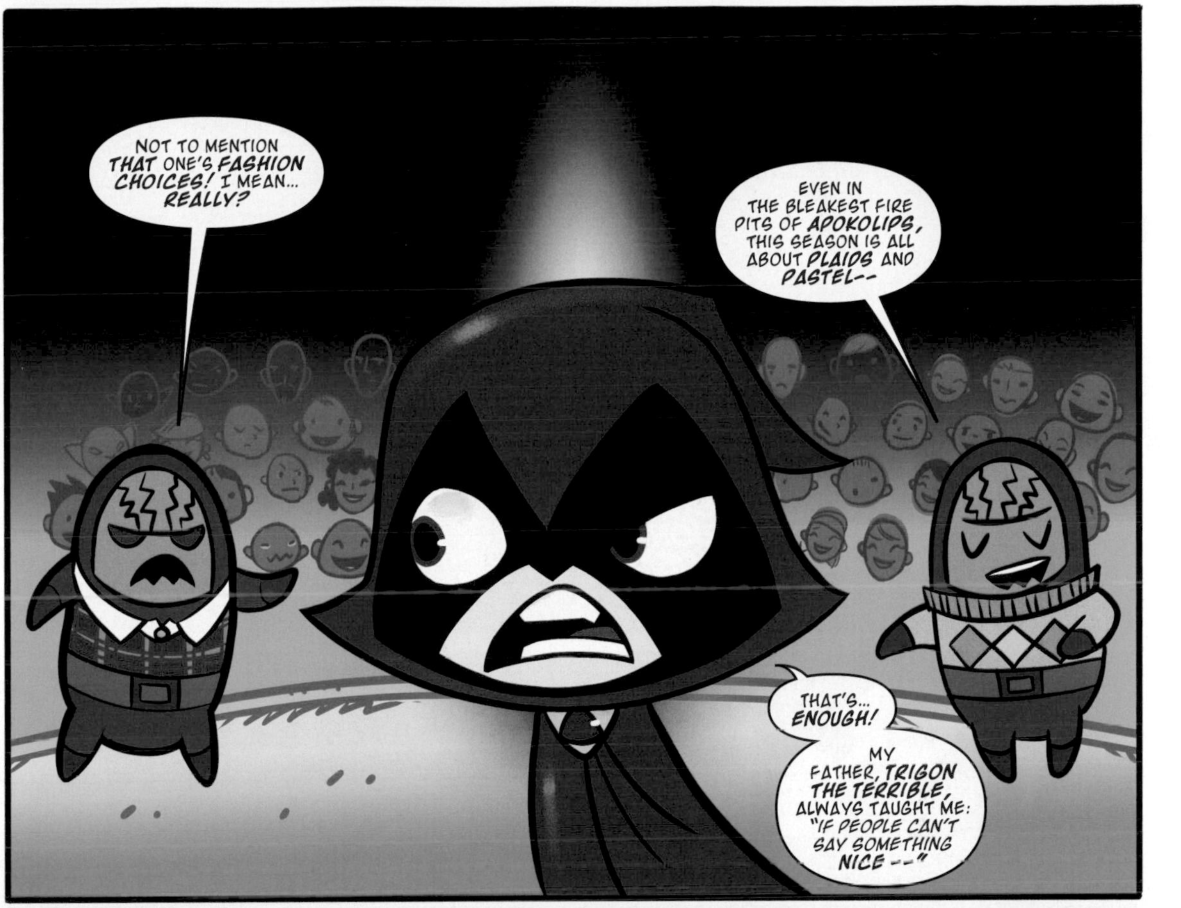
NOT TO MENTION THAT ONE'S FASHION CHOICES! I MEAN... REALLY?
EVEN IN THE BLEAKEST FIRE PITS OF APOKOLIPS, THIS SEASON IS ALL ABOUT PLAIDS AND PASTEL--
THAT'S... ENOUGH!
MY FATHER, TRIGON THE TERRIBLE, ALWAYS TAUGHT ME: "IF PEOPLE CAN'T SAY SOMETHING NICE --"

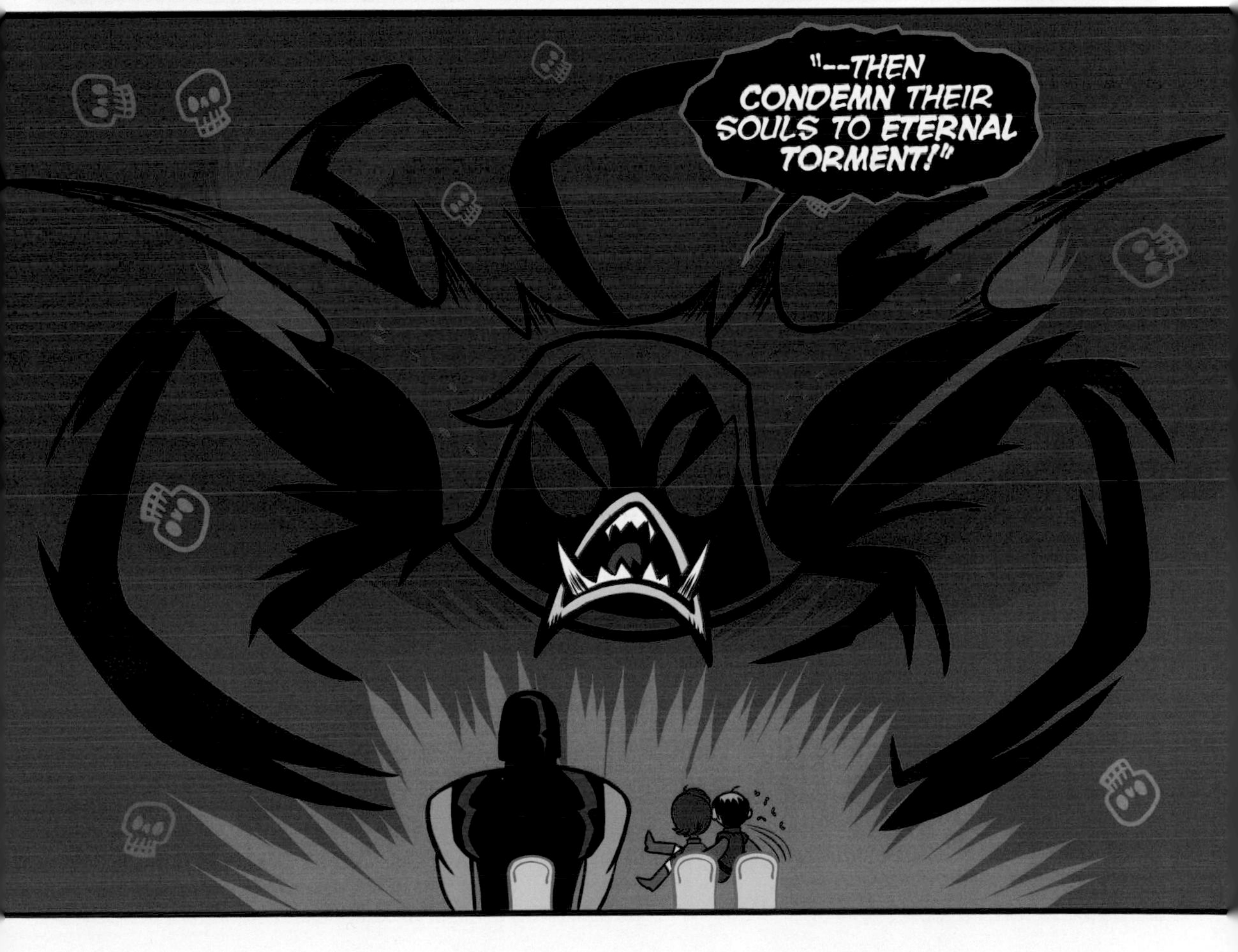
"--THEN CONDEMN THEIR SOULS TO ETERNAL TORMENT!"

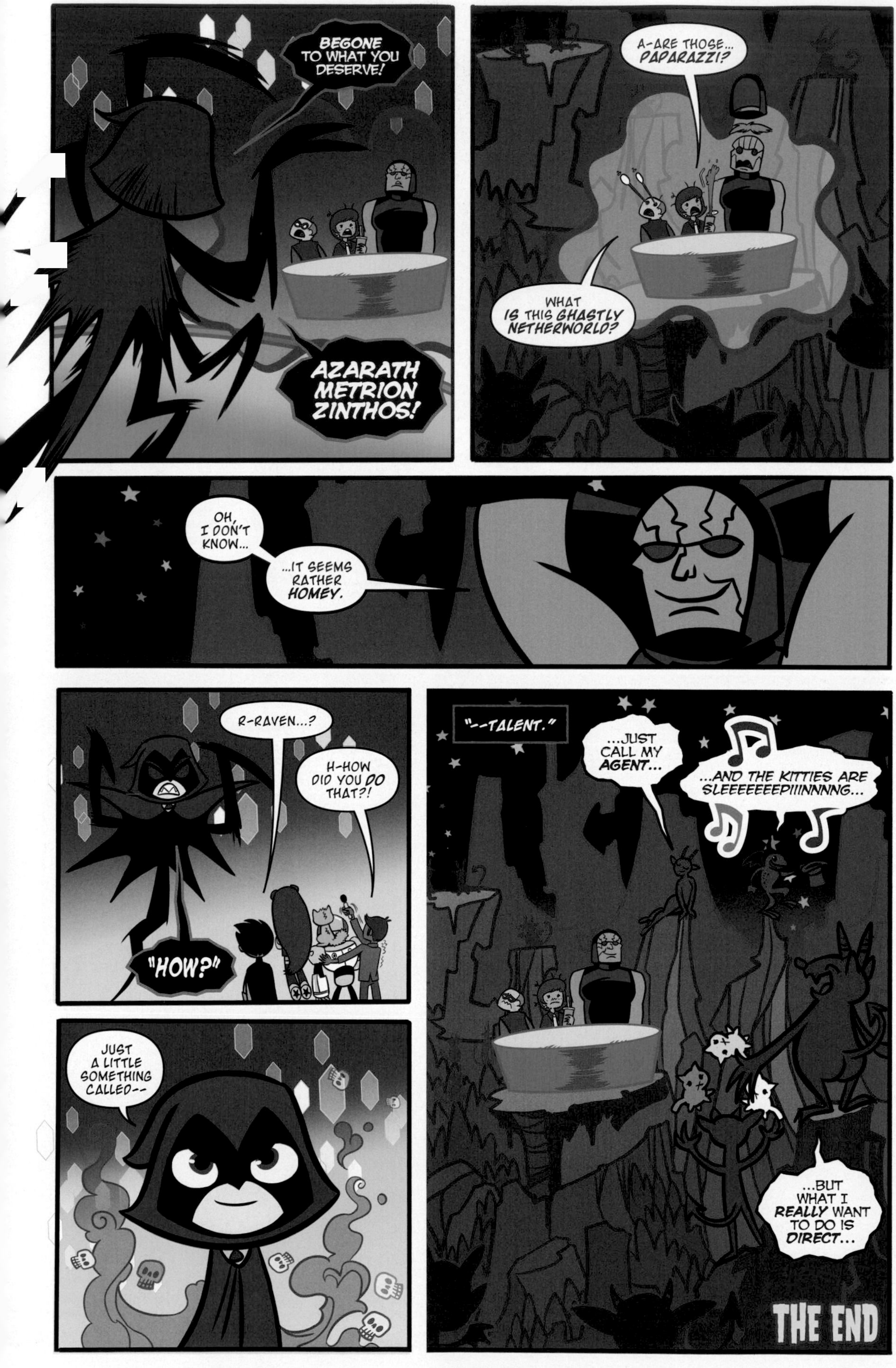
BEGONE TO WHAT YOU DESERVE!
AZARATH METRION ZINTHOS!
A-ARE THOSE... PAPARAZZI!?
WHAT IS THIS GHASTLY NETHERWORLD?
OH, I DON'T KNOW...
...IT SEEMS RATHER HOMEY.
R-RAVEN...?
H-HOW DID YOU DO THAT?!
"HOW?"
JUST A LITTLE SOMETHING CALLED--
"--TALENT."
...JUST CALL MY AGENT...
...AND THE KITTIES ARE SLEEEEEEEPIIINNNNG...
...BUT WHAT I REALLY WANT TO DO IS DIRECT...
THE END

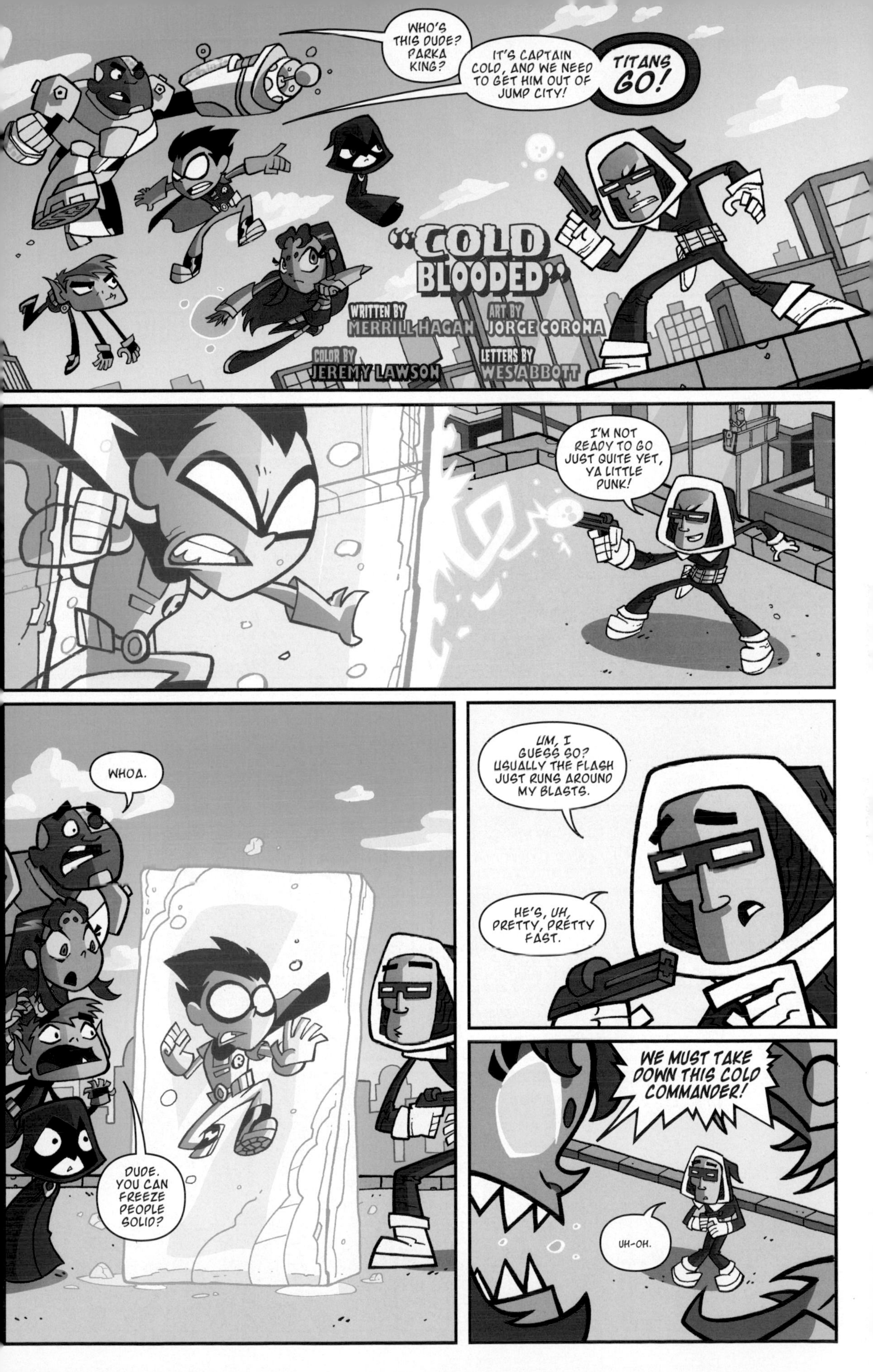

WHO'S THIS DUDE? PARKA KING?
IT'S CAPTAIN COLD, AND WE NEED TO GET HIM OUT OF JUMP CITY!
TITANS GO!
"COLD BLOODED"
WRITTEN BY MERRILL HAGAN
ART BY JORGE CORONA
COLOR BY JEREMY LAWSON
LETTERS BY WES ABBOTT
I'M NOT READY TO GO JUST QUITE YET, YA LITTLE PUNK!
WHOA.
DUDE. YOU CAN FREEZE PEOPLE SOLID?
UM, I GUESS SO? USUALLY THE FLASH JUST RUNS AROUND MY BLASTS.
HE'S, UH, PRETTY, PRETTY FAST.
WE MUST TAKE DOWN THIS COLD COMMANDER!
UH-OH.

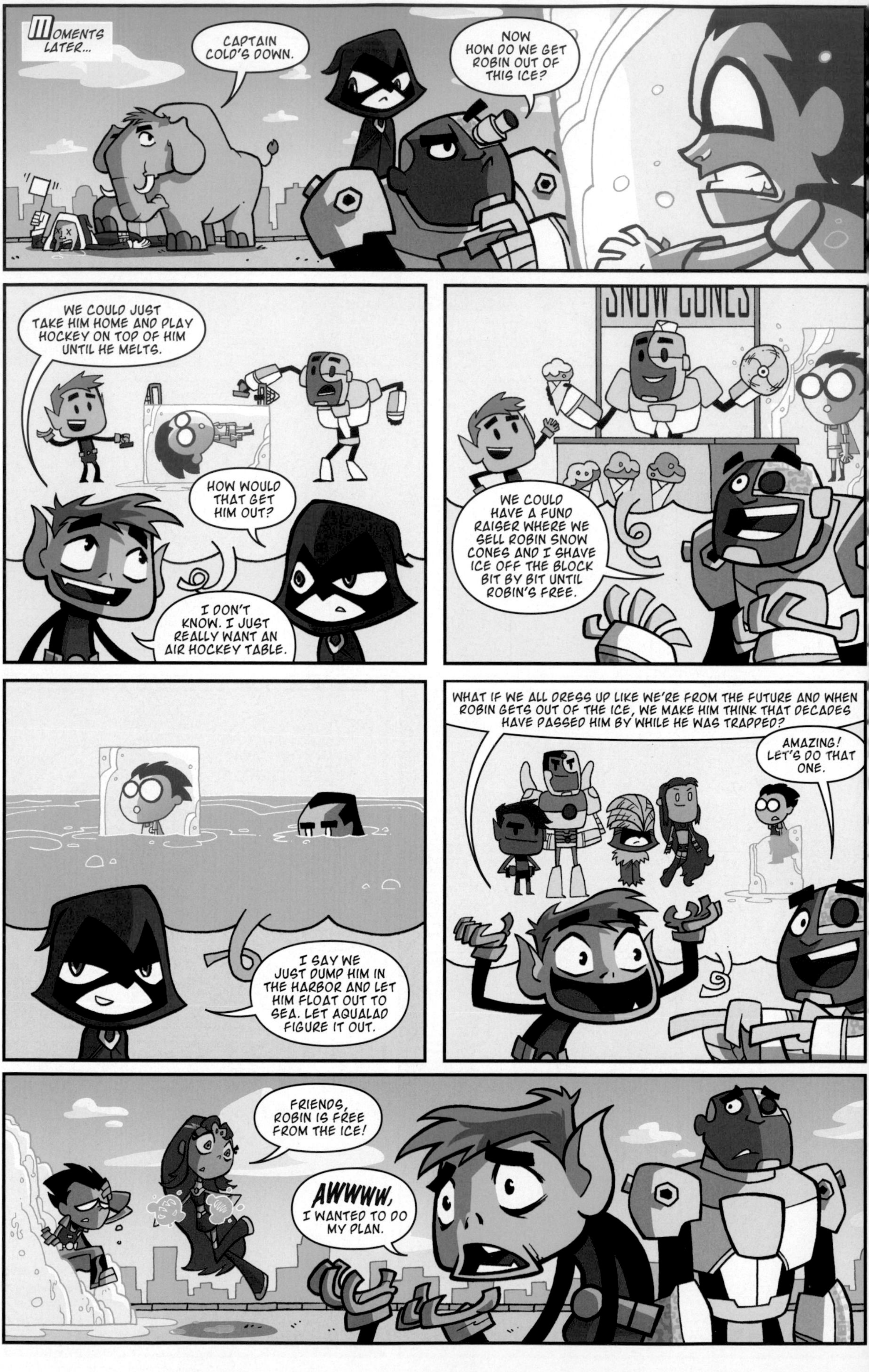
MOMENTS LATER...
CAPTAIN COLD'S DOWN.
NOW HOW DO WE GET ROBIN OUT OF THIS ICE?
WE COULD JUST TAKE HIM HOME AND PLAY HOCKEY ON TOP OF HIM UNTIL HE MELTS.
HOW WOULD THAT GET HIM OUT?
I DON'T KNOW. I JUST REALLY WANT AN AIR HOCKEY TABLE.
SNOW CONES
WE COULD HAVE A FUND RAISER WHERE WE SELL ROBIN SNOW CONES AND I SHAVE ICE OFF THE BLOCK BIT BY BIT UNTIL ROBIN'S FREE.
I SAY WE JUST DUMP HIM IN THE HARBOR AND LET HIM FLOAT OUT TO SEA. LET AQUALAD FIGURE IT OUT.
WHAT IF WE ALL DRESS UP LIKE WE'RE FROM THE FUTURE AND WHEN ROBIN GETS OUT OF THE ICE, WE MAKE HIM THINK THAT DECADES HAVE PASSED HIM BY WHILE HE WAS TRAPPED?
AMAZING! LET'S DO THAT ONE.
FRIENDS, ROBIN IS FREE FROM THE ICE!
AWWWW, I WANTED TO DO MY PLAN.

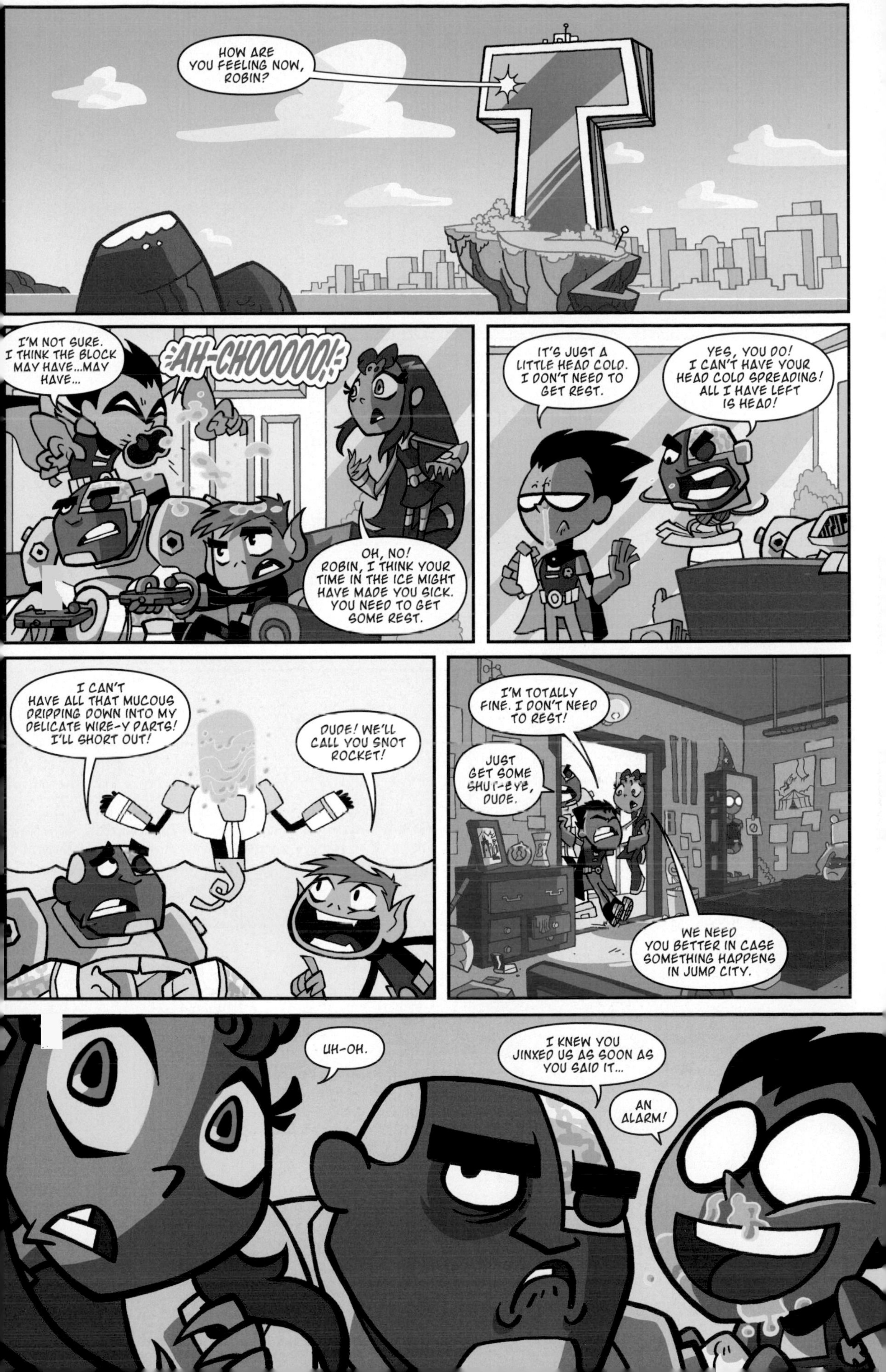
HOW ARE YOU FEELING NOW, ROBIN?
I'M NOT SURE. I THINK THE BLOCK MAY HAVE...MAY HAVE...
AH-CHOOOOOO!
OH, NO! ROBIN, I THINK YOUR TIME IN THE ICE MIGHT HAVE MADE YOU SICK. YOU NEED TO GET SOME REST.
IT'S JUST A LITTLE HEAD COLD. I DON'T NEED TO GET REST.
YES, YOU DO! I CAN'T HAVE YOUR HEAD COLD SPREADING! ALL I HAVE LEFT IS HEAD!
I CAN'T HAVE ALL THAT MUCOUS DRIPPING DOWN INTO MY DELICATE WIRE-Y PARTS! I'LL SHORT OUT!
DUDE! WE'LL CALL YOU SNOT ROCKET!
I'M TOTALLY FINE. I DON'T NEED TO REST!
JUST GET SOME SHUT-EYE, DUDE.
WE NEED YOU BETTER IN CASE SOMETHING HAPPENS IN JUMP CITY.
UH-OH.
I KNEW YOU JINXED US AS SOON AS YOU SAID IT...
AN ALARM!

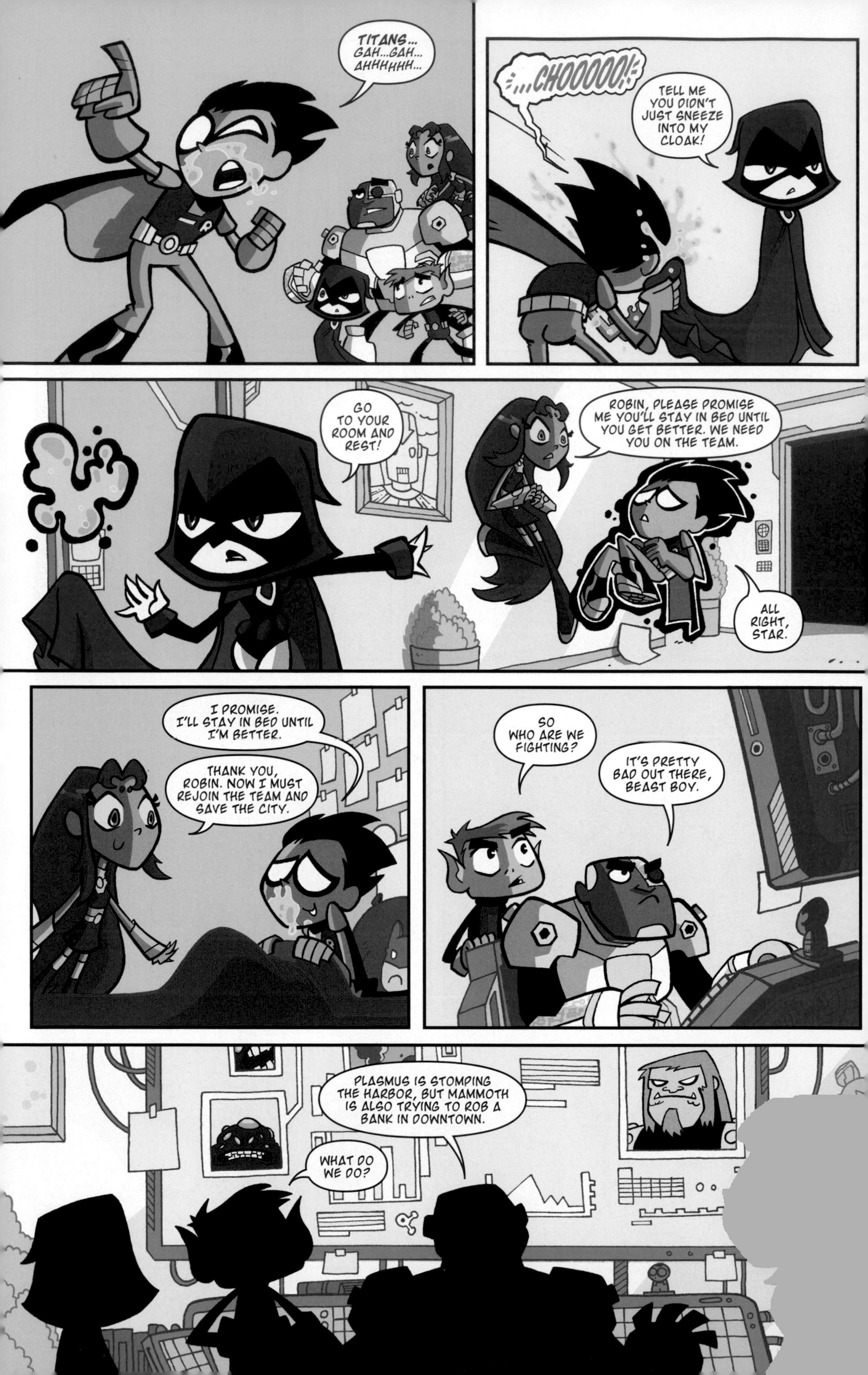
TITANS... GAH...GAH... AHHHHHH...
...CHOOOOO!
TELL ME YOU DIDN'T JUST SNEEZE INTO MY CLOAK!
GO TO YOUR ROOM AND REST!
ROBIN, PLEASE PROMISE ME YOU'LL STAY IN BED UNTIL YOU GET BETTER. WE NEED YOU ON THE TEAM.
ALL RIGHT, STAR.
I PROMISE. I'LL STAY IN BED UNTIL I'M BETTER.
THANK YOU, ROBIN. NOW I MUST REJOIN THE TEAM AND SAVE THE CITY.
SO WHO ARE WE FIGHTING?
IT'S PRETTY BAD OUT THERE, BEAST BOY.
PLASMUS IS STOMPING THE HARBOR, BUT MAMMOTH IS ALSO TRYING TO ROB A BANK IN DOWNTOWN.
WHAT DO WE DO?

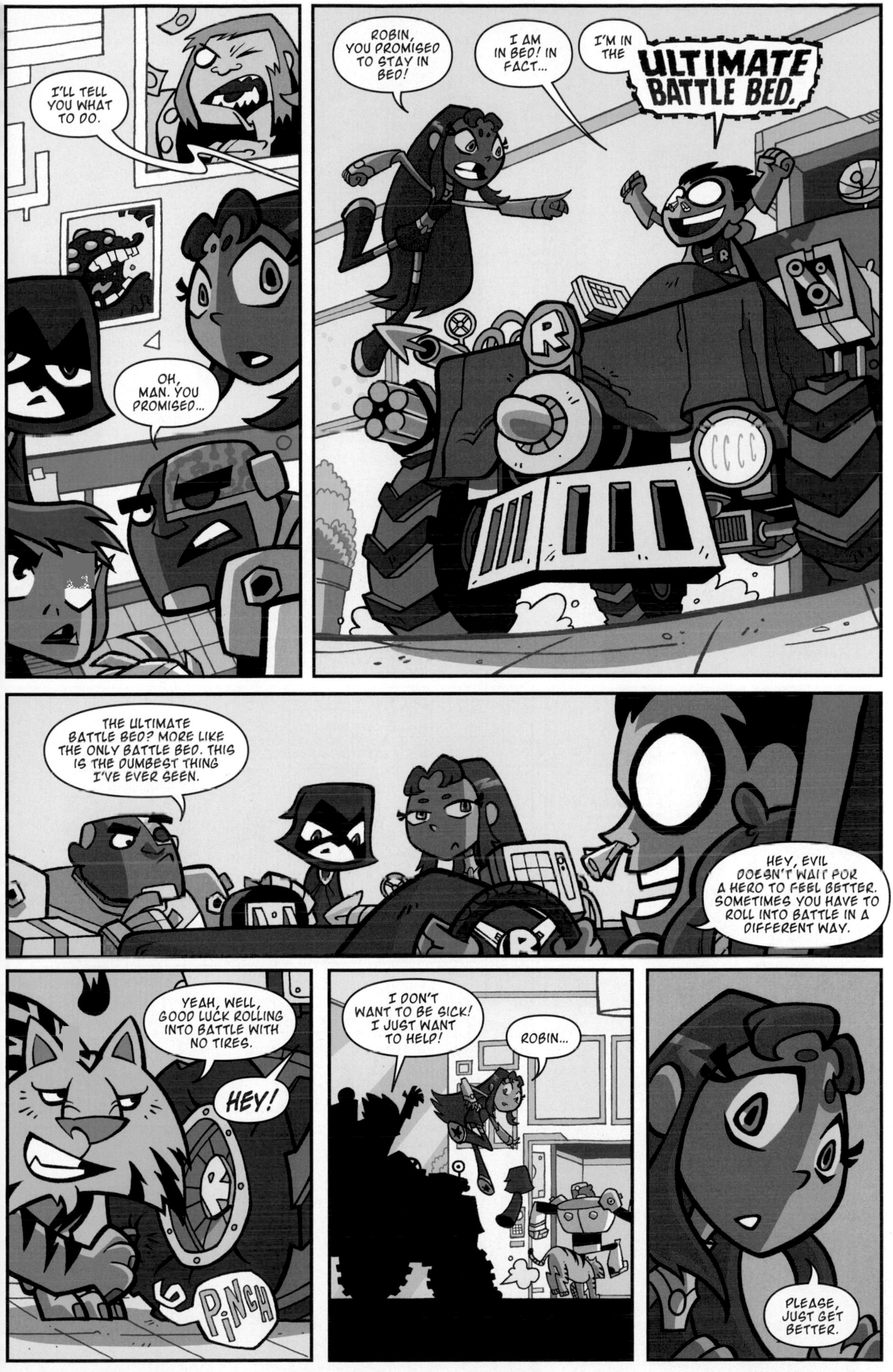
I'LL TELL YOU WHAT TO DO.
OH, MAN. YOU PROMISED...
ROBIN, YOU PROMISED TO STAY IN BED!
I AM IN BED! IN FACT...
I'M IN THE
ULTIMATE BATTLE BED.
THE ULTIMATE BATTLE BED? MORE LIKE THE ONLY BATTLE BED. THIS IS THE DUMBEST THING I'VE EVER SEEN.
HEY, EVIL DOESN'T WAIT FOR A HERO TO FEEL BETTER. SOMETIMES YOU HAVE TO ROLL INTO BATTLE IN A DIFFERENT WAY.
YEAH, WELL, GOOD LUCK ROLLING INTO BATTLE WITH NO TIRES.
HEY!
PINCH
I DON'T WANT TO BE SICK! I JUST WANT TO HELP!
ROBIN...
PLEASE, JUST GET BETTER.

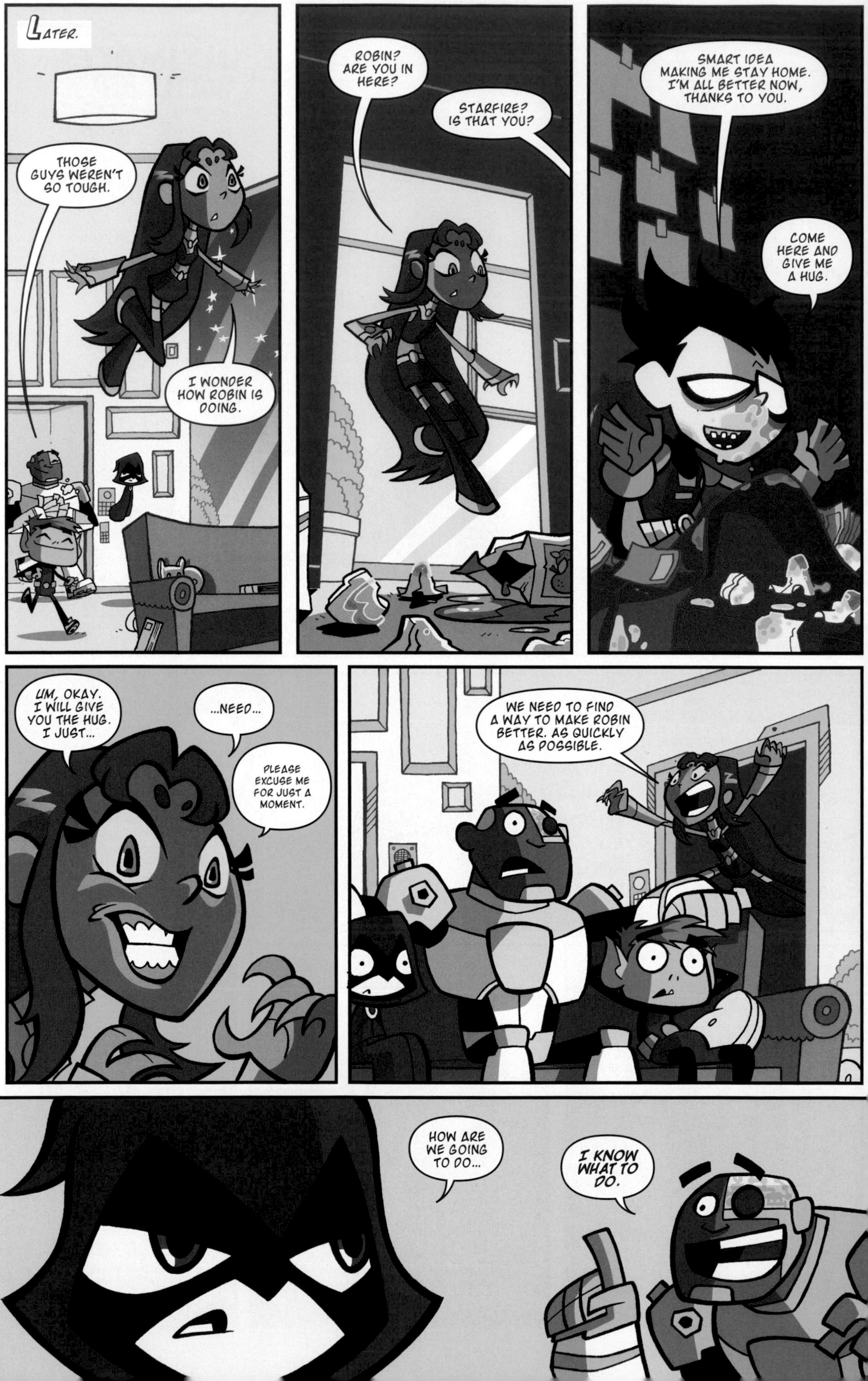
LATER.
THOSE GUYS WEREN'T SO TOUGH.
I WONDER HOW ROBIN IS DOING.
ROBIN? ARE YOU IN HERE?
STARFIRE? IS THAT YOU?
SMART IDEA MAKING ME STAY HOME. I'M ALL BETTER NOW, THANKS TO YOU.
COME HERE AND GIVE ME A HUG.
UM, OKAY. I WILL GIVE YOU THE HUG. I JUST...
...NEED...
PLEASE EXCUSE ME FOR JUST A MOMENT.
WE NEED TO FIND A WAY TO MAKE ROBIN BETTER. AS QUICKLY AS POSSIBLE.
HOW ARE WE GOING TO DO...
I KNOW WHAT TO DO.

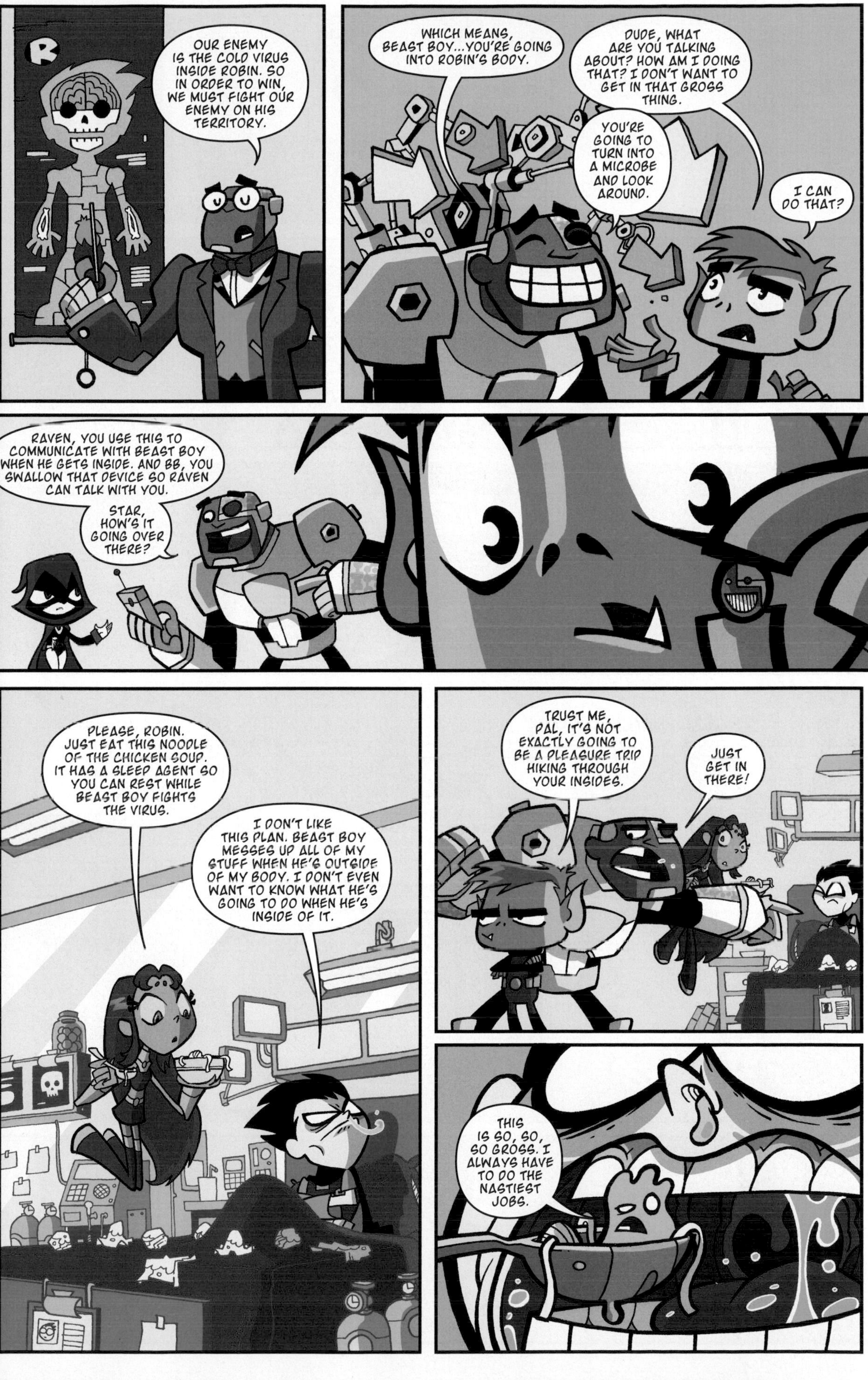
OUR ENEMY IS THE COLD VIRUS INSIDE ROBIN. SO IN ORDER TO WIN, WE MUST FIGHT OUR ENEMY ON HIS TERRITORY.
WHICH MEANS, BEAST BOY...YOU'RE GOING INTO ROBIN'S BODY.
DUDE, WHAT ARE YOU TALKING ABOUT? HOW AM I DOING THAT? I DON'T WANT TO GET IN THAT GROSS THING.
YOU'RE GOING TO TURN INTO A MICROBE AND LOOK AROUND.
I CAN DO THAT?
RAVEN, YOU USE THIS TO COMMUNICATE WITH BEAST BOY WHEN HE GETS INSIDE. AND BB, YOU SWALLOW THAT DEVICE SO RAVEN CAN TALK WITH YOU.
STAR, HOW'S IT GOING OVER THERE?
PLEASE, ROBIN. JUST EAT THIS NOODLE OF THE CHICKEN SOUP. IT HAS A SLEEP AGENT SO YOU CAN REST WHILE BEAST BOY FIGHTS THE VIRUS.
I DON'T LIKE THIS PLAN. BEAST BOY MESSES UP ALL OF MY STUFF WHEN HE'S OUTSIDE OF MY BODY. I DON'T EVEN WANT TO KNOW WHAT HE'S GOING TO DO WHEN HE'S INSIDE OF IT.
TRUST ME, PAL, IT'S NOT EXACTLY GOING TO BE A PLEASURE TRIP HIKING THROUGH YOUR INSIDES.
JUST GET IN THERE!
THIS IS SO, SO, SO GROSS. I ALWAYS HAVE TO DO THE NASTIEST JOBS.

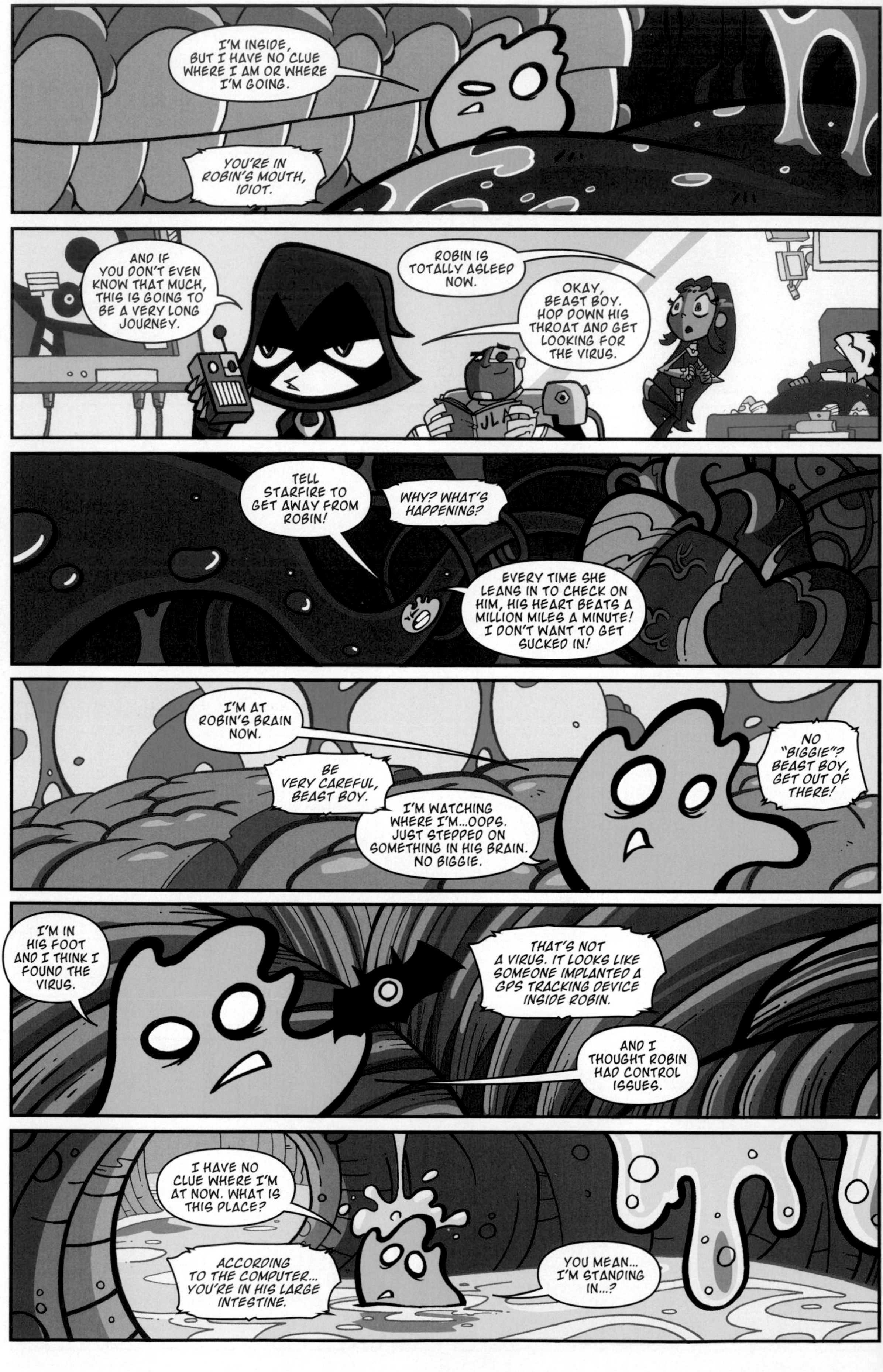
I'M INSIDE, BUT I HAVE NO CLUE WHERE I AM OR WHERE I'M GOING.
YOU'RE IN ROBIN'S MOUTH, IDIOT.
AND IF YOU DON'T EVEN KNOW THAT MUCH, THIS IS GOING TO BE A VERY LONG JOURNEY.
ROBIN IS TOTALLY ASLEEP NOW.
OKAY, BEAST BOY. HOP DOWN HIS THROAT AND GET LOOKING FOR THE VIRUS.
JLA
TELL STARFIRE TO GET AWAY FROM ROBIN!
WHY? WHAT'S HAPPENING?
EVERY TIME SHE LEANS IN TO CHECK ON HIM, HIS HEART BEATS A MILLION MILES A MINUTE! I DON'T WANT TO GET SUCKED IN!
I'M AT ROBIN'S BRAIN NOW.
BE VERY CAREFUL, BEAST BOY.
I'M WATCHING WHERE I'M...OOPS. JUST STEPPED ON SOMETHING IN HIS BRAIN. NO BIGGIE.
NO "BIGGIE"? BEAST BOY, GET OUT OF THERE!
I'M IN HIS FOOT AND I THINK I FOUND THE VIRUS.
THAT'S NOT A VIRUS. IT LOOKS LIKE SOMEONE IMPLANTED A GPS TRACKING DEVICE INSIDE ROBIN.
AND I THOUGHT ROBIN HAD CONTROL ISSUES.
I HAVE NO CLUE WHERE I'M AT NOW. WHAT IS THIS PLACE?
ACCORDING TO THE COMPUTER... YOU'RE IN HIS LARGE INTESTINE.
YOU MEAN... I'M STANDING IN...?

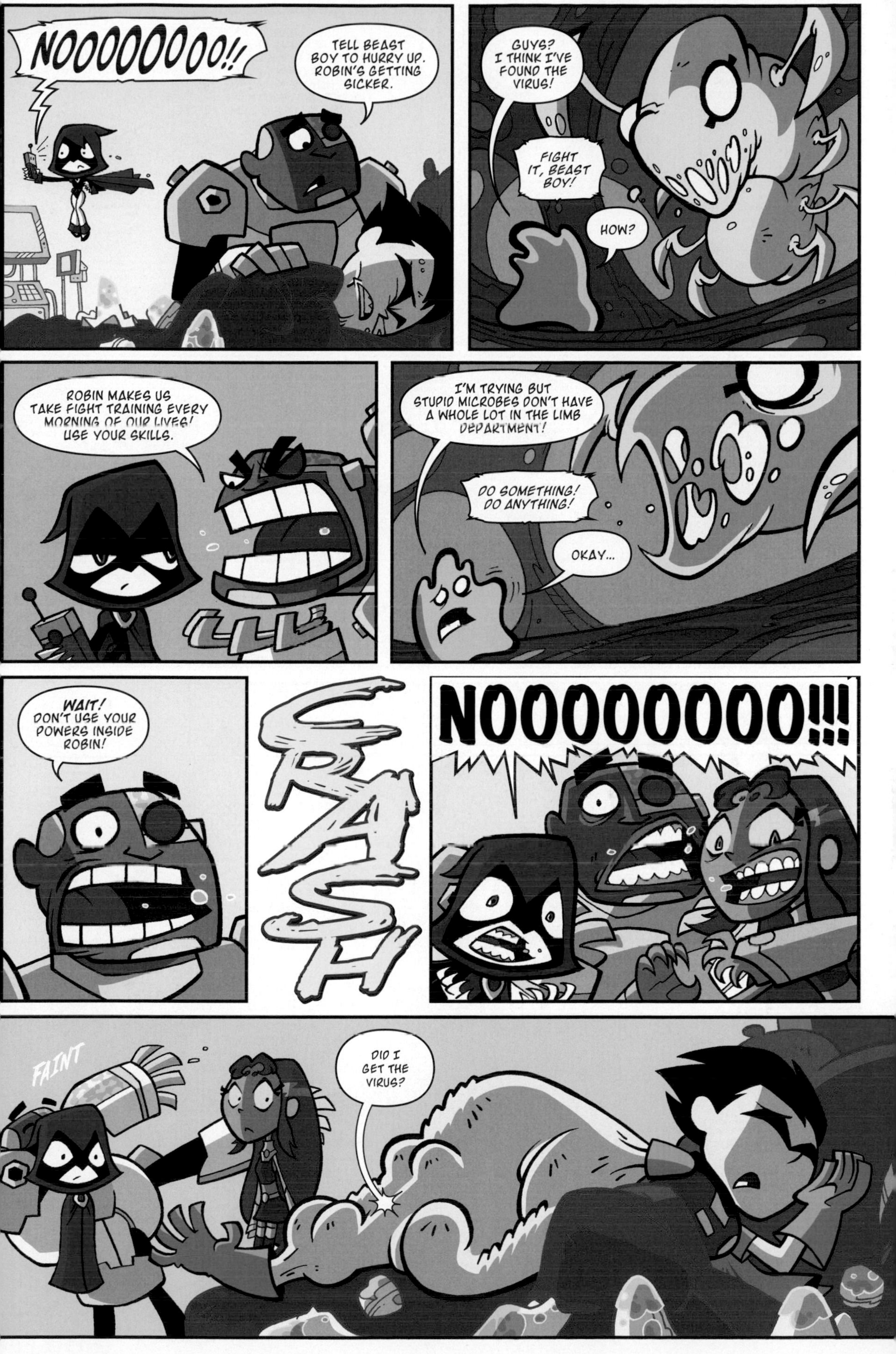
NOOOOOOOO!!
TELL BEAST BOY TO HURRY UP. ROBIN'S GETTING SICKER.
GUYS? I THINK I'VE FOUND THE VIRUS!
FIGHT IT, BEAST BOY!
HOW?
ROBIN MAKES US TAKE FIGHT TRAINING EVERY MORNING OF OUR LIVES! USE YOUR SKILLS.
I'M TRYING BUT STUPID MICROBES DON'T HAVE A WHOLE LOT IN THE LIMB DEPARTMENT!
DO SOMETHING! DO ANYTHING!
OKAY...
WAIT! DON'T USE YOUR POWERS INSIDE ROBIN!
CRASH
NOOOOOOOOO!!!
FAINT
DID I GET THE VIRUS?

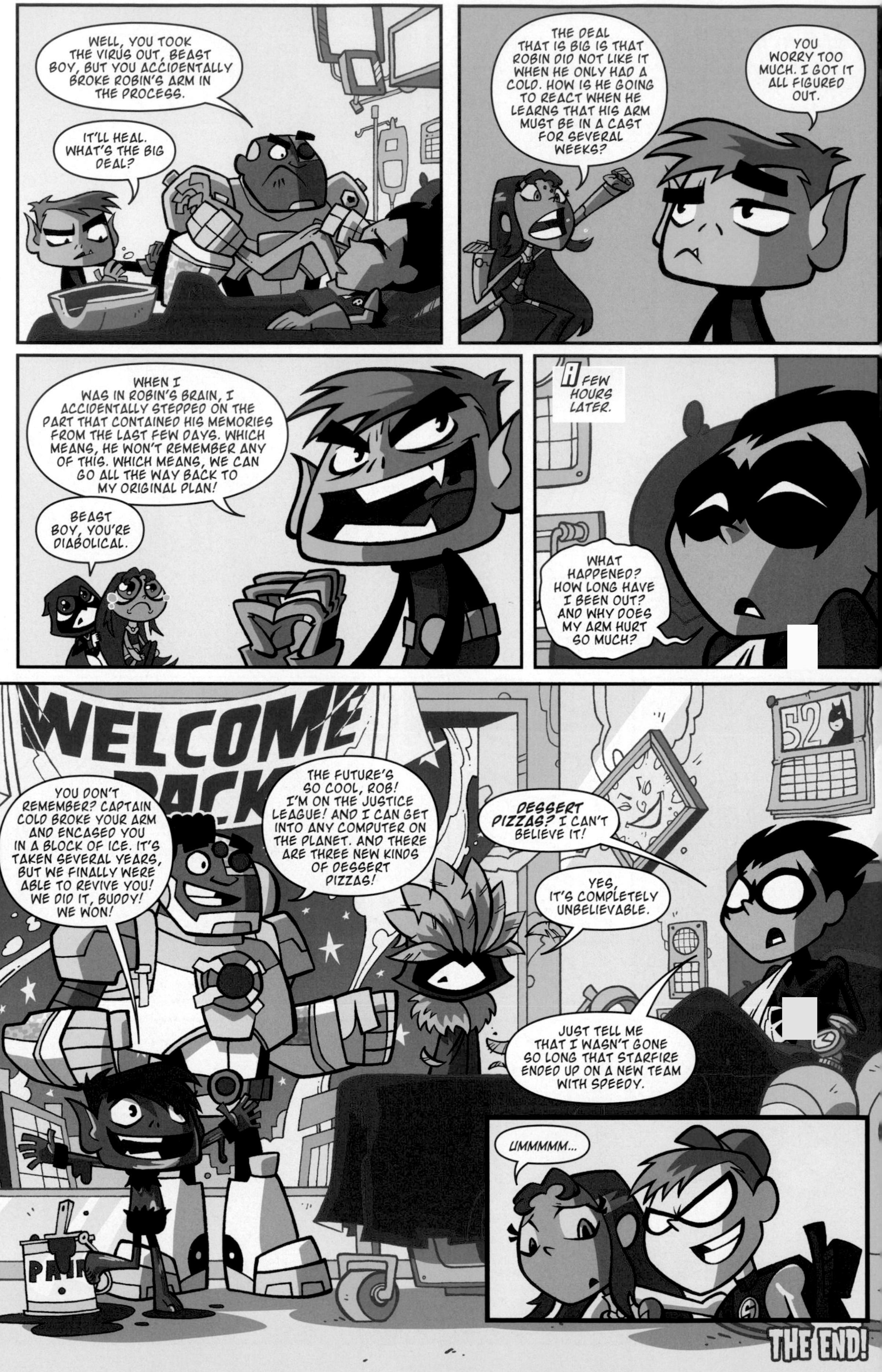
WELL, YOU TOOK THE VIRUS OUT, BEAST BOY, BUT YOU ACCIDENTALLY BROKE ROBIN'S ARM IN THE PROCESS.
IT'LL HEAL. WHAT'S THE BIG DEAL?
THE DEAL THAT IS BIG IS THAT ROBIN DID NOT LIKE IT WHEN HE ONLY HAD A COLD. HOW IS HE GOING TO REACT WHEN HE LEARNS THAT HIS ARM MUST BE IN A CAST FOR SEVERAL WEEKS?
YOU WORRY TOO MUCH. I GOT IT ALL FIGURED OUT.
WHEN I WAS IN ROBIN'S BRAIN, I ACCIDENTALLY STEPPED ON THE PART THAT CONTAINED HIS MEMORIES FROM THE LAST FEW DAYS. WHICH MEANS, HE WON'T REMEMBER ANY OF THIS. WHICH MEANS, WE CAN GO ALL THE WAY BACK TO MY ORIGINAL PLAN!
BEAST BOY, YOU'RE DIABOLICAL.
A FEW HOURS LATER.
WHAT HAPPENED? HOW LONG HAVE I BEEN OUT? AND WHY DOES MY ARM HURT SO MUCH?
WELCOME BACK
YOU DON'T REMEMBER? CAPTAIN COLD BROKE YOUR ARM AND ENCASED YOU IN A BLOCK OF ICE. IT'S TAKEN SEVERAL YEARS, BUT WE FINALLY WERE ABLE TO REVIVE YOU! WE DID IT, BUDDY! WE WON!
THE FUTURE'S SO COOL, ROB! I'M ON THE JUSTICE LEAGUE! AND I CAN GET INTO ANY COMPUTER ON THE PLANET. AND THERE ARE THREE NEW KINDS OF DESSERT PIZZAS!
52
DESSERT PIZZAS? I CAN'T BELIEVE IT!
YES, IT'S COMPLETELY UNBELIEVABLE.
JUST TELL ME THAT I WASN'T GONE SO LONG THAT STARFIRE ENDED UP ON A NEW TEAM WITH SPEEDY.
UMMMMM...
PAINT
THE END!

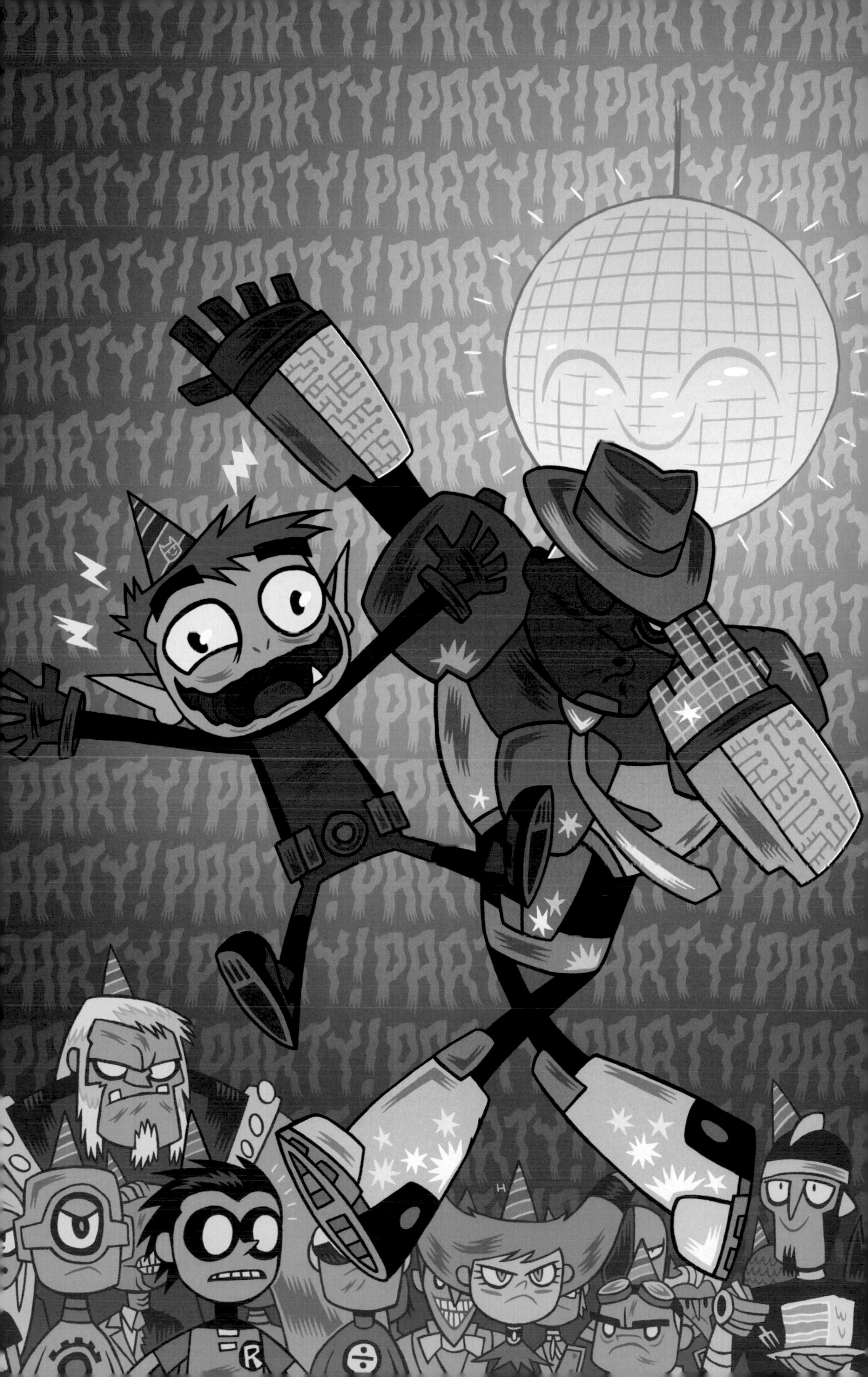
PARTY! PARTY! PARTY! PARTY!

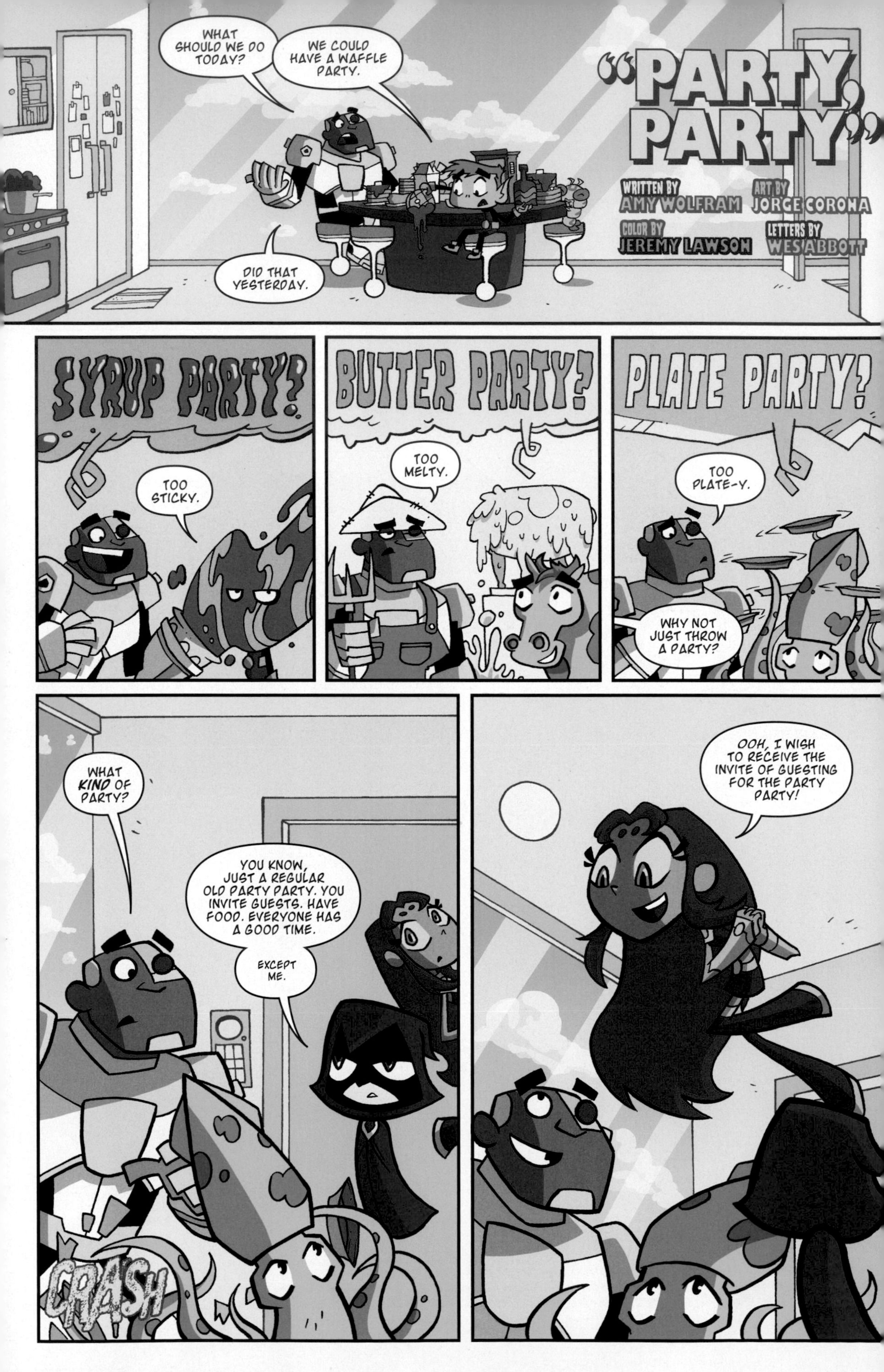

"PARTY, PARTY"
WRITTEN BY AMY WOLFRAM
ART BY JORGE CORONA
COLOR BY JEREMY LAWSON
LETTERS BY WES ABBOTT
WHAT SHOULD WE DO TODAY?
WE COULD HAVE A WAFFLE PARTY.
DID THAT YESTERDAY.
SYRUP PARTY?
TOO STICKY.
BUTTER PARTY?
TOO MELTY.
PLATE PARTY?
TOO PLATE-Y.
WHY NOT JUST THROW A PARTY?
WHAT KIND OF PARTY?
YOU KNOW, JUST A REGULAR OLD PARTY PARTY. YOU INVITE GUESTS. HAVE FOOD. EVERYONE HAS A GOOD TIME.
EXCEPT ME.
CRASH
OOH, I WISH TO RECEIVE THE INVITE OF GUESTING FOR THE PARTY PARTY!

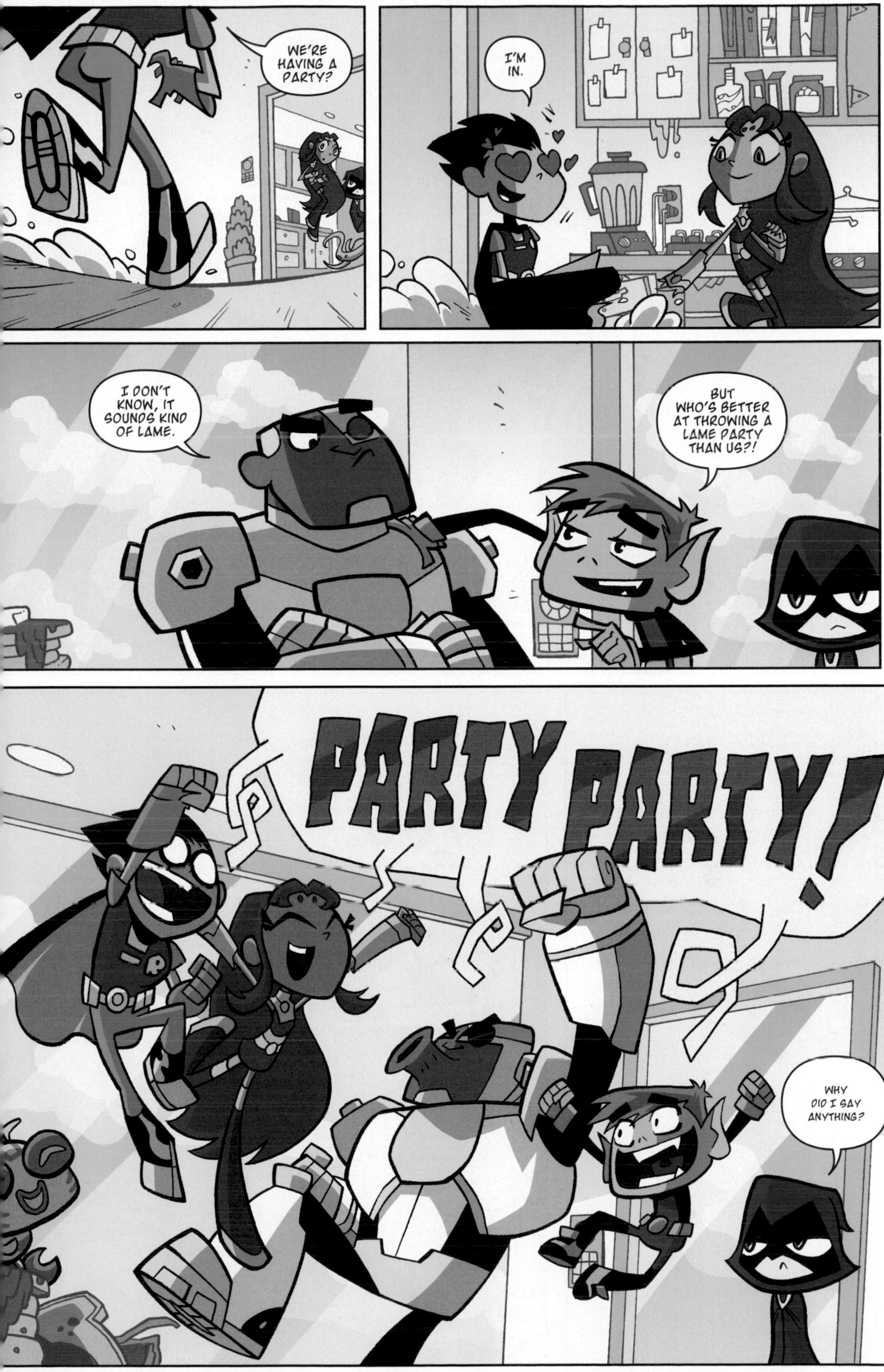
WE'RE HAVING A PARTY?
I'M IN.
I DON'T KNOW, IT SOUNDS KIND OF LAME.
BUT WHO'S BETTER AT THROWING A LAME PARTY THAN US?!
PARTY PARTY!
WHY DID I SAY ANYTHING?

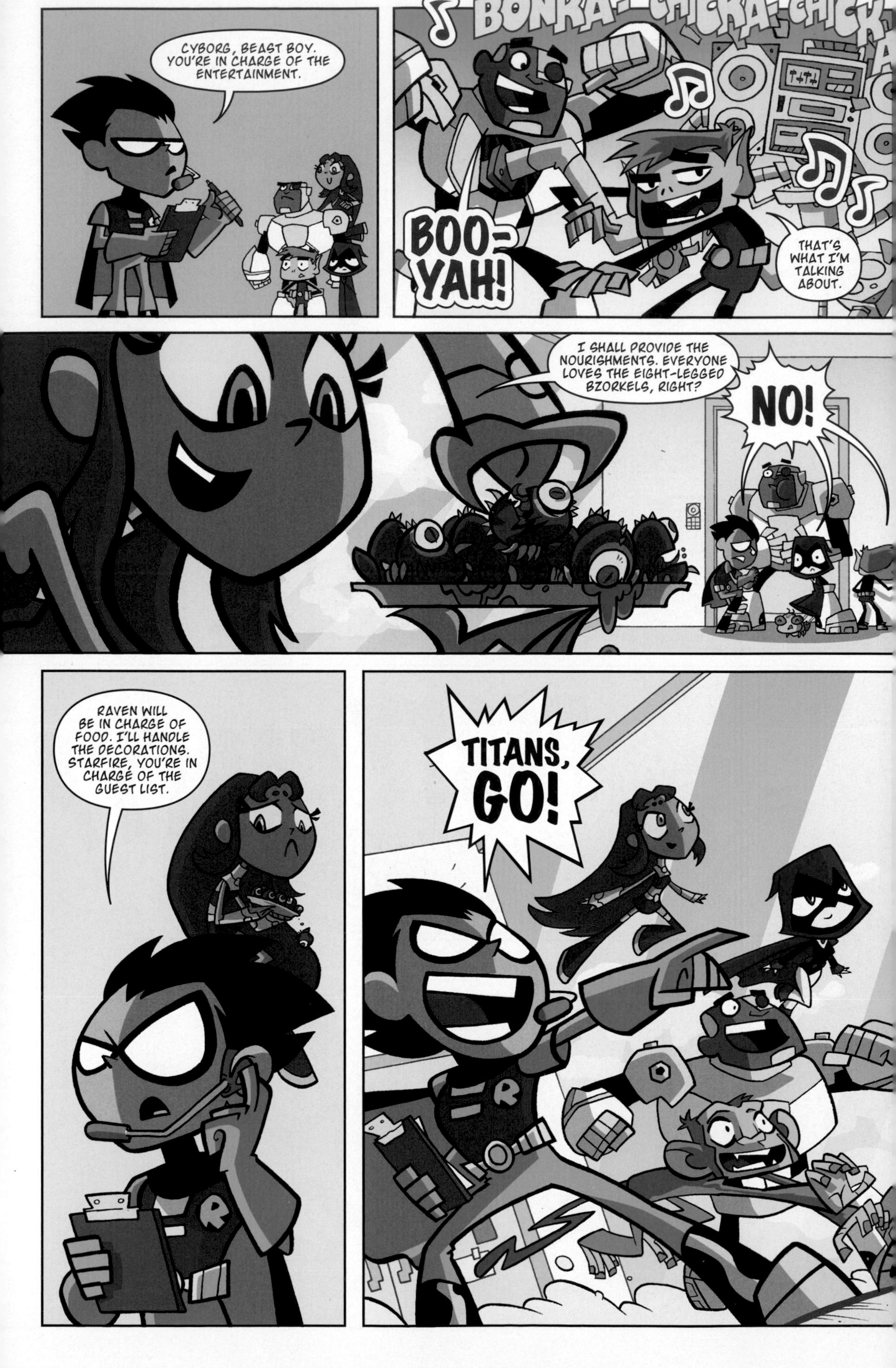
CYBORG, BEAST BOY. YOU'RE IN CHARGE OF THE ENTERTAINMENT.
BONKA-CHICKA-CHICKA
BOO-YAH!
THAT'S WHAT I'M TALKING ABOUT.
I SHALL PROVIDE THE NOURISHMENTS. EVERYONE LOVES THE EIGHT-LEGGED BZORKELS, RIGHT?
NO!
RAVEN WILL BE IN CHARGE OF FOOD. I'LL HANDLE THE DECORATIONS. STARFIRE, YOU'RE IN CHARGE OF THE GUEST LIST.
TITANS, GO!

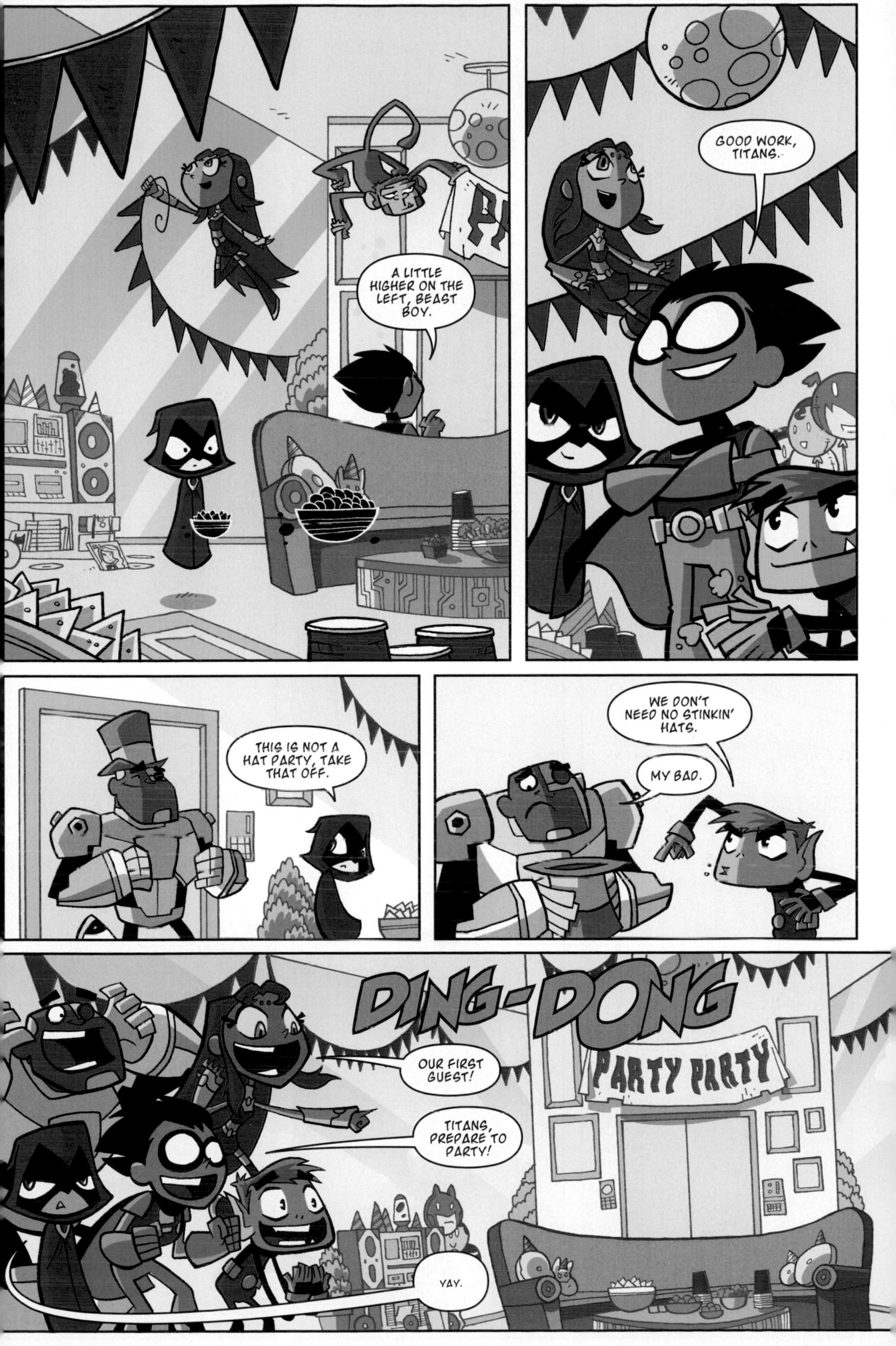
A LITTLE HIGHER ON THE LEFT, BEAST BOY.
GOOD WORK, TITANS.
THIS IS NOT A HAT PARTY, TAKE THAT OFF.
WE DON'T NEED NO STINKIN' HATS.
MY BAD.
DING-DONG
PARTY PARTY
OUR FIRST GUEST!
TITANS, PREPARE TO PARTY!
YAY.

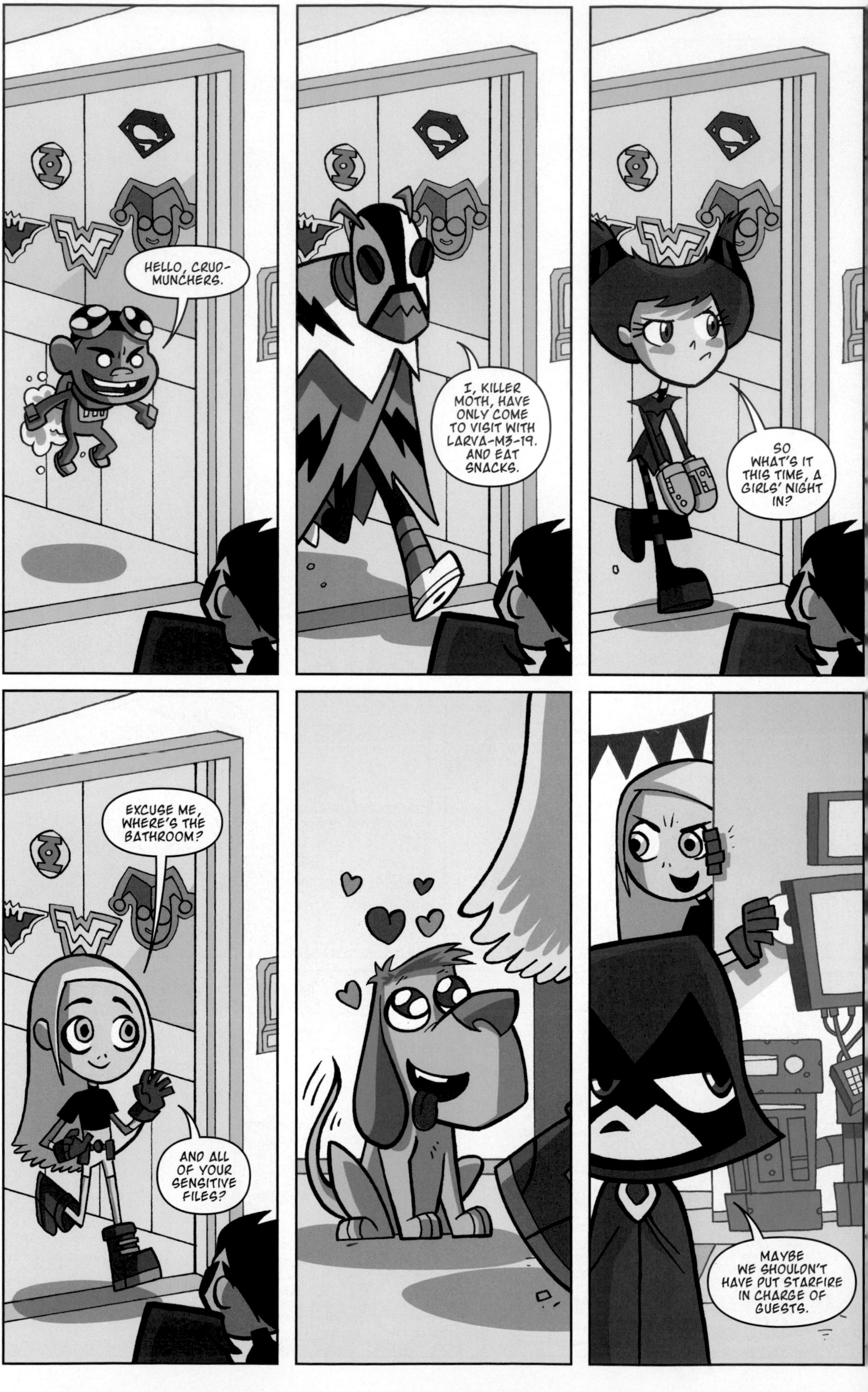
HELLO, CRUD-MUNCHERS.
I, KILLER MOTH, HAVE ONLY COME TO VISIT WITH LARVA-M3-19. AND EAT SNACKS.
SO WHAT'S IT THIS TIME, A GIRLS' NIGHT IN?
EXCUSE ME, WHERE'S THE BATHROOM?
AND ALL OF YOUR SENSITIVE FILES?
MAYBE WE SHOULDN'T HAVE PUT STARFIRE IN CHARGE OF GUESTS.

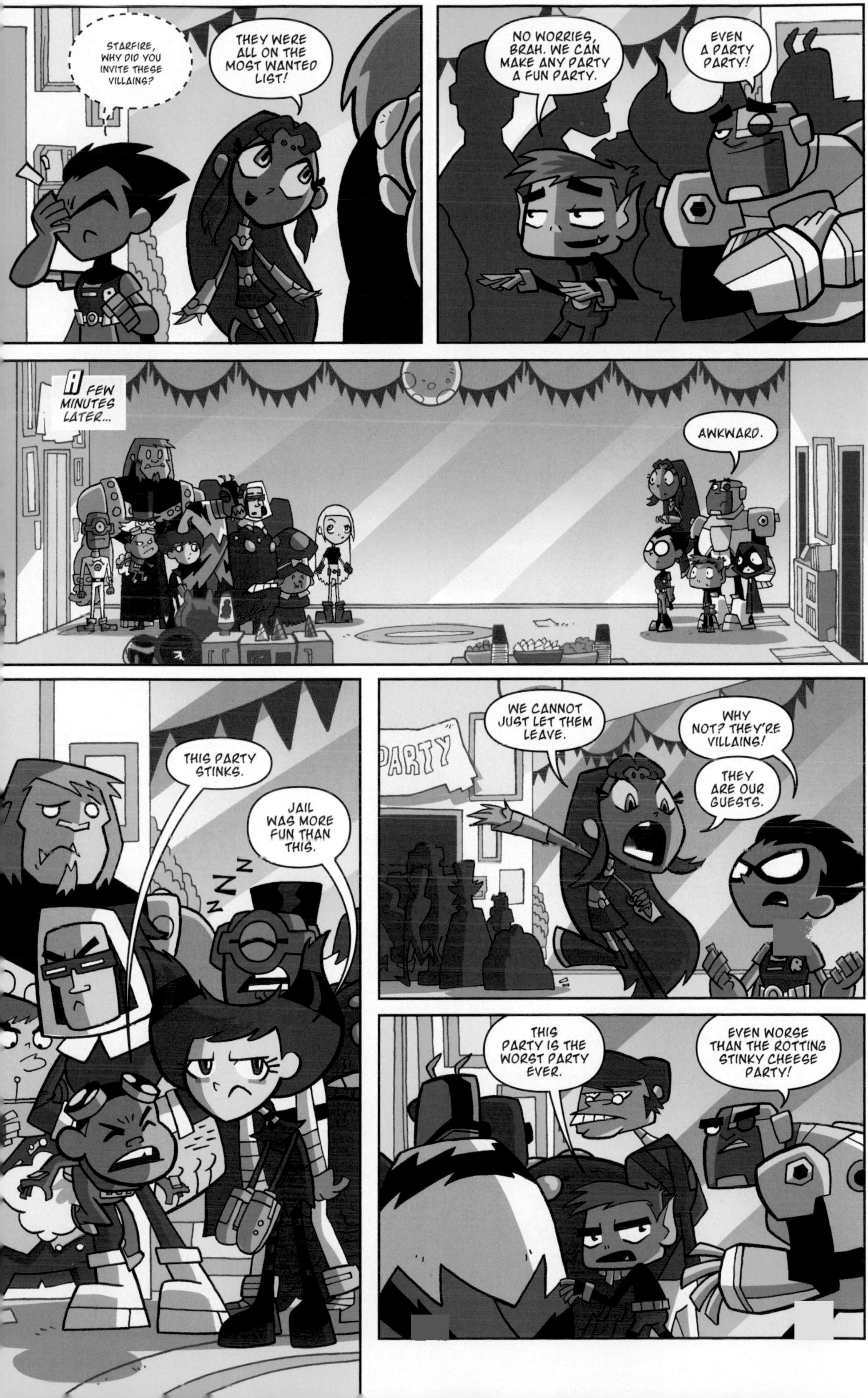
STARFIRE, WHY DID YOU INVITE THESE VILLAINS?
THEY WERE ALL ON THE MOST WANTED LIST!
NO WORRIES, BRAH. WE CAN MAKE ANY PARTY A FUN PARTY.
EVEN A PARTY PARTY!
A FEW MINUTES LATER...
AWKWARD.
THIS PARTY STINKS.
JAIL WAS MORE FUN THAN THIS.
ZZZ
PARTY
WE CANNOT JUST LET THEM LEAVE.
WHY NOT? THEY'RE VILLAINS!
THEY ARE OUR GUESTS.
THIS PARTY IS THE WORST PARTY EVER.
EVEN WORSE THAN THE ROTTING STINKY CHEESE PARTY!

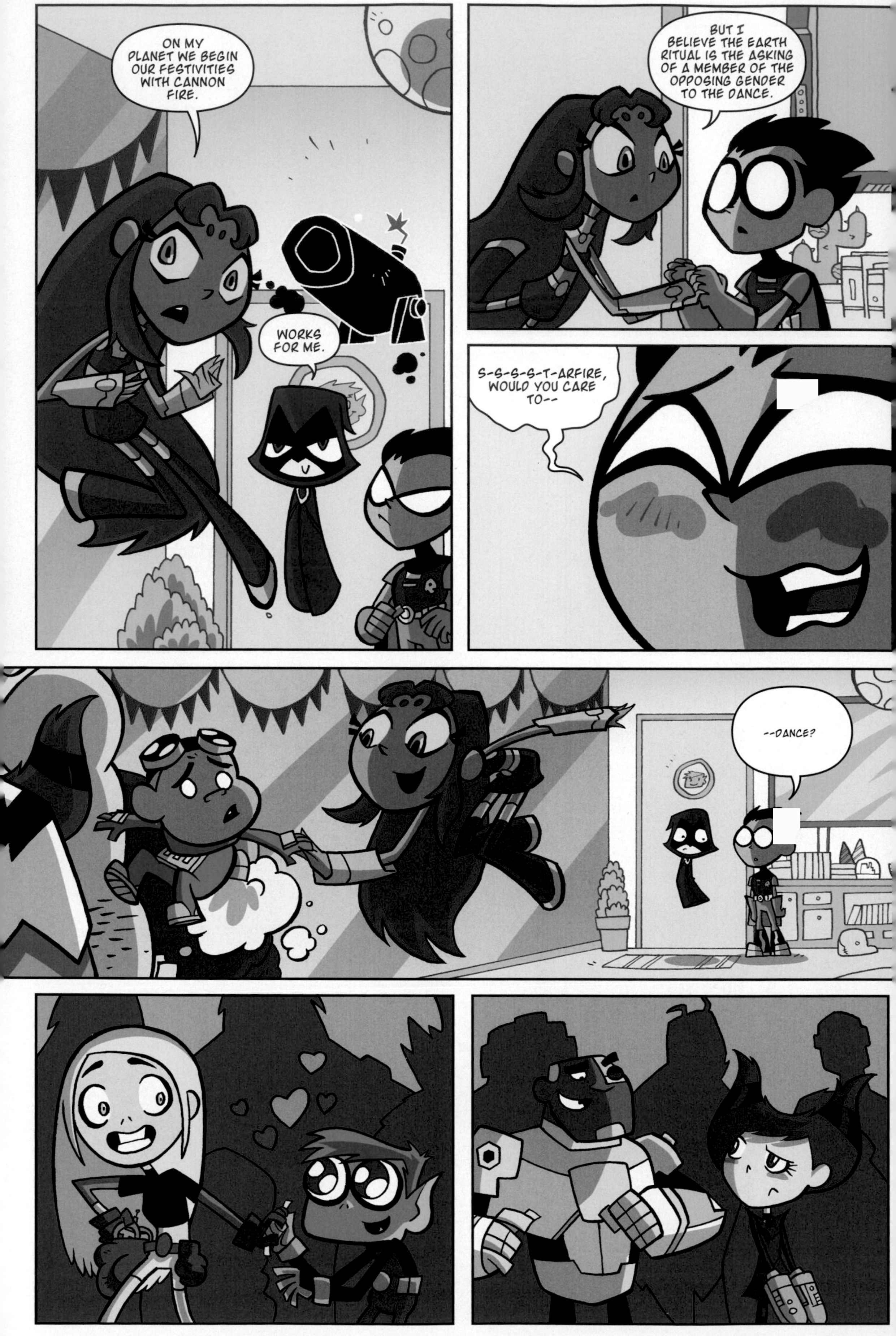
ON MY PLANET WE BEGIN OUR FESTIVITIES WITH CANNON FIRE.
WORKS FOR ME.
BUT I BELIEVE THE EARTH RITUAL IS THE ASKING OF A MEMBER OF THE OPPOSING GENDER TO THE DANCE.
S-S-S-S-T-ARFIRE, WOULD YOU CARE TO--
--DANCE?

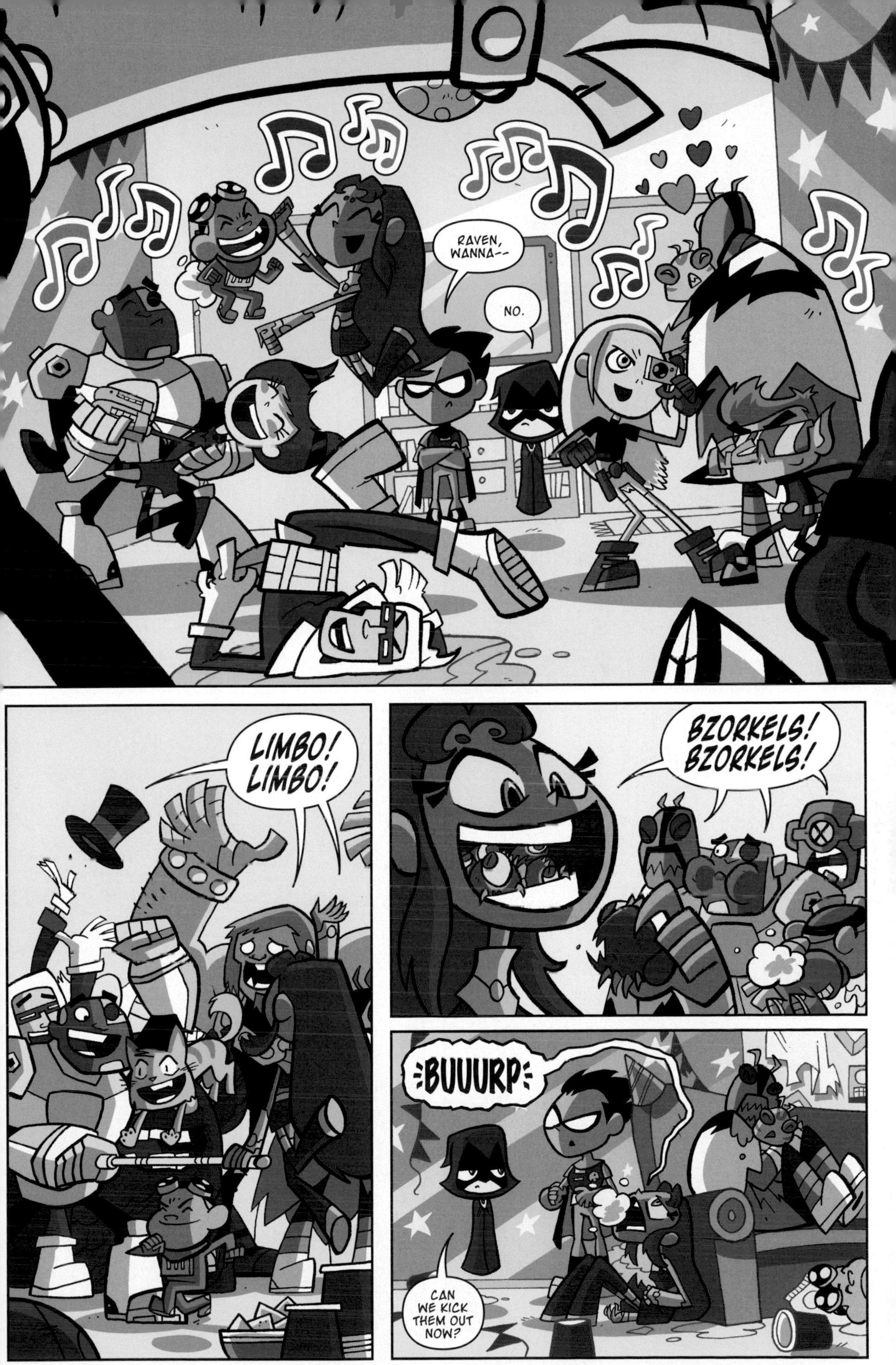
RAVEN, WANNA--
NO.
LIMBO! LIMBO!
BZORKELS! BZORKELS!
BUUURP
CAN WE KICK THEM OUT NOW?

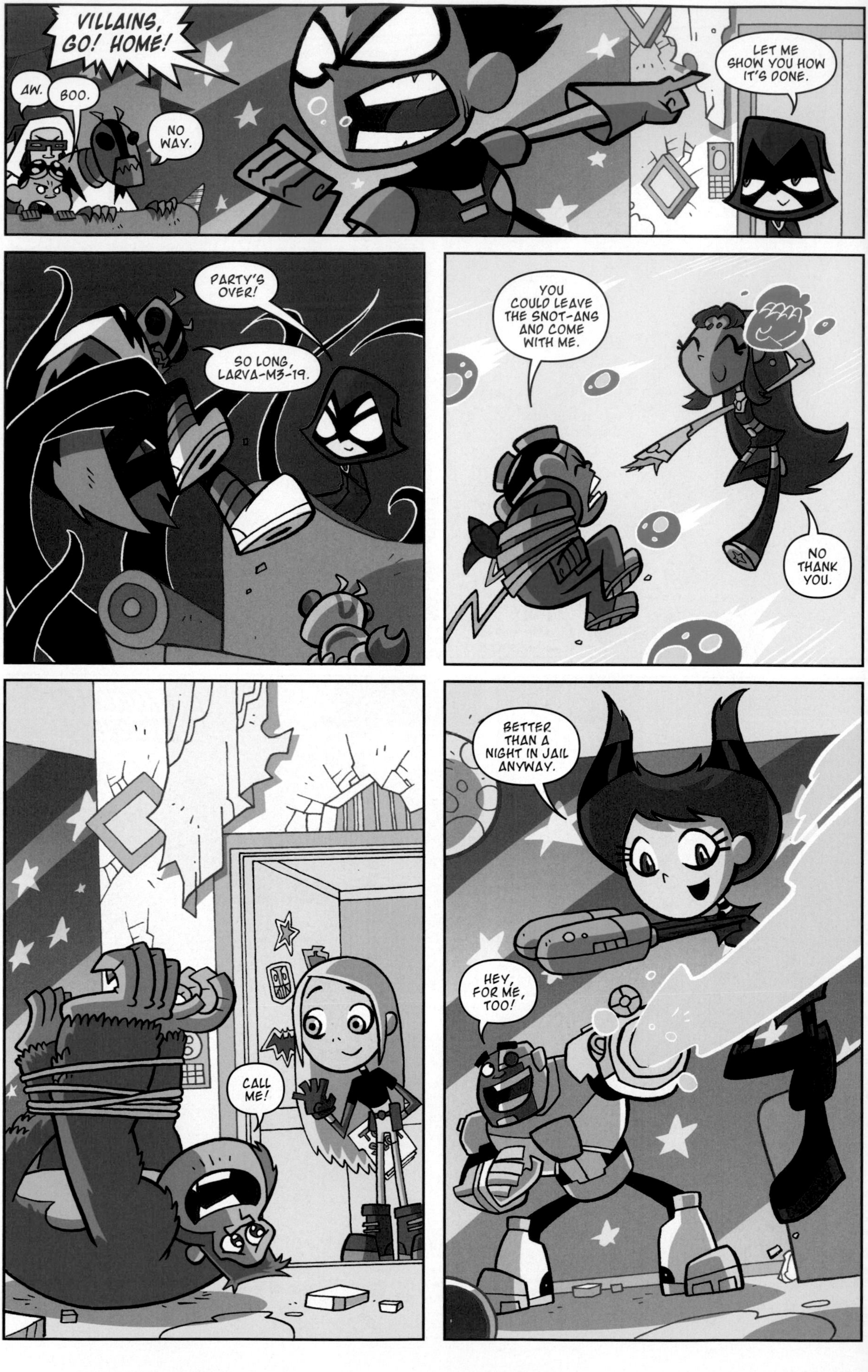
VILLAINS, GO! HOME!
AW.
BOO.
NO WAY.
LET ME SHOW YOU HOW IT'S DONE.
PARTY'S OVER!
SO LONG, LARVA-M3-19.
YOU COULD LEAVE THE SNOT-ANS AND COME WITH ME.
NO THANK YOU.
CALL ME!
BETTER THAN A NIGHT IN JAIL ANYWAY.
HEY, FOR ME, TOO!

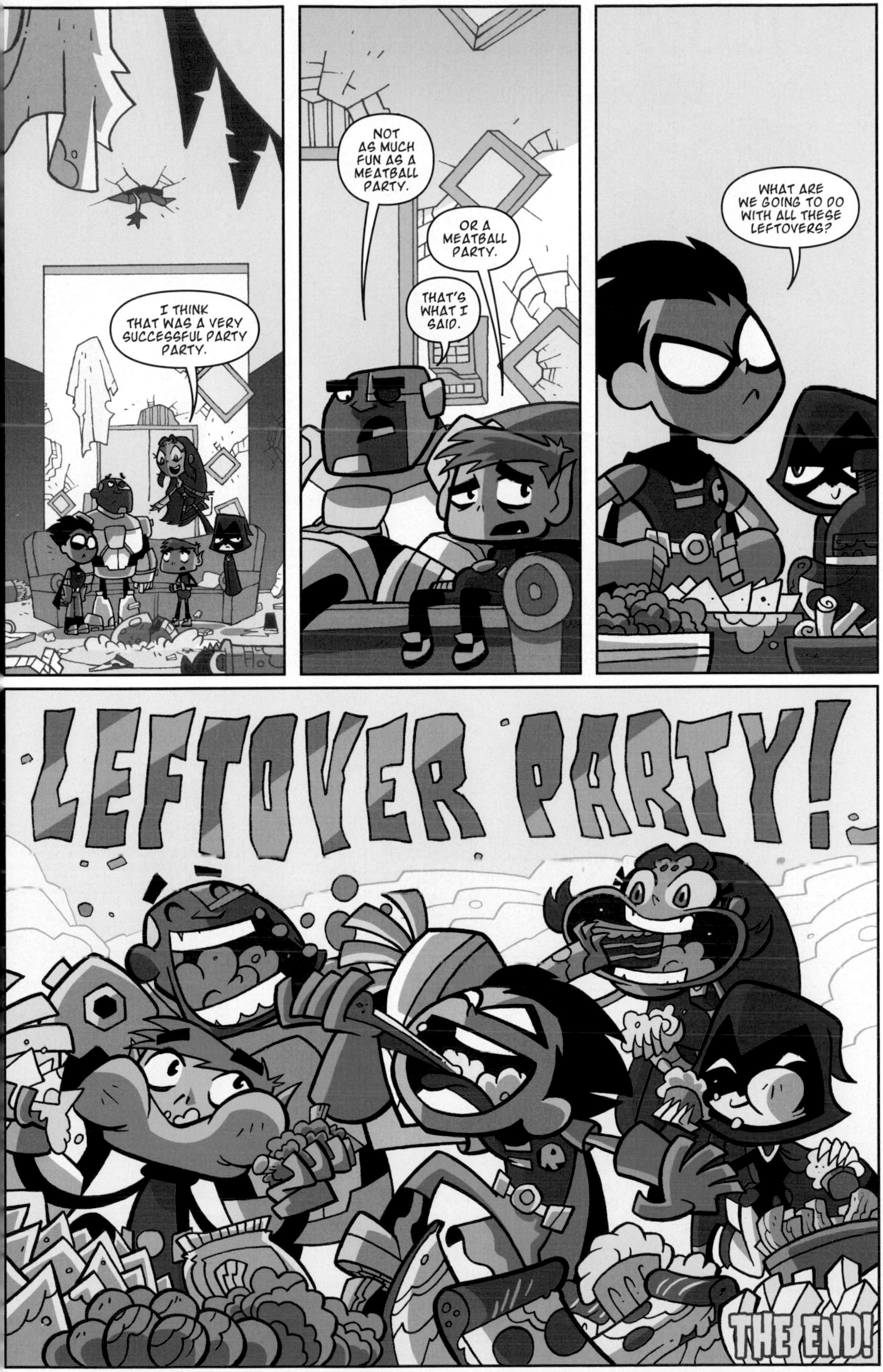
I THINK THAT WAS A VERY SUCCESSFUL PARTY PARTY.
NOT AS MUCH FUN AS A MEATBALL PARTY.
OR A MEATBALL PARTY.
THAT'S WHAT I SAID.
WHAT ARE WE GOING TO DO WITH ALL THESE LEFTOVERS?
LEFTOVER PARTY!
THE END!

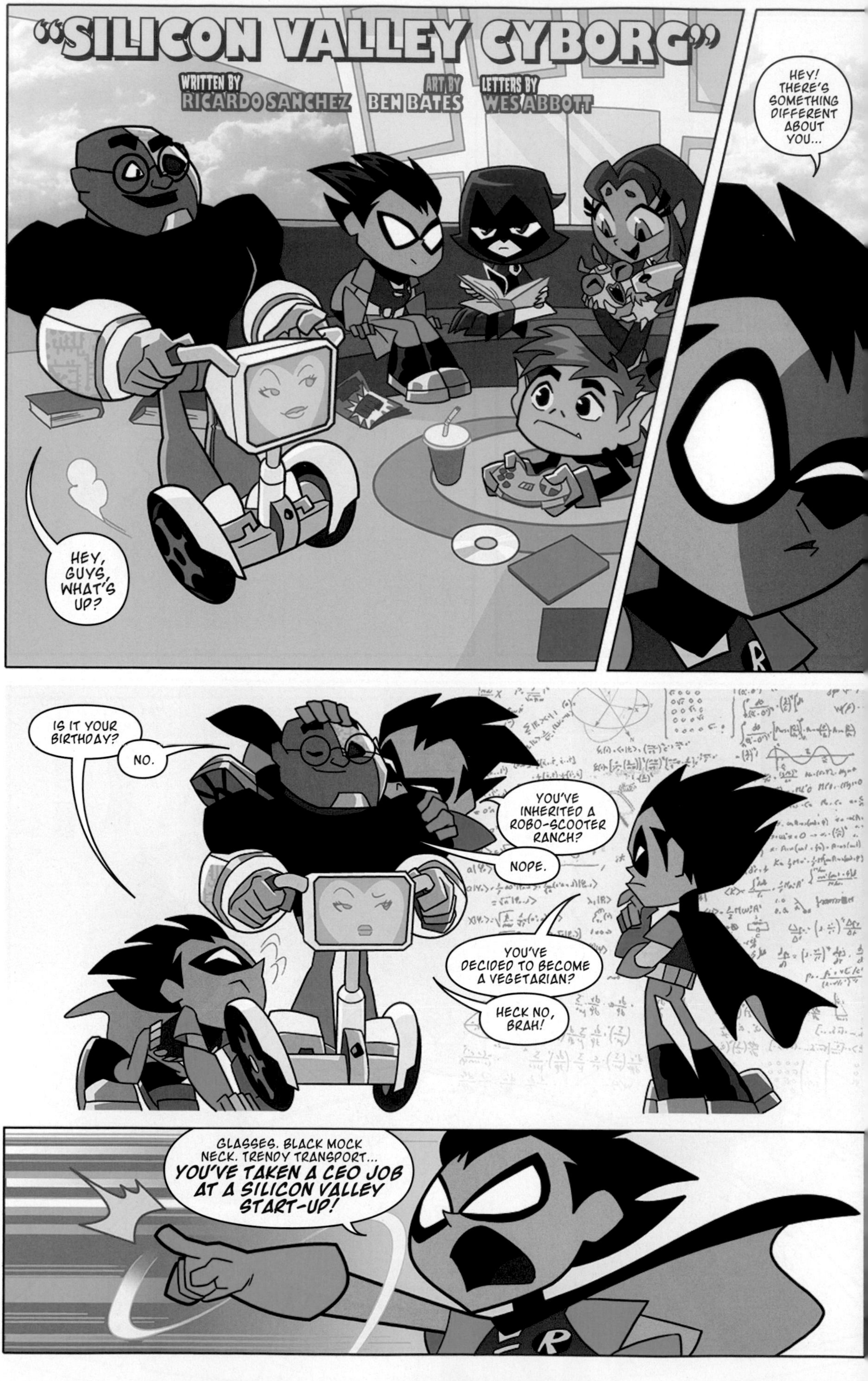
"SILICON VALLEY CYBORG"
WRITTEN BY RICARDO SANCHEZ
ART BY BEN BATES
LETTERS BY WES ABBOTT
HEY, GUYS, WHAT'S UP?
HEY! THERE'S SOMETHING DIFFERENT ABOUT YOU...
IS IT YOUR BIRTHDAY?
NO.
YOU'VE INHERITED A ROBO-SCOOTER RANCH?
NOPE.
YOU'VE DECIDED TO BECOME A VEGETARIAN?
HECK NO, BRAH!
GLASSES. BLACK MOCK NECK. TRENDY TRANSPORT... YOU'VE TAKEN A CEO JOB AT A SILICON VALLEY START-UP!

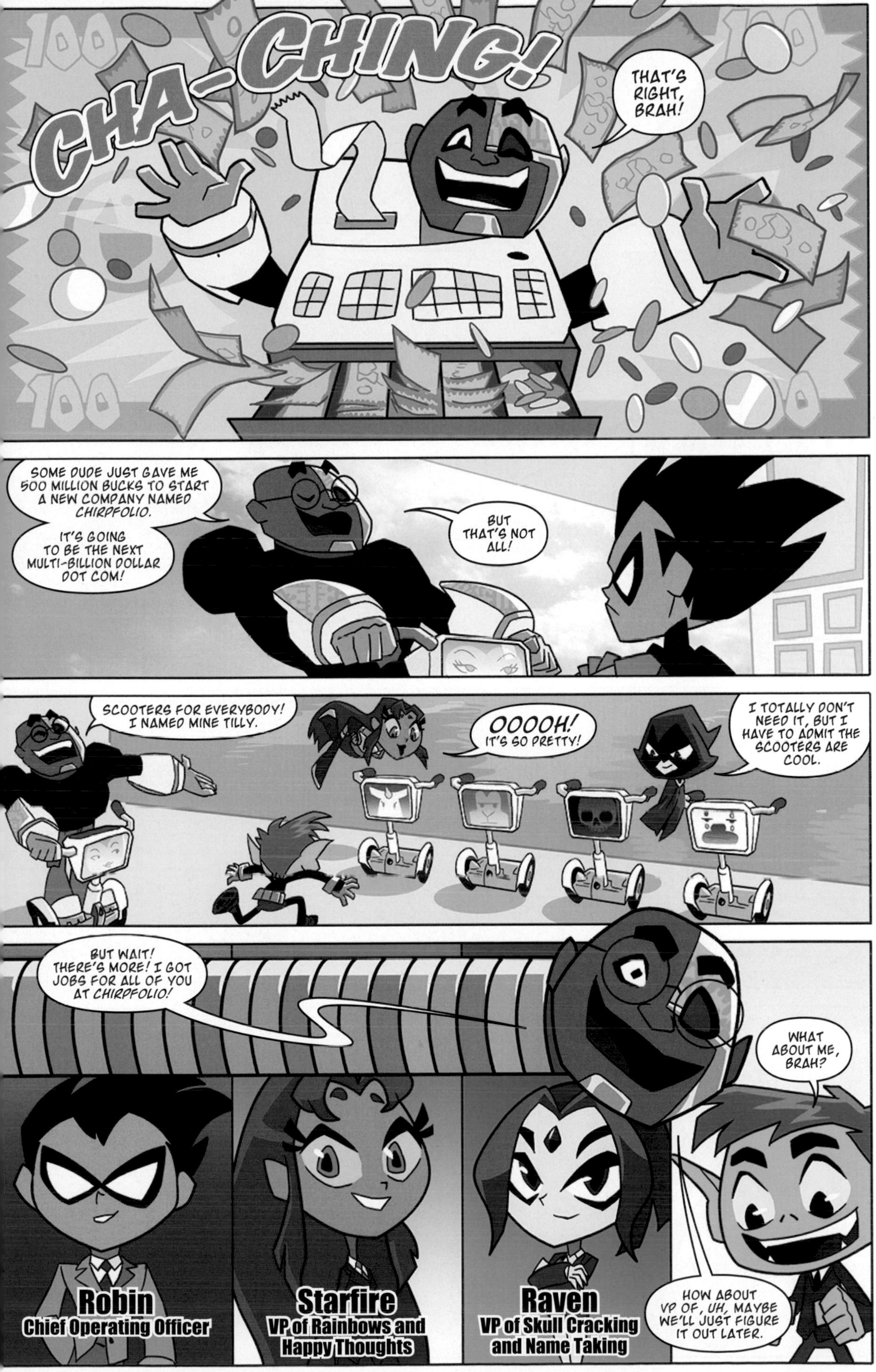
CHA-CHING!
THAT'S RIGHT, BRAH!
SOME DUDE JUST GAVE ME 500 MILLION BUCKS TO START A NEW COMPANY NAMED CHIRPFOLIO.
IT'S GOING TO BE THE NEXT MULTI-BILLION DOLLAR DOT COM!
BUT THAT'S NOT ALL!
SCOOTERS FOR EVERYBODY! I NAMED MINE TILLY.
OOOOH! IT'S SO PRETTY!
I TOTALLY DON'T NEED IT, BUT I HAVE TO ADMIT THE SCOOTERS ARE COOL.
BUT WAIT! THERE'S MORE! I GOT JOBS FOR ALL OF YOU AT CHIRPFOLIO!
WHAT ABOUT ME, BRAH?
Robin
Chief Operating Officer
Starfire
VP of Rainbows and Happy Thoughts
Raven
VP of Skull Cracking and Name Taking
HOW ABOUT VP OF, UH, MAYBE WE'LL JUST FIGURE IT OUT LATER.

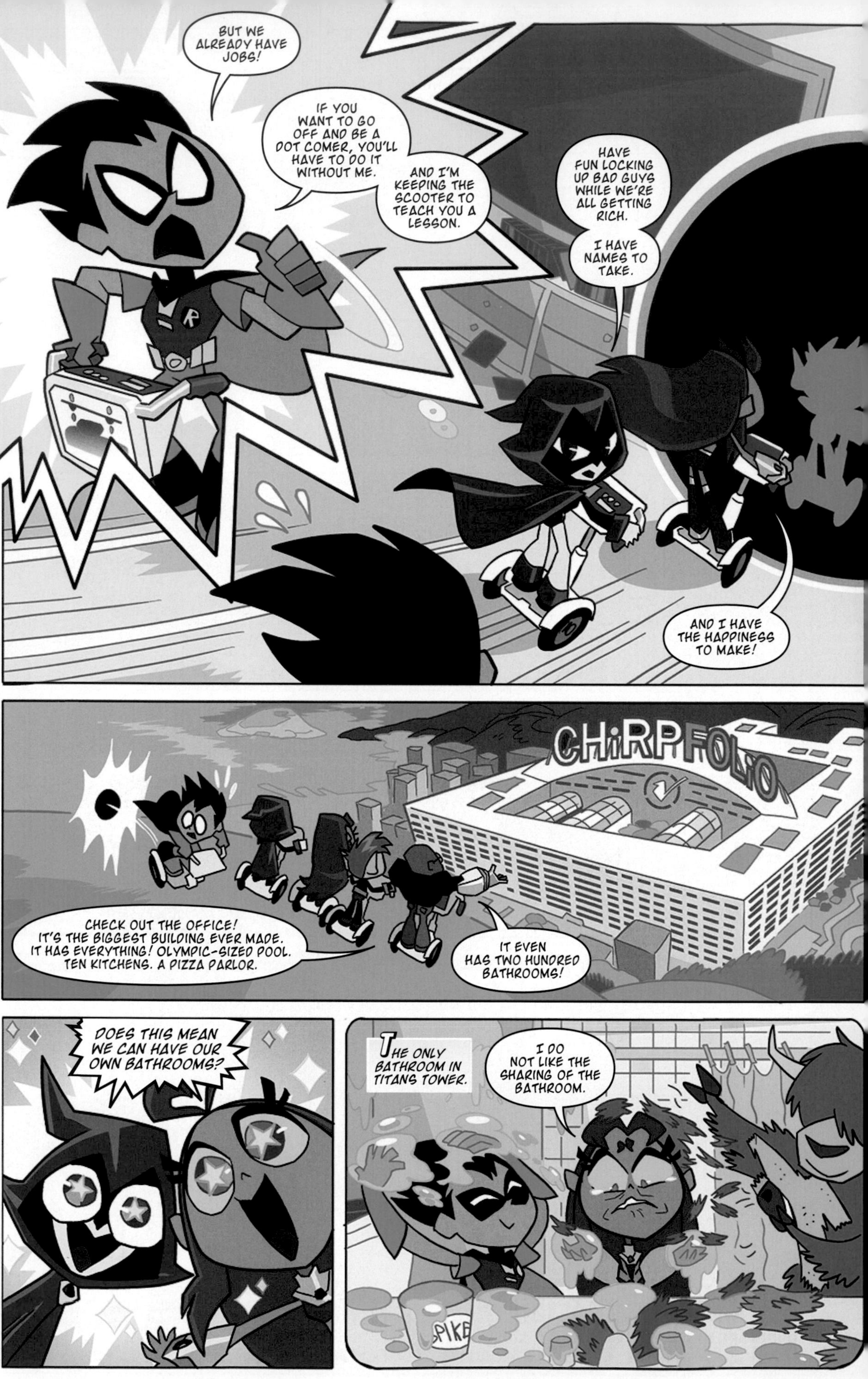
BUT WE ALREADY HAVE JOBS!
IF YOU WANT TO GO OFF AND BE A DOT COMER, YOU'LL HAVE TO DO IT WITHOUT ME.
AND I'M KEEPING THE SCOOTER TO TEACH YOU A LESSON.
HAVE FUN LOCKING UP BAD GUYS WHILE WE'RE ALL GETTING RICH.
I HAVE NAMES TO TAKE.
AND I HAVE THE HAPPINESS TO MAKE!
CHiRPFOLiO
CHECK OUT THE OFFICE! IT'S THE BIGGEST BUILDING EVER MADE. IT HAS EVERYTHING! OLYMPIC-SIZED POOL. TEN KITCHENS. A PIZZA PARLOR.
IT EVEN HAS TWO HUNDRED BATHROOMS!
DOES THIS MEAN WE CAN HAVE OUR OWN BATHROOMS?
THE ONLY BATHROOM IN TITANS TOWER.
I DO NOT LIKE THE SHARING OF THE BATHROOM.
SPIKE

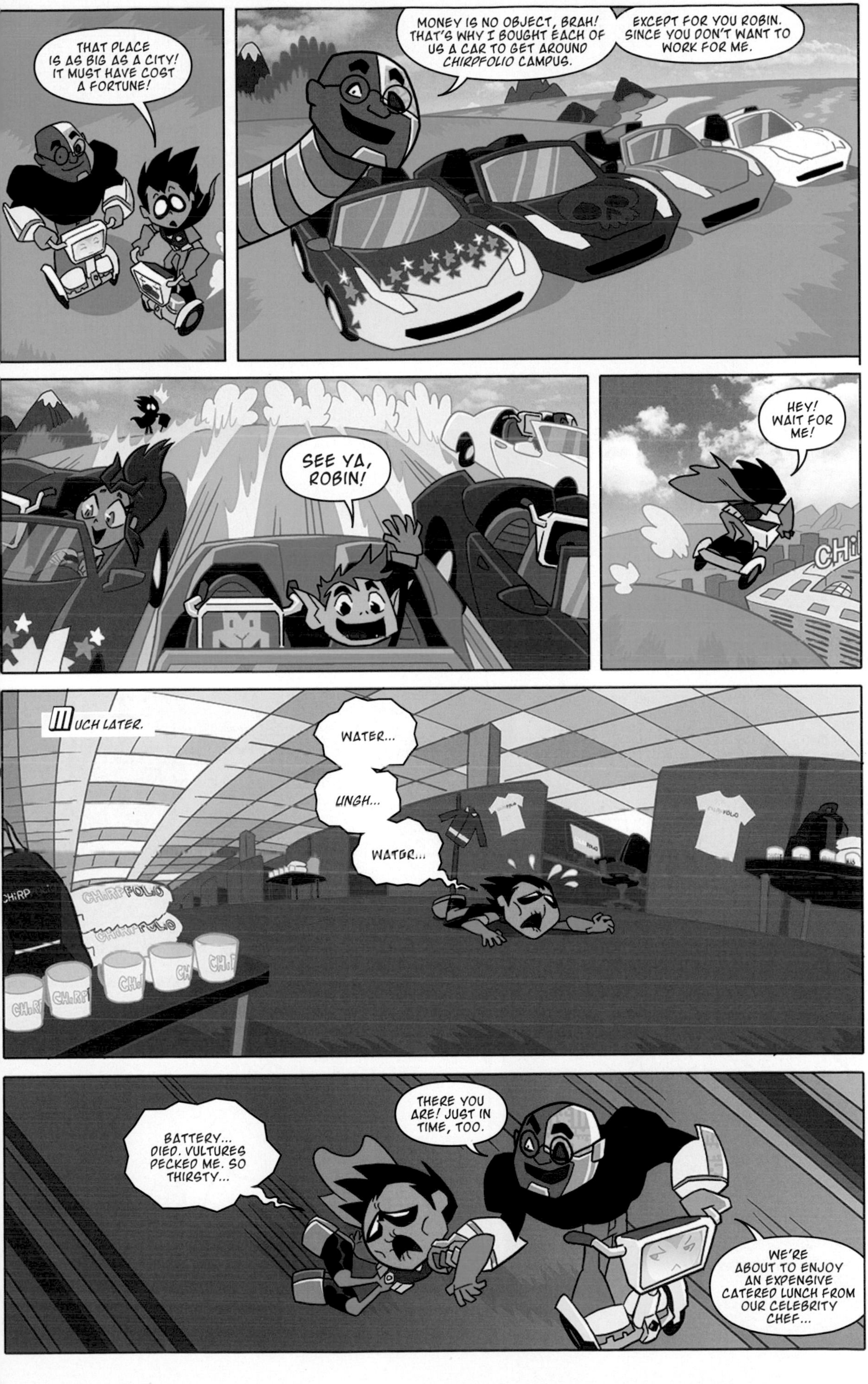
THAT PLACE IS AS BIG AS A CITY! IT MUST HAVE COST A FORTUNE!
MONEY IS NO OBJECT, BRAH! THAT'S WHY I BOUGHT EACH OF US A CAR TO GET AROUND CHIRPFOLIO CAMPUS.
EXCEPT FOR YOU ROBIN. SINCE YOU DON'T WANT TO WORK FOR ME.
SEE YA, ROBIN!
HEY! WAIT FOR ME!
MUCH LATER.
WATER...
UNGH...
WATER...
THERE YOU ARE! JUST IN TIME, TOO.
BATTERY... DIED. VULTURES PECKED ME. SO THIRSTY...
WE'RE ABOUT TO ENJOY AN EXPENSIVE CATERED LUNCH FROM OUR CELEBRITY CHEF...

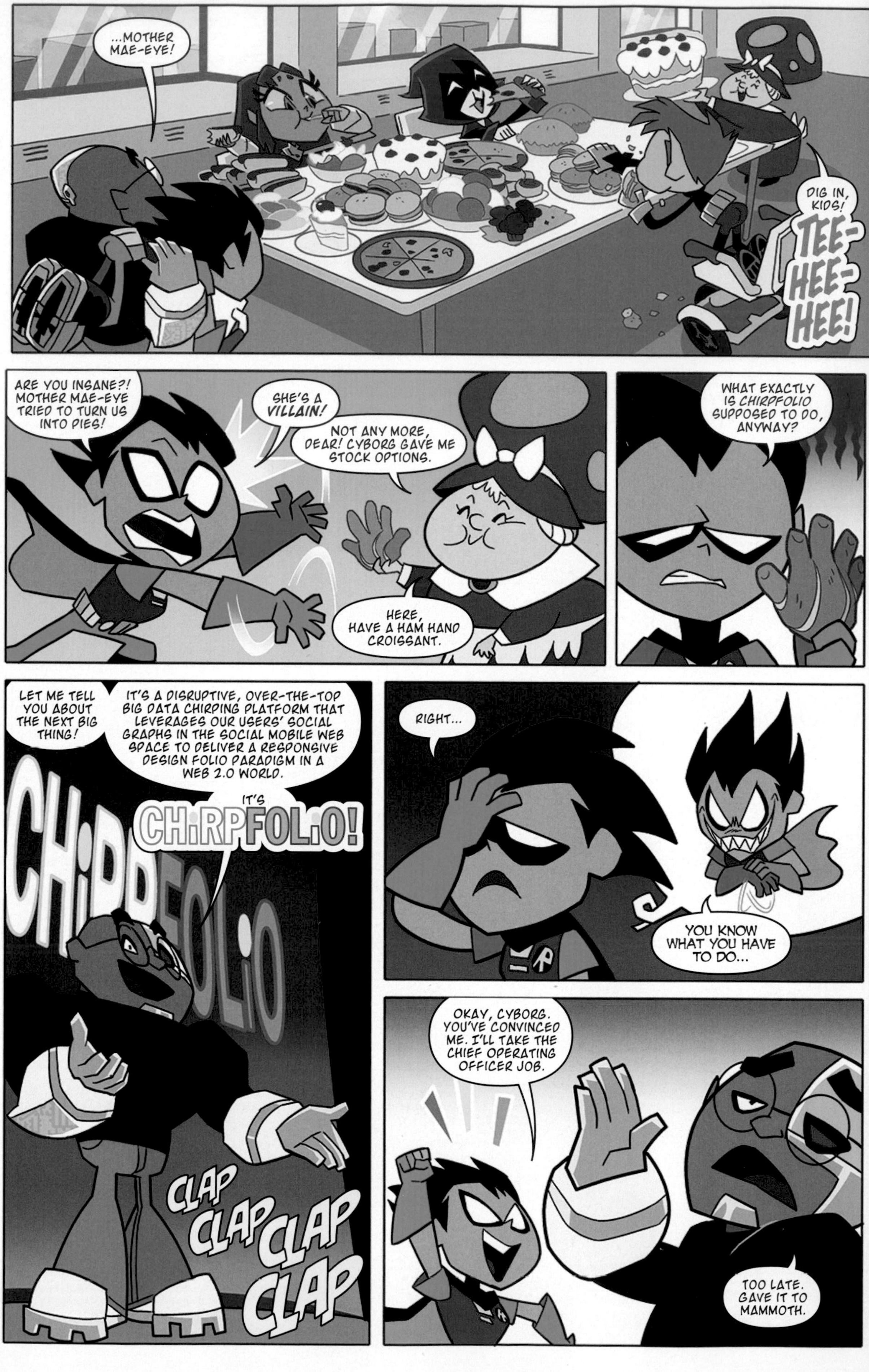

...MOTHER MAE-EYE!
DIG IN, KIDS!
TEE-HEE-HEE!
ARE YOU INSANE?! MOTHER MAE-EYE TRIED TO TURN US INTO PIES!
SHE'S A VILLAIN!
NOT ANY MORE, DEAR! CYBORG GAVE ME STOCK OPTIONS.
HERE, HAVE A HAM HAND CROISSANT.
WHAT EXACTLY IS CHIRPFOLIO SUPPOSED TO DO, ANYWAY?
LET ME TELL YOU ABOUT THE NEXT BIG THING!
IT'S A DISRUPTIVE, OVER-THE-TOP BIG DATA CHIRPING PLATFORM THAT LEVERAGES OUR USERS' SOCIAL GRAPHS IN THE SOCIAL MOBILE WEB SPACE TO DELIVER A RESPONSIVE DESIGN FOLIO PARADIGM IN A WEB 2.0 WORLD.
IT'S CHIRPFOLIO!
CHIRPFOLIO
CLAP CLAP CLAP CLAP
RIGHT...
YOU KNOW WHAT YOU HAVE TO DO...
OKAY, CYBORG. YOU'VE CONVINCED ME. I'LL TAKE THE CHIEF OPERATING OFFICER JOB.
TOO LATE. GAVE IT TO MAMMOTH.

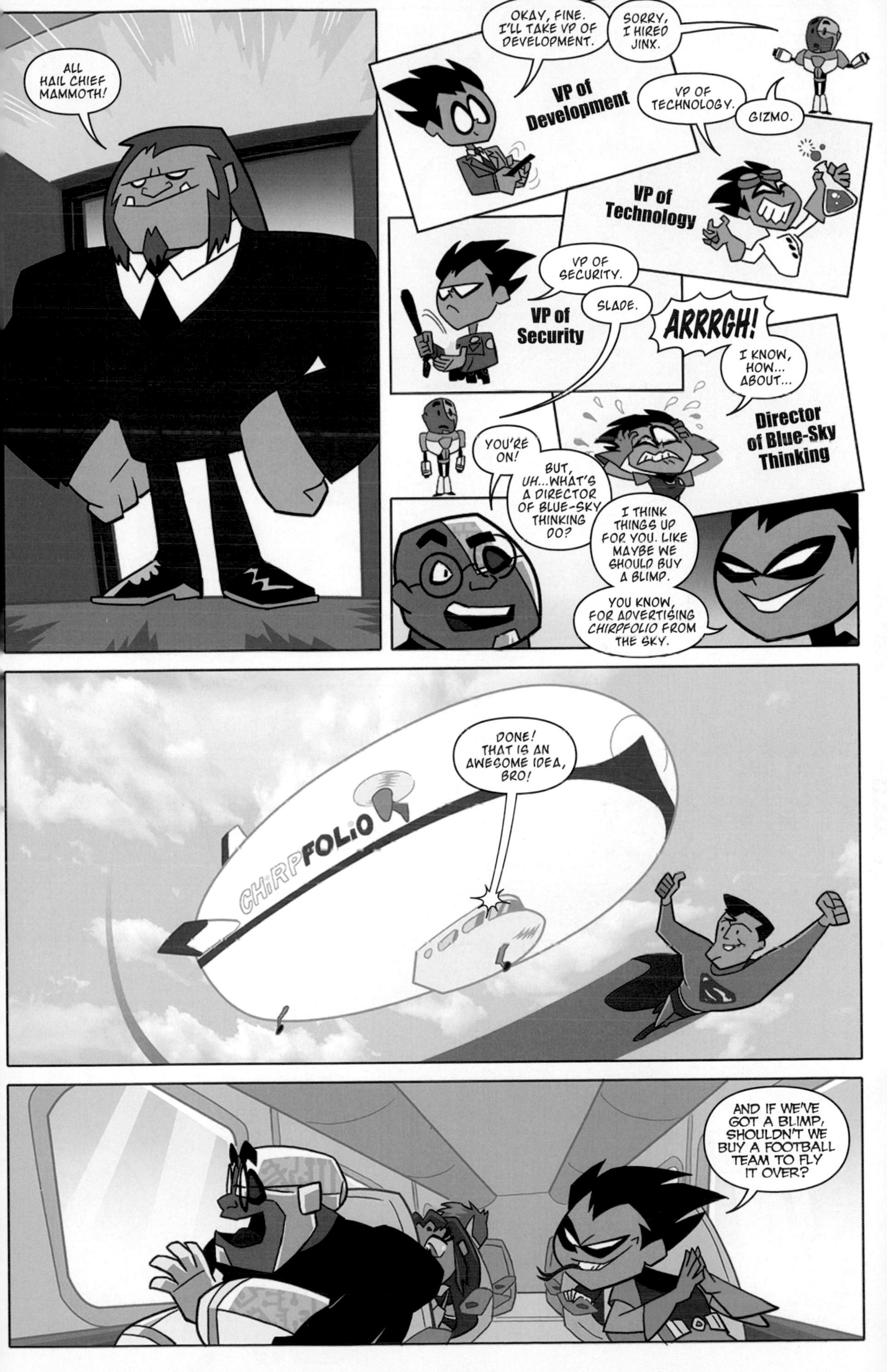
ALL HAIL CHIEF MAMMOTH!
OKAY, FINE. I'LL TAKE VP OF DEVELOPMENT.
SORRY, I HIRED JINX.
VP of Development
VP OF TECHNOLOGY.
GIZMO.
VP of Technology
VP OF SECURITY.
SLADE.
VP of Security
ARRRGH!
I KNOW, HOW... ABOUT...
Director of Blue-Sky Thinking
YOU'RE ON!
BUT, UH...WHAT'S A DIRECTOR OF BLUE-SKY THINKING DO?
I THINK THINGS UP FOR YOU. LIKE MAYBE WE SHOULD BUY A BLIMP.
YOU KNOW, FOR ADVERTISING CHIRPFOLIO FROM THE SKY.
DONE! THAT IS AN AWESOME IDEA, BRO!
CHIRPFOLIO
AND IF WE'VE GOT A BLIMP, SHOULDN'T WE BUY A FOOTBALL TEAM TO FLY IT OVER?

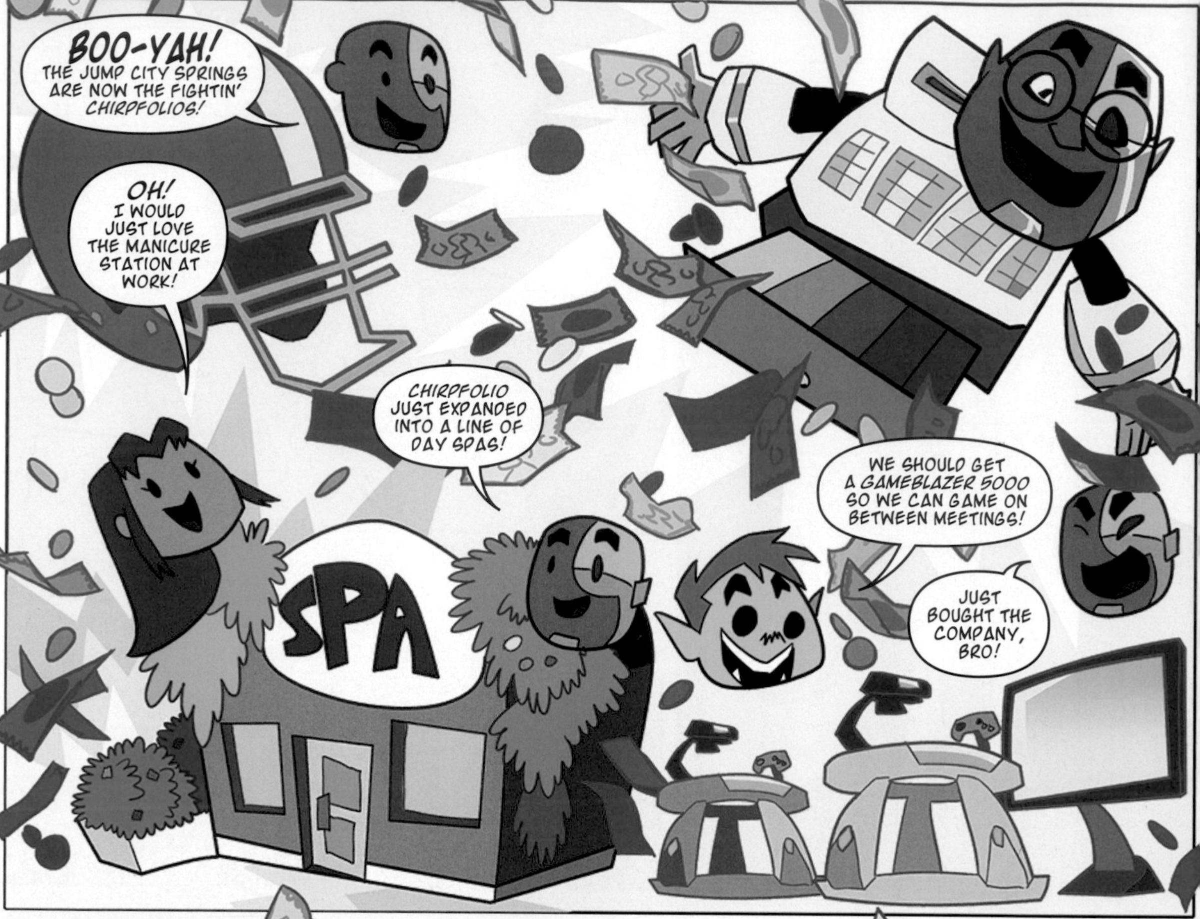
BOO-YAH!
THE JUMP CITY SPRINGS ARE NOW THE FIGHTIN' CHIRPFOLIOS!
OH! I WOULD JUST LOVE THE MANICURE STATION AT WORK!
CHIRPFOLIO JUST EXPANDED INTO A LINE OF DAY SPAS!
SPA
WE SHOULD GET A GAMEBLAZER 5000 SO WE CAN GAME ON BETWEEN MEETINGS!
JUST BOUGHT THE COMPANY, BRO!

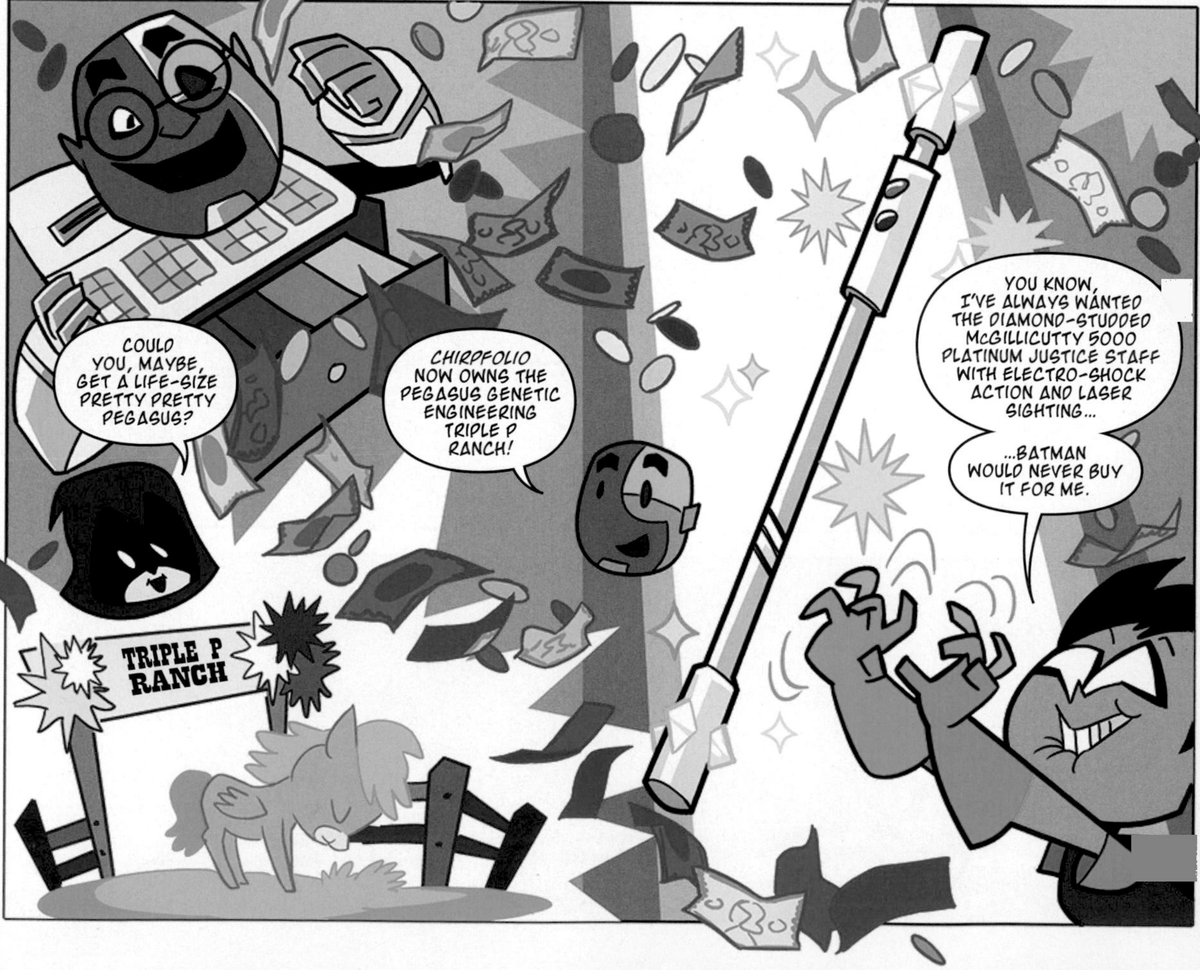
COULD YOU, MAYBE, GET A LIFE-SIZE PRETTY PRETTY PEGASUS?
CHIRPFOLIO NOW OWNS THE PEGASUS GENETIC ENGINEERING TRIPLE P RANCH!
TRIPLE P RANCH
YOU KNOW, I'VE ALWAYS WANTED THE DIAMOND-STUDDED McGILLICUTTY 5000 PLATINUM JUSTICE STAFF WITH ELECTRO-SHOCK ACTION AND LASER SIGHTING...
...BATMAN WOULD NEVER BUY IT FOR ME.

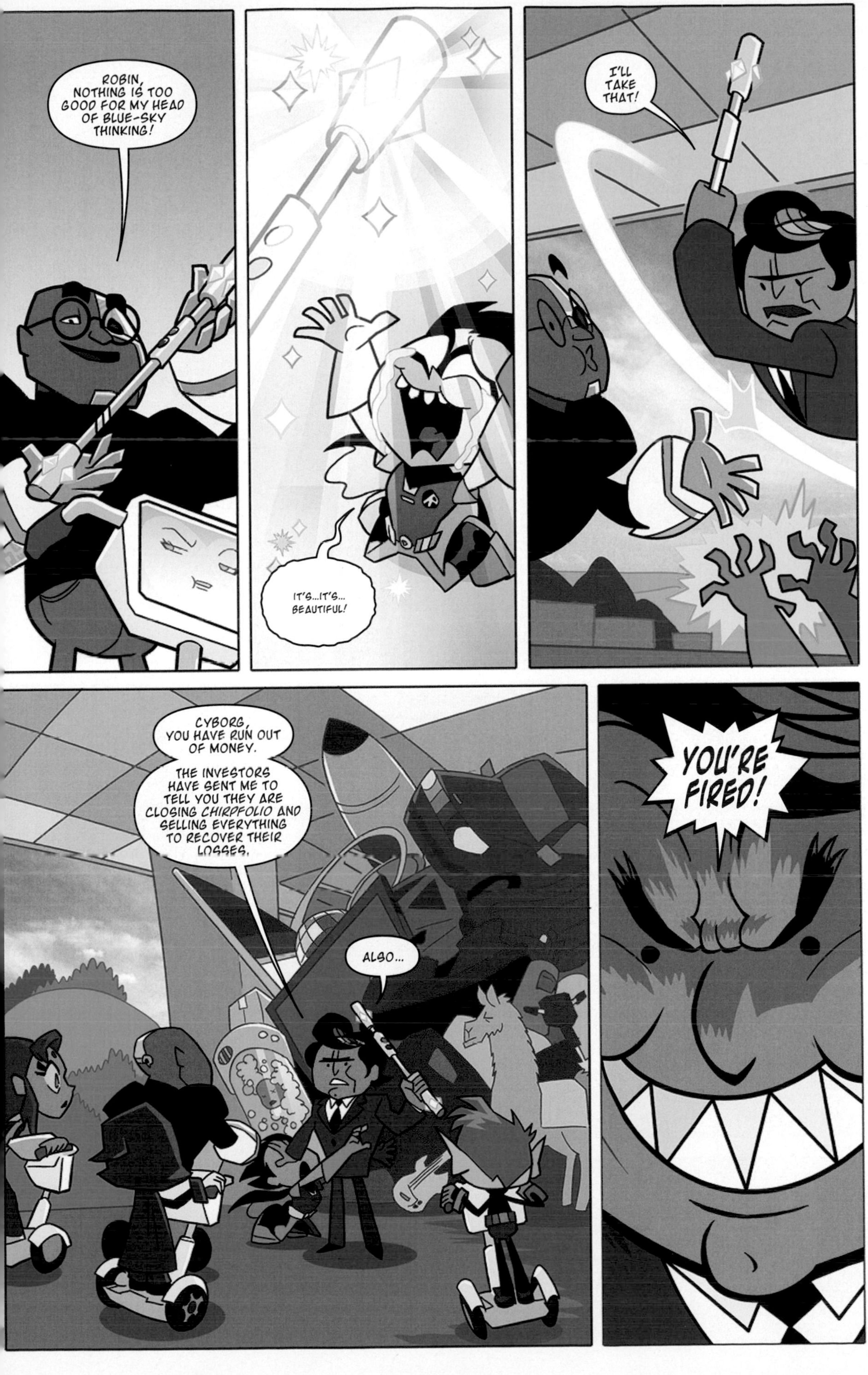
ROBIN, NOTHING IS TOO GOOD FOR MY HEAD OF BLUE-SKY THINKING!
IT'S...IT'S... BEAUTIFUL!
I'LL TAKE THAT!
CYBORG, YOU HAVE RUN OUT OF MONEY.
THE INVESTORS HAVE SENT ME TO TELL YOU THEY ARE CLOSING CHIRPFOLIO AND SELLING EVERYTHING TO RECOVER THEIR LOSSES.
ALSO...
YOU'RE FIRED!

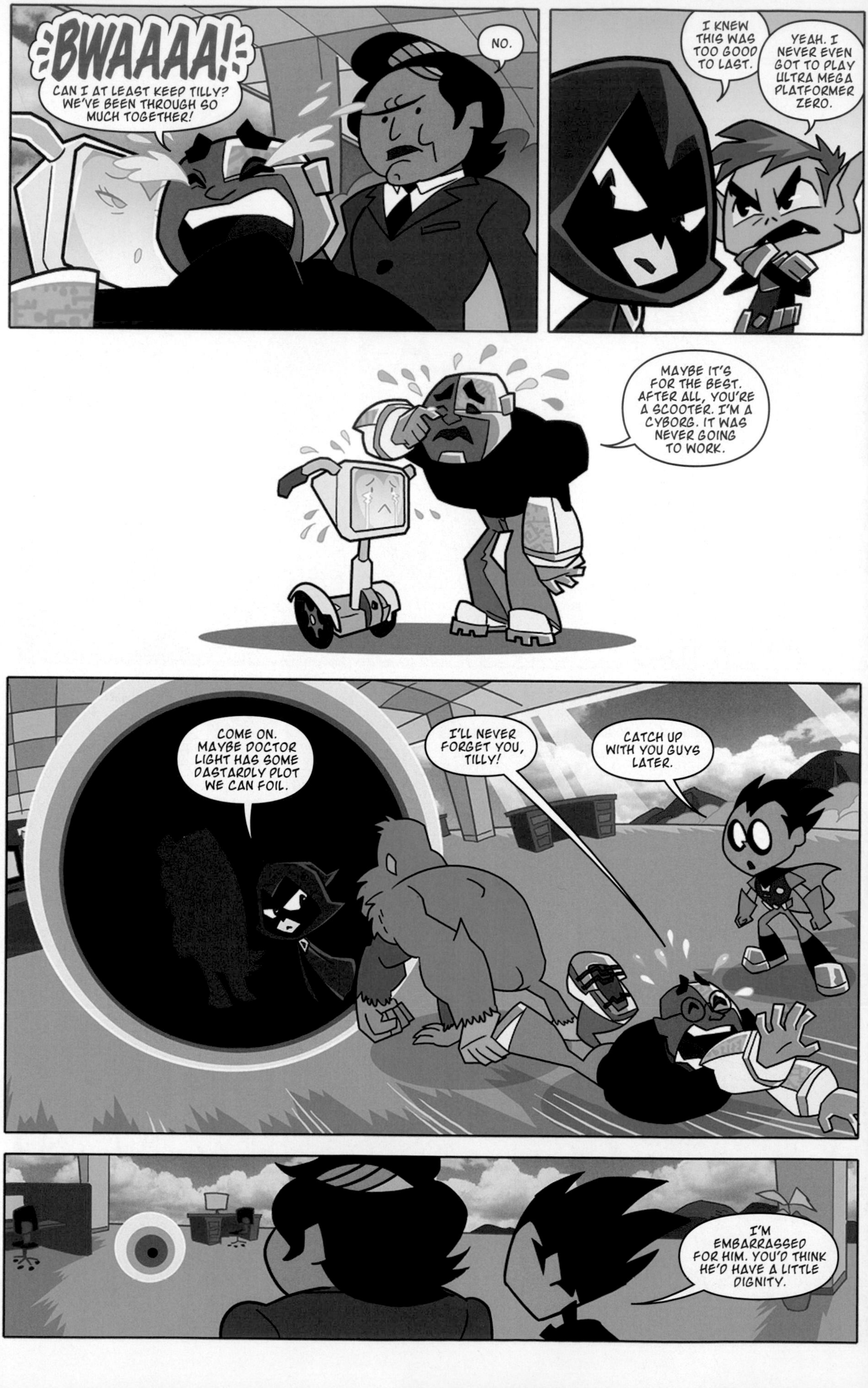
BWAAAA!
CAN I AT LEAST KEEP TILLY? WE'VE BEEN THROUGH SO MUCH TOGETHER!
NO.
I KNEW THIS WAS TOO GOOD TO LAST.
YEAH. I NEVER EVEN GOT TO PLAY ULTRA MEGA PLATFORMER ZERO.
MAYBE IT'S FOR THE BEST. AFTER ALL, YOU'RE A SCOOTER. I'M A CYBORG. IT WAS NEVER GOING TO WORK.
COME ON. MAYBE DOCTOR LIGHT HAS SOME DASTARDLY PLOT WE CAN FOIL.
I'LL NEVER FORGET YOU, TILLY!
CATCH UP WITH YOU GUYS LATER.
I'M EMBARRASSED FOR HIM. YOU'D THINK HE'D HAVE A LITTLE DIGNITY.

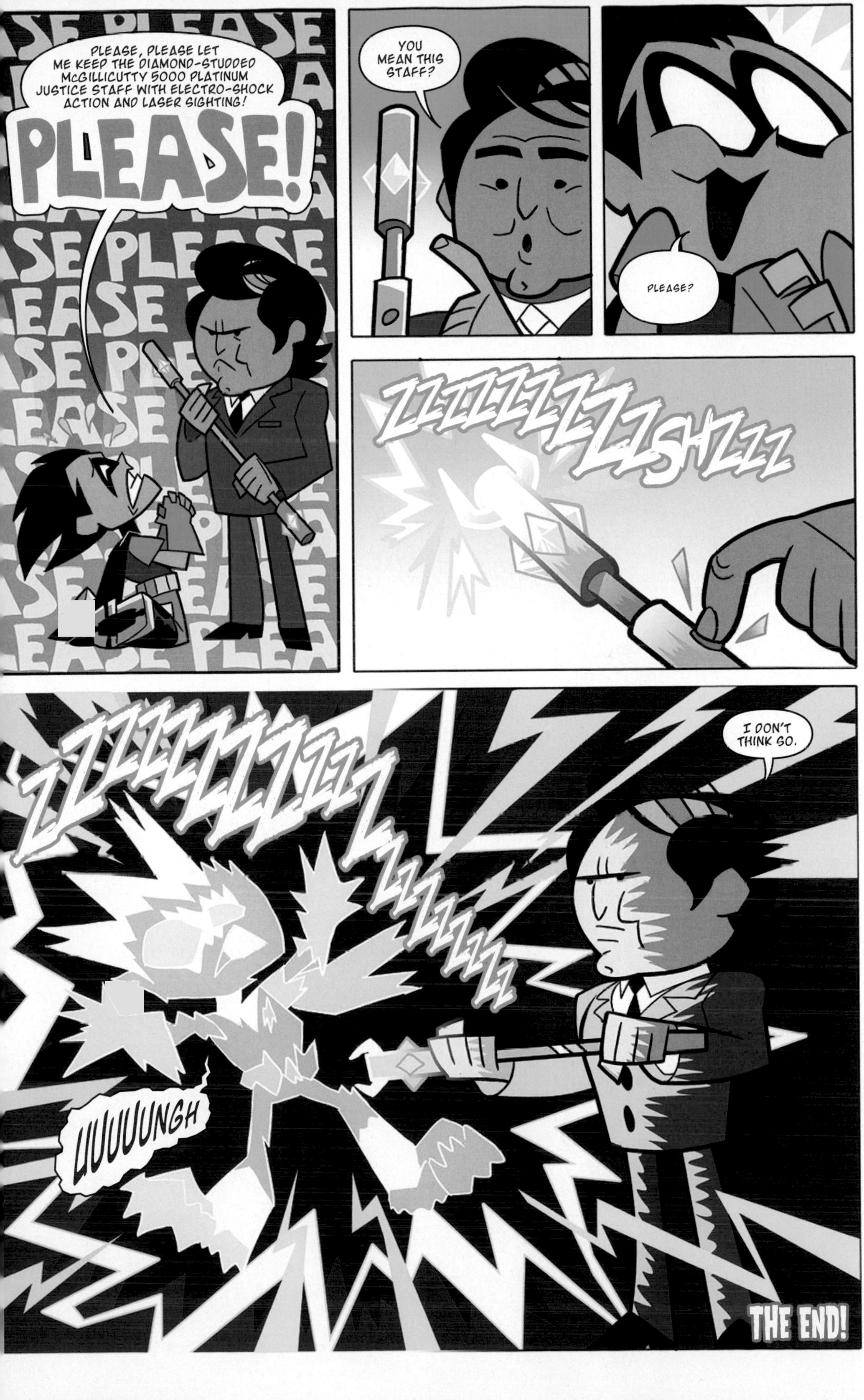
PLEASE, PLEASE LET ME KEEP THE DIAMOND-STUDDED McGILLICUTTY 5000 PLATINUM JUSTICE STAFF WITH ELECTRO-SHOCK ACTION AND LASER SIGHTING!
PLEASE!
YOU MEAN THIS STAFF?
PLEASE?
ZZZZZZZZZZZZSHZZZ
I DON'T THINK SO.
UUUUUNGH
THE END!

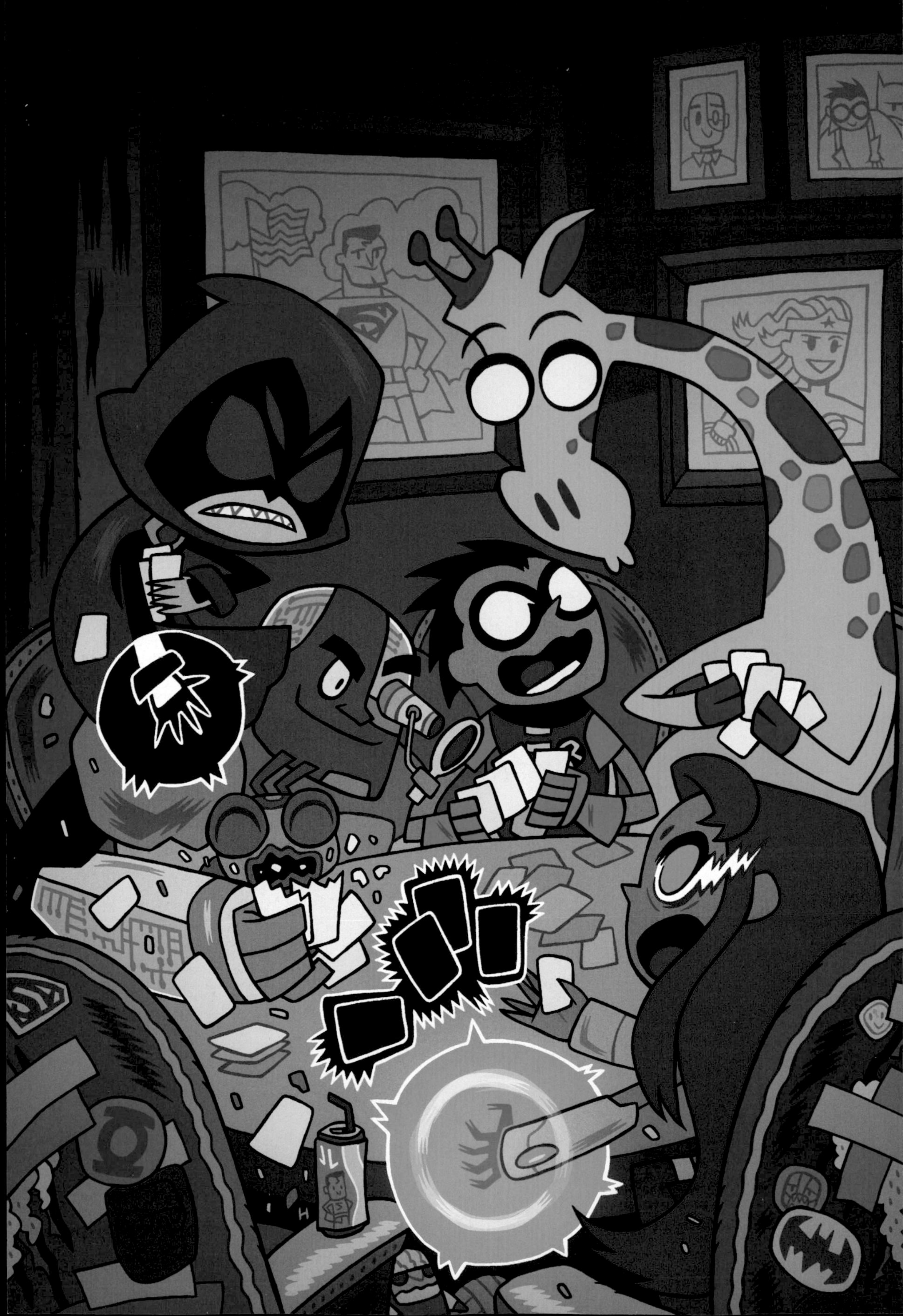
JL

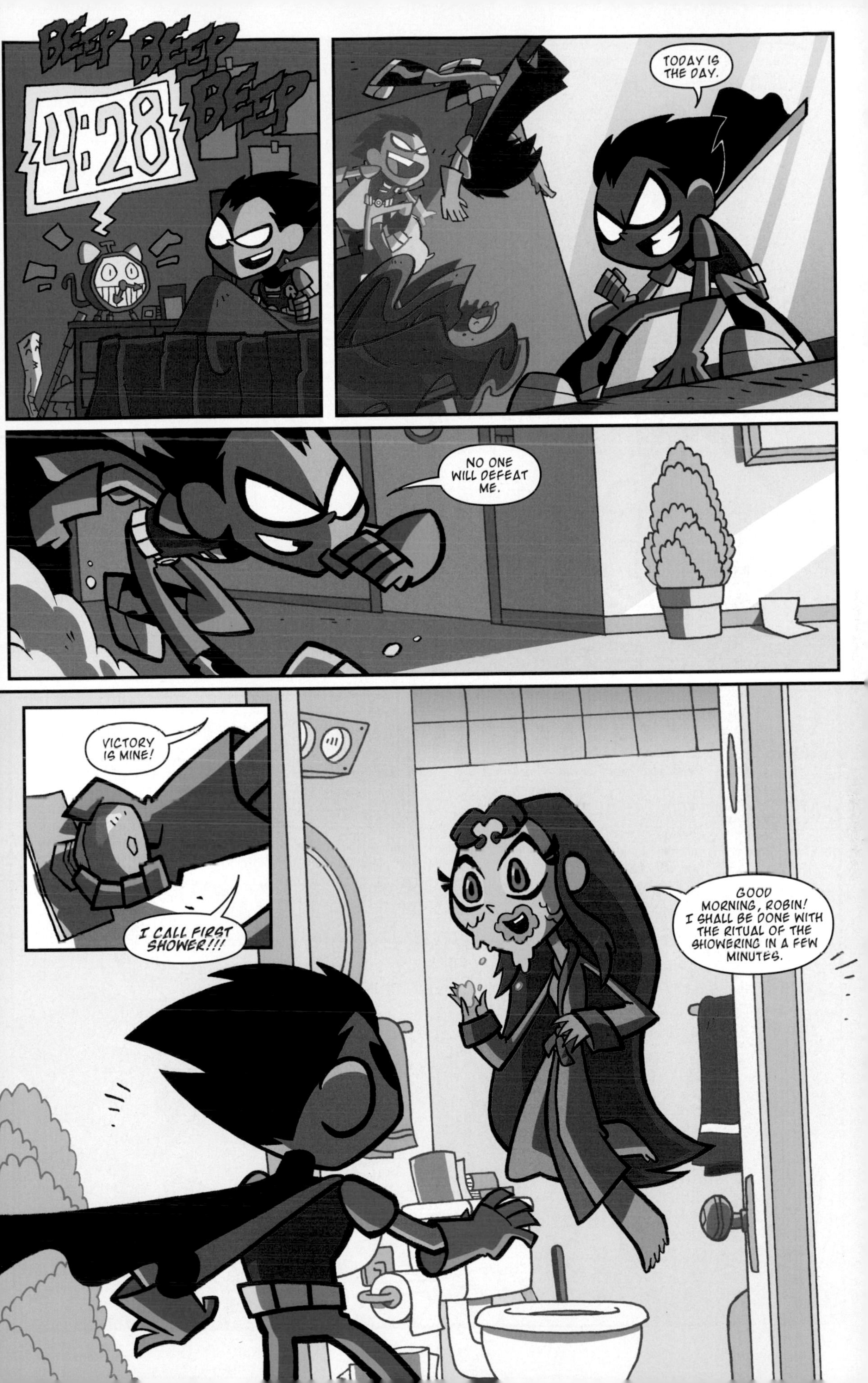
BEEP BEEP BEEP
4:28
TODAY IS THE DAY.
NO ONE WILL DEFEAT ME.
VICTORY IS MINE!
I CALL FIRST SHOWER!!!
GOOD MORNING, ROBIN! I SHALL BE DONE WITH THE RITUAL OF THE SHOWERING IN A FEW MINUTES.

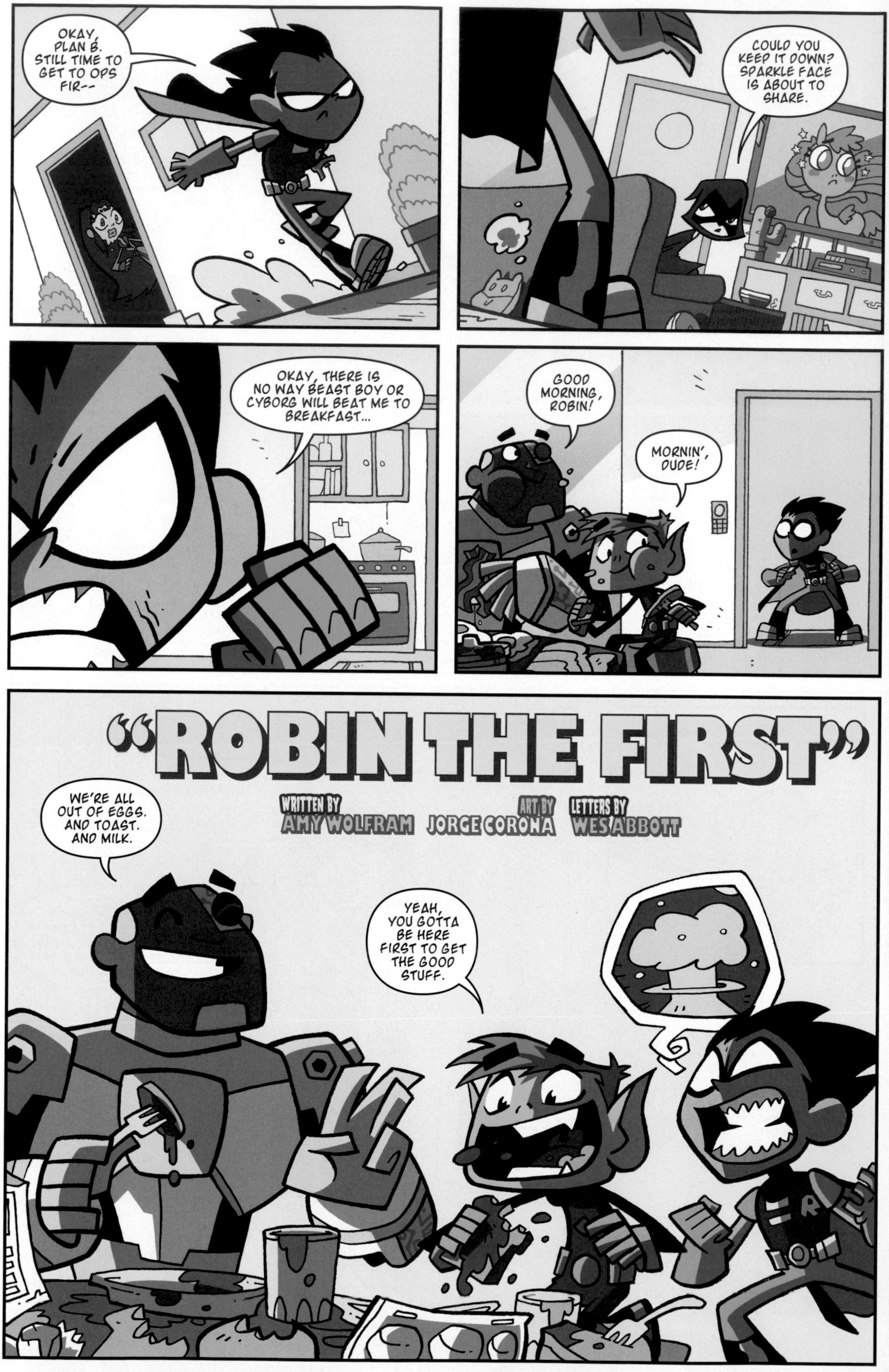
OKAY, PLAN B. STILL TIME TO GET TO OPS FIR--
COULD YOU KEEP IT DOWN? SPARKLE FACE IS ABOUT TO SHARE.
OKAY, THERE IS NO WAY BEAST BOY OR CYBORG WILL BEAT ME TO BREAKFAST...
GOOD MORNING, ROBIN!
MORNIN', DUDE!
"ROBIN THE FIRST"
WRITTEN BY AMY WOLFRAM
ART BY JORGE CORONA
LETTERS BY WES ABBOTT
WE'RE ALL OUT OF EGGS. AND TOAST. AND MILK.
YEAH, YOU GOTTA BE HERE FIRST TO GET THE GOOD STUFF.

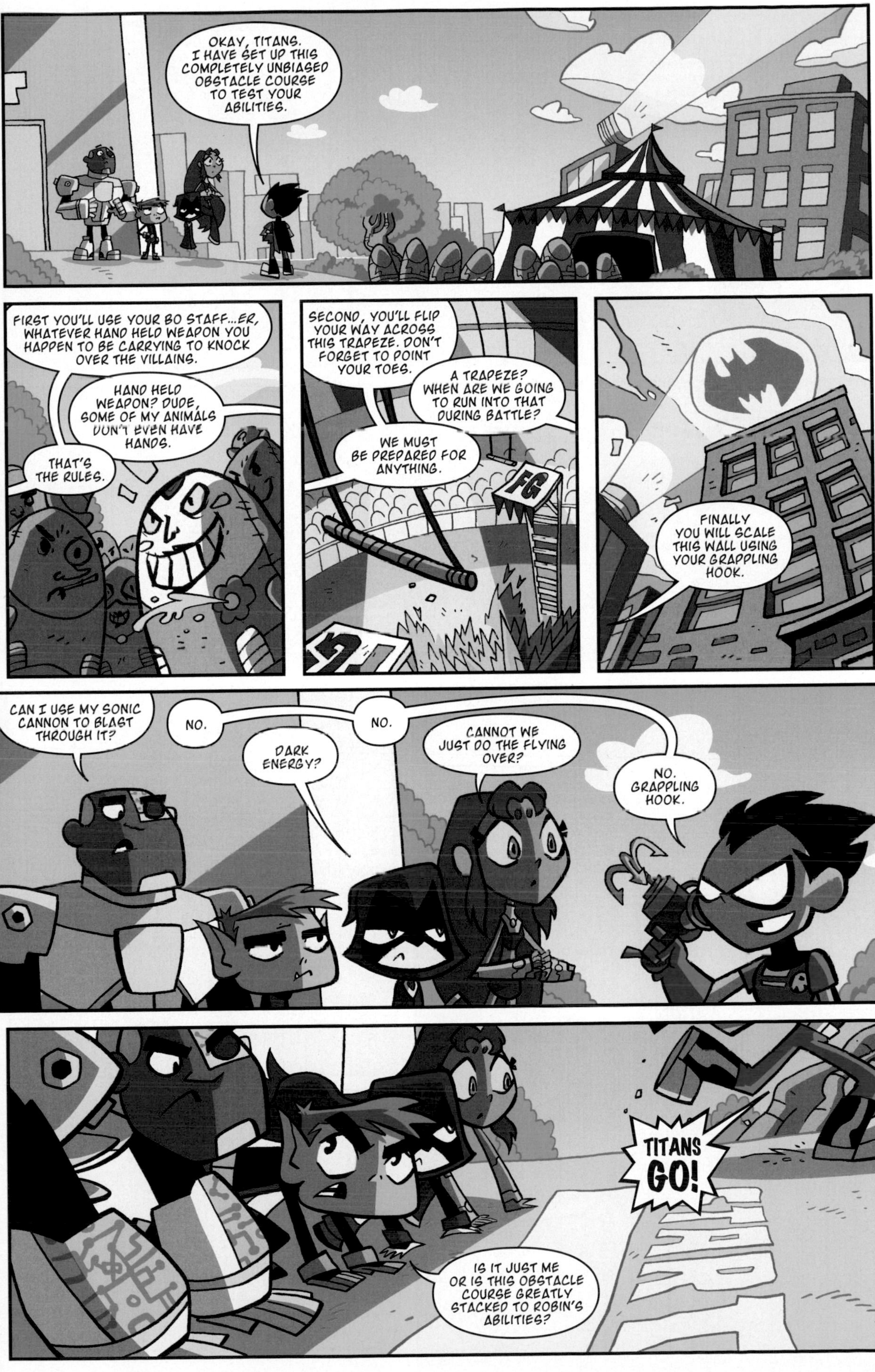
OKAY, TITANS. I HAVE SET UP THIS COMPLETELY UNBIASED OBSTACLE COURSE TO TEST YOUR ABILITIES.
FIRST YOU'LL USE YOUR BO STAFF...ER, WHATEVER HAND HELD WEAPON YOU HAPPEN TO BE CARRYING TO KNOCK OVER THE VILLAINS.
HAND HELD WEAPON? DUDE, SOME OF MY ANIMALS DON'T EVEN HAVE HANDS.
THAT'S THE RULES.
SECOND, YOU'LL FLIP YOUR WAY ACROSS THIS TRAPEZE. DON'T FORGET TO POINT YOUR TOES.
A TRAPEZE? WHEN ARE WE GOING TO RUN INTO THAT DURING BATTLE?
WE MUST BE PREPARED FOR ANYTHING.
FG
FINALLY YOU WILL SCALE THIS WALL USING YOUR GRAPPLING HOOK.
CAN I USE MY SONIC CANNON TO BLAST THROUGH IT?
NO.
DARK ENERGY?
NO.
CANNOT WE JUST DO THE FLYING OVER?
NO. GRAPPLING HOOK.
TITANS GO!
IS IT JUST ME OR IS THIS OBSTACLE COURSE GREATLY STACKED TO ROBIN'S ABILITIES?

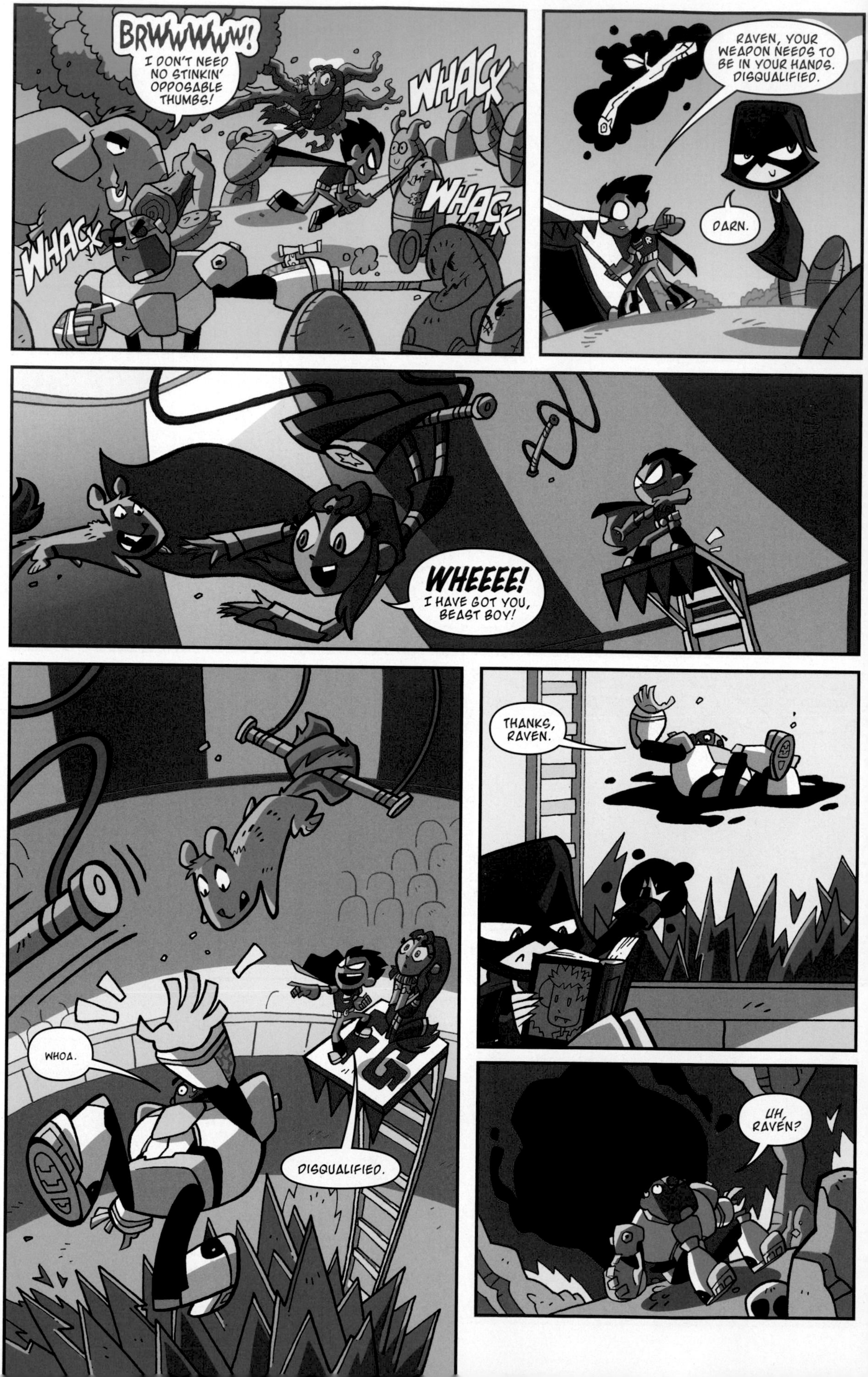

BRWWWWW!
I DON'T NEED NO STINKIN' OPPOSABLE THUMBS!
WHACK
WHACK
WHACK
RAVEN, YOUR WEAPON NEEDS TO BE IN YOUR HANDS. DISQUALIFIED.
DARN.
WHEEEE!
I HAVE GOT YOU, BEAST BOY!
WHOA.
DISQUALIFIED.
THANKS, RAVEN.
UH, RAVEN?

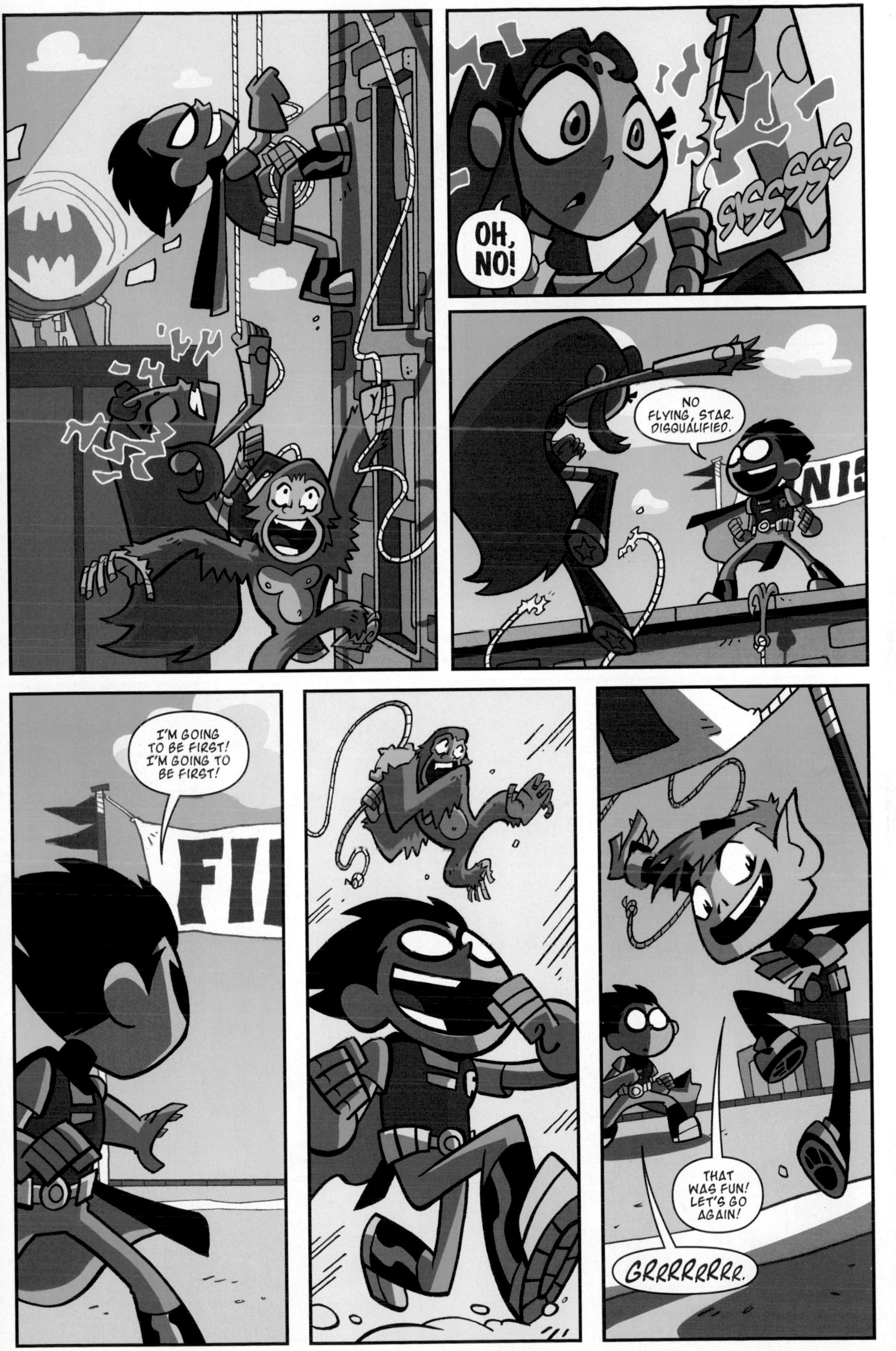

OH, NO!
SISSSSS
NO FLYING, STAR. DISQUALIFIED.
I'M GOING TO BE FIRST! I'M GOING TO BE FIRST!
THAT WAS FUN! LET'S GO AGAIN!
GRRRRRRRR.

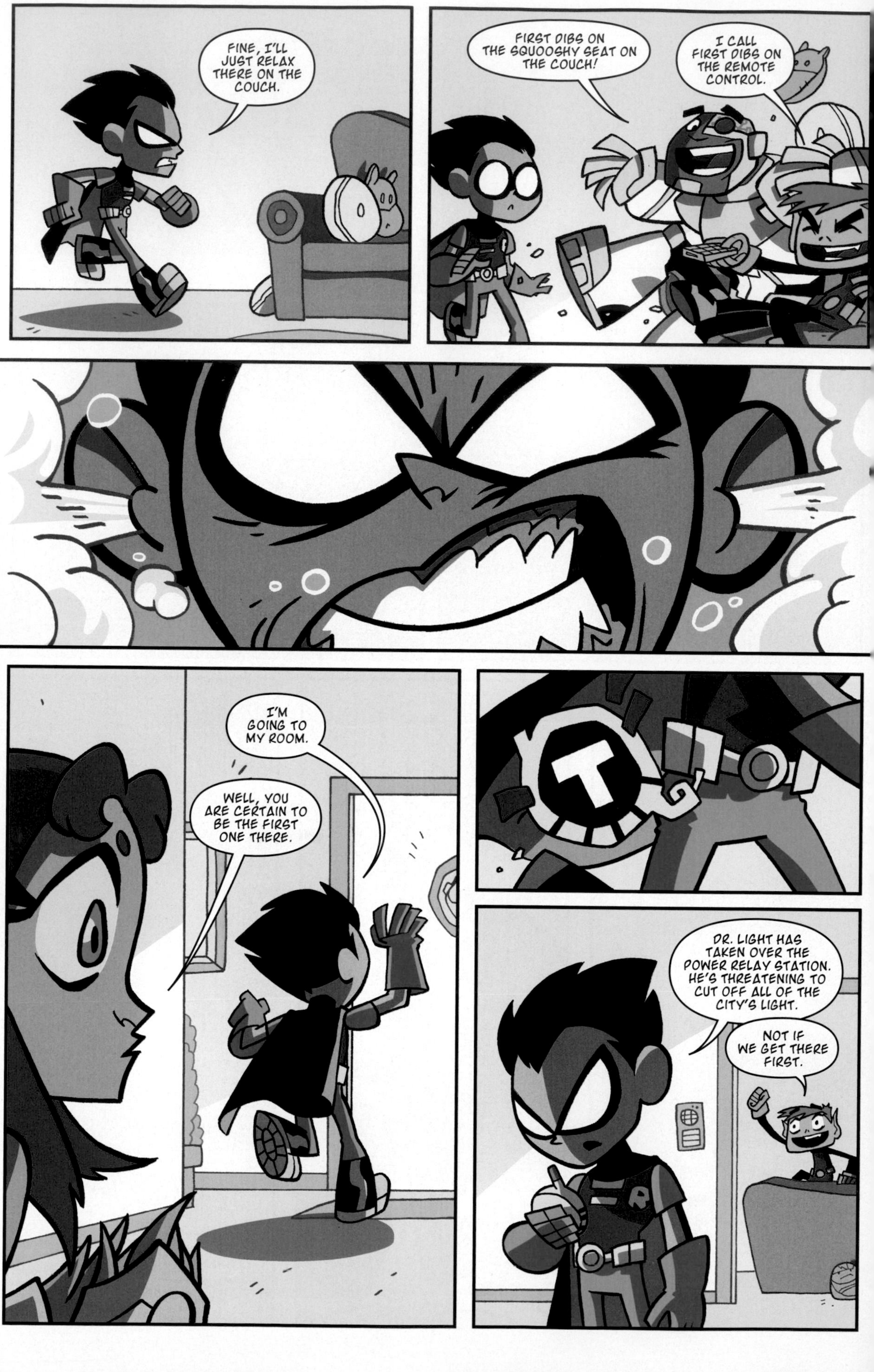
FINE, I'LL JUST RELAX THERE ON THE COUCH.
FIRST DIBS ON THE SQUOOSHY SEAT ON THE COUCH!
I CALL FIRST DIBS ON THE REMOTE CONTROL.
I'M GOING TO MY ROOM.
WELL, YOU ARE CERTAIN TO BE THE FIRST ONE THERE.
DR. LIGHT HAS TAKEN OVER THE POWER RELAY STATION. HE'S THREATENING TO CUT OFF ALL OF THE CITY'S LIGHT.
NOT IF WE GET THERE FIRST.

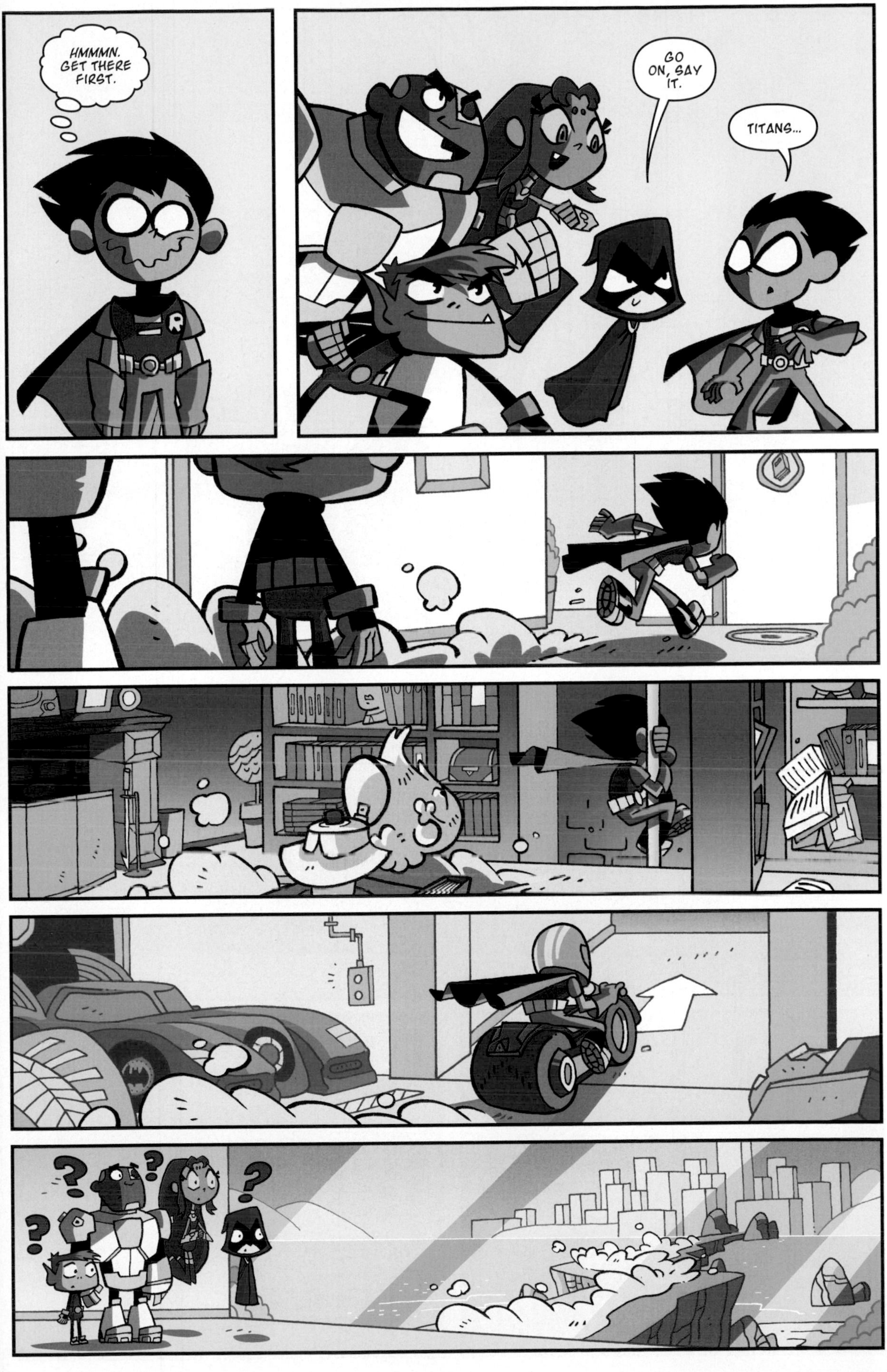
HMMMN. GET THERE FIRST.
GO ON, SAY IT.
TITANS...

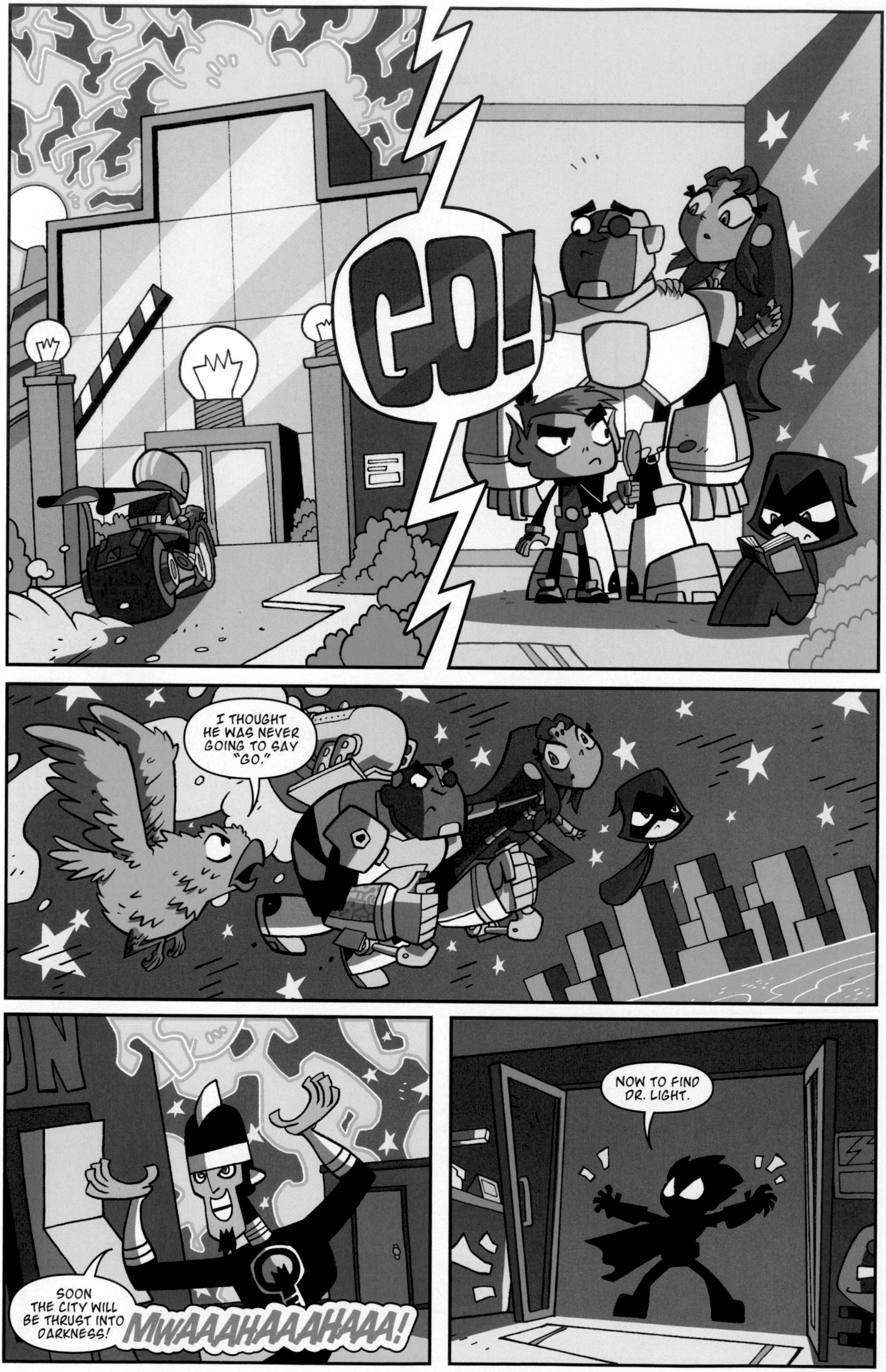
GO!
I THOUGHT HE WAS NEVER GOING TO SAY "GO."
SOON THE CITY WILL BE THRUST INTO DARKNESS!
MWAAAHAAAAHAAA!
NOW TO FIND DR. LIGHT.

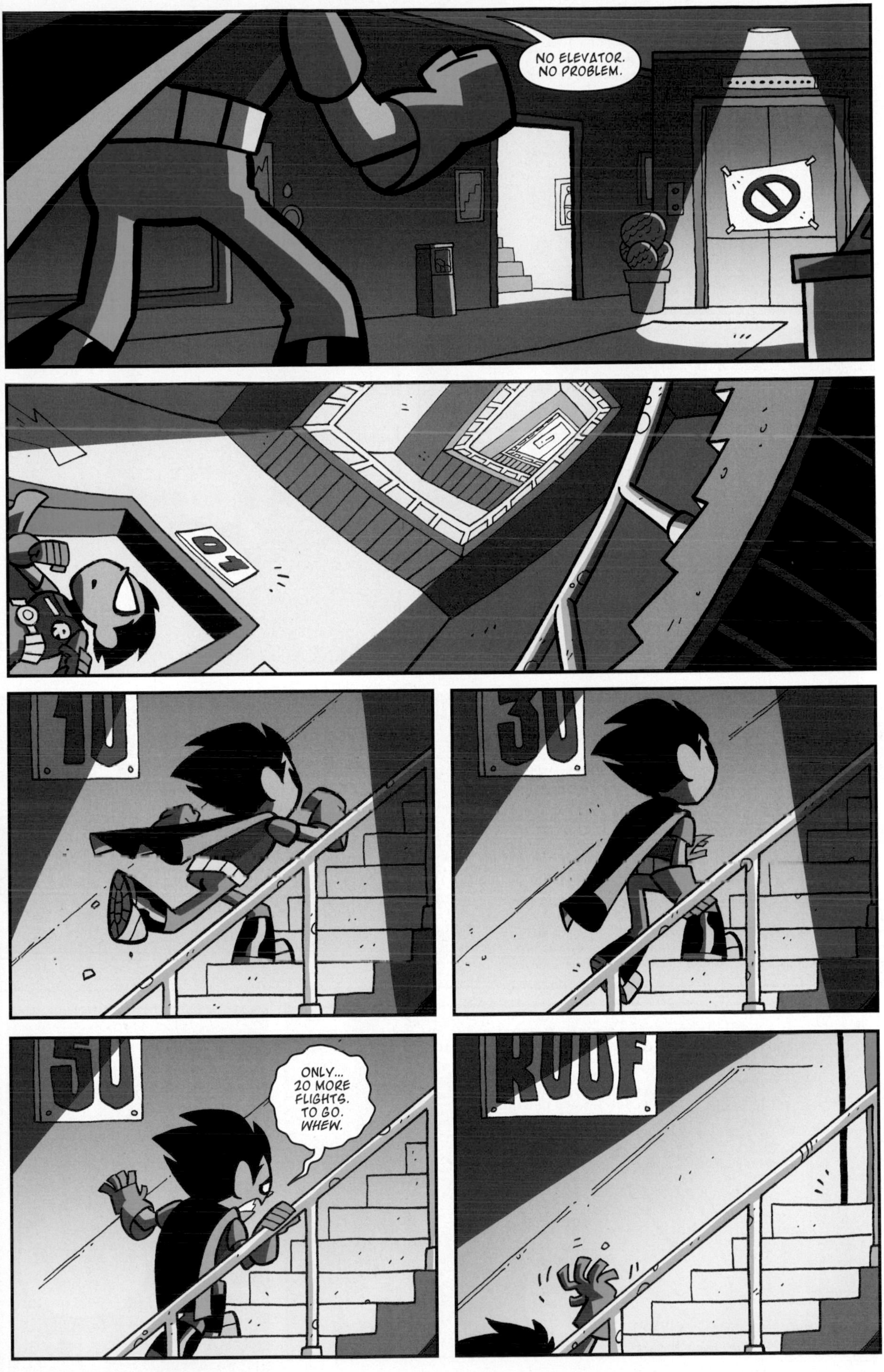
NO ELEVATOR. NO PROBLEM.
10
30
50
ONLY... 20 MORE FLIGHTS. TO GO. WHEW.
ROOF

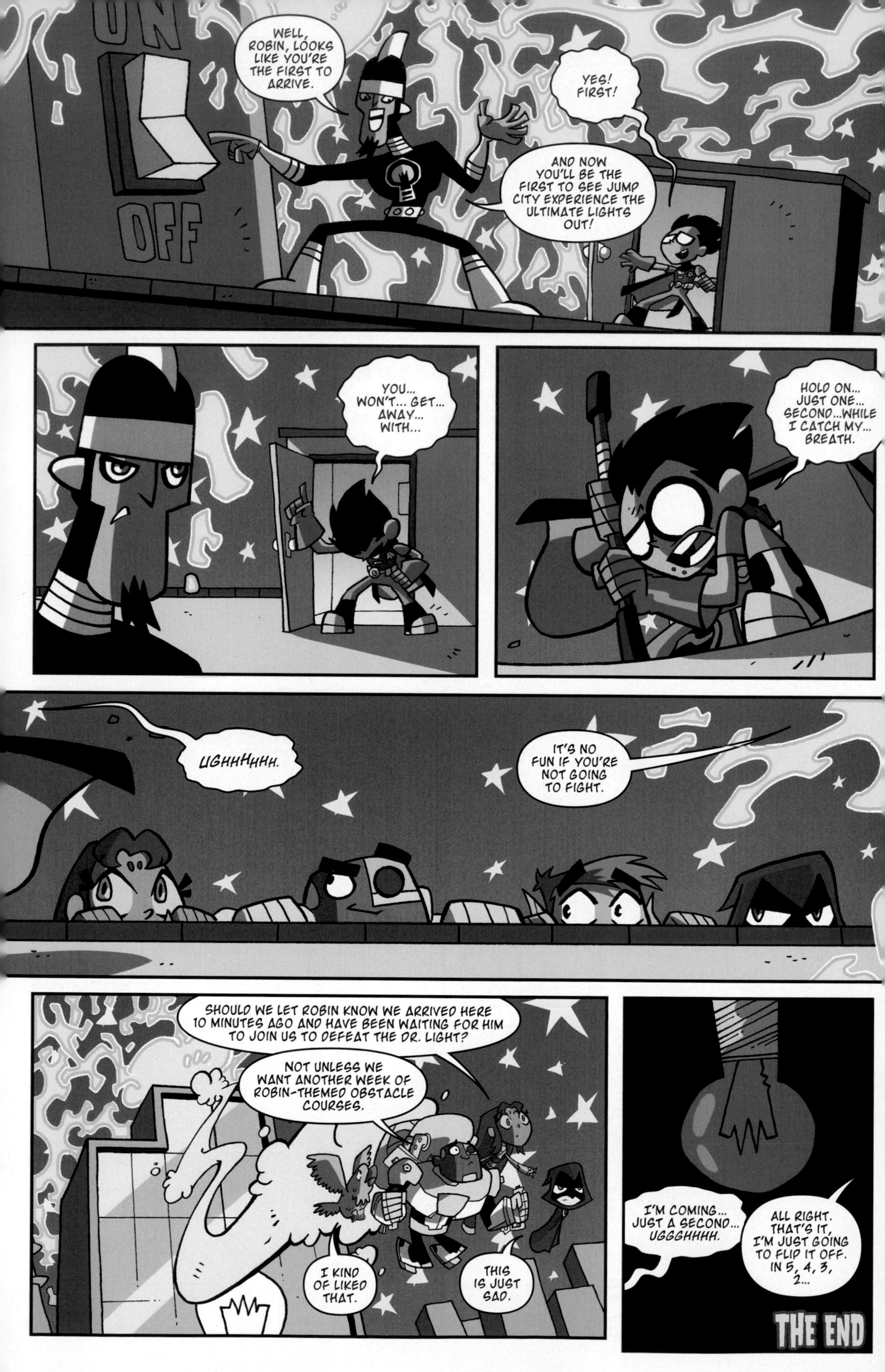
WELL, ROBIN, LOOKS LIKE YOU'RE THE FIRST TO ARRIVE.
YES! FIRST!
AND NOW YOU'LL BE THE FIRST TO SEE JUMP CITY EXPERIENCE THE ULTIMATE LIGHTS OUT!
ON
OFF
YOU... WON'T... GET... AWAY... WITH...
HOLD ON... JUST ONE... SECOND...WHILE I CATCH MY... BREATH.
UGHHHhhh.
IT'S NO FUN IF YOU'RE NOT GOING TO FIGHT.
SHOULD WE LET ROBIN KNOW WE ARRIVED HERE 10 MINUTES AGO AND HAVE BEEN WAITING FOR HIM TO JOIN US TO DEFEAT THE DR. LIGHT?
NOT UNLESS WE WANT ANOTHER WEEK OF ROBIN-THEMED OBSTACLE COURSES.
I KIND OF LIKED THAT.
THIS IS JUST SAD.
I'M COMING... JUST A SECOND... UGGGHHHH.
ALL RIGHT. THAT'S IT, I'M JUST GOING TO FLIP IT OFF. IN 5, 4, 3, 2...
THE END

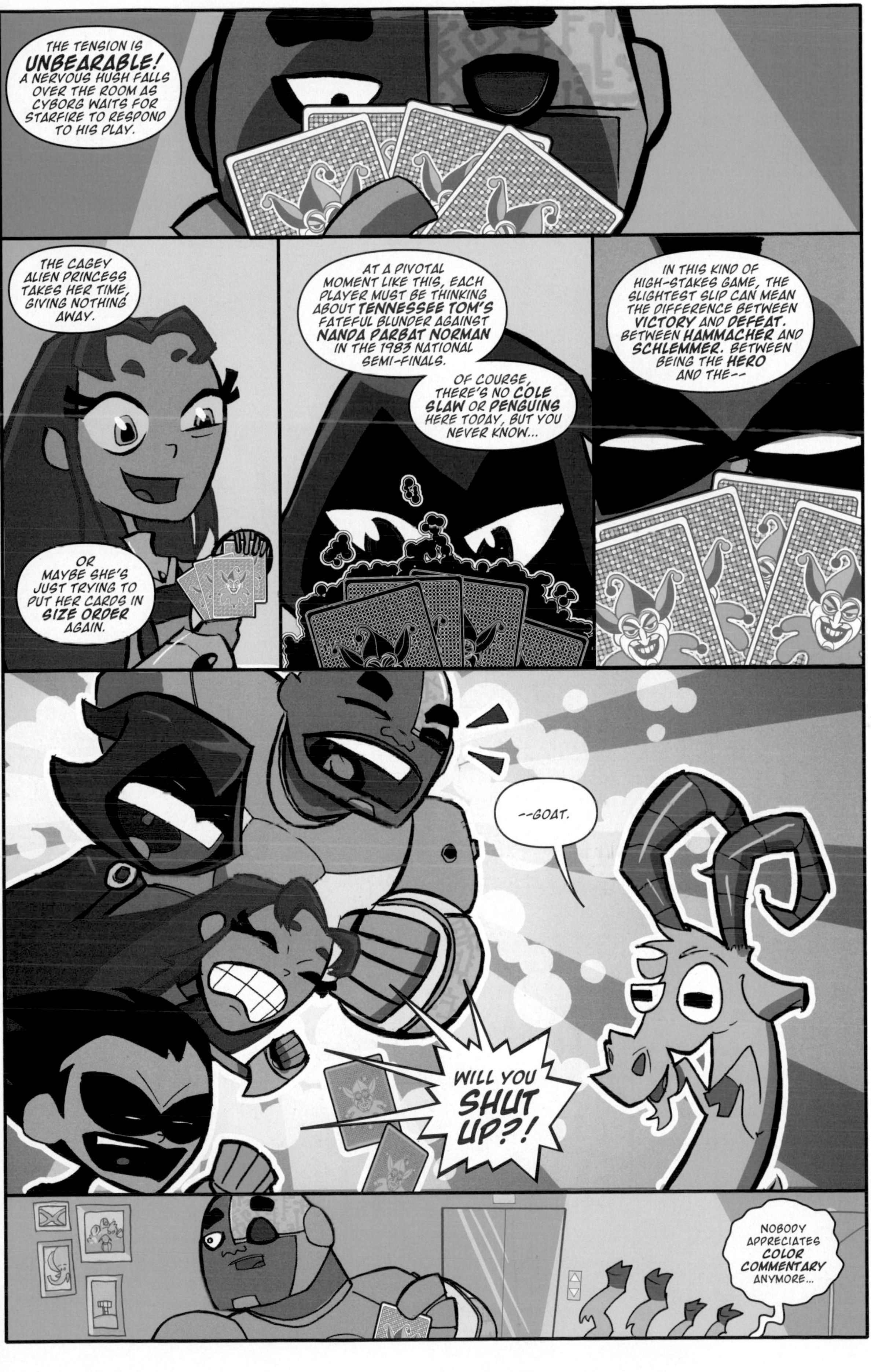
THE TENSION IS UNBEARABLE! A NERVOUS HUSH FALLS OVER THE ROOM AS CYBORG WAITS FOR STARFIRE TO RESPOND TO HIS PLAY.
THE CAGEY ALIEN PRINCESS TAKES HER TIME, GIVING NOTHING AWAY.
OR MAYBE SHE'S JUST TRYING TO PUT HER CARDS IN SIZE ORDER AGAIN.
AT A PIVOTAL MOMENT LIKE THIS, EACH PLAYER MUST BE THINKING ABOUT TENNESSEE TOM'S FATEFUL BLUNDER AGAINST NANDA PARBAT NORMAN IN THE 1983 NATIONAL SEMI-FINALS.
OF COURSE, THERE'S NO COLE SLAW OR PENGUINS HERE TODAY, BUT YOU NEVER KNOW...
IN THIS KIND OF HIGH-STAKES GAME, THE SLIGHTEST SLIP CAN MEAN THE DIFFERENCE BETWEEN VICTORY AND DEFEAT. BETWEEN HAMMACHER AND SCHLEMMER. BETWEEN BEING THE HERO AND THE--
--GOAT.
WILL YOU SHUT UP?!
NOBODY APPRECIATES COLOR COMMENTARY ANYMORE...

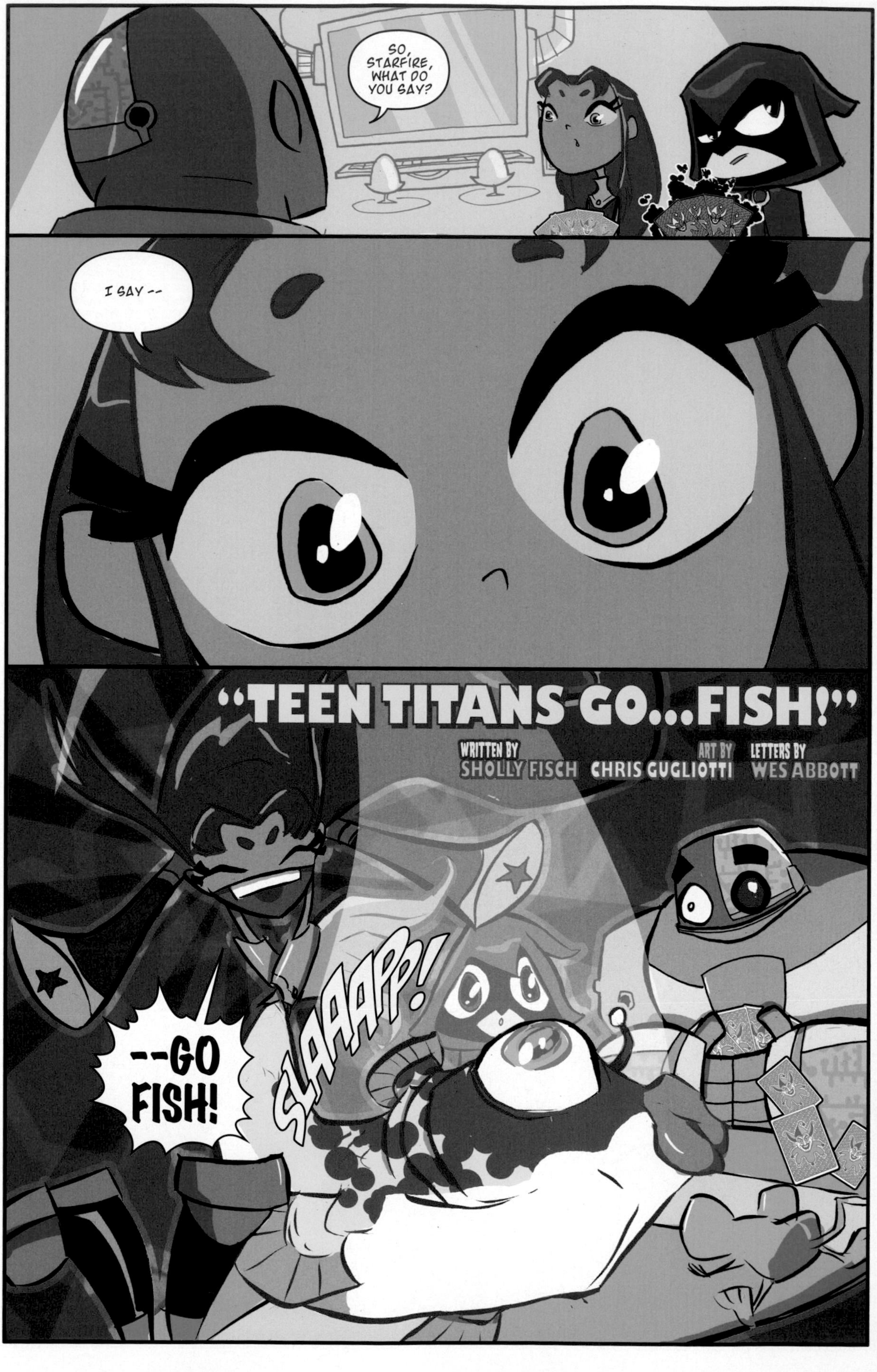
SO, STARFIRE, WHAT DO YOU SAY?
I SAY --
"TEEN TITANS GO...FISH!"
WRITTEN BY SHOLLY FISCH
ART BY CHRIS GUGLIOTTI
LETTERS BY WES ABBOTT
--GO FISH!
SLAAAPP!

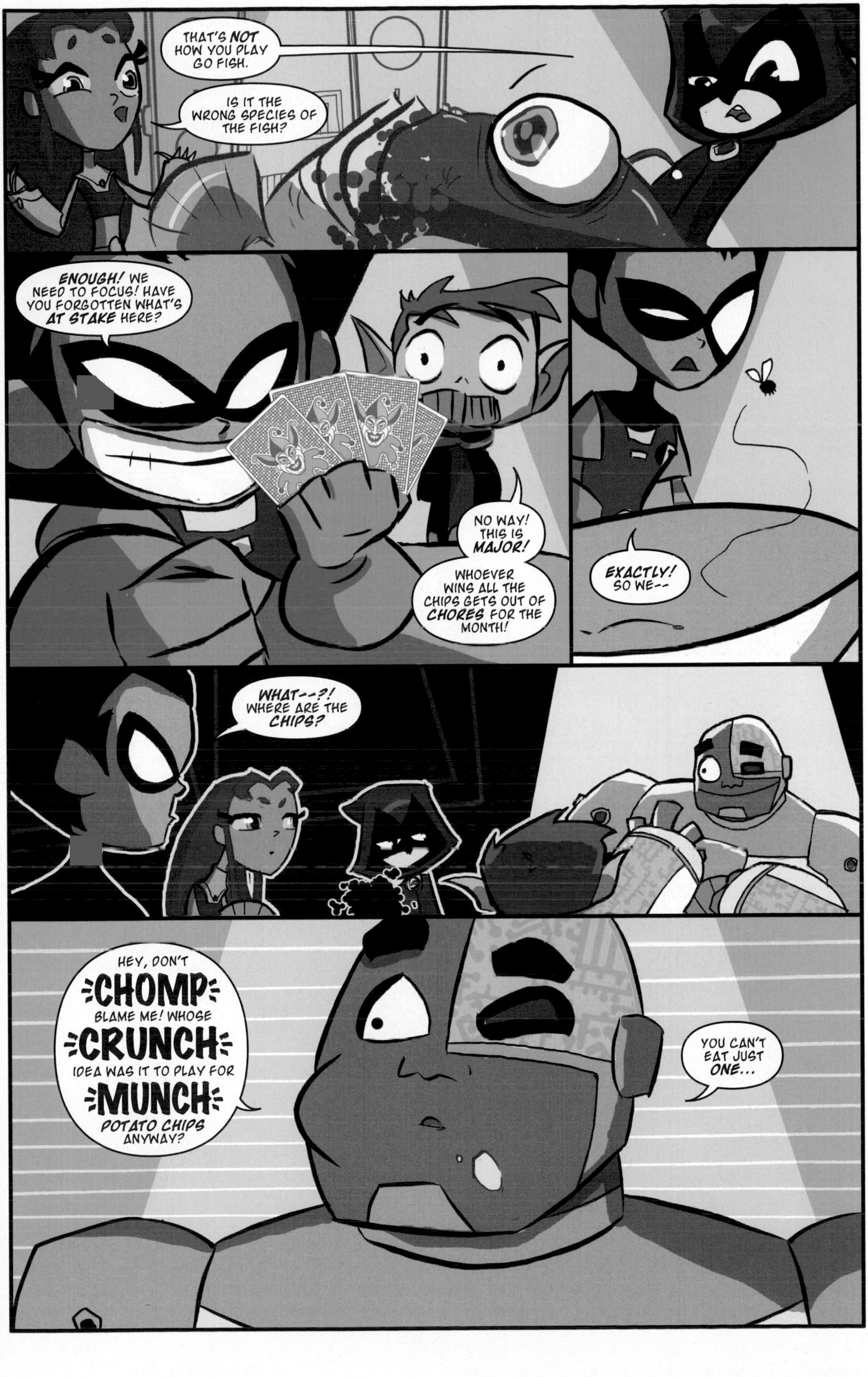
THAT'S NOT HOW YOU PLAY GO FISH.
IS IT THE WRONG SPECIES OF THE FISH?
ENOUGH! WE NEED TO FOCUS! HAVE YOU FORGOTTEN WHAT'S AT STAKE HERE?
NO WAY! THIS IS MAJOR!
WHOEVER WINS ALL THE CHIPS GETS OUT OF CHORES FOR THE MONTH!
EXACTLY! SO WE--
WHAT--?! WHERE ARE THE CHIPS?
HEY, DON'T CHOMP BLAME ME! WHOSE CRUNCH IDEA WAS IT TO PLAY FOR MUNCH POTATO CHIPS ANYWAY?
YOU CAN'T EAT JUST ONE...

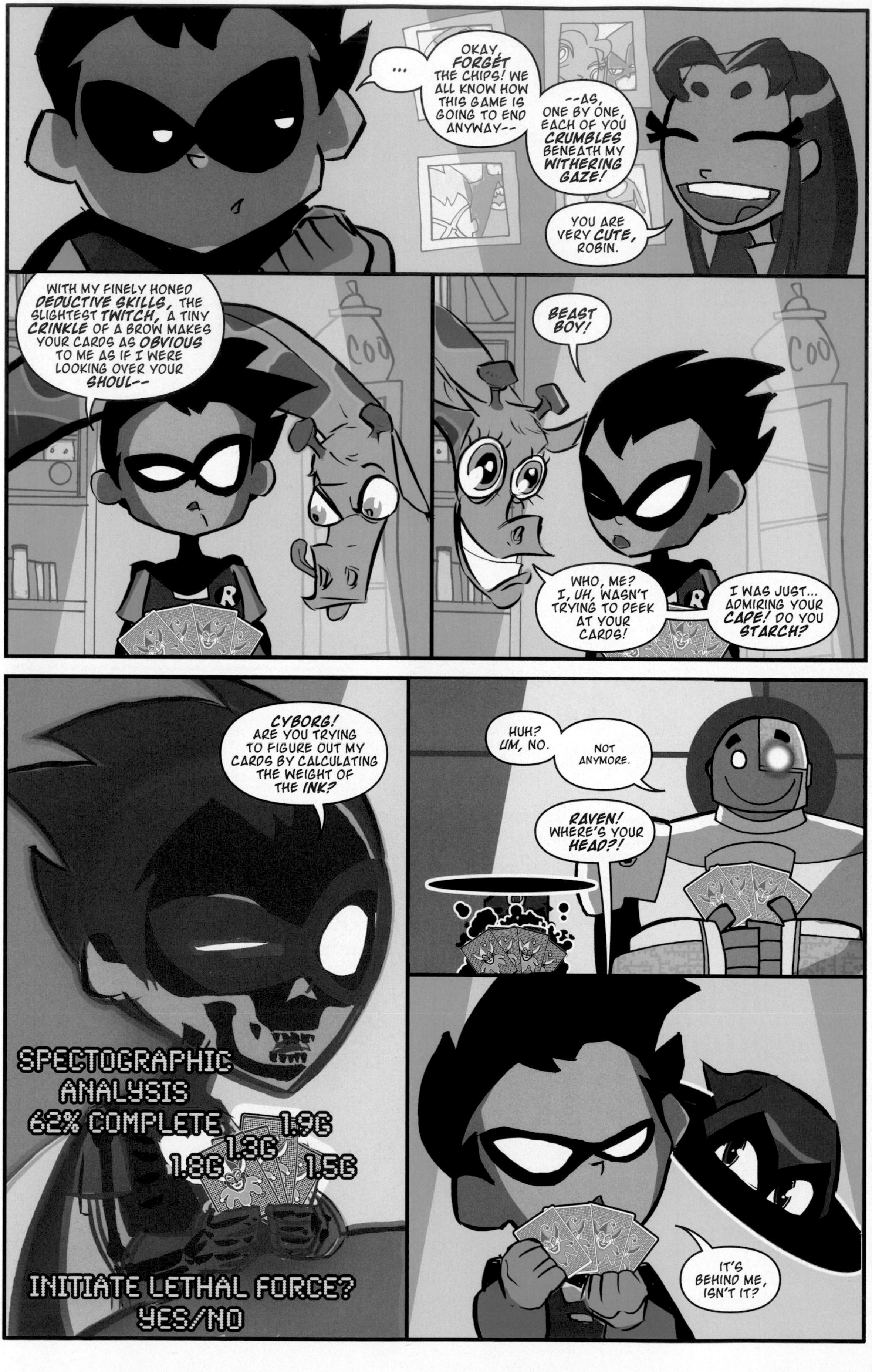
...
OKAY, FORGET THE CHIPS! WE ALL KNOW HOW THIS GAME IS GOING TO END ANYWAY--
--AS, ONE BY ONE, EACH OF YOU CRUMBLES BENEATH MY WITHERING GAZE!
YOU ARE VERY CUTE, ROBIN.
WITH MY FINELY HONED DEDUCTIVE SKILLS, THE SLIGHTEST TWITCH, A TINY CRINKLE OF A BROW MAKES YOUR CARDS AS OBVIOUS TO ME AS IF I WERE LOOKING OVER YOUR SHOUL--
BEAST BOY!
WHO, ME? I, UH, WASN'T TRYING TO PEEK AT YOUR CARDS!
I WAS JUST... ADMIRING YOUR CAPE! DO YOU STARCH?
CYBORG! ARE YOU TRYING TO FIGURE OUT MY CARDS BY CALCULATING THE WEIGHT OF THE INK?
SPECTOGRAPHIC ANALYSIS 62% COMPLETE
1.9G
1.3G
1.8G
1.5G
INITIATE LETHAL FORCE? YES/NO
HUH? UM, NO.
NOT ANYMORE.
RAVEN! WHERE'S YOUR HEAD?!
IT'S BEHIND ME, ISN'T IT?

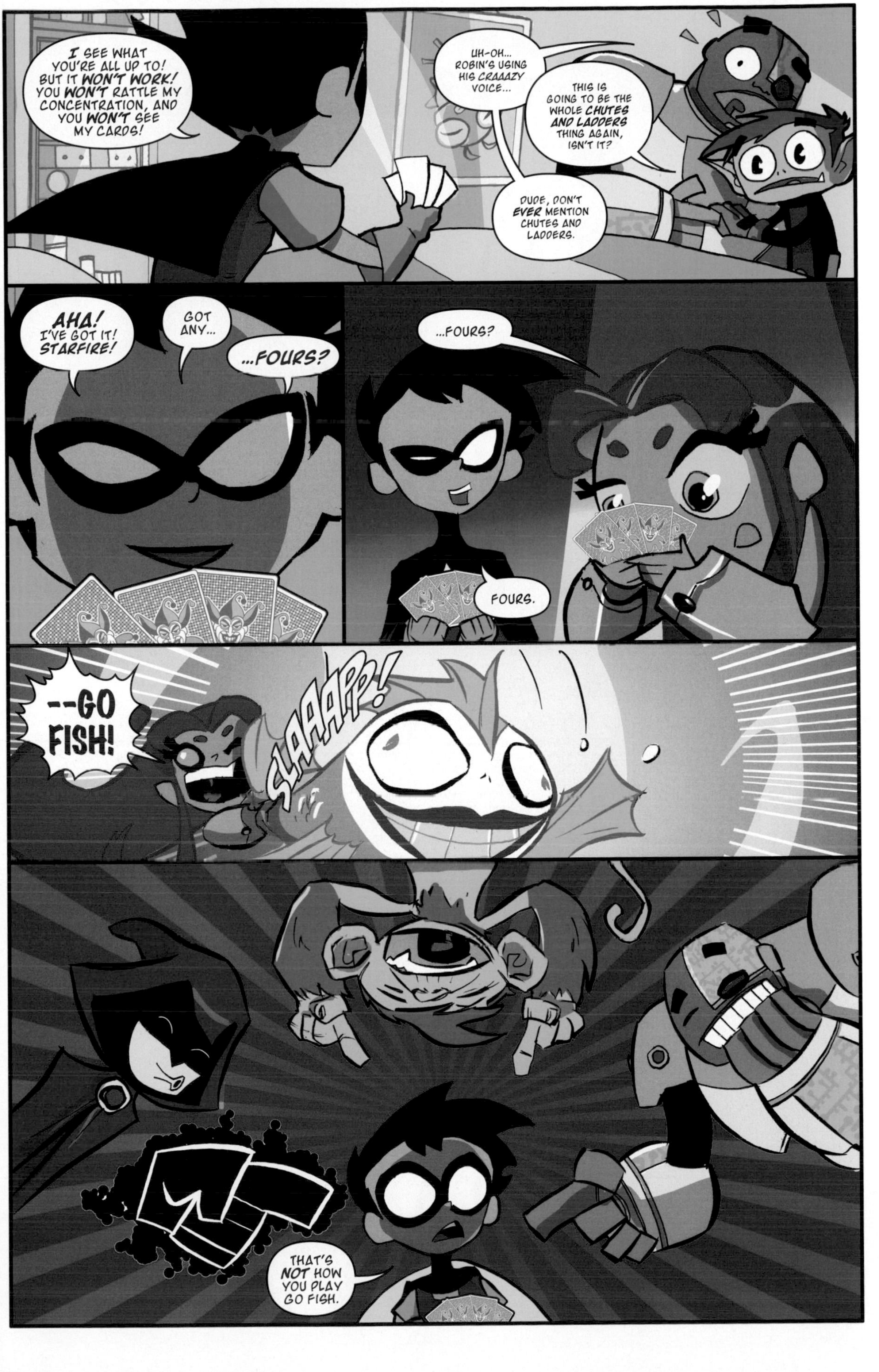

I SEE WHAT YOU'RE ALL UP TO! BUT IT WON'T WORK! YOU WON'T RATTLE MY CONCENTRATION, AND YOU WON'T SEE MY CARDS!
UH-OH... ROBIN'S USING HIS CRAAAZY VOICE...
THIS IS GOING TO BE THE WHOLE CHUTES AND LADDERS THING AGAIN, ISN'T IT?
DUDE, DON'T EVER MENTION CHUTES AND LADDERS.
AHA! I'VE GOT IT! STARFIRE!
GOT ANY...
...FOURS?
...FOURS?
FOURS.
--GO FISH!
SLAAAPP!
THAT'S NOT HOW YOU PLAY GO FISH.

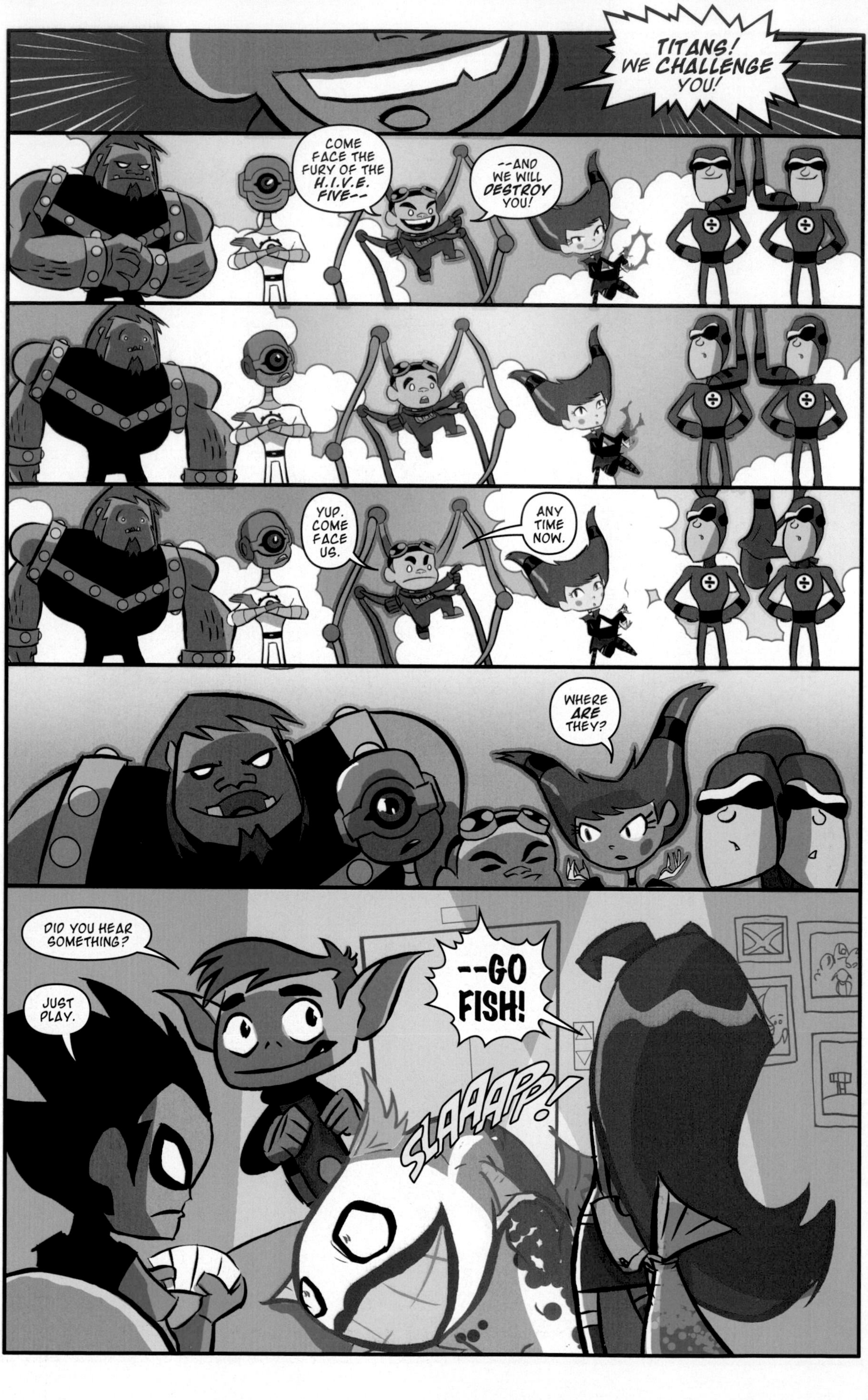
TITANS! WE CHALLENGE YOU!
COME FACE THE FURY OF THE H.I.V.E. FIVE--
--AND WE WILL DESTROY YOU!
YUP. COME FACE US.
ANY TIME NOW.
WHERE ARE THEY?
DID YOU HEAR SOMETHING?
JUST PLAY.
--GO FISH!
SLAAAP!

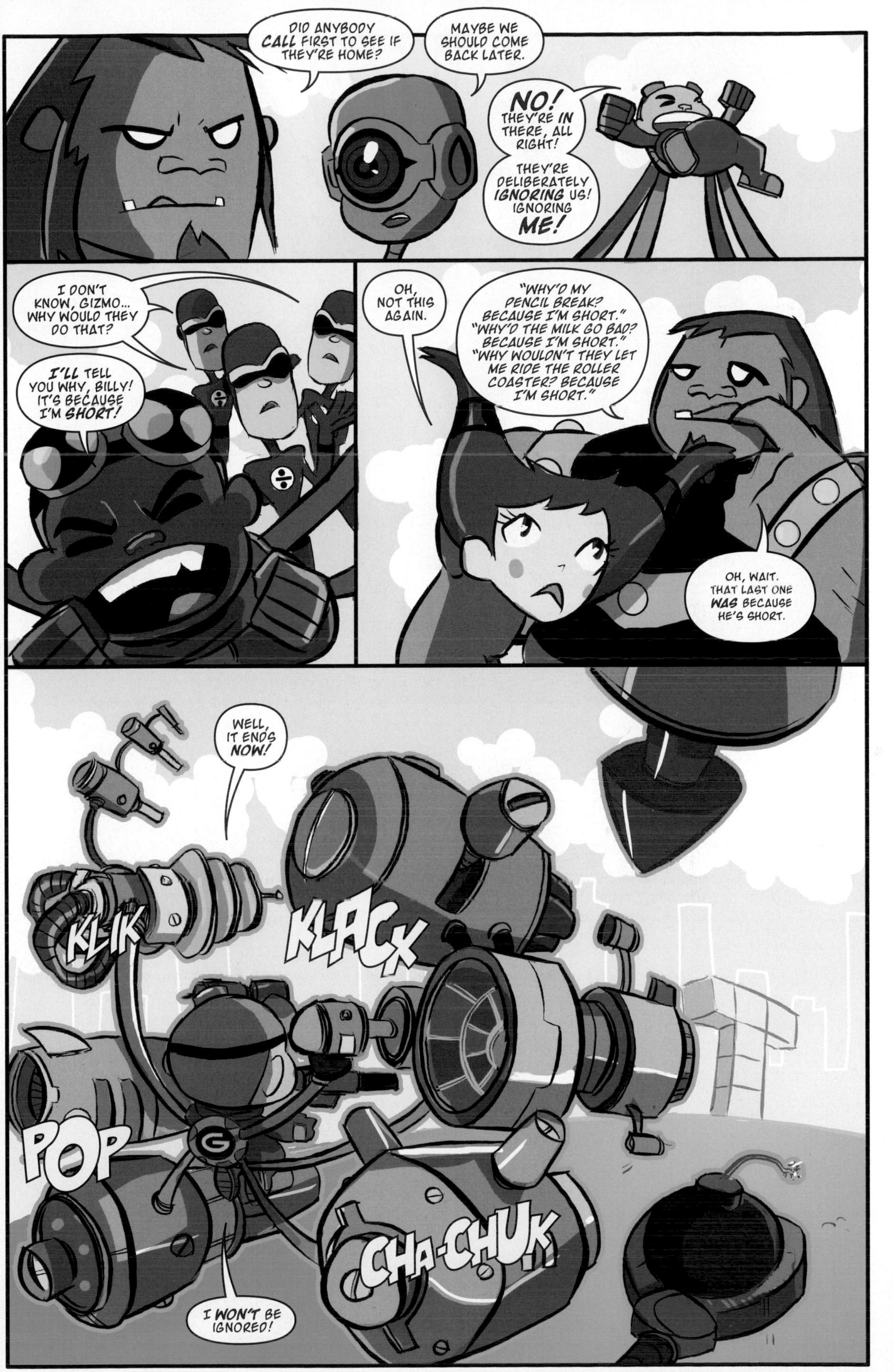
DID ANYBODY CALL FIRST TO SEE IF THEY'RE HOME?
MAYBE WE SHOULD COME BACK LATER.
NO! THEY'RE IN THERE, ALL RIGHT!
THEY'RE DELIBERATELY IGNORING US! IGNORING ME!
I DON'T KNOW, GIZMO... WHY WOULD THEY DO THAT?
I'LL TELL YOU WHY, BILLY! IT'S BECAUSE I'M SHORT!
OH, NOT THIS AGAIN.
"WHY'D MY PENCIL BREAK? BECAUSE I'M SHORT." "WHY'D THE MILK GO BAD? BECAUSE I'M SHORT." "WHY WOULDN'T THEY LET ME RIDE THE ROLLER COASTER? BECAUSE I'M SHORT."
OH, WAIT. THAT LAST ONE WAS BECAUSE HE'S SHORT.
WELL, IT ENDS NOW!
KLIK
KLACK
POP
CHA-CHUK
I WON'T BE IGNORED!

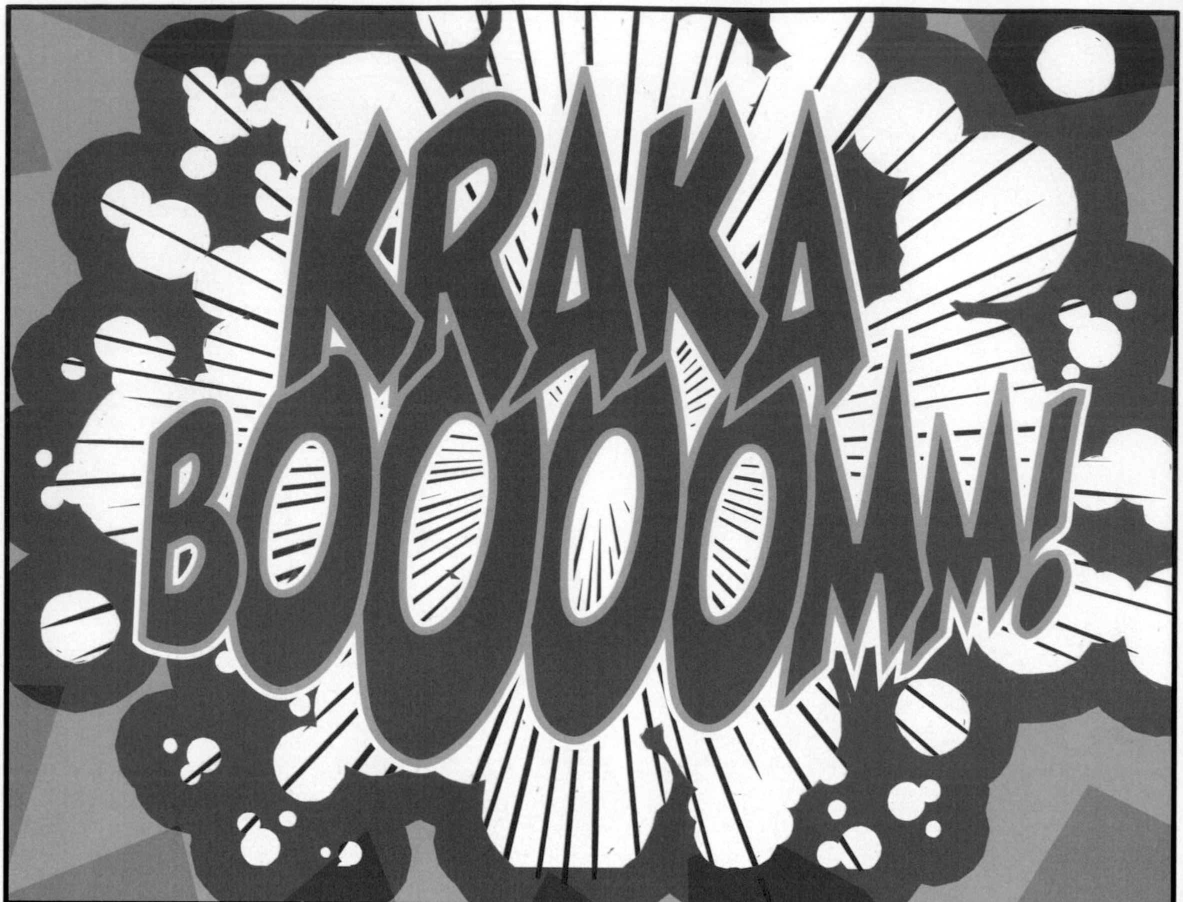
KRAKA BOOOOM!!!
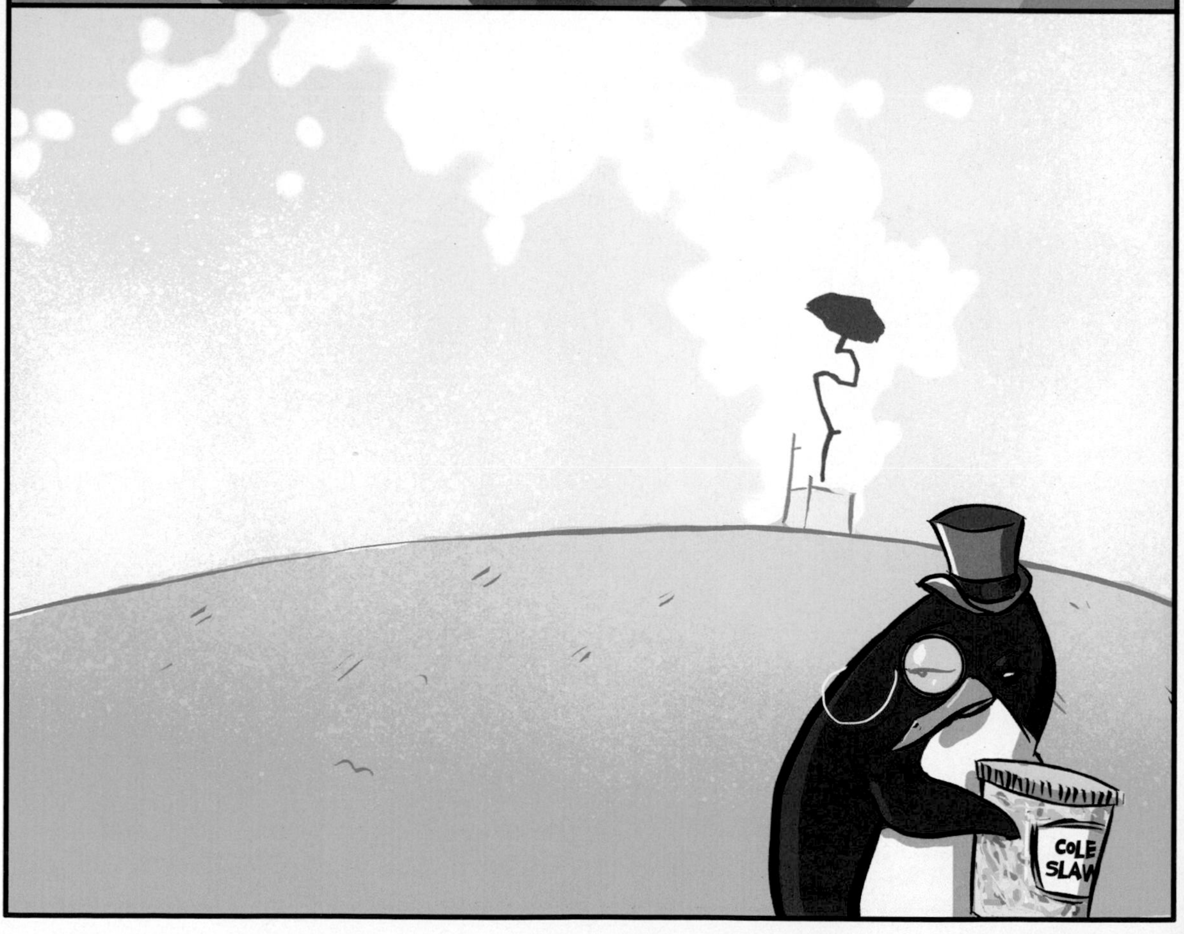
COLE SLAW

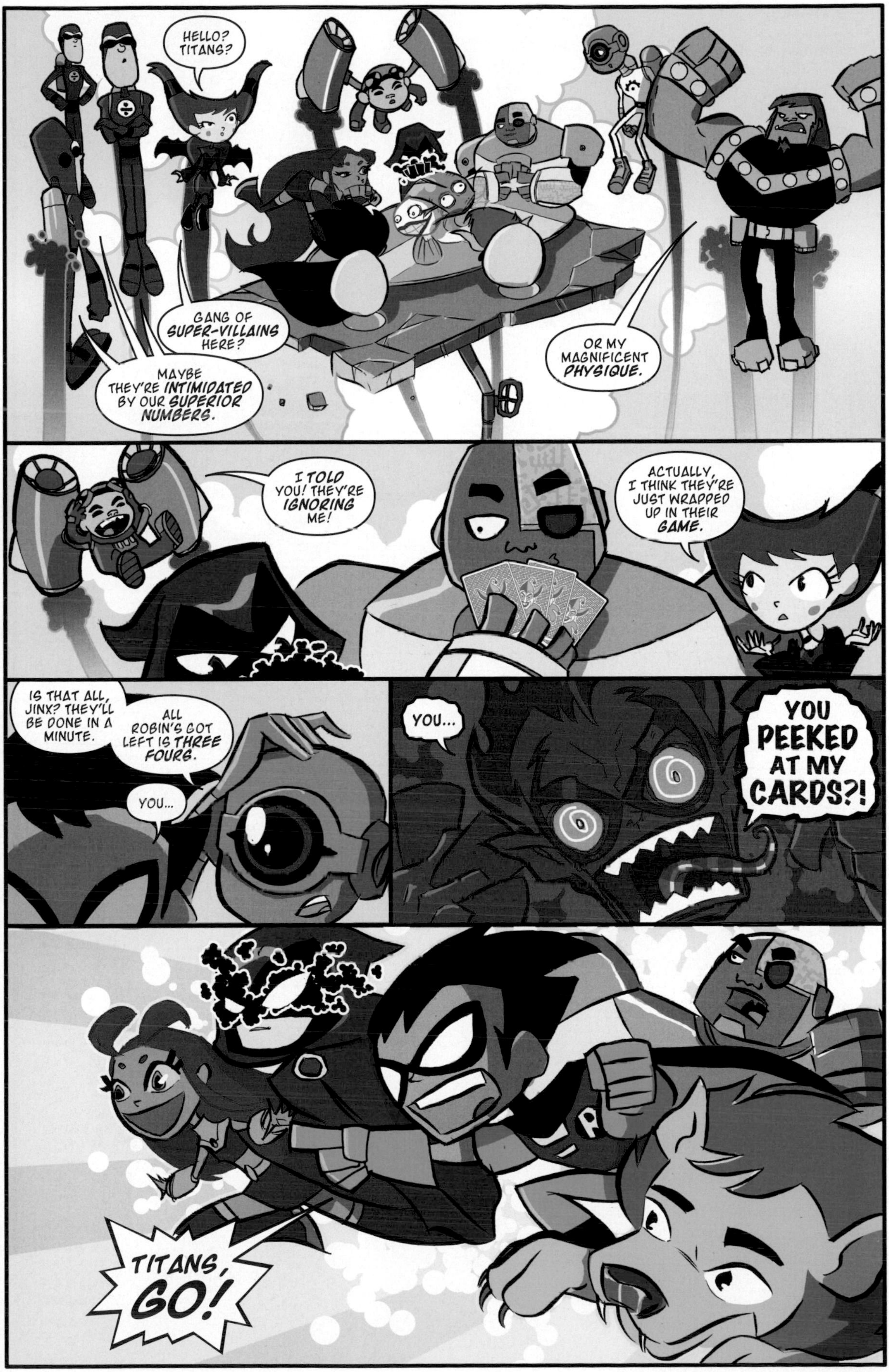
HELLO? TITANS?
GANG OF SUPER-VILLAINS HERE?
MAYBE THEY'RE INTIMIDATED BY OUR SUPERIOR NUMBERS.
OR MY MAGNIFICENT PHYSIQUE.
I TOLD YOU! THEY'RE IGNORING ME!
ACTUALLY, I THINK THEY'RE JUST WRAPPED UP IN THEIR GAME.
IS THAT ALL, JINX? THEY'LL BE DONE IN A MINUTE.
ALL ROBIN'S GOT LEFT IS THREE FOURS.
YOU...
YOU...
YOU PEEKED AT MY CARDS?!
TITANS, GO!

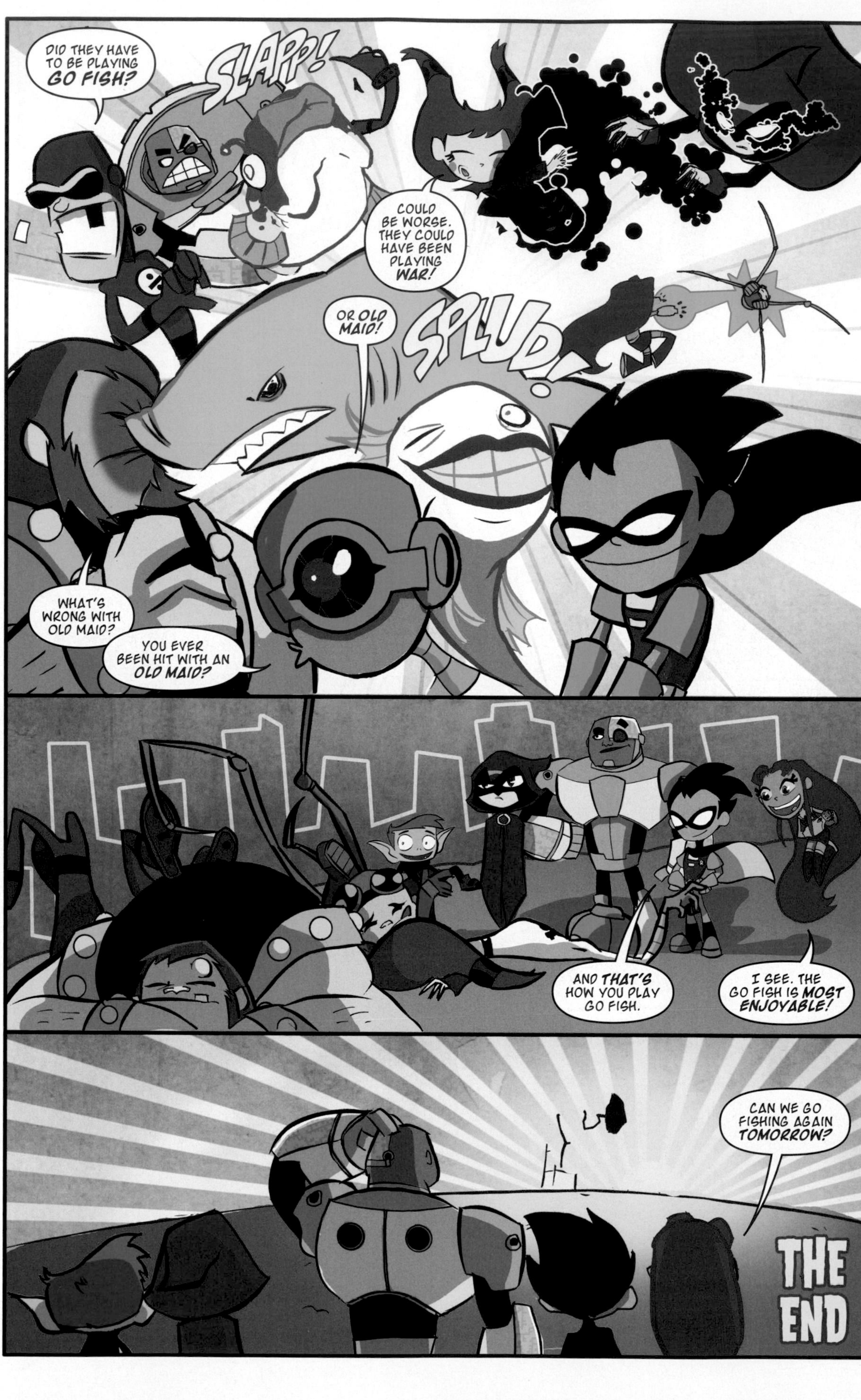
DID THEY HAVE TO BE PLAYING GO FISH?
SLAPP!
COULD BE WORSE. THEY COULD HAVE BEEN PLAYING WAR!
OR OLD MAID!
SPLUD!
WHAT'S WRONG WITH OLD MAID?
YOU EVER BEEN HIT WITH AN OLD MAID?
AND THAT'S HOW YOU PLAY GO FISH.
I SEE. THE GO FISH IS MOST ENJOYABLE!
CAN WE GO FISHING AGAIN TOMORROW?
THE END

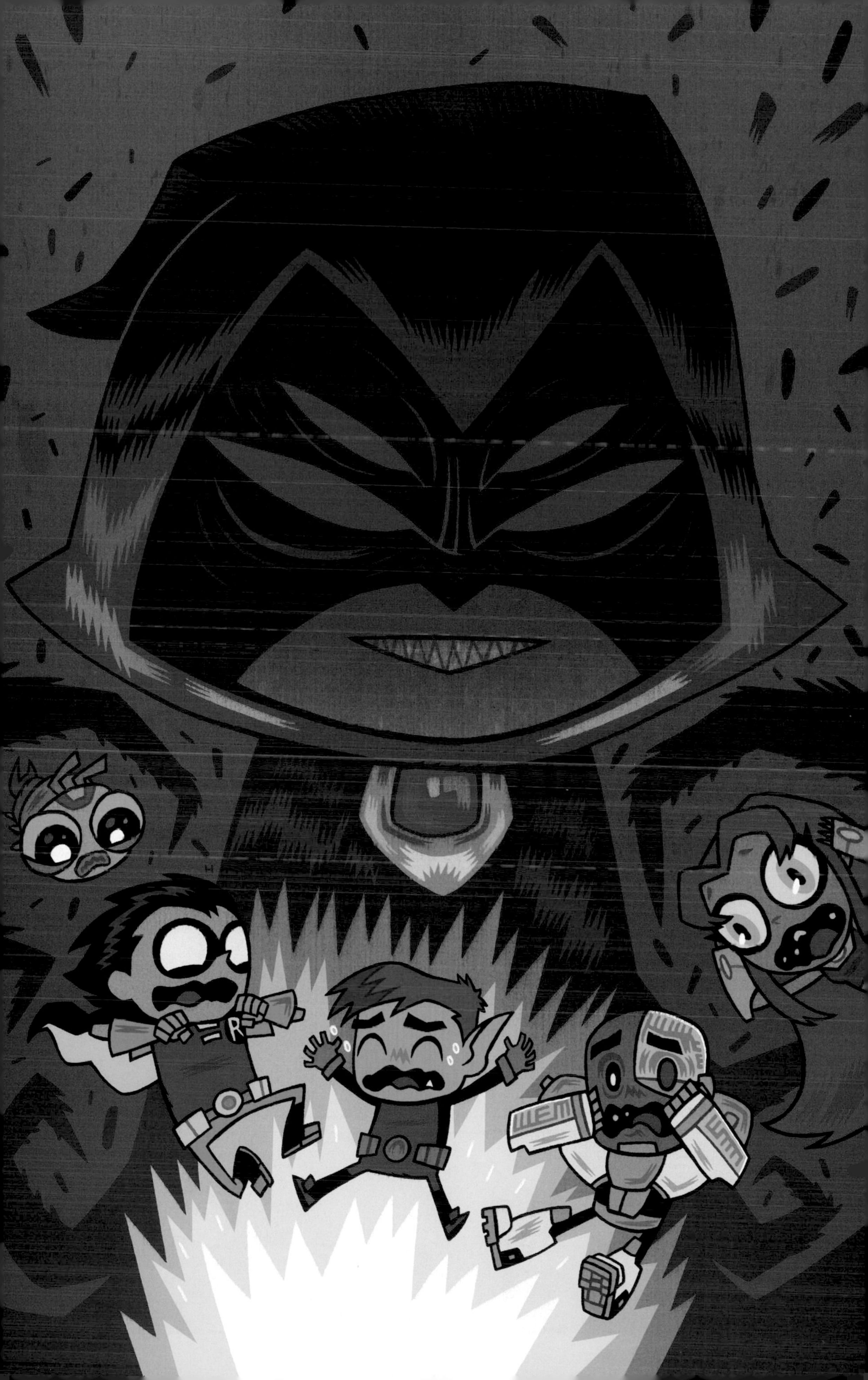

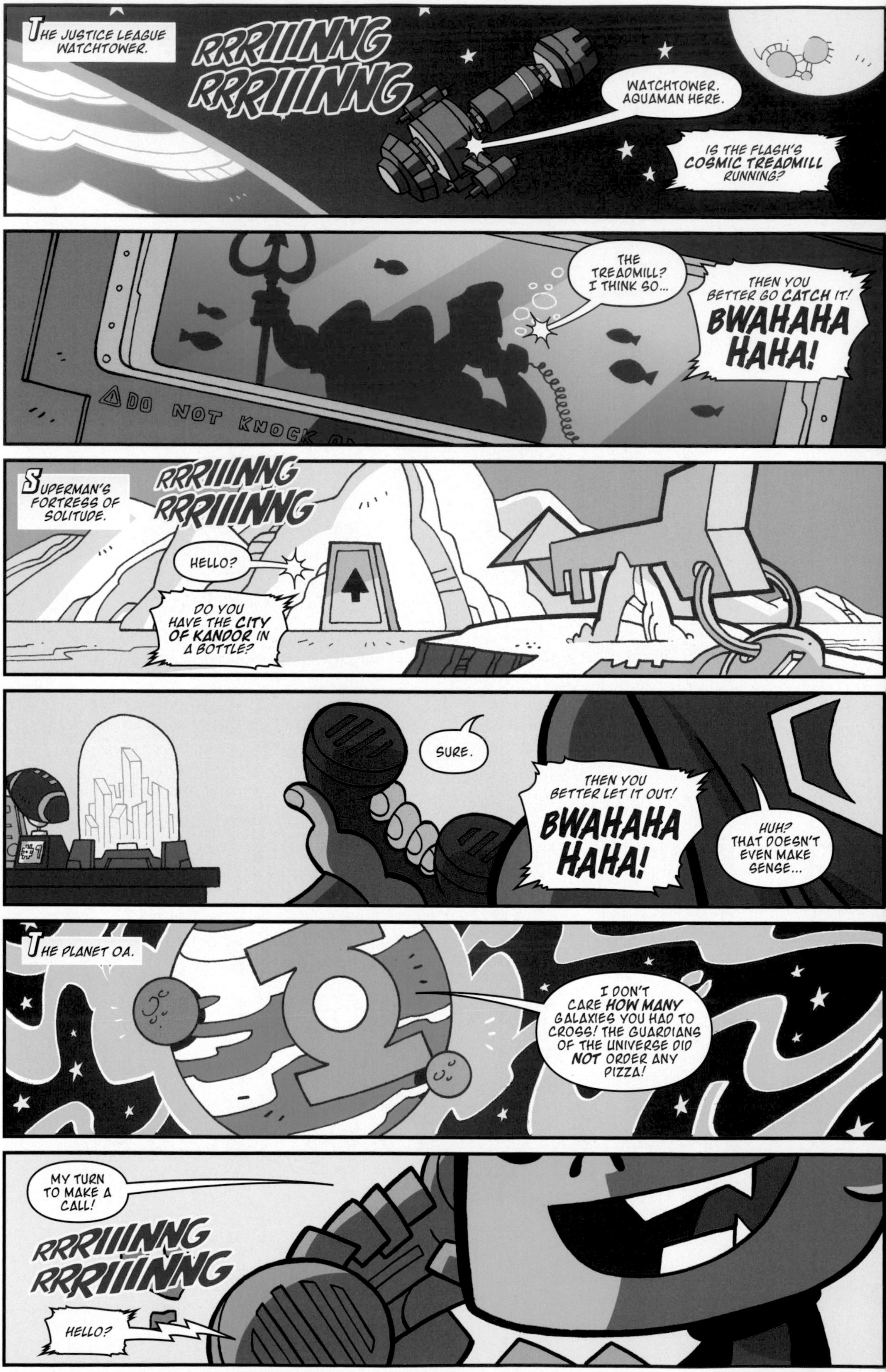
THE JUSTICE LEAGUE WATCHTOWER.
RRRIIINNG RRRIIINNG
WATCHTOWER. AQUAMAN HERE.
IS THE FLASH'S COSMIC TREADMILL RUNNING?
THE TREADMILL? I THINK SO...
THEN YOU BETTER GO CATCH IT! BWAHAHA HAHA!
DO NOT KNOCK
SUPERMAN'S FORTRESS OF SOLITUDE.
RRRIIINNG RRRIIINNG
HELLO?
DO YOU HAVE THE CITY OF KANDOR IN A BOTTLE?
SURE.
THEN YOU BETTER LET IT OUT! BWAHAHA HAHA!
HUH? THAT DOESN'T EVEN MAKE SENSE...
#1
THE PLANET OA.
I DON'T CARE HOW MANY GALAXIES YOU HAD TO CROSS! THE GUARDIANS OF THE UNIVERSE DID NOT ORDER ANY PIZZA!
MY TURN TO MAKE A CALL!
RRRIIINNG RRRIIINNG
HELLO?

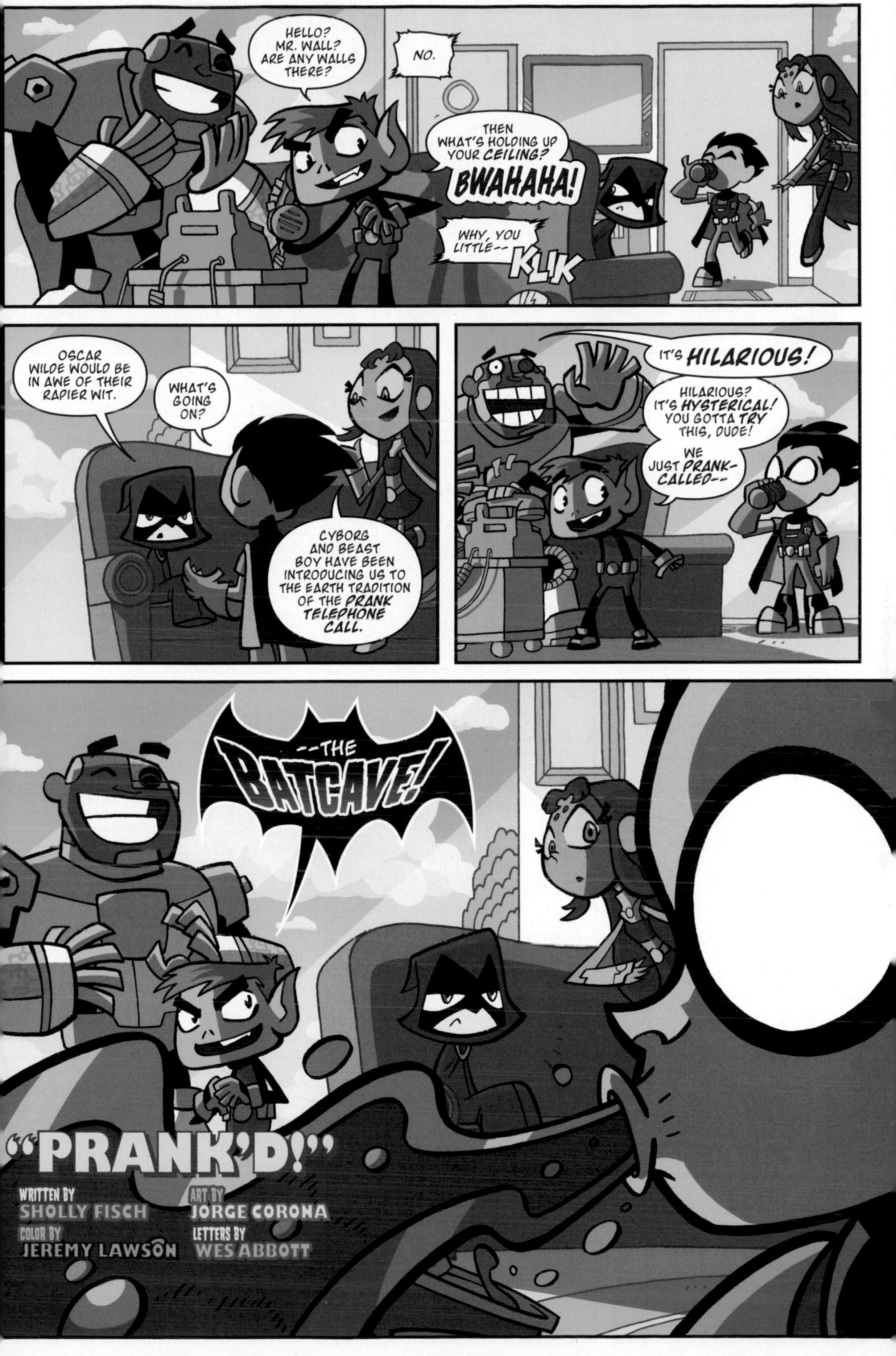
HELLO? MR. WALL? ARE ANY WALLS THERE?
NO.
THEN WHAT'S HOLDING UP YOUR CEILING? BWAHAHA!
WHY, YOU LITTLE--
KLIK
OSCAR WILDE WOULD BE IN AWE OF THEIR RAPIER WIT.
WHAT'S GOING ON?
CYBORG AND BEAST BOY HAVE BEEN INTRODUCING US TO THE EARTH TRADITION OF THE PRANK TELEPHONE CALL.
IT'S HILARIOUS!
HILARIOUS? IT'S HYSTERICAL! YOU GOTTA TRY THIS, DUDE!
WE JUST PRANK-CALLED--
--THE BATCAVE!
"PRANK'D!"
WRITTEN BY SHOLLY FISCH
ART BY JORGE CORONA
COLOR BY JEREMY LAWSON
LETTERS BY WES ABBOTT

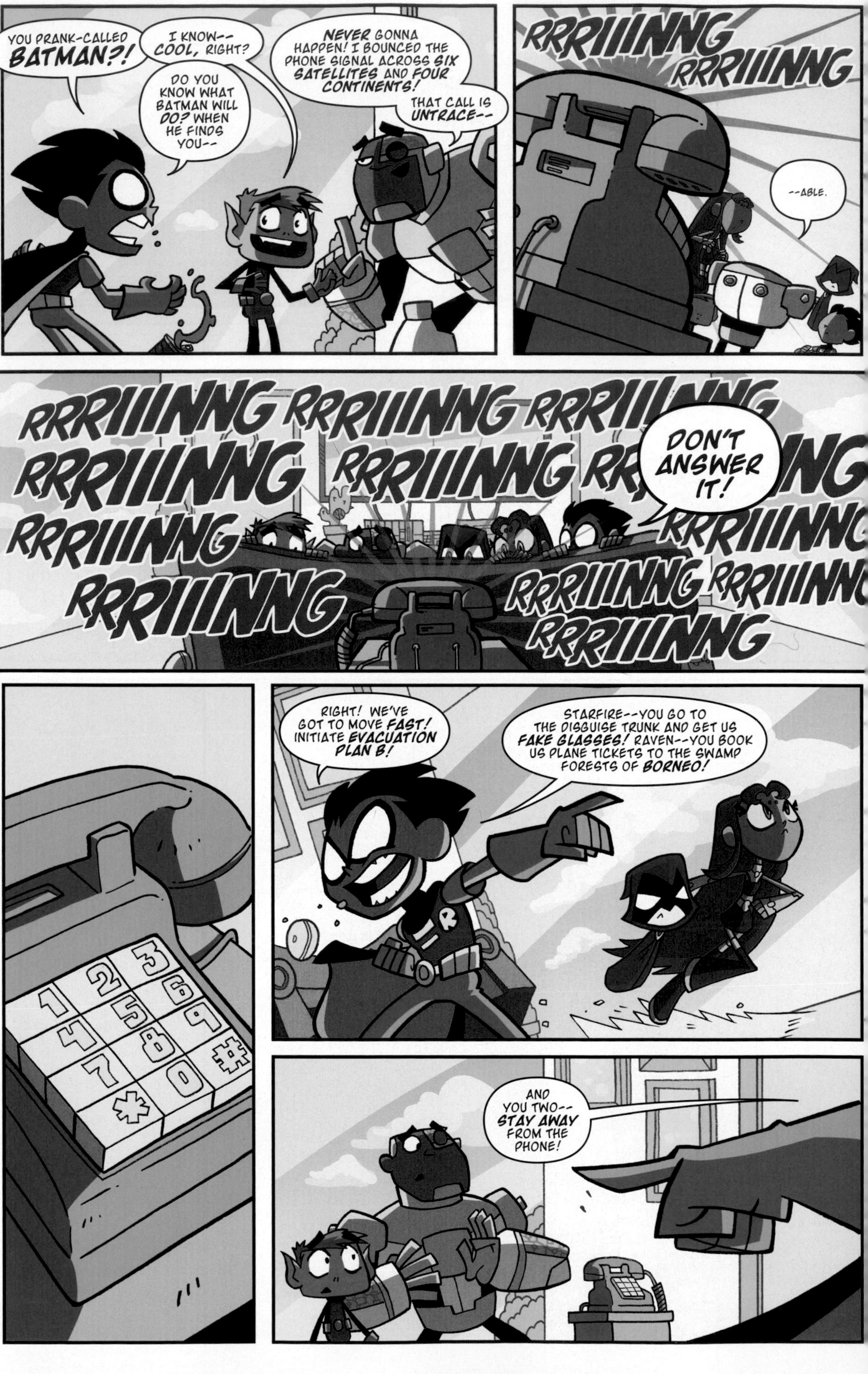
YOU PRANK-CALLED BATMAN?!
I KNOW-- COOL, RIGHT?
DO YOU KNOW WHAT BATMAN WILL DO? WHEN HE FINDS YOU--
NEVER GONNA HAPPEN! I BOUNCED THE PHONE SIGNAL ACROSS SIX SATELLITES AND FOUR CONTINENTS!
THAT CALL IS UNTRACE--
RRRIIINNG
RRRIIINNG
--ABLE.
RRRIIINNG RRRIIINNG RRRIIINNG
RRRIIINNG RRRIIINNG
DON'T ANSWER IT!
RRRIIINNG
RRRIIINNG
RRRIIINNG RRRIIINNG
RRRIIINNG
RIGHT! WE'VE GOT TO MOVE FAST! INITIATE EVACUATION PLAN B!
STARFIRE--YOU GO TO THE DISGUISE TRUNK AND GET US FAKE GLASSES! RAVEN--YOU BOOK US PLANE TICKETS TO THE SWAMP FORESTS OF BORNEO!
AND YOU TWO-- STAY AWAY FROM THE PHONE!

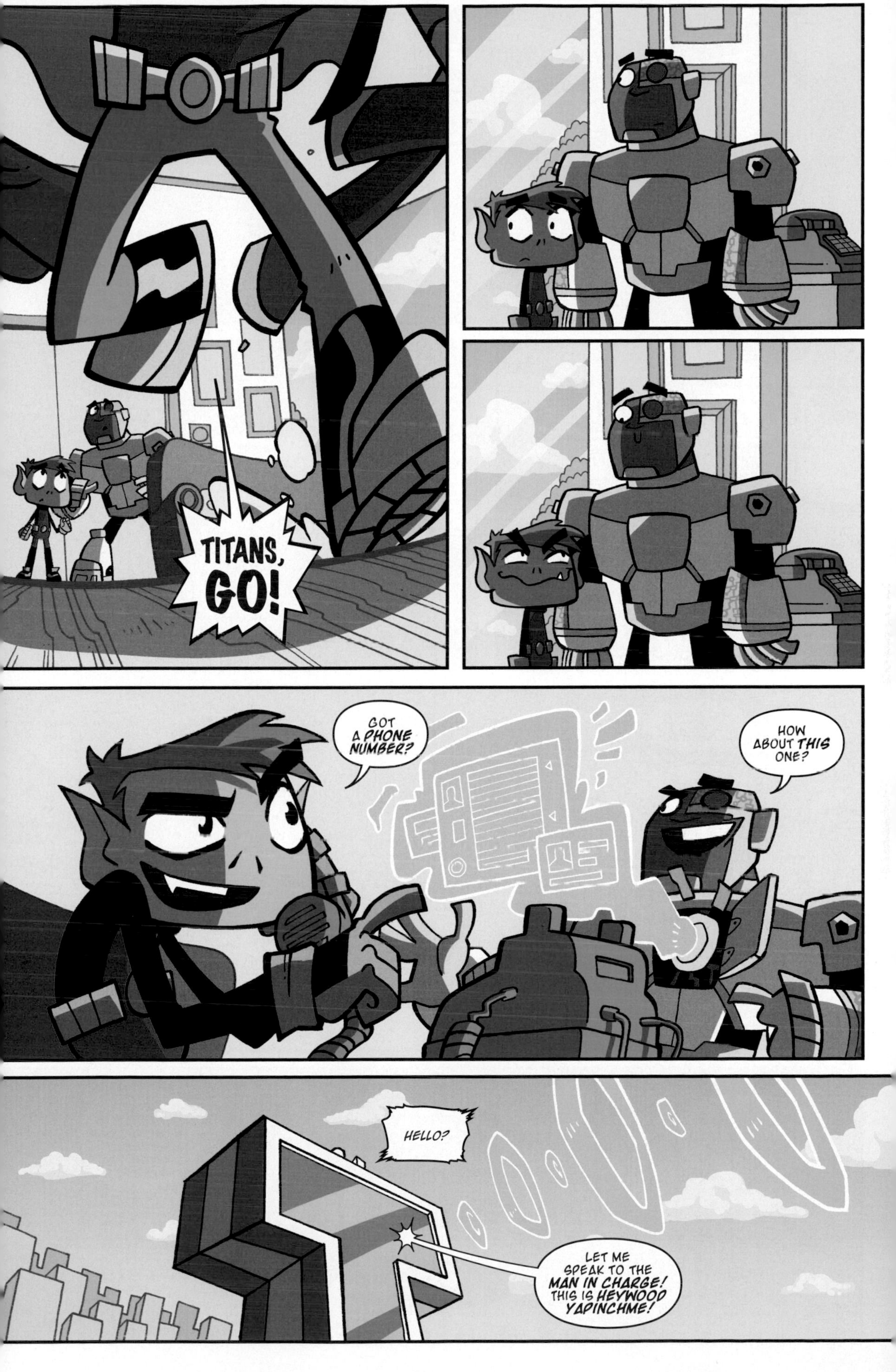
TITANS, GO!
GOT A PHONE NUMBER?
HOW ABOUT THIS ONE?
HELLO?
LET ME SPEAK TO THE MAN IN CHARGE! THIS IS HEYWOOD YAPINCHME!

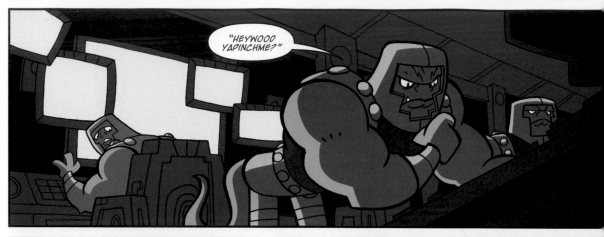

"HEYWOOD YAPINCHME?"

OW!

WHAT? YOU *ASKED* ME TO.

"HEY, WOULD YOU PINCH ME?"

WHERE DID THAT TRANSMISSION ORIGINATE?

EARTH, SIR.

CHANGE COURSE!

BUT, COMMANDER--

--WE HAVEN'T FINISHED *DESTROYING* THE PLANET *HNY'XX* YET!

THE HNY'XXIANS WILL JUST HAVE TO *WAIT THEIR TURN!*

THIS IS AN *INSULT* TO THE GORDANIAN HOMEWORLD! WE GO TO *EARTH!*

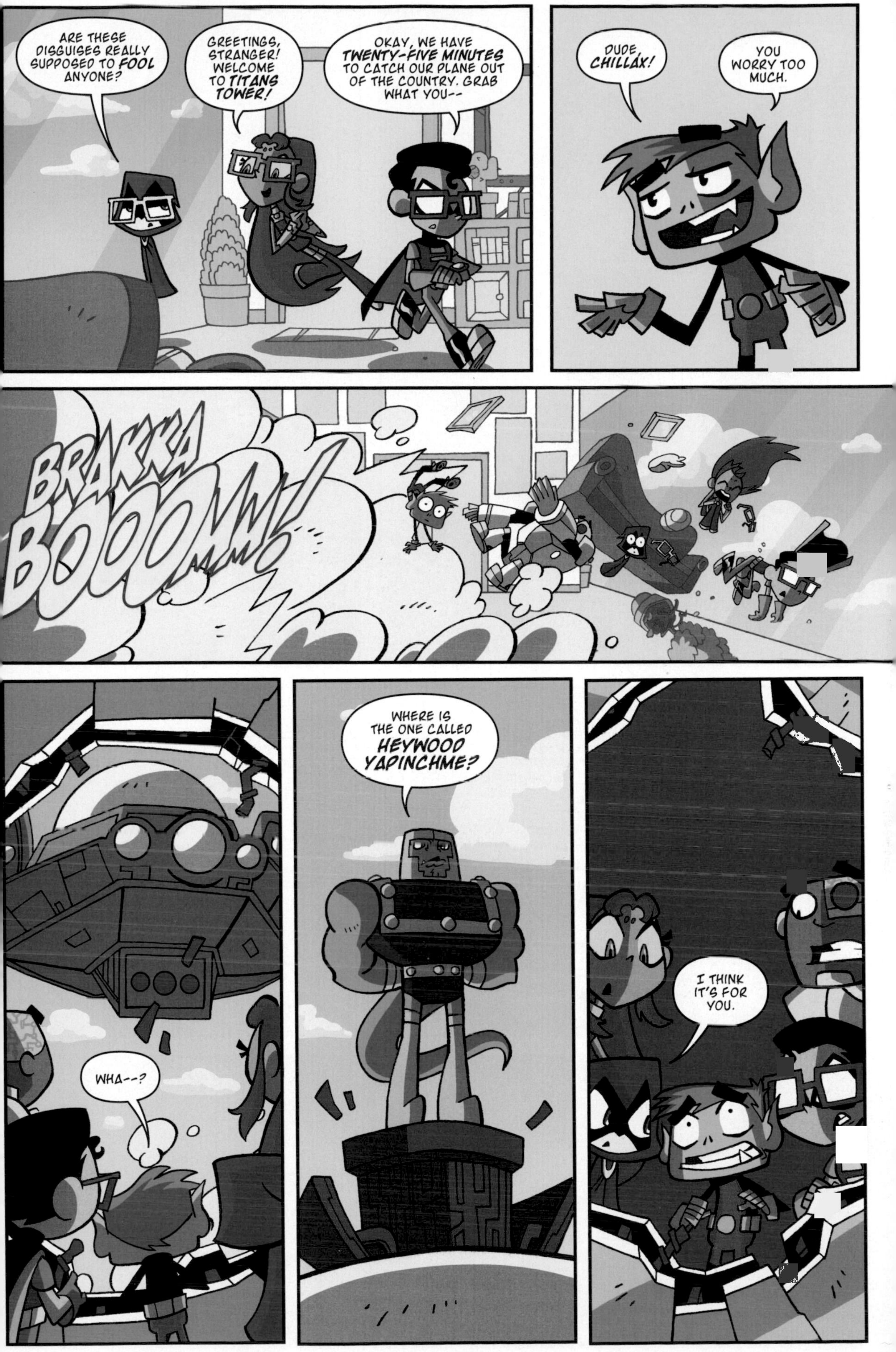
ARE THESE DISGUISES REALLY SUPPOSED TO FOOL ANYONE?
GREETINGS, STRANGER! WELCOME TO TITANS TOWER!
OKAY, WE HAVE TWENTY-FIVE MINUTES TO CATCH OUR PLANE OUT OF THE COUNTRY. GRAB WHAT YOU--
DUDE, CHILLAX!
YOU WORRY TOO MUCH.
BRAKKA BOOOOM!
WHA--?
WHERE IS THE ONE CALLED HEYWOOD YAPINCHME?
I THINK IT'S FOR YOU.

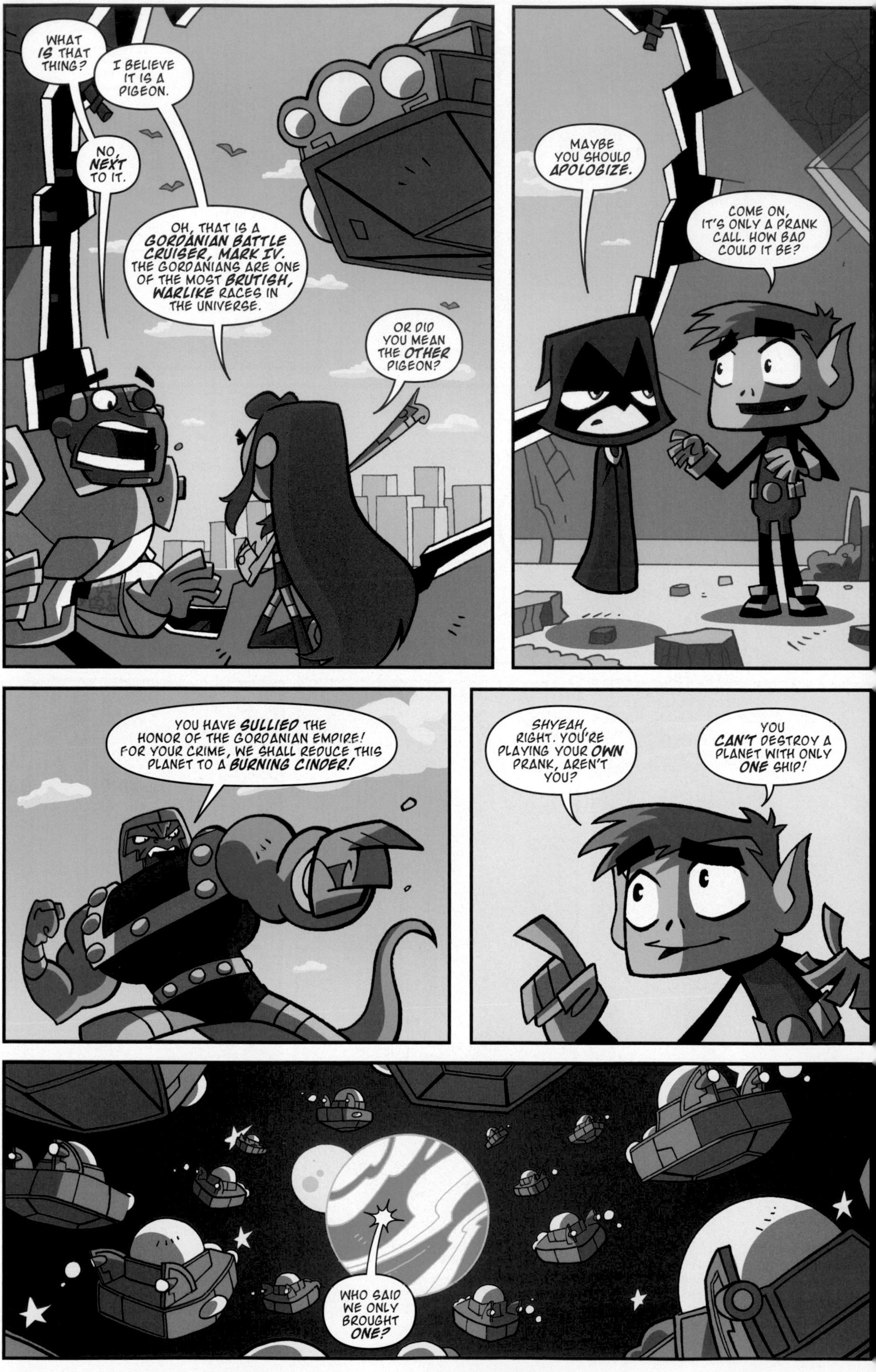

WHAT IS THAT THING?
I BELIEVE IT IS A PIGEON.
NO, NEXT TO IT.
OH, THAT IS A GORDANIAN BATTLE CRUISER, MARK IV. THE GORDANIANS ARE ONE OF THE MOST BRUTISH, WARLIKE RACES IN THE UNIVERSE.
OR DID YOU MEAN THE OTHER PIGEON?
MAYBE YOU SHOULD APOLOGIZE.
COME ON, IT'S ONLY A PRANK CALL. HOW BAD COULD IT BE?
YOU HAVE SULLIED THE HONOR OF THE GORDANIAN EMPIRE! FOR YOUR CRIME, WE SHALL REDUCE THIS PLANET TO A BURNING CINDER!
SHYEAH, RIGHT. YOU'RE PLAYING YOUR OWN PRANK, AREN'T YOU?
YOU CAN'T DESTROY A PLANET WITH ONLY ONE SHIP!
WHO SAID WE ONLY BROUGHT ONE?

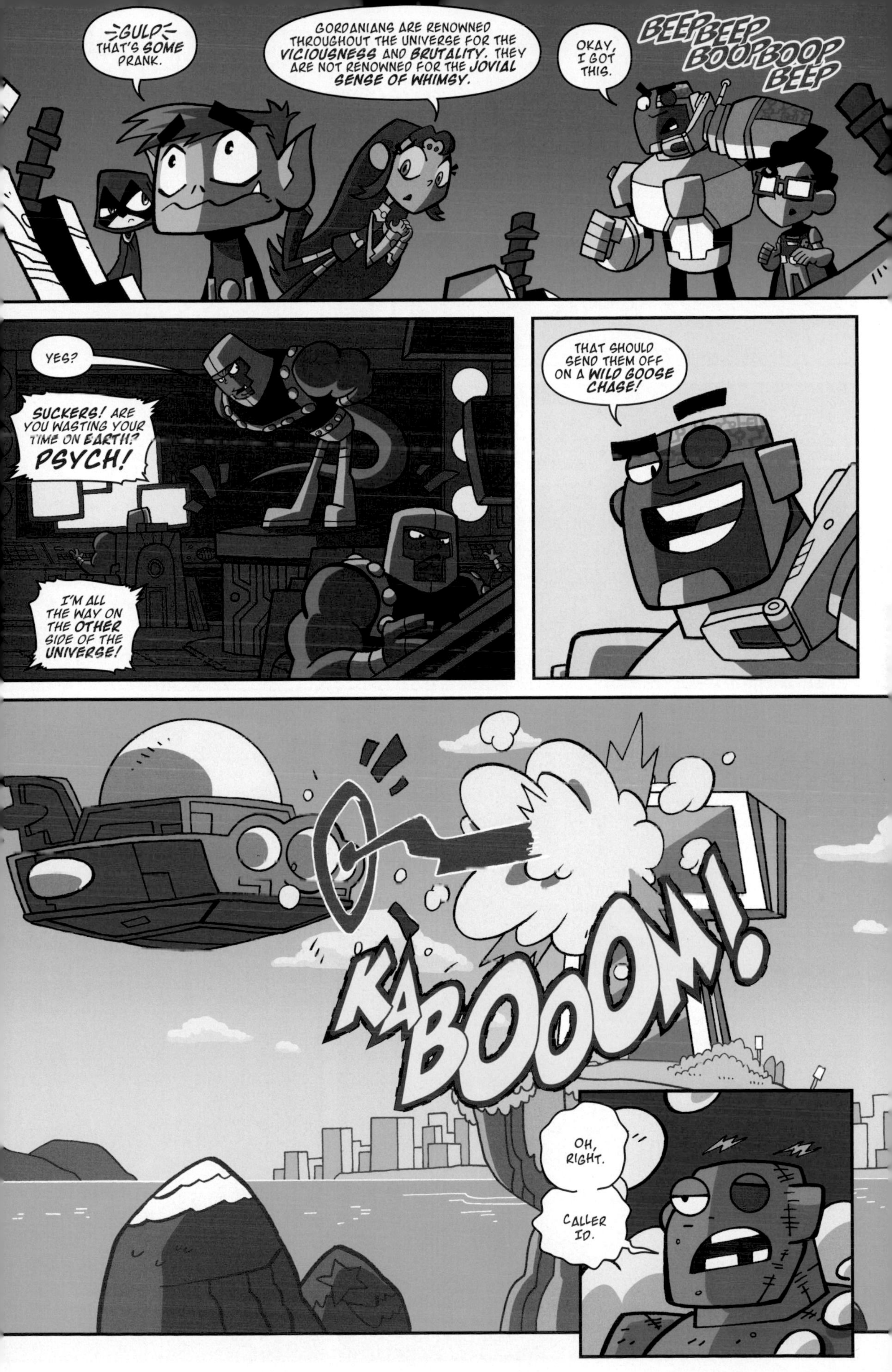
-GULP- THAT'S SOME PRANK.
GORDANIANS ARE RENOWNED THROUGHOUT THE UNIVERSE FOR THE VICIOUSNESS AND BRUTALITY. THEY ARE NOT RENOWNED FOR THE JOVIAL SENSE OF WHIMSY.
OKAY, I GOT THIS.
BEEP BEEP BOOP BOOP BEEP
YES?
SUCKERS! ARE YOU WASTING YOUR TIME ON EARTH? PSYCH!
I'M ALL THE WAY ON THE OTHER SIDE OF THE UNIVERSE!
THAT SHOULD SEND THEM OFF ON A WILD GOOSE CHASE!
KABOOOM!
OH, RIGHT.
CALLER ID.

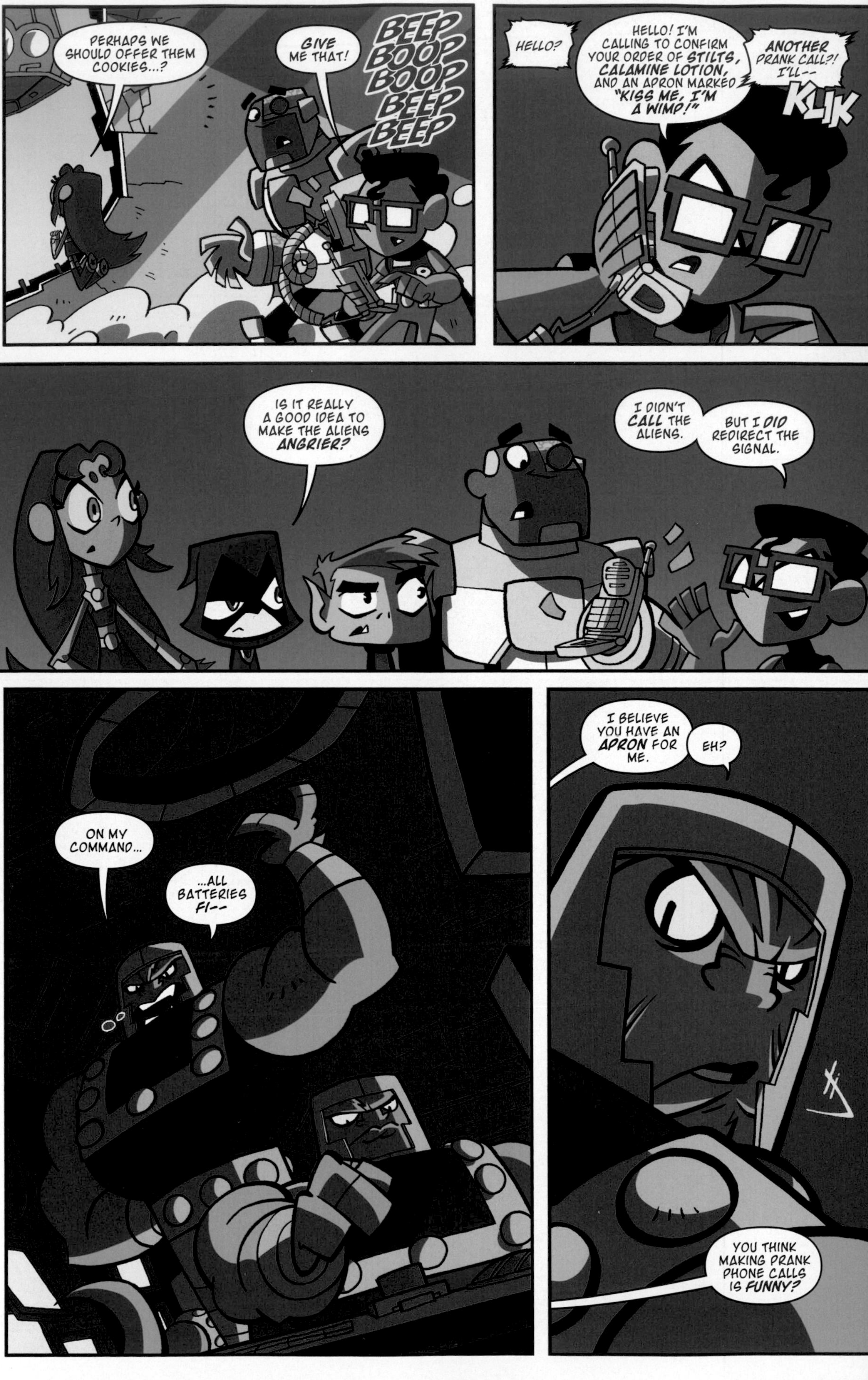
PERHAPS WE SHOULD OFFER THEM COOKIES...?
GIVE ME THAT!
BEEP BOOP BOOP BEEP BEEP
HELLO?
HELLO! I'M CALLING TO CONFIRM YOUR ORDER OF STILTS, CALAMINE LOTION, AND AN APRON MARKED "KISS ME, I'M A WIMP!"
ANOTHER PRANK CALL?! I'LL--
KLIK
IS IT REALLY A GOOD IDEA TO MAKE THE ALIENS ANGRIER?
I DIDN'T CALL THE ALIENS.
BUT I DID REDIRECT THE SIGNAL.
ON MY COMMAND...
...ALL BATTERIES FI--
I BELIEVE YOU HAVE AN APRON FOR ME.
EH?
YOU THINK MAKING PRANK PHONE CALLS IS FUNNY?

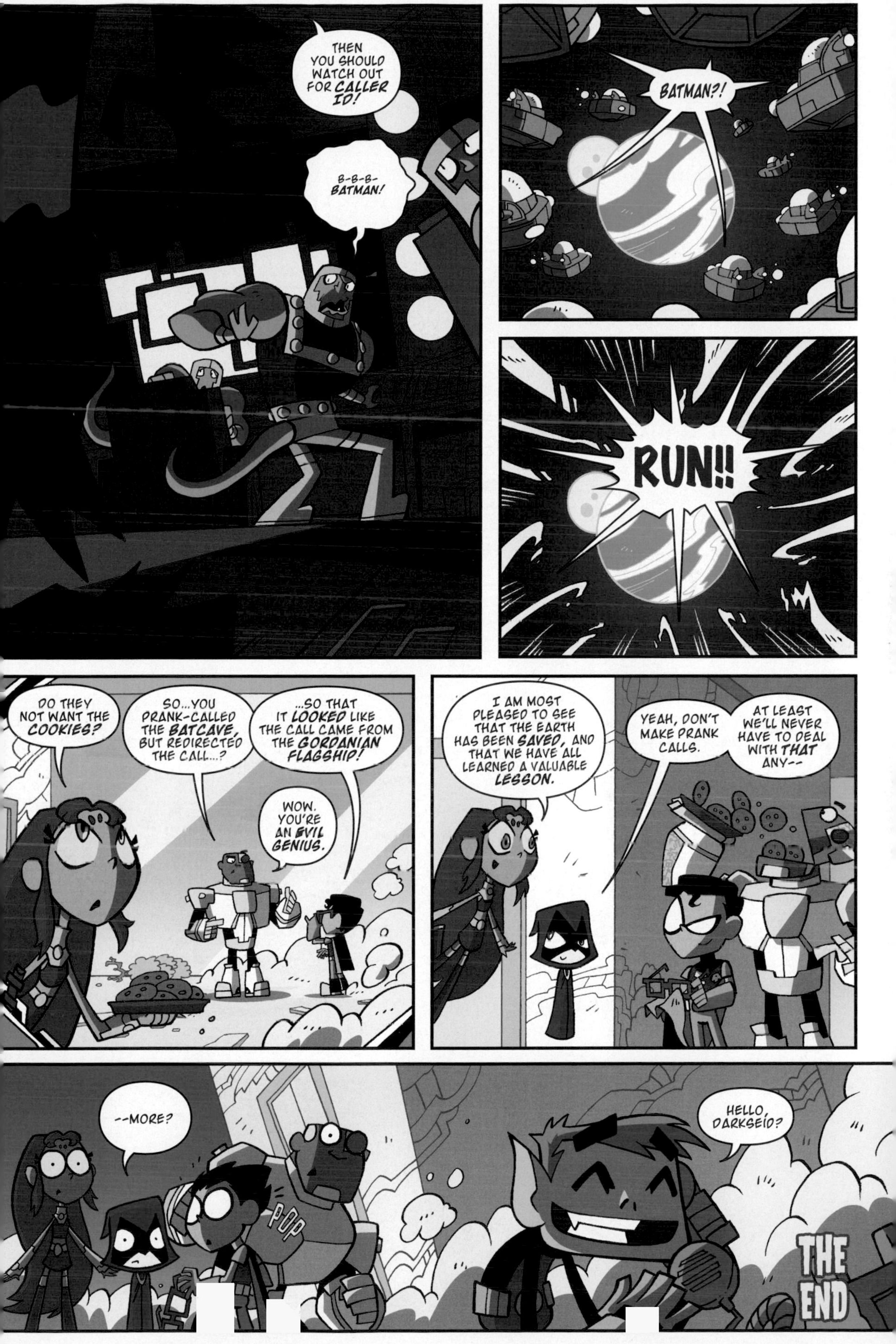
THEN YOU SHOULD WATCH OUT FOR CALLER ID!
B-B-B-BATMAN!
BATMAN?!
RUN!!
DO THEY NOT WANT THE COOKIES?
SO...YOU PRANK-CALLED THE BATCAVE, BUT REDIRECTED THE CALL...?
...SO THAT IT LOOKED LIKE THE CALL CAME FROM THE GORDANIAN FLAGSHIP!
WOW. YOU'RE AN EVIL GENIUS.
I AM MOST PLEASED TO SEE THAT THE EARTH HAS BEEN SAVED, AND THAT WE HAVE ALL LEARNED A VALUABLE LESSON.
YEAH, DON'T MAKE PRANK CALLS.
AT LEAST WE'LL NEVER HAVE TO DEAL WITH THAT ANY--
--MORE?
POP
HELLO, DARKSEID?
THE END

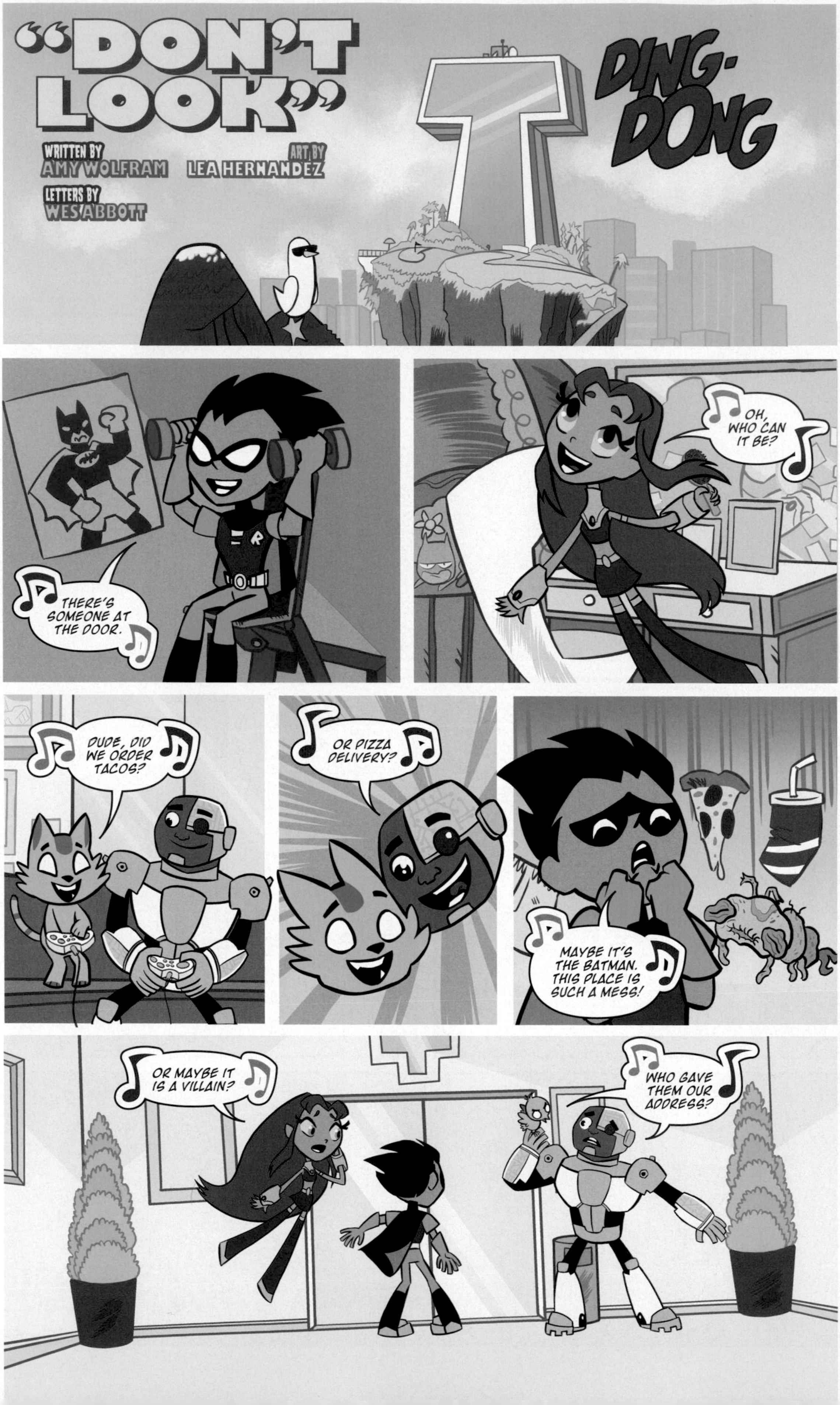

"DON'T LOOK"
WRITTEN BY AMY WOLFRAM
ART BY LEA HERNANDEZ
LETTERS BY WES ABBOTT
DING-DONG
THERE'S SOMEONE AT THE DOOR.
OH, WHO CAN IT BE?
DUDE, DID WE ORDER TACOS?
OR PIZZA DELIVERY?
MAYBE IT'S THE BATMAN. THIS PLACE IS SUCH A MESS!
OR MAYBE IT IS A VILLAIN?
WHO GAVE THEM OUR ADDRESS?

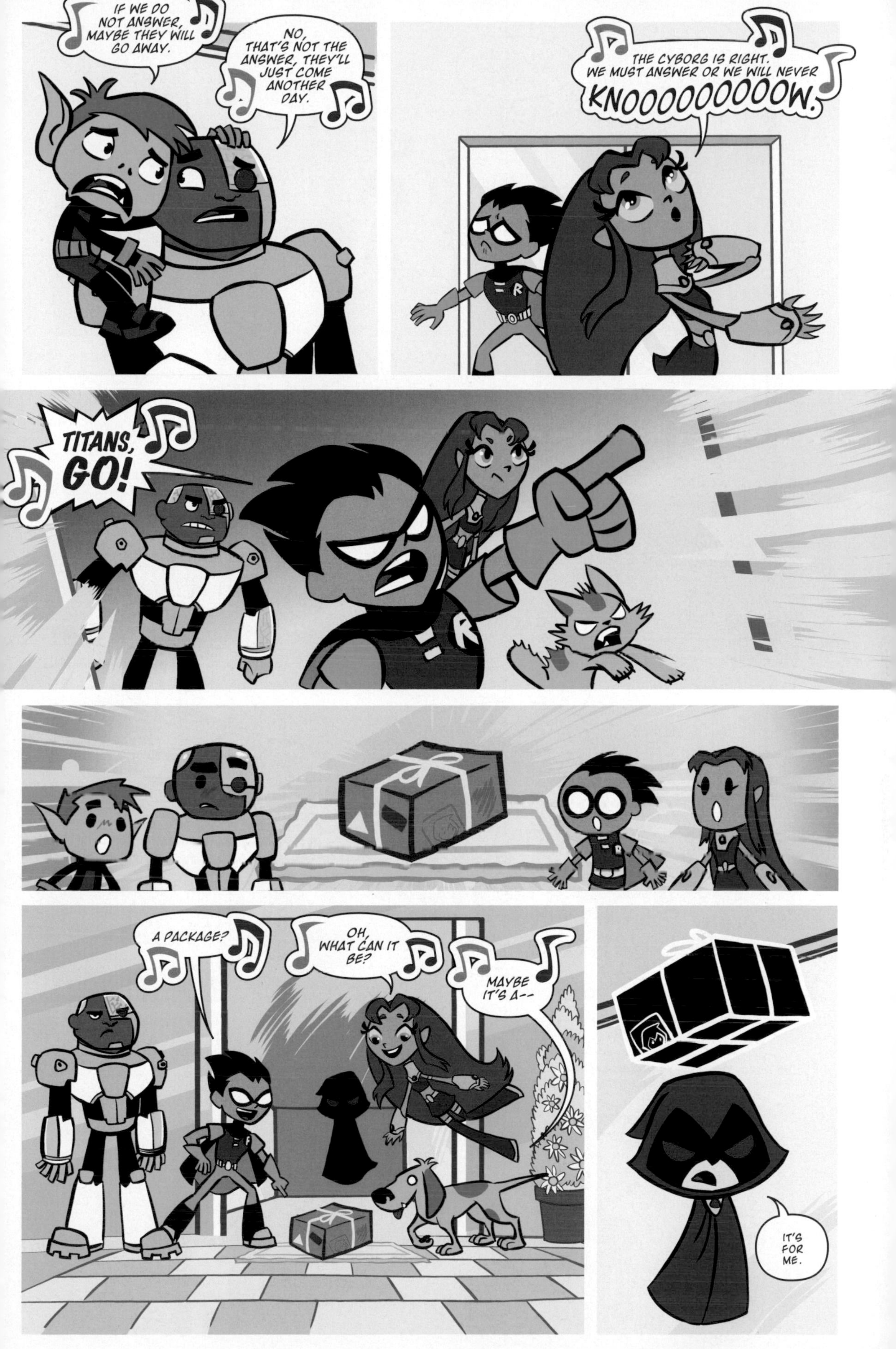

IF WE DO NOT ANSWER, MAYBE THEY WILL GO AWAY.
NO, THAT'S NOT THE ANSWER, THEY'LL JUST COME ANOTHER DAY.
THE CYBORG IS RIGHT. WE MUST ANSWER OR WE WILL NEVER KNOOOOOOOOOW.
TITANS, GO!
A PACKAGE?
OH, WHAT CAN IT BE?
MAYBE IT'S A--
IT'S FOR ME.

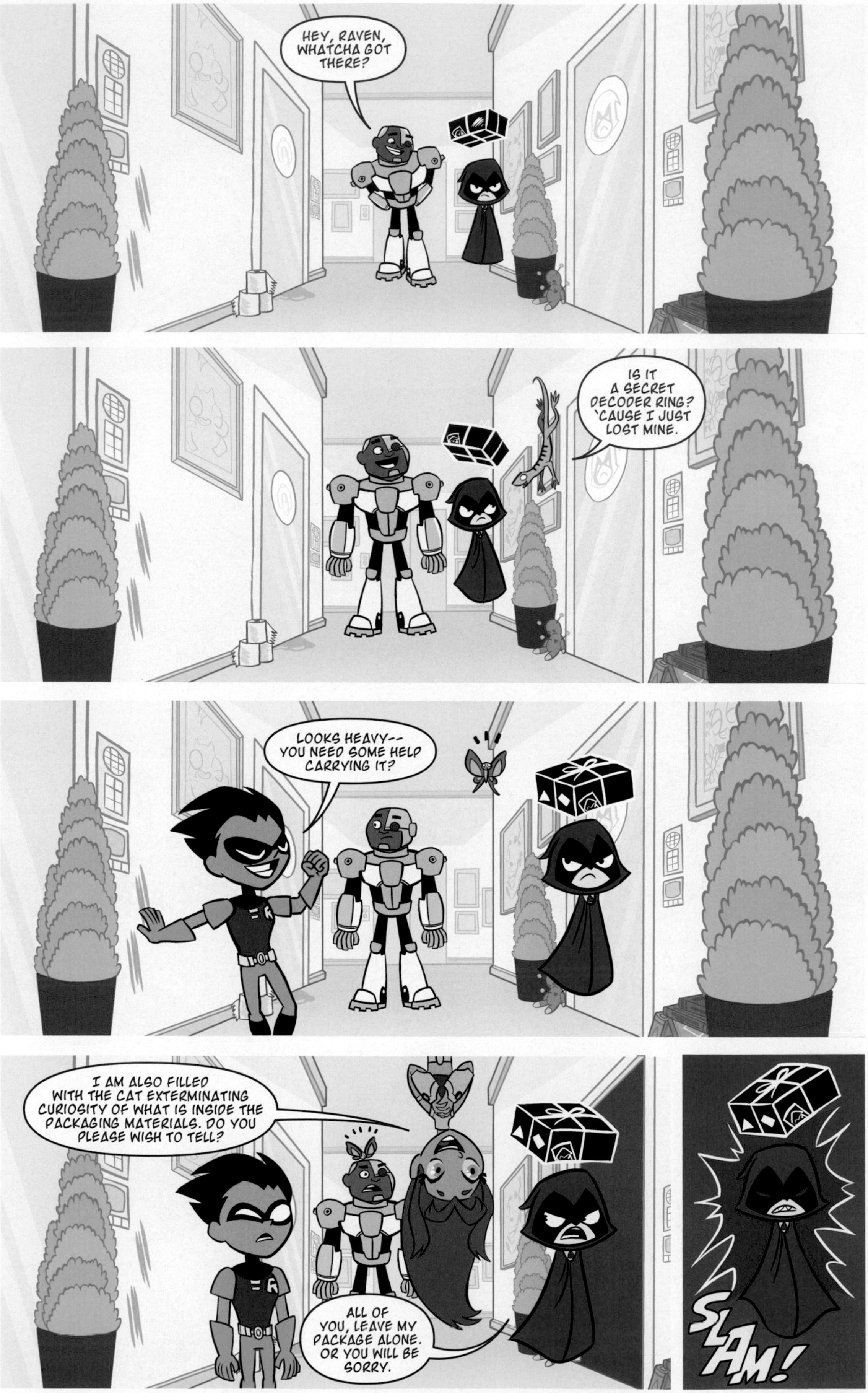
HEY, RAVEN, WHATCHA GOT THERE?
IS IT A SECRET DECODER RING? 'CAUSE I JUST LOST MINE.
LOOKS HEAVY-- YOU NEED SOME HELP CARRYING IT?
I AM ALSO FILLED WITH THE CAT EXTERMINATING CURIOSITY OF WHAT IS INSIDE THE PACKAGING MATERIALS. DO YOU PLEASE WISH TO TELL?
ALL OF YOU, LEAVE MY PACKAGE ALONE. OR YOU WILL BE SORRY.
SLAM!

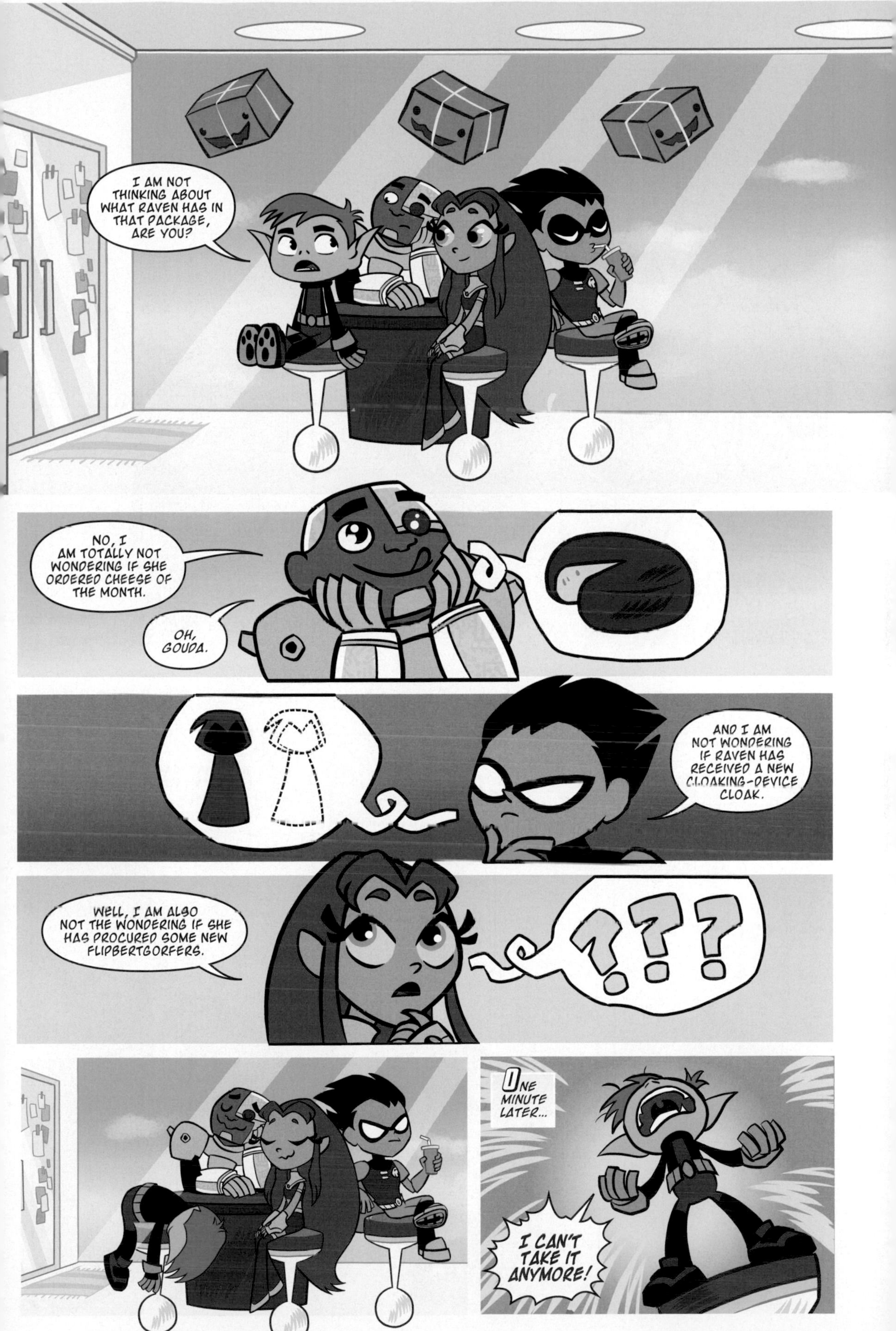
I AM NOT THINKING ABOUT WHAT RAVEN HAS IN THAT PACKAGE, ARE YOU?
NO, I AM TOTALLY NOT WONDERING IF SHE ORDERED CHEESE OF THE MONTH.
OH, GOUDA.
AND I AM NOT WONDERING IF RAVEN HAS RECEIVED A NEW CLOAKING-DEVICE CLOAK.
WELL, I AM ALSO NOT THE WONDERING IF SHE HAS PROCURED SOME NEW FLIPBERTGORFERS.
???
ONE MINUTE LATER...
I CAN'T TAKE IT ANYMORE!

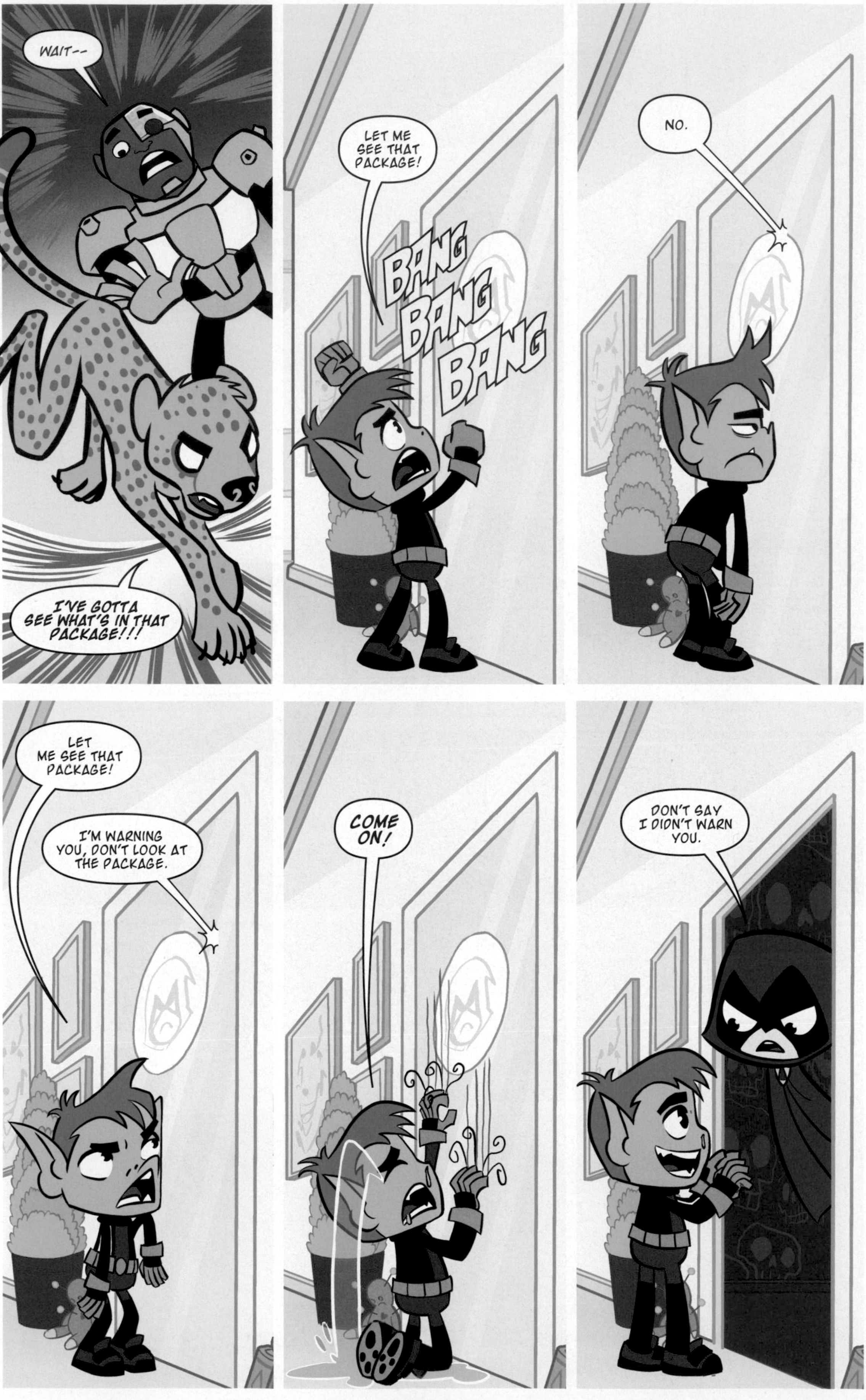
WAIT--
I'VE GOTTA SEE WHAT'S IN THAT PACKAGE!!!
LET ME SEE THAT PACKAGE!
BANG BANG BANG
NO.
LET ME SEE THAT PACKAGE!
I'M WARNING YOU, DON'T LOOK AT THE PACKAGE.
COME ON!
DON'T SAY I DIDN'T WARN YOU.

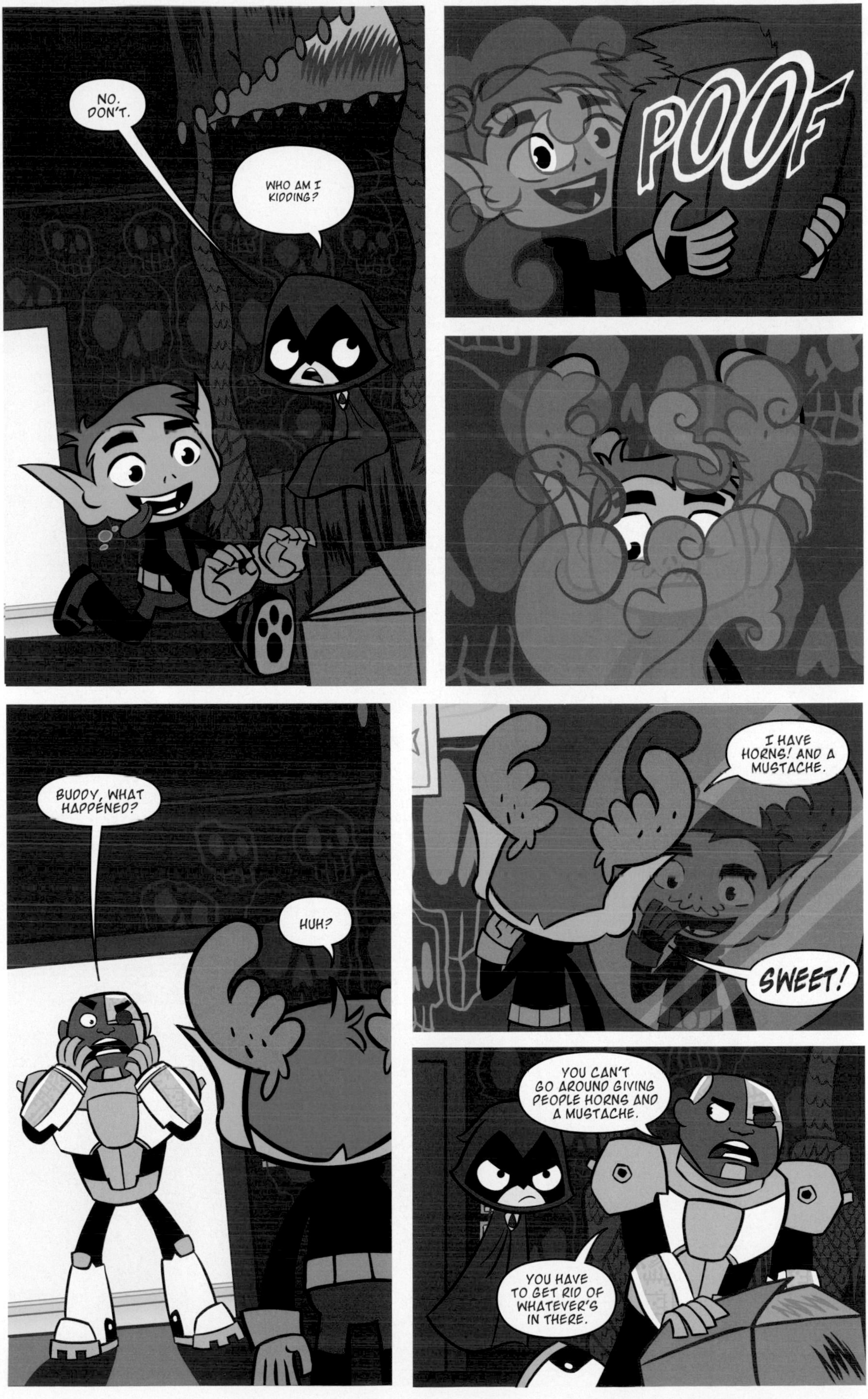
NO. DON'T.
WHO AM I KIDDING?
POOF
BUDDY, WHAT HAPPENED?
HUH?
I HAVE HORNS! AND A MUSTACHE.
SWEET!
YOU CAN'T GO AROUND GIVING PEOPLE HORNS AND A MUSTACHE.
YOU HAVE TO GET RID OF WHATEVER'S IN THERE.

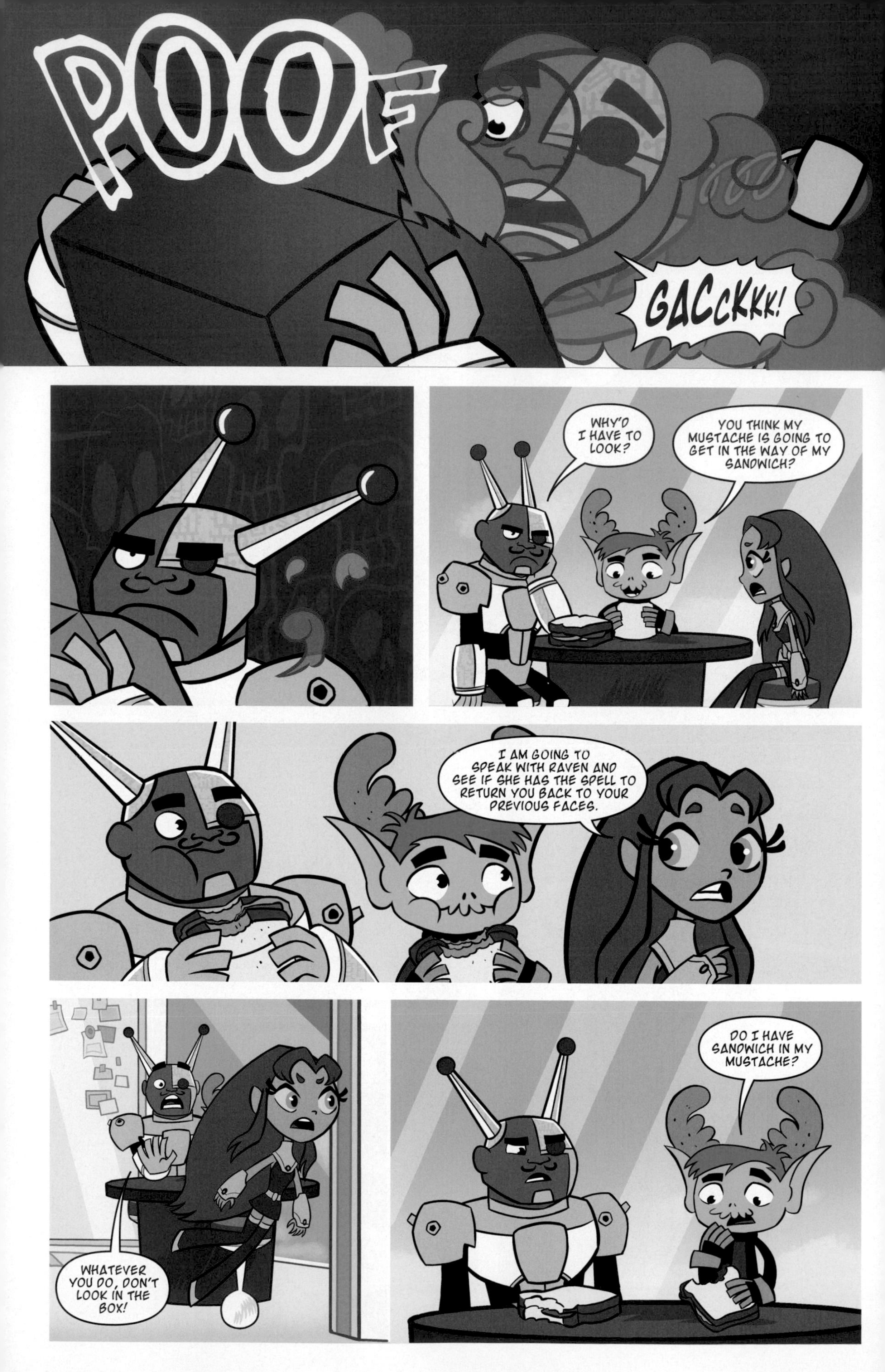
POOF
GACCKKK!
WHY'D I HAVE TO LOOK?
YOU THINK MY MUSTACHE IS GOING TO GET IN THE WAY OF MY SANDWICH?
I AM GOING TO SPEAK WITH RAVEN AND SEE IF SHE HAS THE SPELL TO RETURN YOU BACK TO YOUR PREVIOUS FACES.
WHATEVER YOU DO, DON'T LOOK IN THE BOX!
DO I HAVE SANDWICH IN MY MUSTACHE?

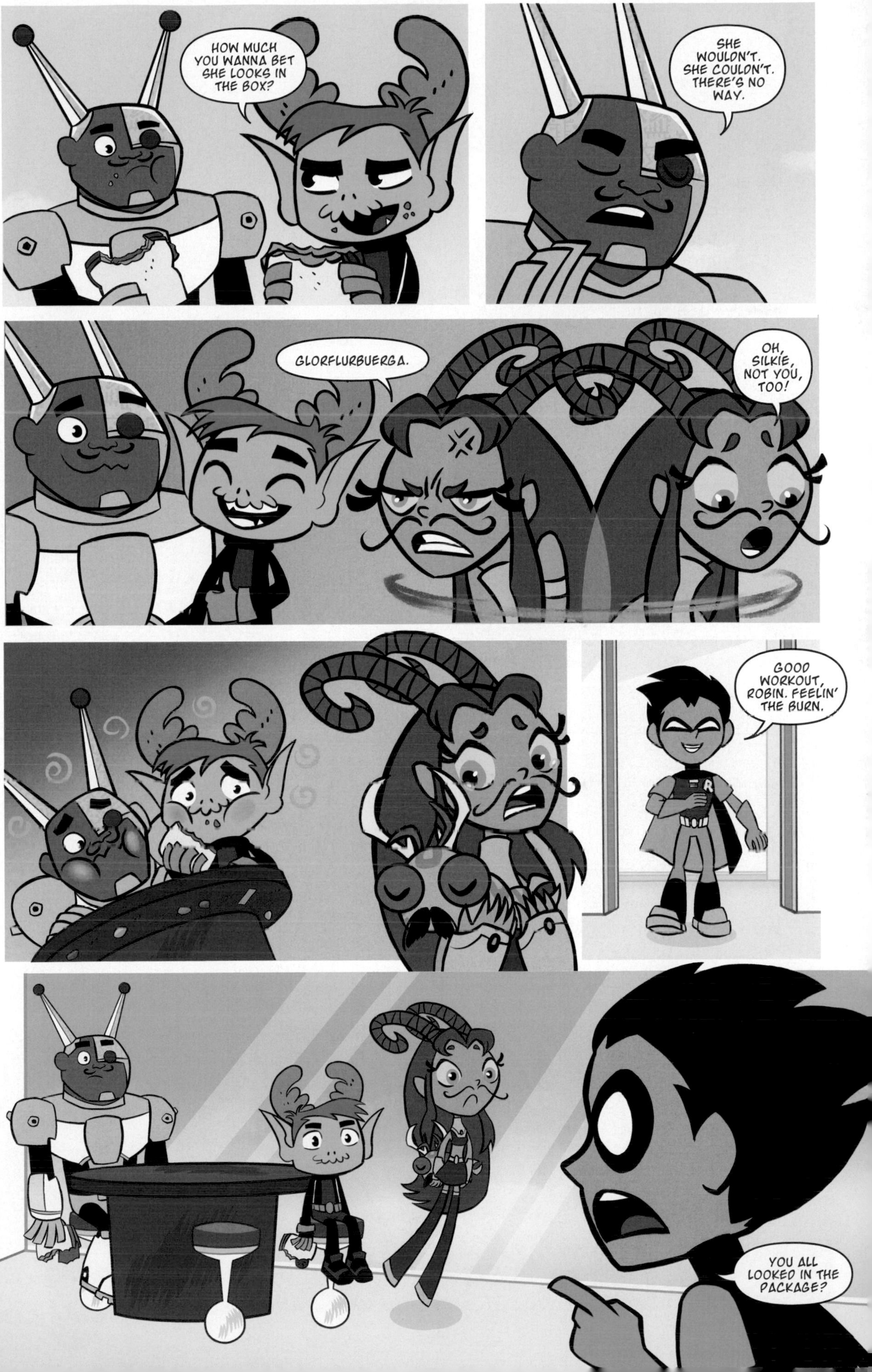
HOW MUCH YOU WANNA BET SHE LOOKS IN THE BOX?
SHE WOULDN'T. SHE COULDN'T. THERE'S NO WAY.
GLORFLURBUERGA.
OH, SILKIE, NOT YOU, TOO!
GOOD WORKOUT, ROBIN. FEELIN' THE BURN.
YOU ALL LOOKED IN THE PACKAGE?

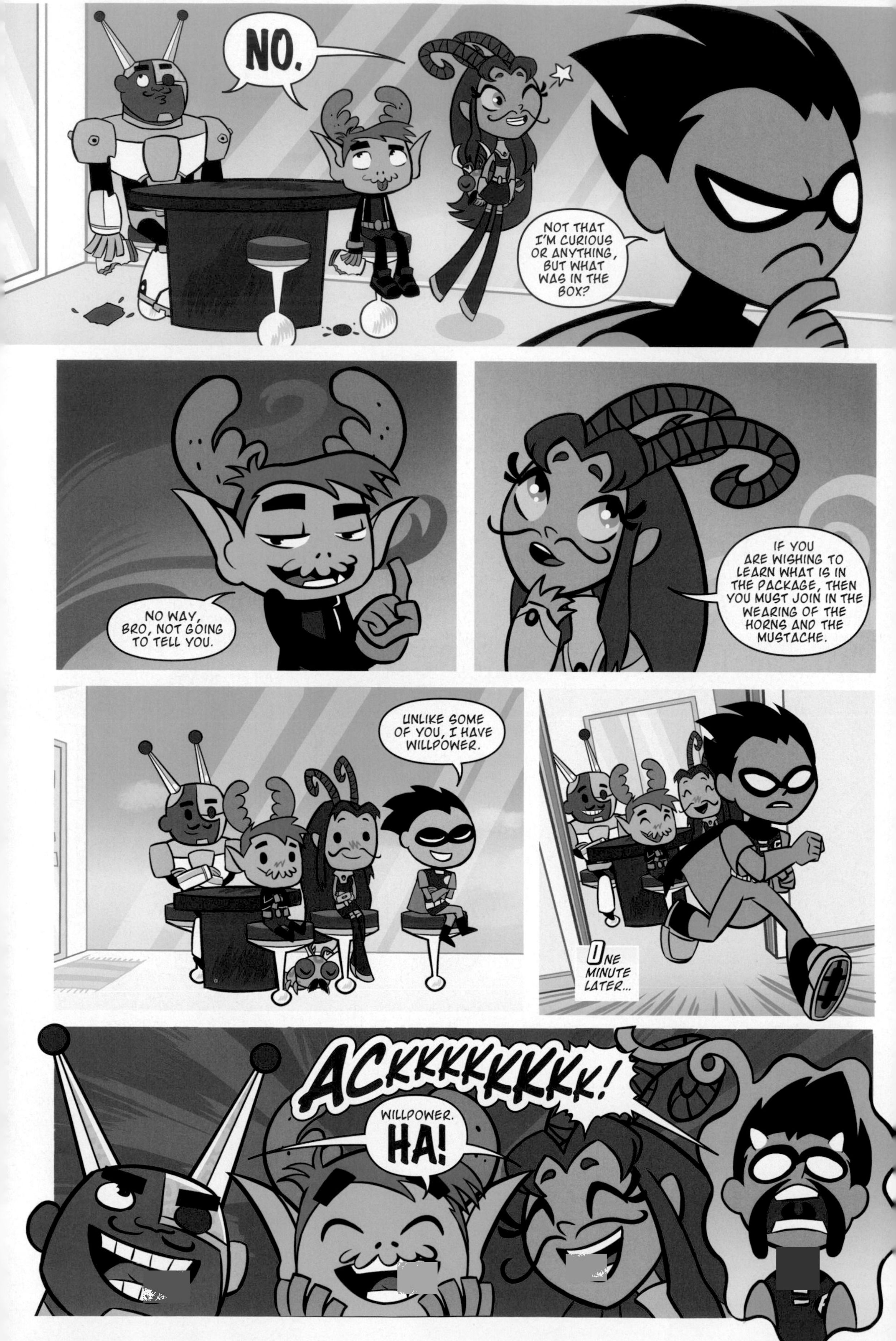
NO.
NOT THAT I'M CURIOUS OR ANYTHING, BUT WHAT WAS IN THE BOX?
NO WAY, BRO, NOT GOING TO TELL YOU.
IF YOU ARE WISHING TO LEARN WHAT IS IN THE PACKAGE, THEN YOU MUST JOIN IN THE WEARING OF THE HORNS AND THE MUSTACHE.
UNLIKE SOME OF YOU, I HAVE WILLPOWER.
ONE MINUTE LATER...
ACKKKKKKKK!
WILLPOWER. HA!

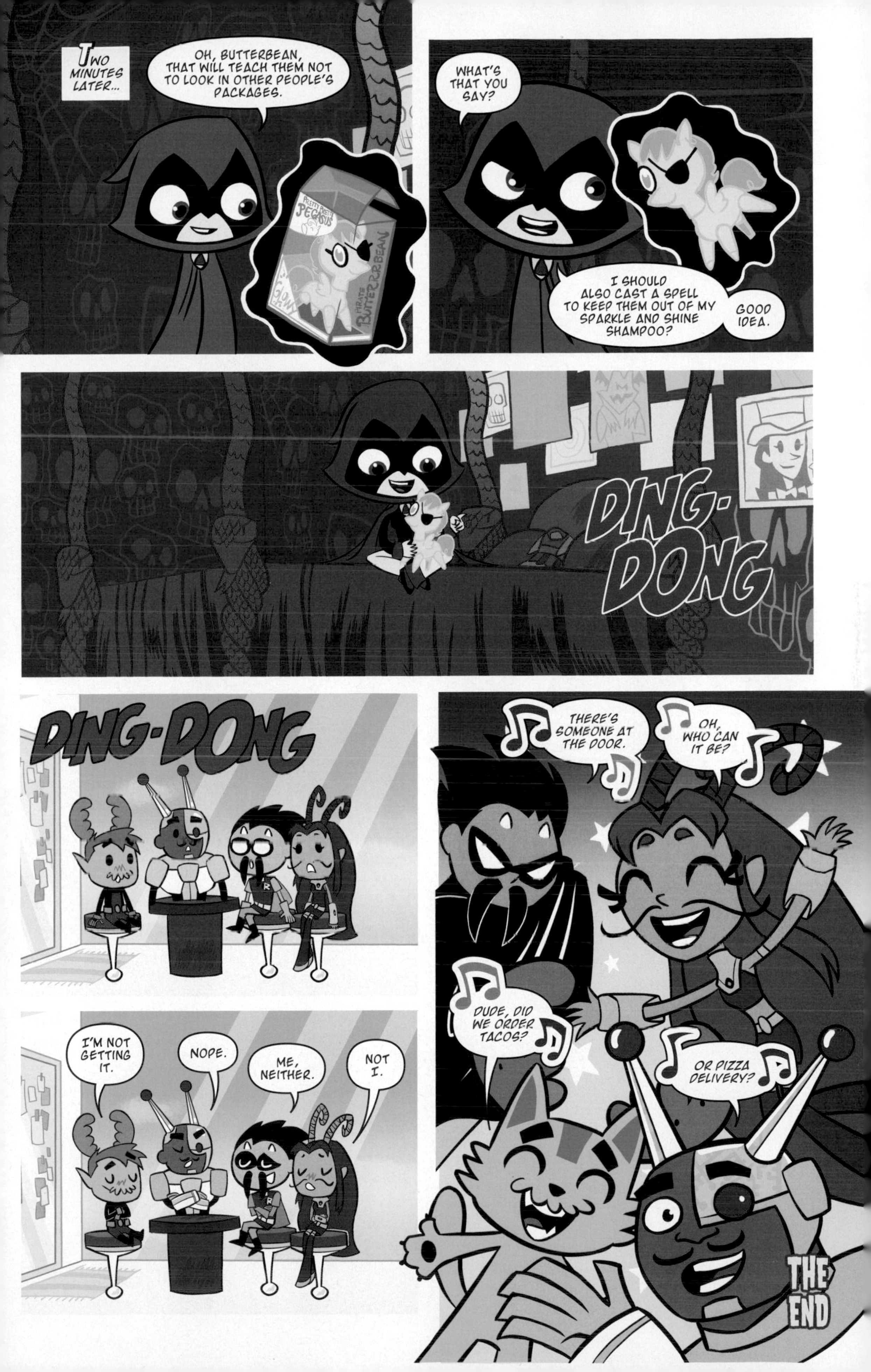
TWO MINUTES LATER...
OH, BUTTERBEAN, THAT WILL TEACH THEM NOT TO LOOK IN OTHER PEOPLE'S PACKAGES.
PRETTY PRETTY PEGASUS
PIRATE BUTTERRRBEAN
GLOWS
WHAT'S THAT YOU SAY?
I SHOULD ALSO CAST A SPELL TO KEEP THEM OUT OF MY SPARKLE AND SHINE SHAMPOO?
GOOD IDEA.
DING-DONG
DING-DONG
THERE'S SOMEONE AT THE DOOR.
OH, WHO CAN IT BE?
DUDE, DID WE ORDER TACOS?
OR PIZZA DELIVERY?
I'M NOT GETTING IT.
NOPE.
ME, NEITHER.
NOT I.
THE END

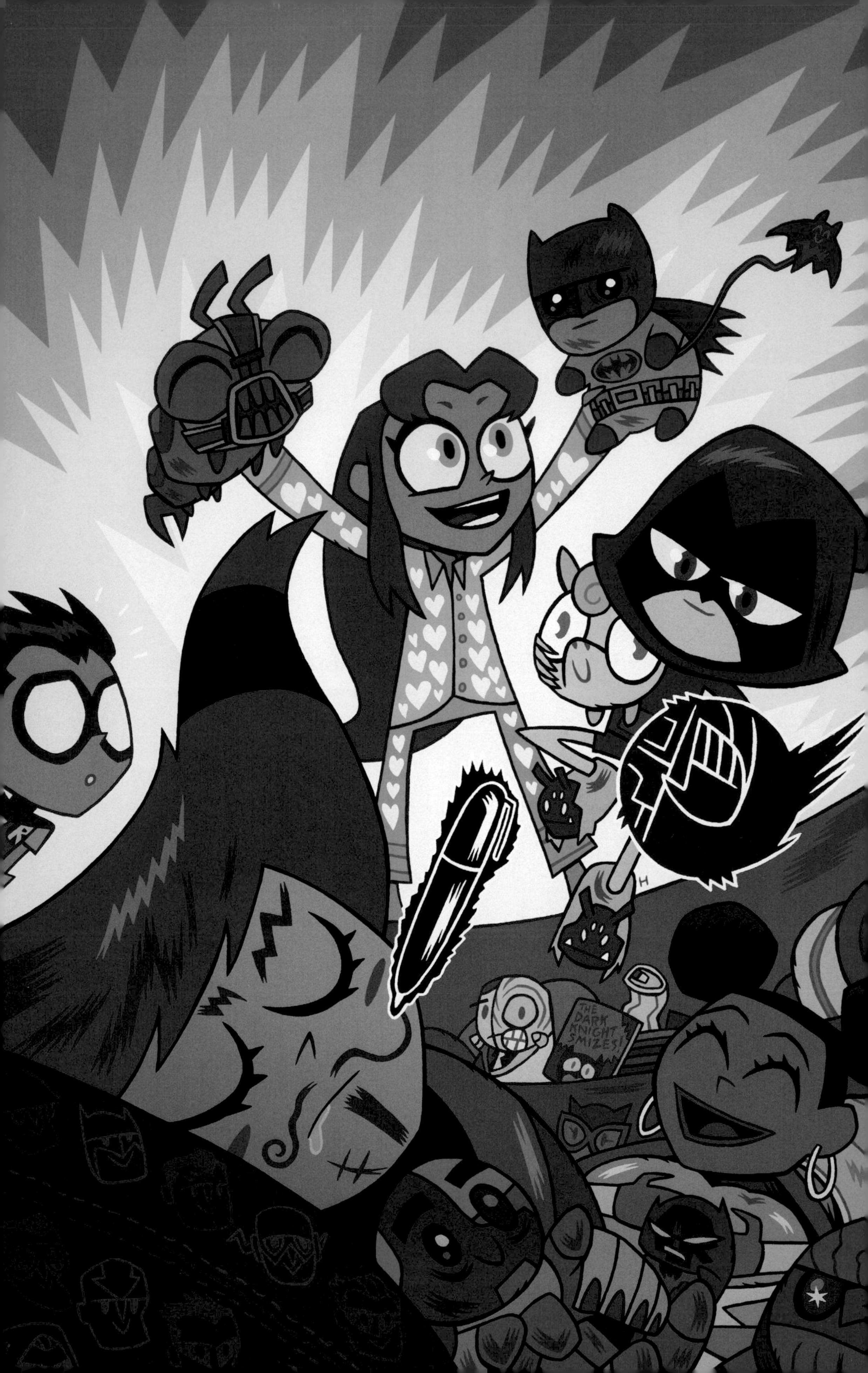
THE DARK KNIGHT SMIZES!

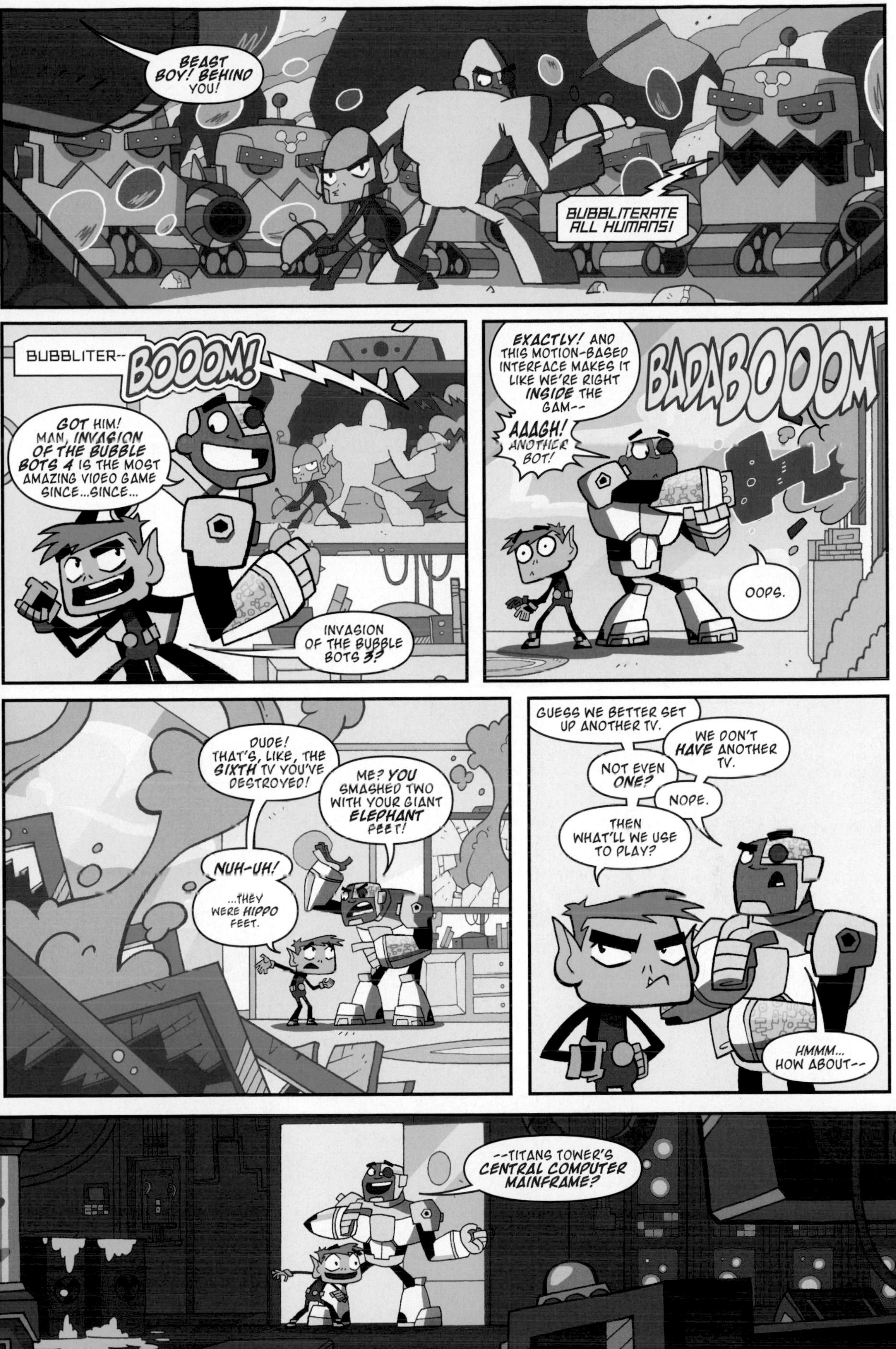
BEAST BOY! BEHIND YOU!
BUBBLITERATE ALL HUMANS!
BUBBLITER--
BOOOM!
GOT HIM! MAN, INVASION OF THE BUBBLE BOTS 4 IS THE MOST AMAZING VIDEO GAME SINCE...SINCE...
INVASION OF THE BUBBLE BOTS 3?
EXACTLY! AND THIS MOTION-BASED INTERFACE MAKES IT LIKE WE'RE RIGHT INSIDE THE GAM--
BADABOOOM
AAAGH! ANOTHER BOT!
OOPS.
DUDE! THAT'S, LIKE, THE SIXTH TV YOU'VE DESTROYED!
ME? YOU SMASHED TWO WITH YOUR GIANT ELEPHANT FEET!
NUH-UH!
...THEY WERE HIPPO FEET.
GUESS WE BETTER SET UP ANOTHER TV.
WE DON'T HAVE ANOTHER TV.
NOT EVEN ONE?
NOPE.
THEN WHAT'LL WE USE TO PLAY?
HMMM... HOW ABOUT--
--TITANS TOWER'S CENTRAL COMPUTER MAINFRAME?

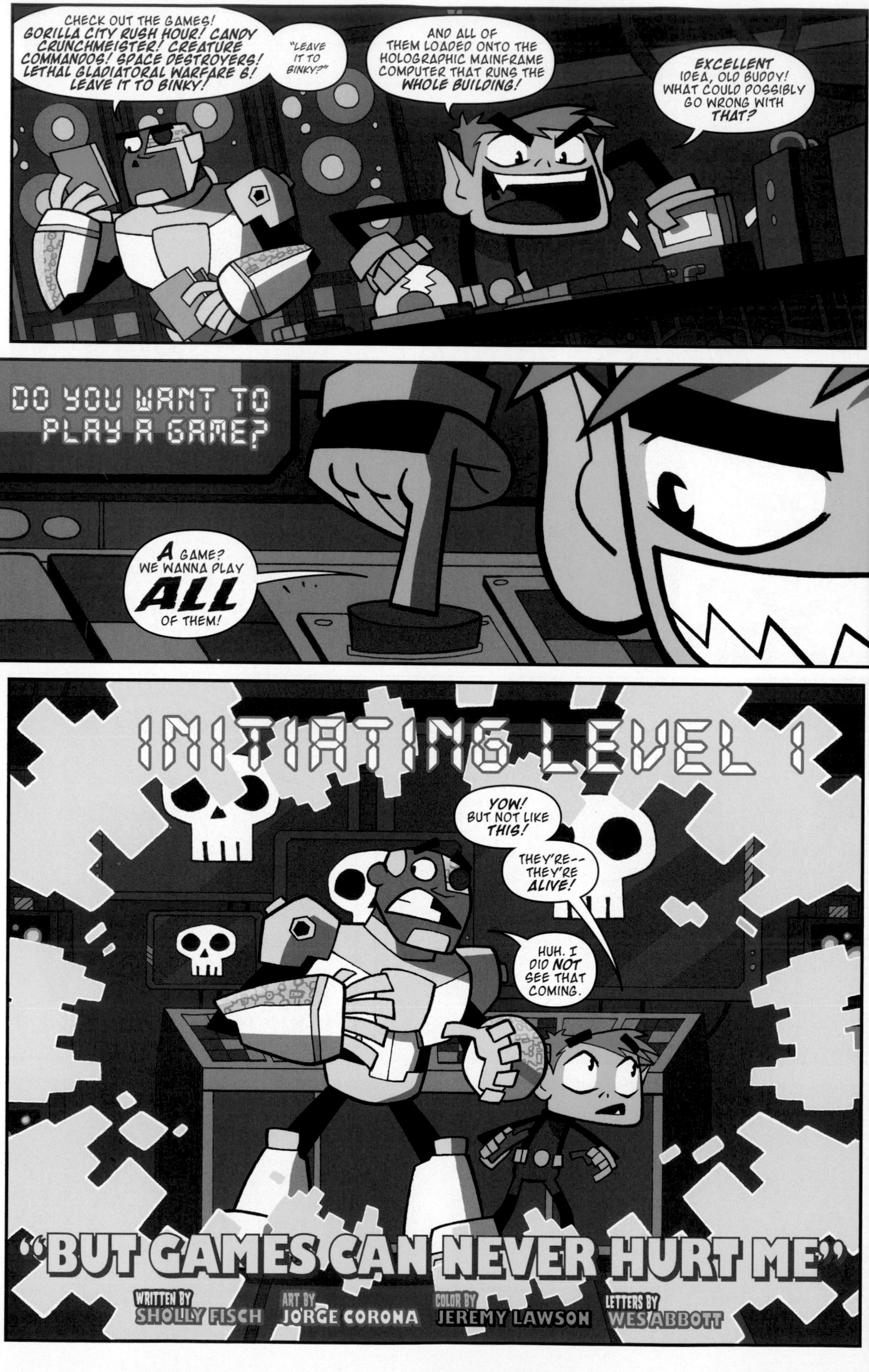
CHECK OUT THE GAMES! GORILLA CITY RUSH HOUR! CANDY CRUNCHMEISTER! CREATURE COMMANDOS! SPACE DESTROYERS! LETHAL GLADIATORAL WARFARE 6! LEAVE IT TO BINKY!
"LEAVE IT TO BINKY?"
AND ALL OF THEM LOADED ONTO THE HOLOGRAPHIC MAINFRAME COMPUTER THAT RUNS THE WHOLE BUILDING!
EXCELLENT IDEA, OLD BUDDY! WHAT COULD POSSIBLY GO WRONG WITH THAT?
DO YOU WANT TO PLAY A GAME?
A GAME? WE WANNA PLAY ALL OF THEM!
INITIATING LEVEL 1
YOW! BUT NOT LIKE THIS!
THEY'RE-- THEY'RE ALIVE!
HUH. I DID NOT SEE THAT COMING.
"BUT GAMES CAN NEVER HURT ME"
WRITTEN BY SHOLLY FISCH
ART BY JORGE CORONA
COLOR BY JEREMY LAWSON
LETTERS BY WES ABBOTT

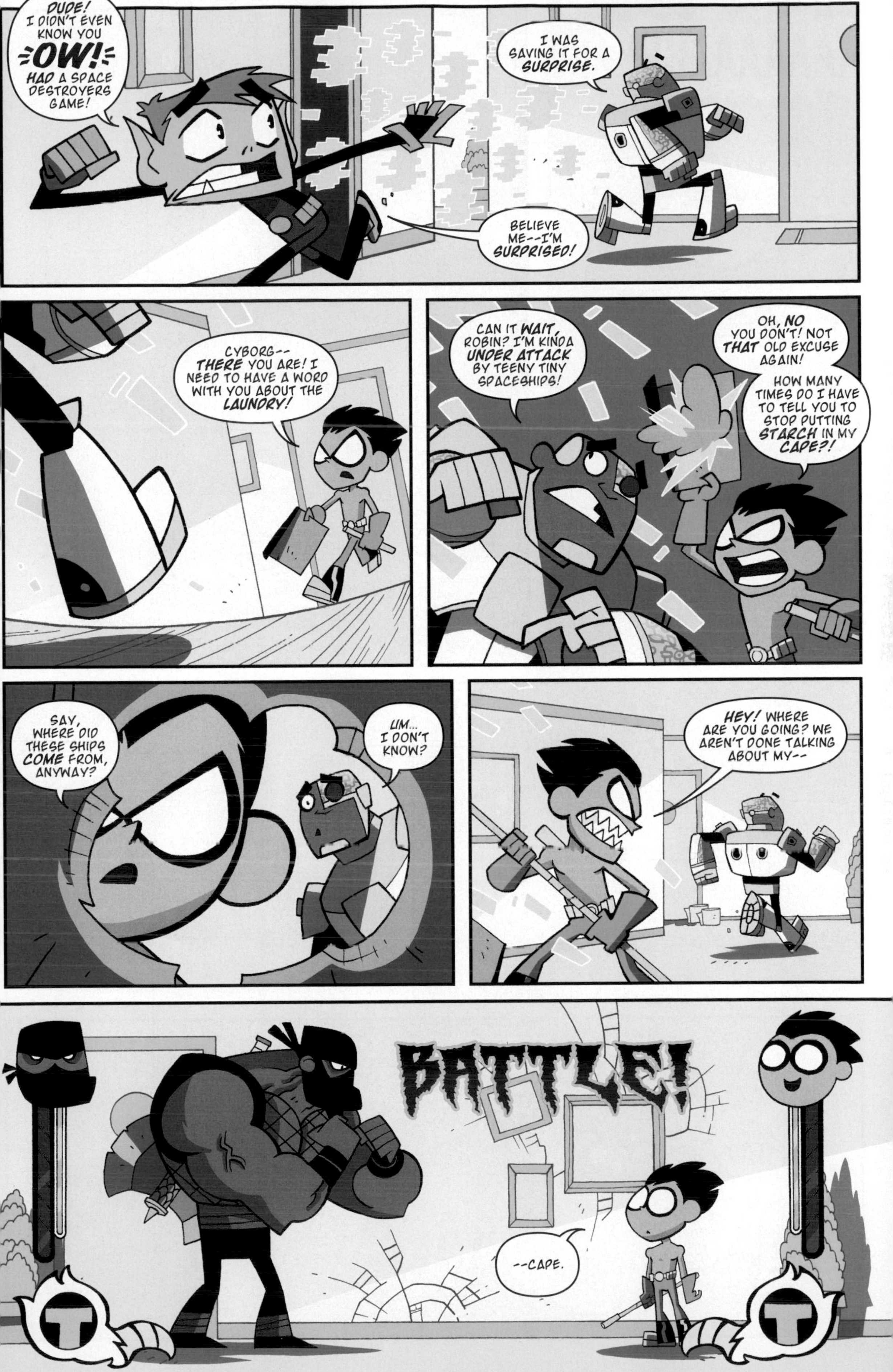
DUDE! I DIDN'T EVEN KNOW YOU OW! HAD A SPACE DESTROYERS GAME!
I WAS SAVING IT FOR A SURPRISE.
BELIEVE ME--I'M SURPRISED!
CYBORG-- THERE YOU ARE! I NEED TO HAVE A WORD WITH YOU ABOUT THE LAUNDRY!
CAN IT WAIT, ROBIN? I'M KINDA UNDER ATTACK BY TEENY TINY SPACESHIPS!
OH, NO YOU DON'T! NOT THAT OLD EXCUSE AGAIN!
HOW MANY TIMES DO I HAVE TO TELL YOU TO STOP PUTTING STARCH IN MY CAPE?!
SAY, WHERE DID THESE SHIPS COME FROM, ANYWAY?
UM... I DON'T KNOW?
HEY! WHERE ARE YOU GOING? WE AREN'T DONE TALKING ABOUT MY--
BATTLE!
--CAPE.

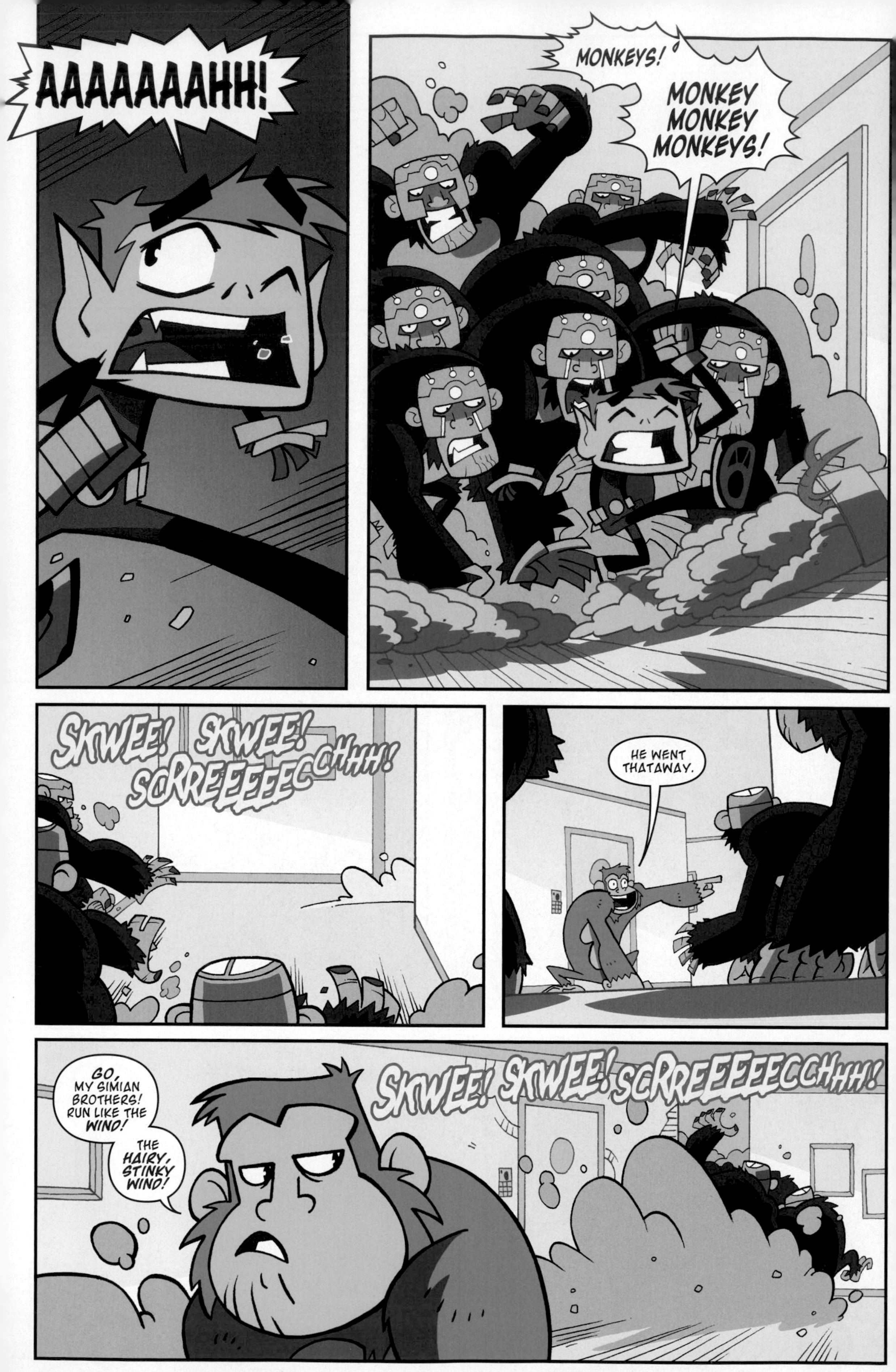
AAAAAAAHH!
MONKEYS!
MONKEY MONKEY MONKEYS!
SKWEE! SKWEE! SCRREEEEECCHHH!
HE WENT THATAWAY.
GO, MY SIMIAN BROTHERS! RUN LIKE THE WIND!
THE HAIRY, STINKY WIND!
SKWEE! SKWEE! SCRREEEEECCHHH!

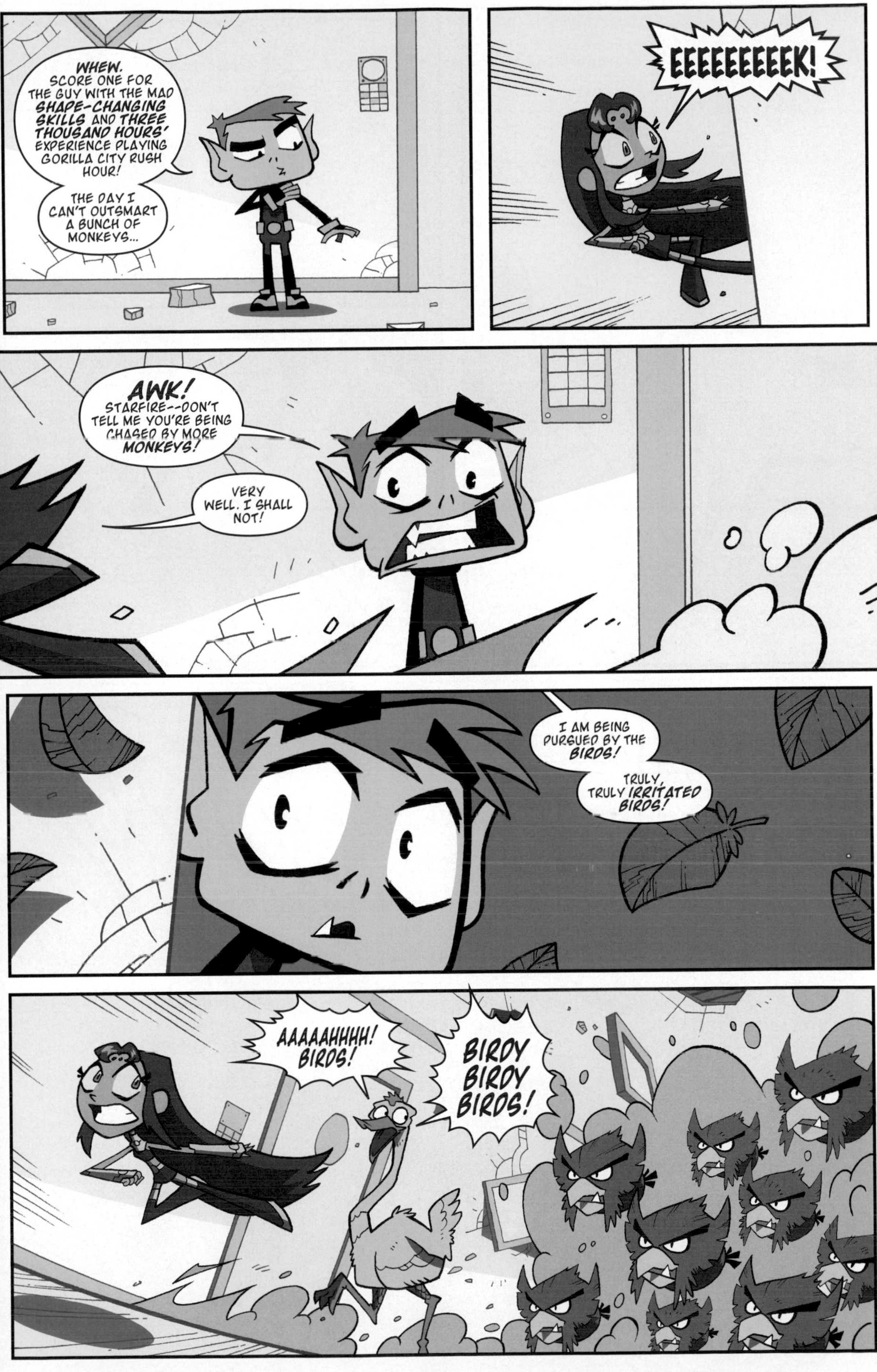
WHEW. SCORE ONE FOR THE GUY WITH THE MAD SHAPE-CHANGING SKILLS AND THREE THOUSAND HOURS' EXPERIENCE PLAYING GORILLA CITY RUSH HOUR!
THE DAY I CAN'T OUTSMART A BUNCH OF MONKEYS...
EEEEEEEEEK!
AWK! STARFIRE--DON'T TELL ME YOU'RE BEING CHASED BY MORE MONKEYS!
VERY WELL. I SHALL NOT!
I AM BEING PURSUED BY THE BIRDS!
TRULY, TRULY IRRITATED BIRDS!
AAAAAHHHH! BIRDS!
BIRDY BIRDY BIRDS!

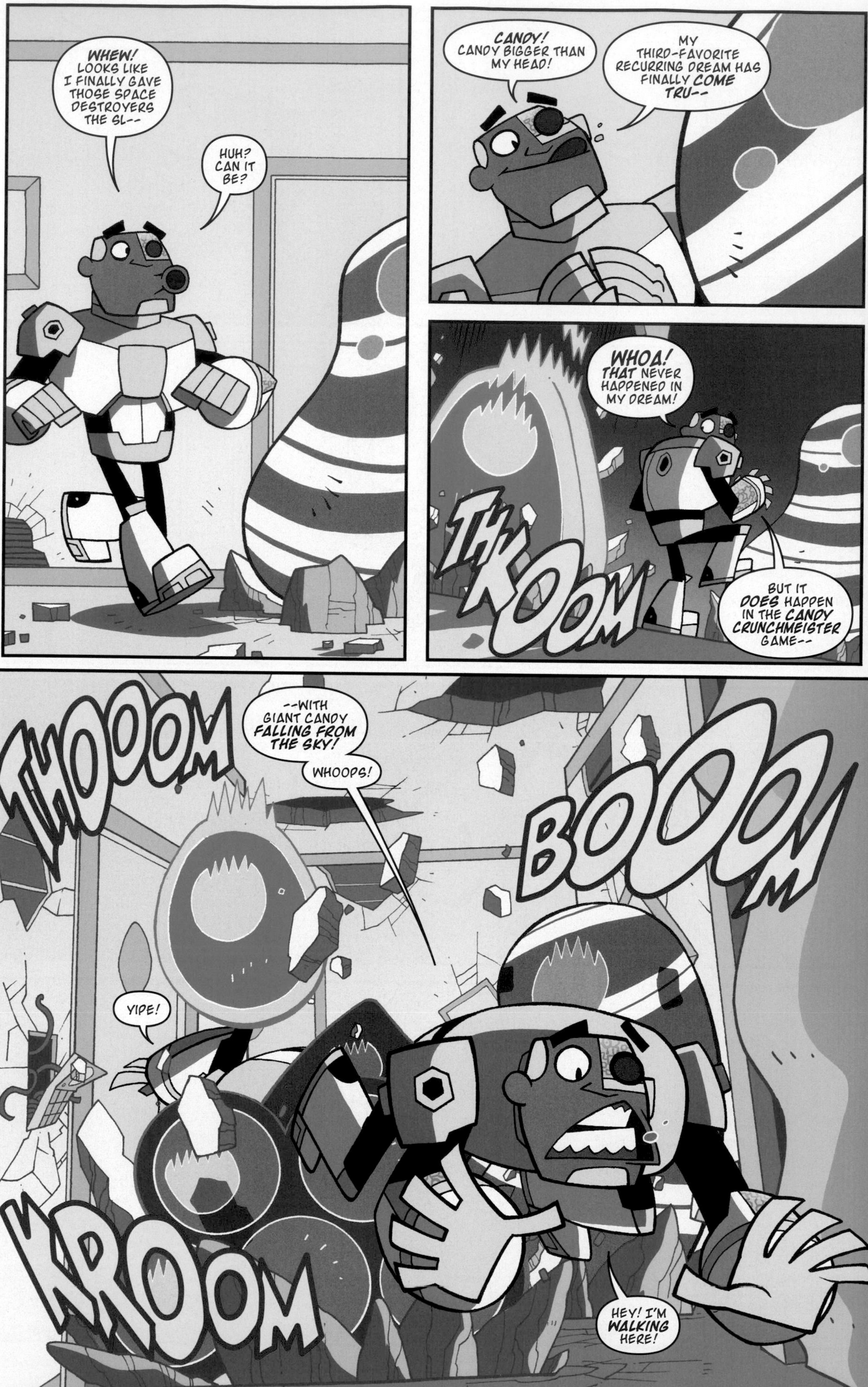
WHEW! LOOKS LIKE I FINALLY GAVE THOSE SPACE DESTROYERS THE SL--
HUH? CAN IT BE?
CANDY! CANDY BIGGER THAN MY HEAD!
MY THIRD-FAVORITE RECURRING DREAM HAS FINALLY COME TRU--
WHOA! THAT NEVER HAPPENED IN MY DREAM!
THKOOOM
BUT IT DOES HAPPEN IN THE CANDY CRUNCHMEISTER GAME--
THOOOM
--WITH GIANT CANDY FALLING FROM THE SKY!
WHOOPS!
BOOOM
YIPE!
KROOOM
HEY! I'M WALKING HERE!

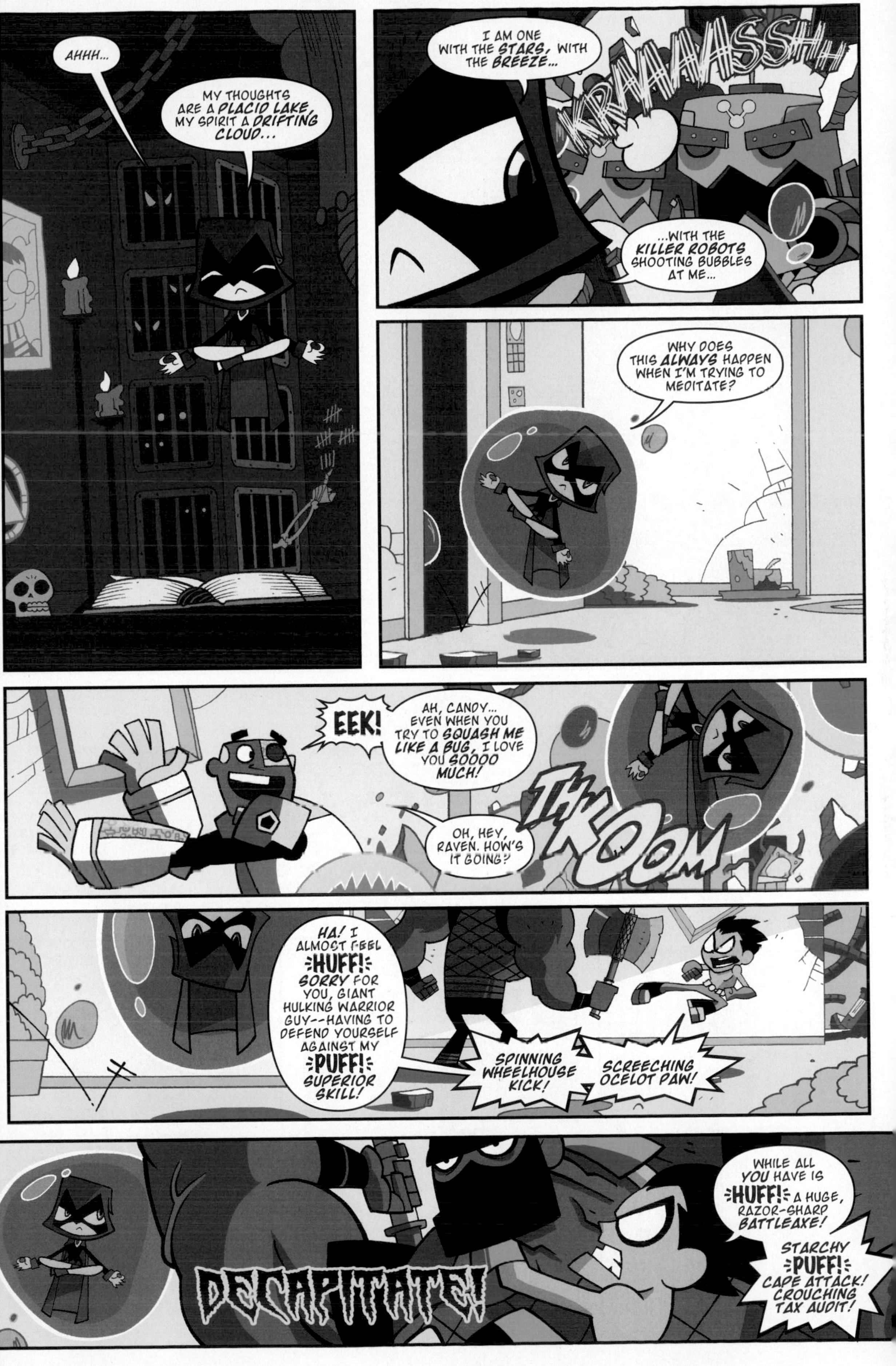
AHHH...
MY THOUGHTS ARE A PLACID LAKE, MY SPIRIT A DRIFTING CLOUD...
I AM ONE WITH THE STARS, WITH THE BREEZE...
KRAAAASSHH
...WITH THE KILLER ROBOTS SHOOTING BUBBLES AT ME...
WHY DOES THIS ALWAYS HAPPEN WHEN I'M TRYING TO MEDITATE?
EEK!
AH, CANDY... EVEN WHEN YOU TRY TO SQUASH ME LIKE A BUG, I LOVE YOU SOOOO MUCH!
OH, HEY, RAVEN. HOW'S IT GOING?
THOOM
HA! I ALMOST FEEL HUFF! SORRY FOR YOU, GIANT HULKING WARRIOR GUY--HAVING TO DEFEND YOURSELF AGAINST MY PUFF! SUPERIOR SKILL!
SPINNING WHEELHOUSE KICK!
SCREECHING OCELOT PAW!
DECAPITATE!
WHILE ALL YOU HAVE IS HUFF! A HUGE, RAZOR-SHARP BATTLEAXE!
STARCHY PUFF! CAPE ATTACK! CROUCHING TAX AUDIT!

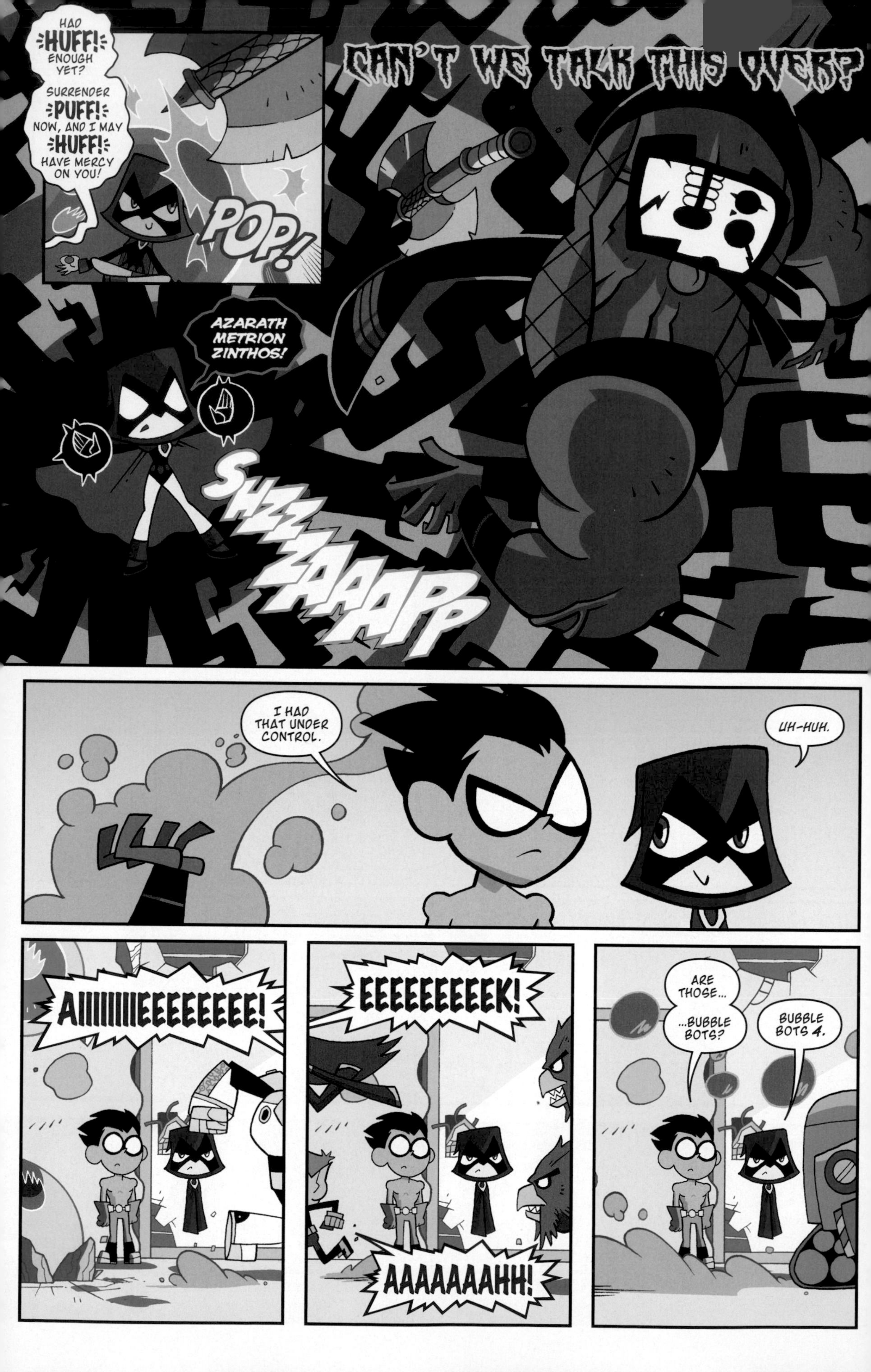
CAN'T WE TALK THIS OVER?
HAD HUFF! ENOUGH YET?
SURRENDER PUFF! NOW, AND I MAY HUFF! HAVE MERCY ON YOU!
POP!
AZARATH METRION ZINTHOS!
SHZZZAAAAPP
I HAD THAT UNDER CONTROL.
UH-HUH.
AIIIIIIIIEEEEEEEE!
EEEEEEEEEK!
AAAAAAAHH!
ARE THOSE...
...BUBBLE BOTS?
BUBBLE BOTS 4.

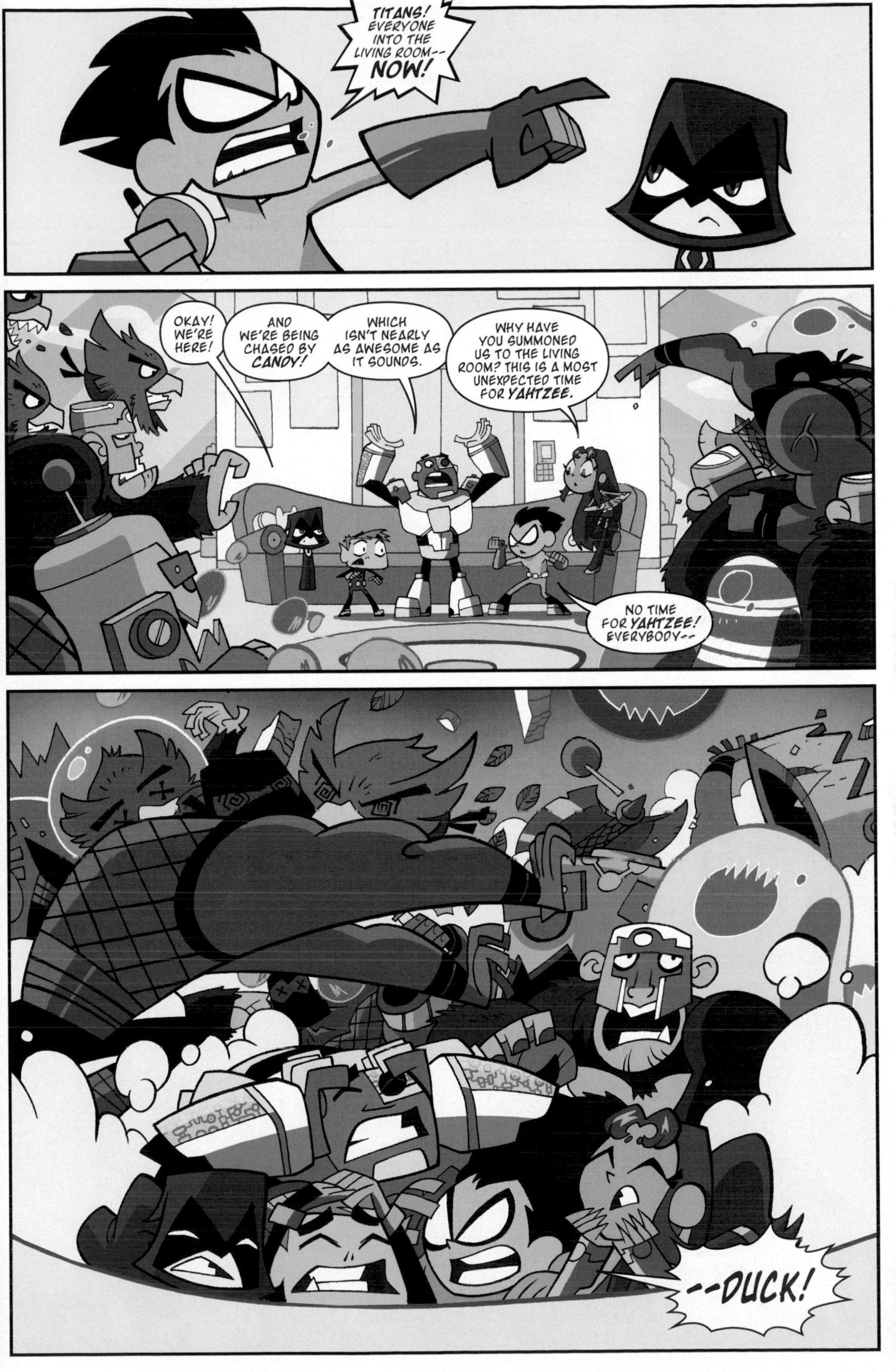

TITANS! EVERYONE INTO THE LIVING ROOM-- NOW!
OKAY! WE'RE HERE!
AND WE'RE BEING CHASED BY CANDY!
WHICH ISN'T NEARLY AS AWESOME AS IT SOUNDS.
WHY HAVE YOU SUMMONED US TO THE LIVING ROOM? THIS IS A MOST UNEXPECTED TIME FOR YAHTZEE.
NO TIME FOR YAHTZEE! EVERYBODY--
--DUCK!

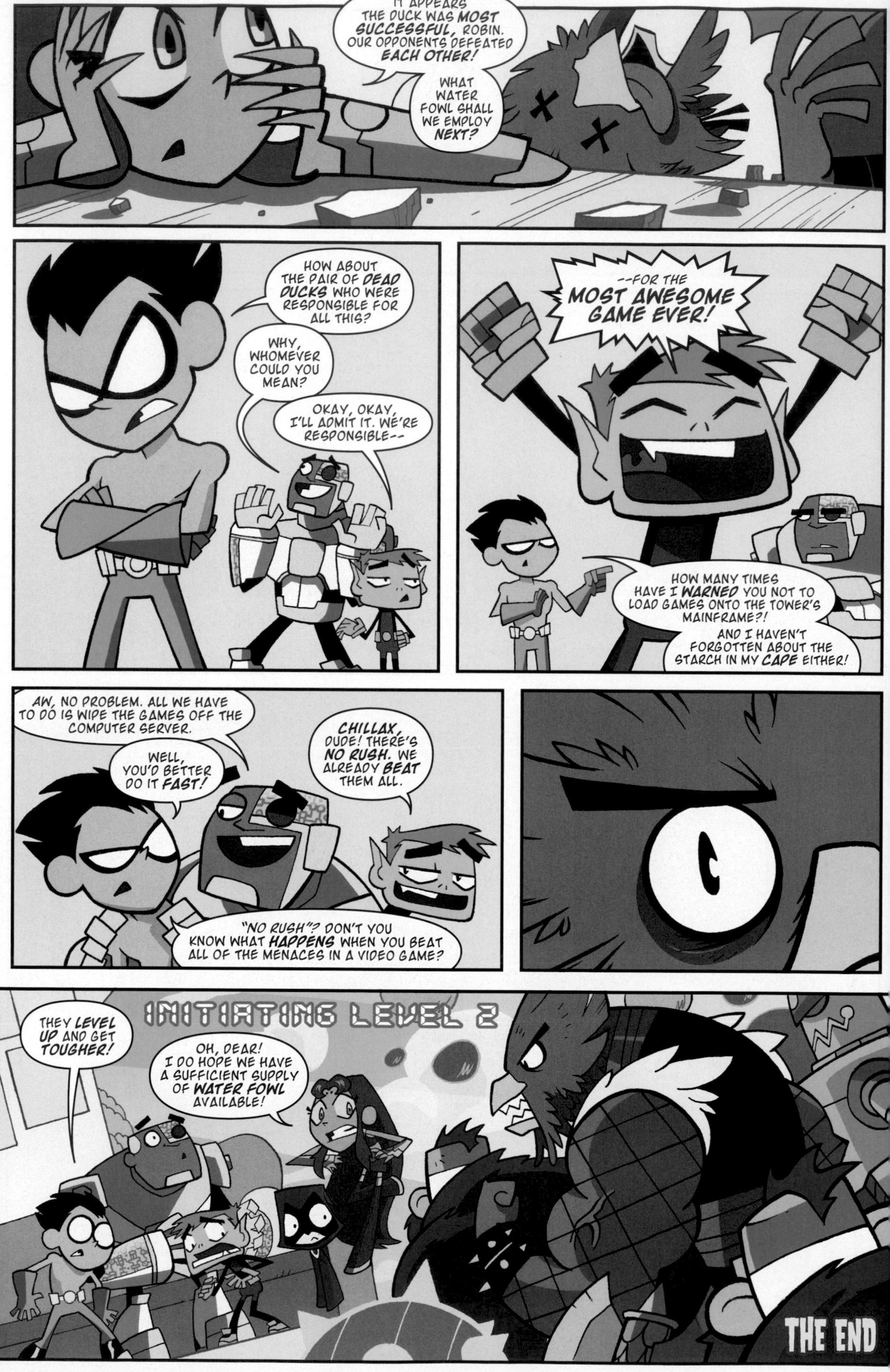
IT APPEARS THE DUCK WAS MOST SUCCESSFUL, ROBIN. OUR OPPONENTS DEFEATED EACH OTHER!
WHAT WATER FOWL SHALL WE EMPLOY NEXT?
HOW ABOUT THE PAIR OF DEAD DUCKS WHO WERE RESPONSIBLE FOR ALL THIS?
WHY, WHOMEVER COULD YOU MEAN?
OKAY, OKAY, I'LL ADMIT IT. WE'RE RESPONSIBLE--
--FOR THE MOST AWESOME GAME EVER!
HOW MANY TIMES HAVE I WARNED YOU NOT TO LOAD GAMES ONTO THE TOWER'S MAINFRAME?!
AND I HAVEN'T FORGOTTEN ABOUT THE STARCH IN MY CAPE EITHER!
AW, NO PROBLEM. ALL WE HAVE TO DO IS WIPE THE GAMES OFF THE COMPUTER SERVER.
WELL, YOU'D BETTER DO IT FAST!
CHILLAX, DUDE! THERE'S NO RUSH. WE ALREADY BEAT THEM ALL.
"NO RUSH"? DON'T YOU KNOW WHAT HAPPENS WHEN YOU BEAT ALL OF THE MENACES IN A VIDEO GAME?
INITIATING LEVEL 2
THEY LEVEL UP AND GET TOUGHER!
OH, DEAR! I DO HOPE WE HAVE A SUFFICIENT SUPPLY OF WATER FOWL AVAILABLE!
THE END

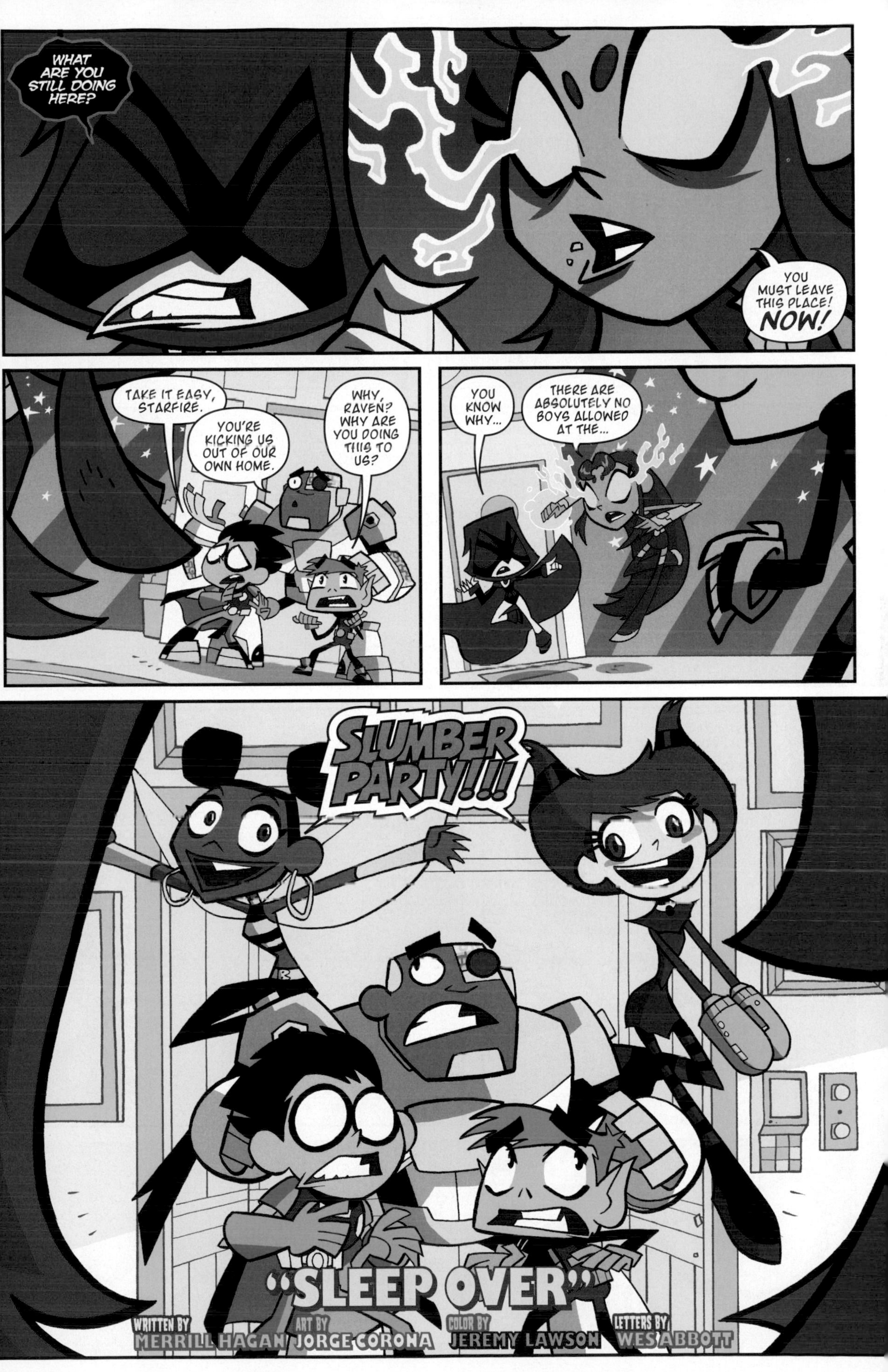
WHAT ARE YOU STILL DOING HERE?
YOU MUST LEAVE THIS PLACE! NOW!
TAKE IT EASY, STARFIRE.
YOU'RE KICKING US OUT OF OUR OWN HOME.
WHY, RAVEN? WHY ARE YOU DOING THIS TO US?
YOU KNOW WHY...
THERE ARE ABSOLUTELY NO BOYS ALLOWED AT THE...
SLUMBER PARTY!!!
"SLEEP OVER"
WRITTEN BY MERRILL HAGAN
ART BY JORGE CORONA
COLOR BY JEREMY LAWSON
LETTERS BY WES ABBOTT

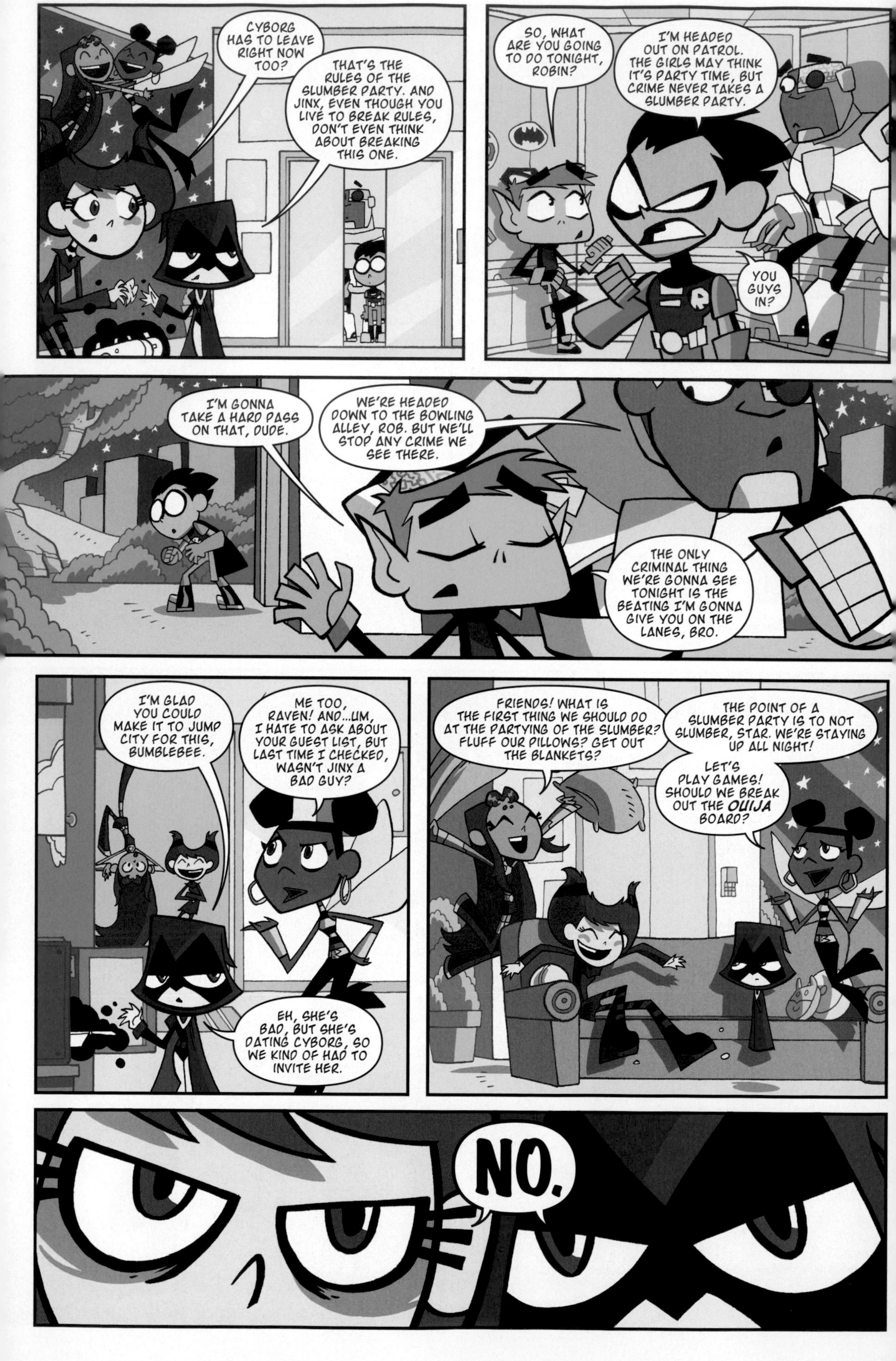
CYBORG HAS TO LEAVE RIGHT NOW TOO?
THAT'S THE RULES OF THE SLUMBER PARTY. AND JINX, EVEN THOUGH YOU LIVE TO BREAK RULES, DON'T EVEN THINK ABOUT BREAKING THIS ONE.
SO, WHAT ARE YOU GOING TO DO TONIGHT, ROBIN?
I'M HEADED OUT ON PATROL. THE GIRLS MAY THINK IT'S PARTY TIME, BUT CRIME NEVER TAKES A SLUMBER PARTY.
YOU GUYS IN?
I'M GONNA TAKE A HARD PASS ON THAT, DUDE.
WE'RE HEADED DOWN TO THE BOWLING ALLEY, ROB. BUT WE'LL STOP ANY CRIME WE SEE THERE.
THE ONLY CRIMINAL THING WE'RE GONNA SEE TONIGHT IS THE BEATING I'M GONNA GIVE YOU ON THE LANES, BRO.
I'M GLAD YOU COULD MAKE IT TO JUMP CITY FOR THIS, BUMBLEBEE.
ME TOO, RAVEN! AND...UM, I HATE TO ASK ABOUT YOUR GUEST LIST, BUT LAST TIME I CHECKED, WASN'T JINX A BAD GUY?
EH, SHE'S BAD, BUT SHE'S DATING CYBORG, SO WE KIND OF HAD TO INVITE HER.
FRIENDS! WHAT IS THE FIRST THING WE SHOULD DO AT THE PARTYING OF THE SLUMBER? FLUFF OUR PILLOWS? GET OUT THE BLANKETS?
THE POINT OF A SLUMBER PARTY IS TO NOT SLUMBER, STAR. WE'RE STAYING UP ALL NIGHT!
LET'S PLAY GAMES! SHOULD WE BREAK OUT THE OUIJA BOARD?
NO.

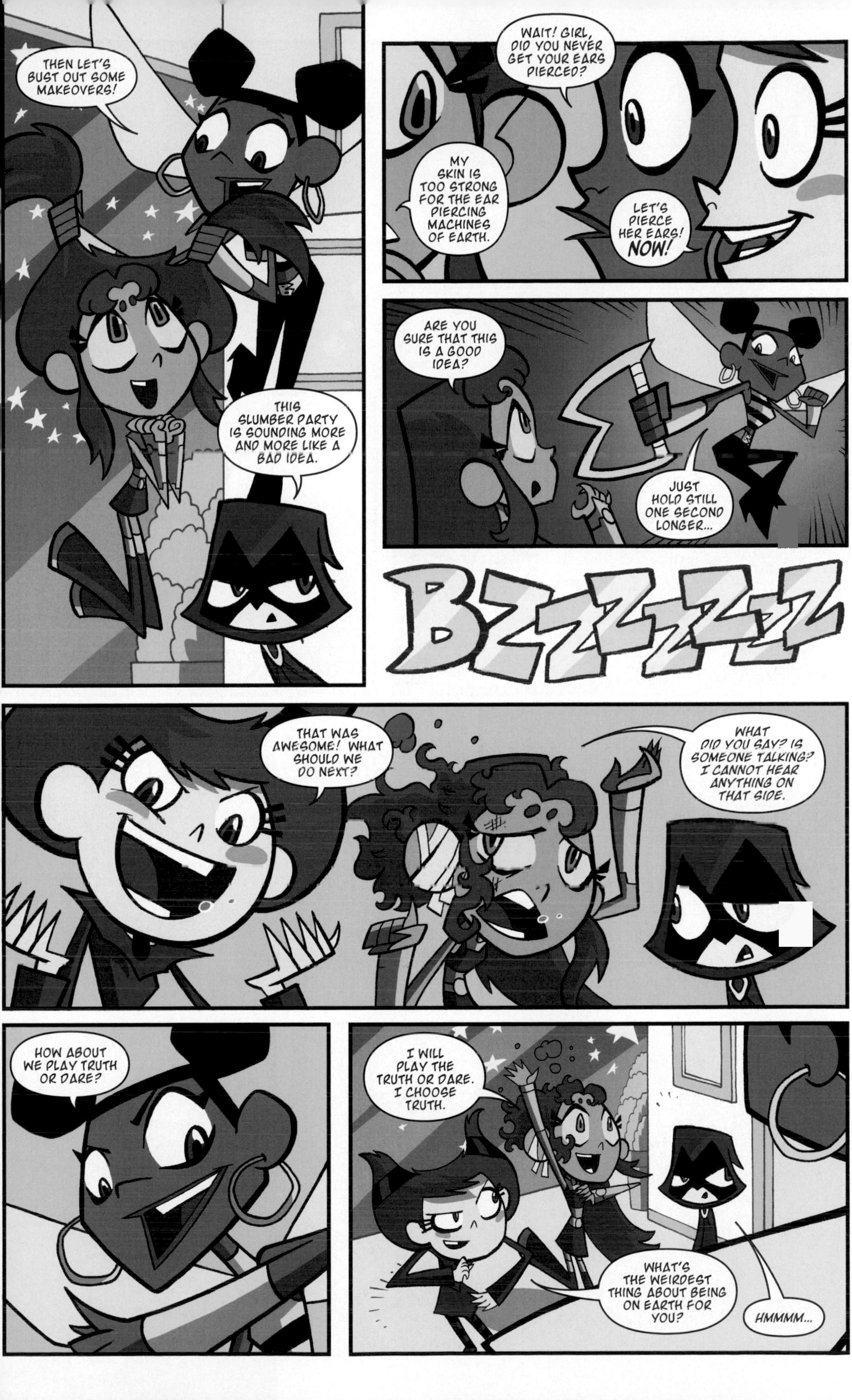
THEN LET'S BUST OUT SOME MAKEOVERS!
THIS SLUMBER PARTY IS SOUNDING MORE AND MORE LIKE A BAD IDEA.
WAIT! GIRL, DID YOU NEVER GET YOUR EARS PIERCED?
MY SKIN IS TOO STRONG FOR THE EAR PIERCING MACHINES OF EARTH.
LET'S PIERCE HER EARS! NOW!
ARE YOU SURE THAT THIS IS A GOOD IDEA?
JUST HOLD STILL ONE SECOND LONGER...
BZZZZZZ
THAT WAS AWESOME! WHAT SHOULD WE DO NEXT?
WHAT DID YOU SAY? IS SOMEONE TALKING? I CANNOT HEAR ANYTHING ON THAT SIDE.
HOW ABOUT WE PLAY TRUTH OR DARE?
I WILL PLAY THE TRUTH OR DARE. I CHOOSE TRUTH.
WHAT'S THE WEIRDEST THING ABOUT BEING ON EARTH FOR YOU?
HMMMM...

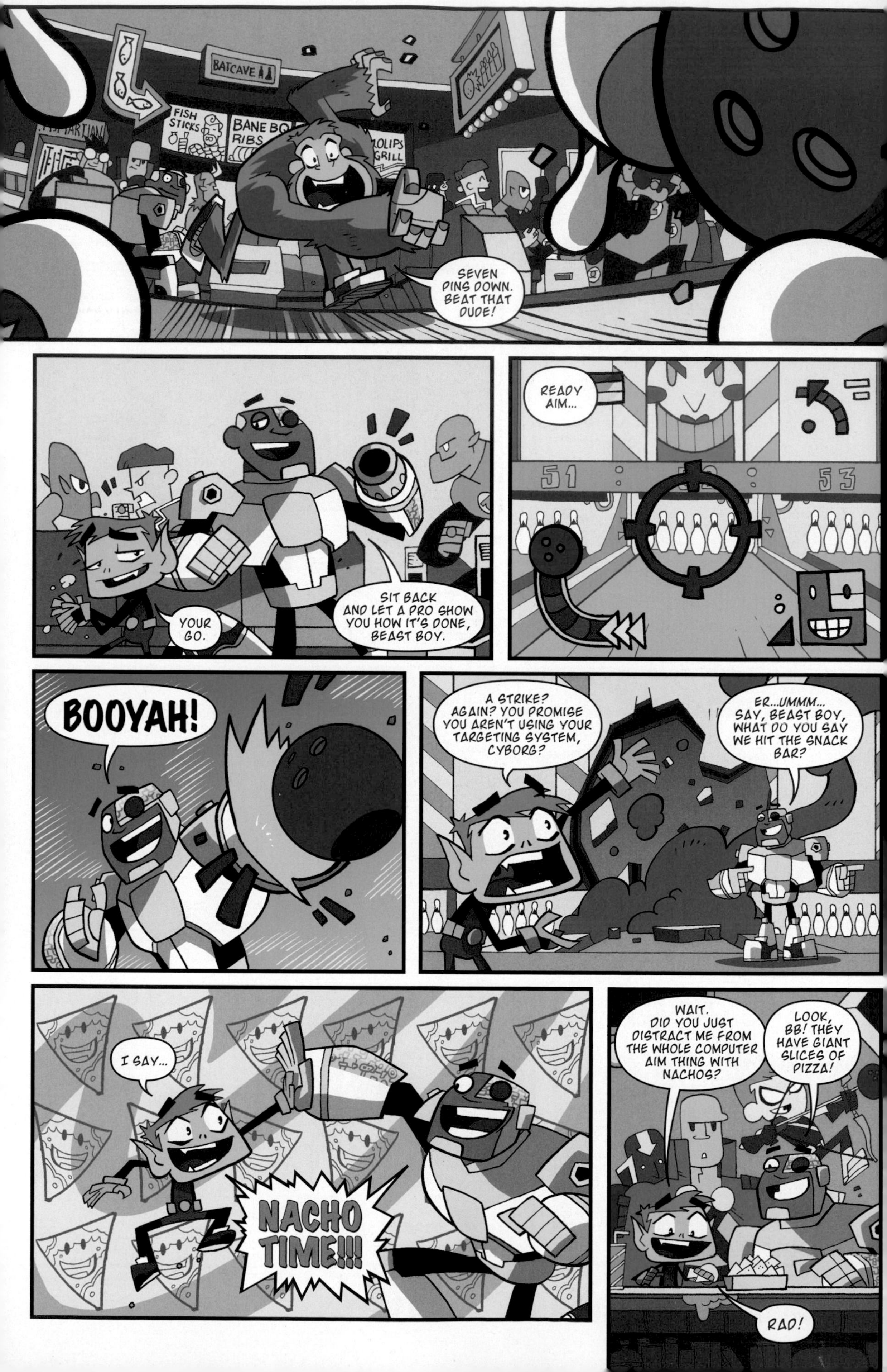
BATCAVE
FISH STICKS
BANE BQ RIBS
APOKOLIPS GRILL
SEVEN PINS DOWN. BEAT THAT DUDE!
YOUR GO.
SIT BACK AND LET A PRO SHOW YOU HOW IT'S DONE, BEAST BOY.
READY AIM...
51
53
BOOYAH!
A STRIKE? AGAIN? YOU PROMISE YOU AREN'T USING YOUR TARGETING SYSTEM, CYBORG?
ER...UMMM... SAY, BEAST BOY, WHAT DO YOU SAY WE HIT THE SNACK BAR?
I SAY...
NACHO TIME!!!
WAIT. DID YOU JUST DISTRACT ME FROM THE WHOLE COMPUTER AIM THING WITH NACHOS?
LOOK, BB! THEY HAVE GIANT SLICES OF PIZZA!
RAD!

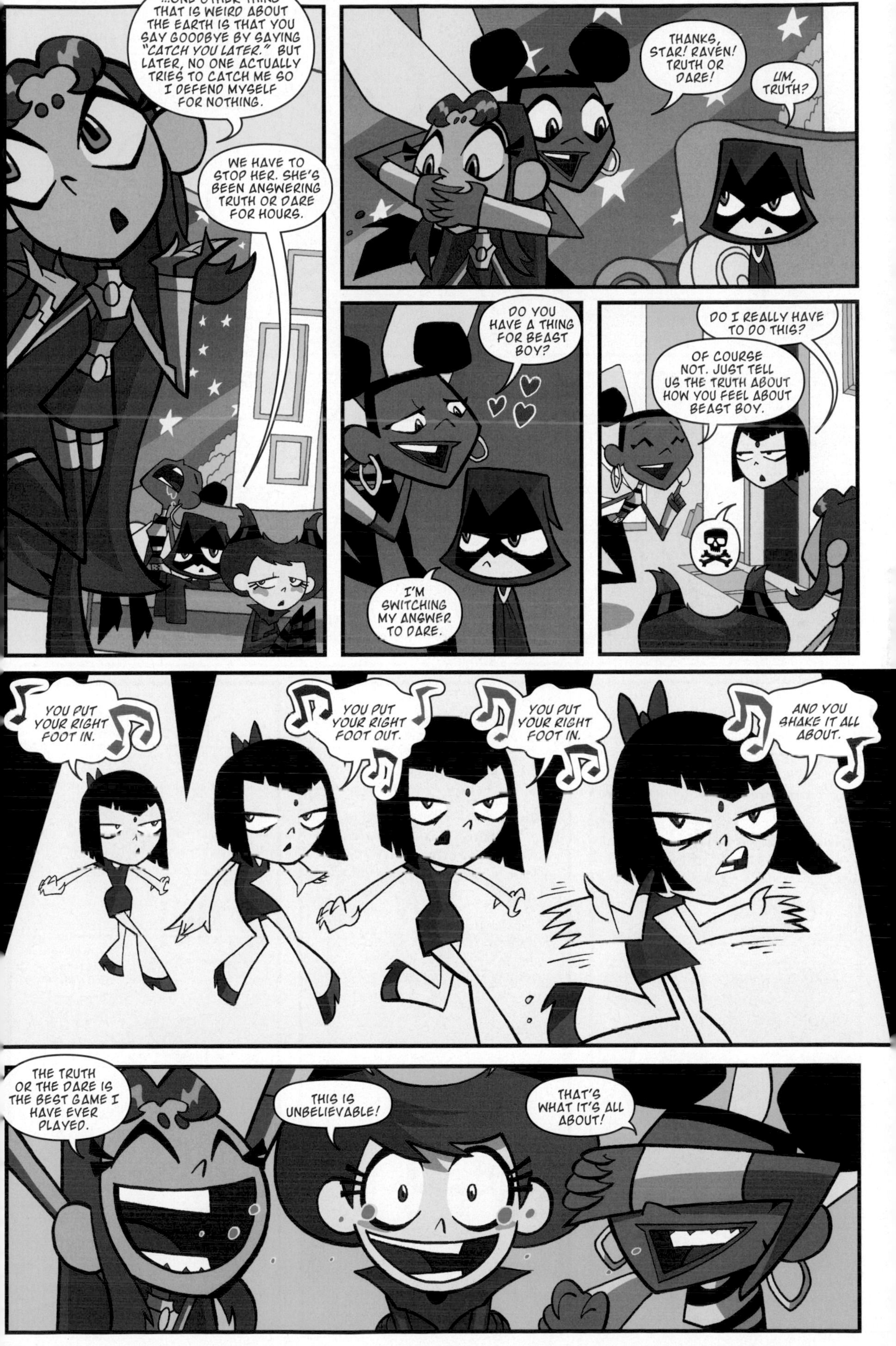
...ONE OTHER THING THAT IS WEIRD ABOUT THE EARTH IS THAT YOU SAY GOODBYE BY SAYING "CATCH YOU LATER." BUT LATER, NO ONE ACTUALLY TRIES TO CATCH ME SO I DEFEND MYSELF FOR NOTHING.
WE HAVE TO STOP HER. SHE'S BEEN ANSWERING TRUTH OR DARE FOR HOURS.
THANKS, STAR! RAVEN! TRUTH OR DARE!
UM, TRUTH?
DO YOU HAVE A THING FOR BEAST BOY?
I'M SWITCHING MY ANSWER TO DARE.
DO I REALLY HAVE TO DO THIS?
OF COURSE NOT. JUST TELL US THE TRUTH ABOUT HOW YOU FEEL ABOUT BEAST BOY.
YOU PUT YOUR RIGHT FOOT IN.
YOU PUT YOUR RIGHT FOOT OUT.
YOU PUT YOUR RIGHT FOOT IN.
AND YOU SHAKE IT ALL ABOUT.
THE TRUTH OR THE DARE IS THE BEST GAME I HAVE EVER PLAYED.
THIS IS UNBELIEVABLE!
THAT'S WHAT IT'S ALL ABOUT!

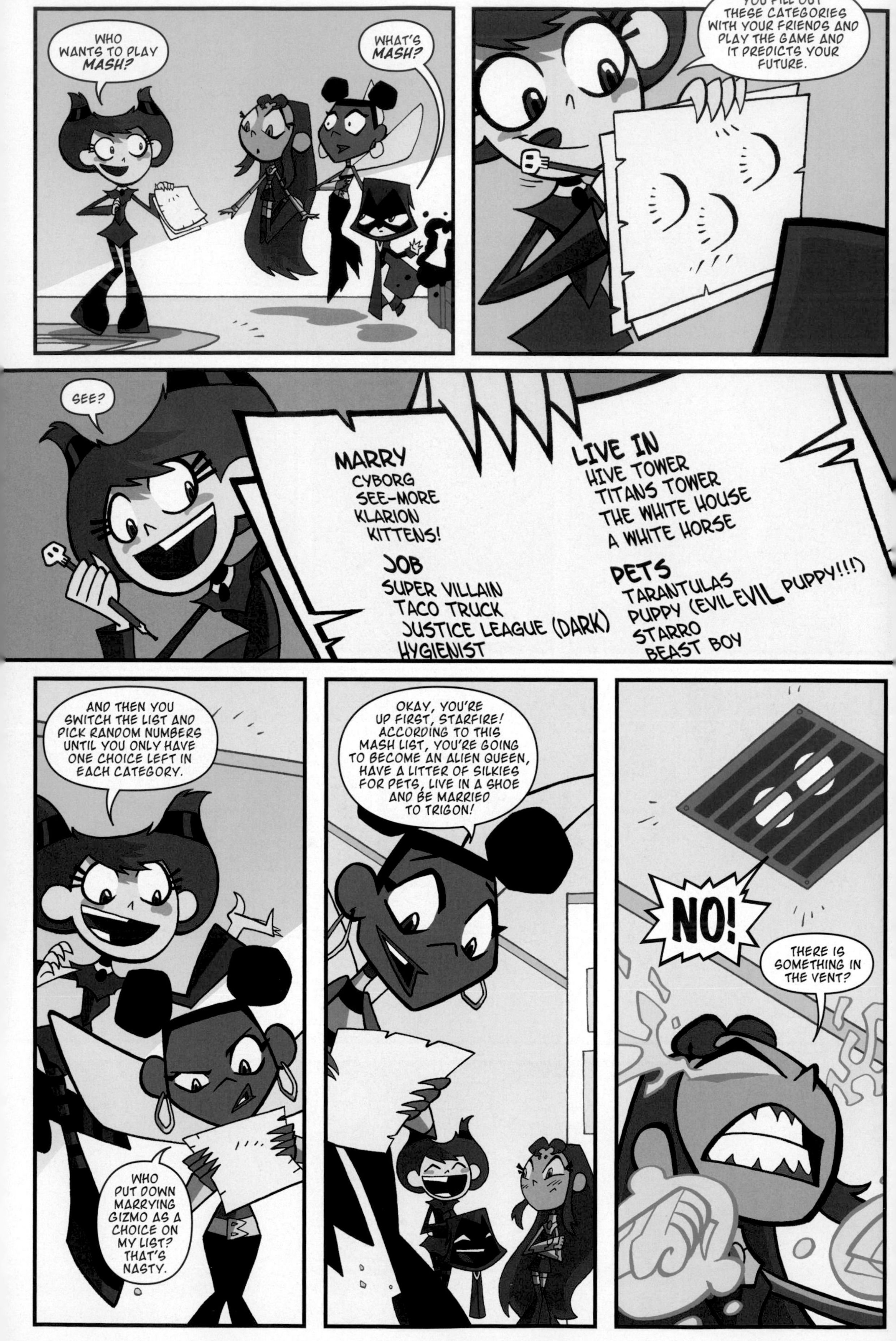
WHO WANTS TO PLAY MASH?
WHAT'S MASH?
YOU FILL OUT THESE CATEGORIES WITH YOUR FRIENDS AND PLAY THE GAME AND IT PREDICTS YOUR FUTURE.
SEE?
MARRY
CYBORG
SEE-MORE
KLARION
KITTENS!
LIVE IN
HIVE TOWER
TITANS TOWER
THE WHITE HOUSE
A WHITE HORSE
JOB
SUPER VILLAIN
TACO TRUCK
JUSTICE LEAGUE (DARK)
HYGIENIST
PETS
TARANTULAS
PUPPY (EVIL EVIL PUPPY!!!)
STARRO
BEAST BOY
AND THEN YOU SWITCH THE LIST AND PICK RANDOM NUMBERS UNTIL YOU ONLY HAVE ONE CHOICE LEFT IN EACH CATEGORY.
WHO PUT DOWN MARRYING GIZMO AS A CHOICE ON MY LIST? THAT'S NASTY.
OKAY, YOU'RE UP FIRST, STARFIRE! ACCORDING TO THIS MASH LIST, YOU'RE GOING TO BECOME AN ALIEN QUEEN, HAVE A LITTER OF SILKIES FOR PETS, LIVE IN A SHOE AND BE MARRIED TO TRIGON!
NO!
THERE IS SOMETHING IN THE VENT?

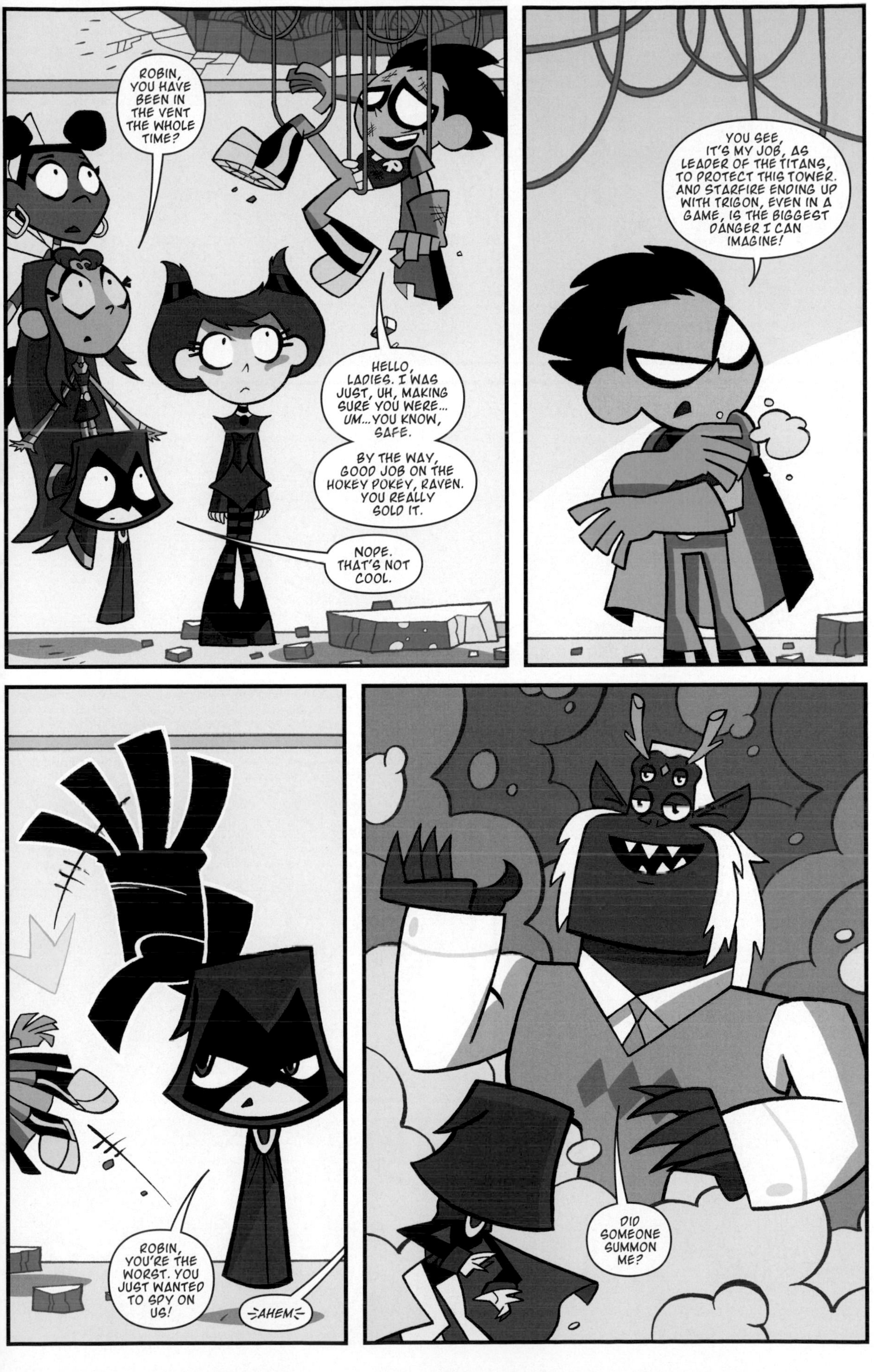
ROBIN, YOU HAVE BEEN IN THE VENT THE WHOLE TIME?
HELLO, LADIES. I WAS JUST, UH, MAKING SURE YOU WERE... UM... YOU KNOW, SAFE.
BY THE WAY, GOOD JOB ON THE HOKEY POKEY, RAVEN. YOU REALLY SOLD IT.
NOPE. THAT'S NOT COOL.
YOU SEE, IT'S MY JOB, AS LEADER OF THE TITANS, TO PROTECT THIS TOWER. AND STARFIRE ENDING UP WITH TRIGON, EVEN IN A GAME, IS THE BIGGEST DANGER I CAN IMAGINE!
ROBIN, YOU'RE THE WORST. YOU JUST WANTED TO SPY ON US!
AHEM
DID SOMEONE SUMMON ME?

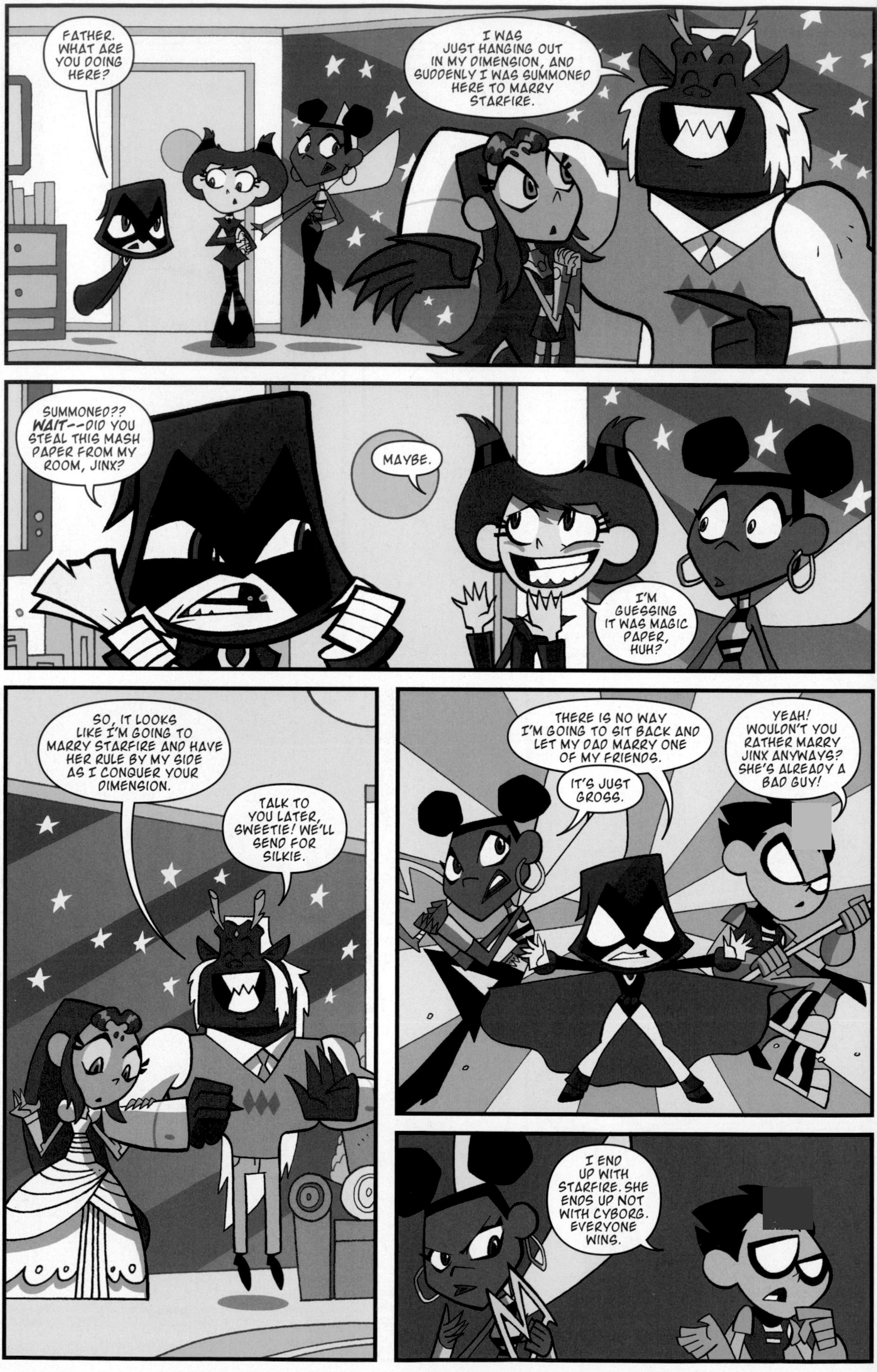

FATHER. WHAT ARE YOU DOING HERE?
I WAS JUST HANGING OUT IN MY DIMENSION, AND SUDDENLY I WAS SUMMONED HERE TO MARRY STARFIRE.
SUMMONED?? WAIT--DID YOU STEAL THIS MASH PAPER FROM MY ROOM, JINX?
MAYBE.
I'M GUESSING IT WAS MAGIC PAPER, HUH?
SO, IT LOOKS LIKE I'M GOING TO MARRY STARFIRE AND HAVE HER RULE BY MY SIDE AS I CONQUER YOUR DIMENSION.
TALK TO YOU LATER, SWEETIE! WE'LL SEND FOR SILKIE.
THERE IS NO WAY I'M GOING TO SIT BACK AND LET MY DAD MARRY ONE OF MY FRIENDS.
IT'S JUST GROSS.
YEAH! WOULDN'T YOU RATHER MARRY JINX ANYWAYS? SHE'S ALREADY A BAD GUY!
I END UP WITH STARFIRE. SHE ENDS UP NOT WITH CYBORG. EVERYONE WINS.

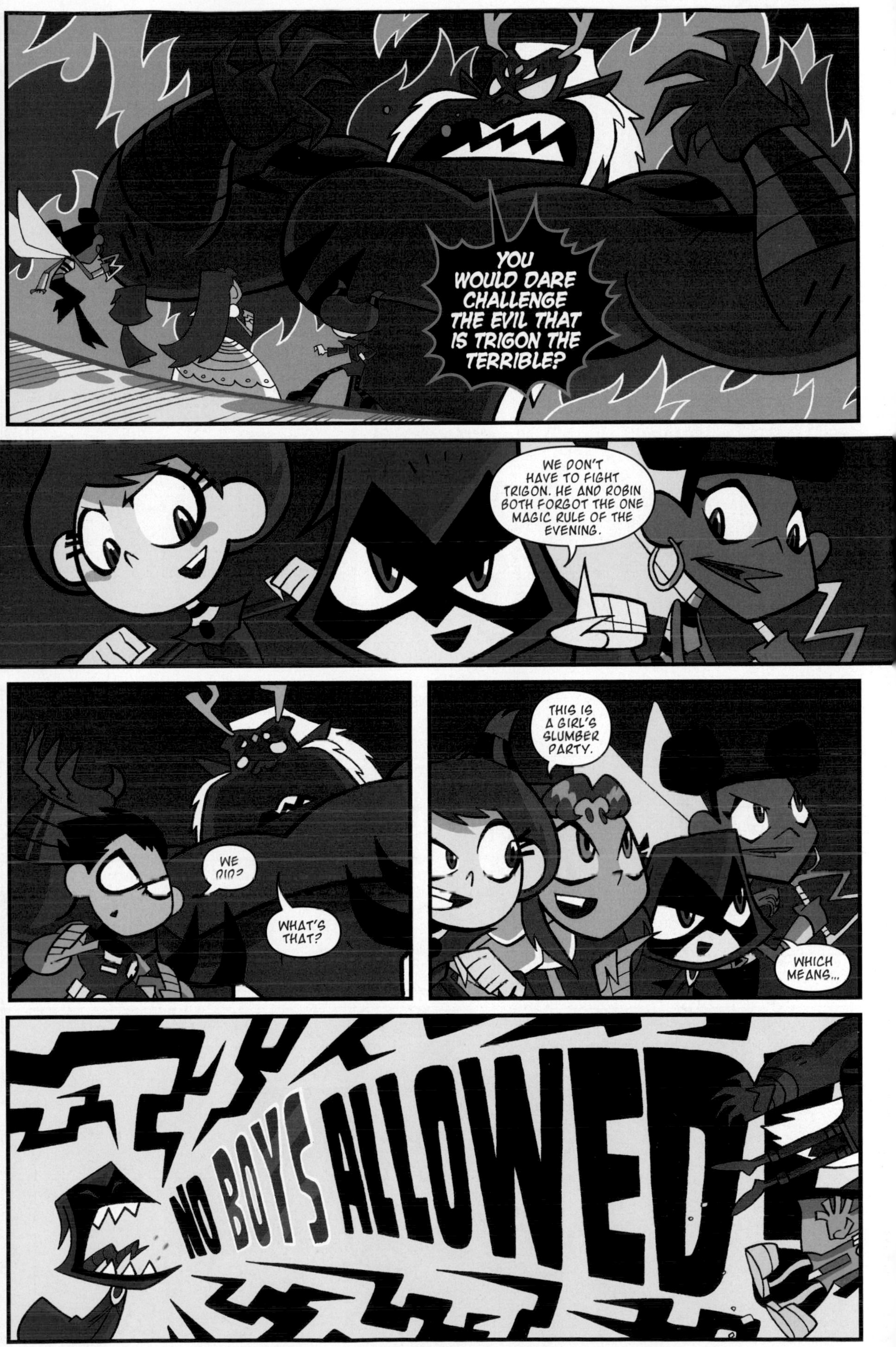
YOU WOULD DARE CHALLENGE THE EVIL THAT IS TRIGON THE TERRIBLE?
WE DON'T HAVE TO FIGHT TRIGON. HE AND ROBIN BOTH FORGOT THE ONE MAGIC RULE OF THE EVENING.
WE DID?
WHAT'S THAT?
THIS IS A GIRL'S SLUMBER PARTY.
WHICH MEANS...
NO BOYS ALLOWED!

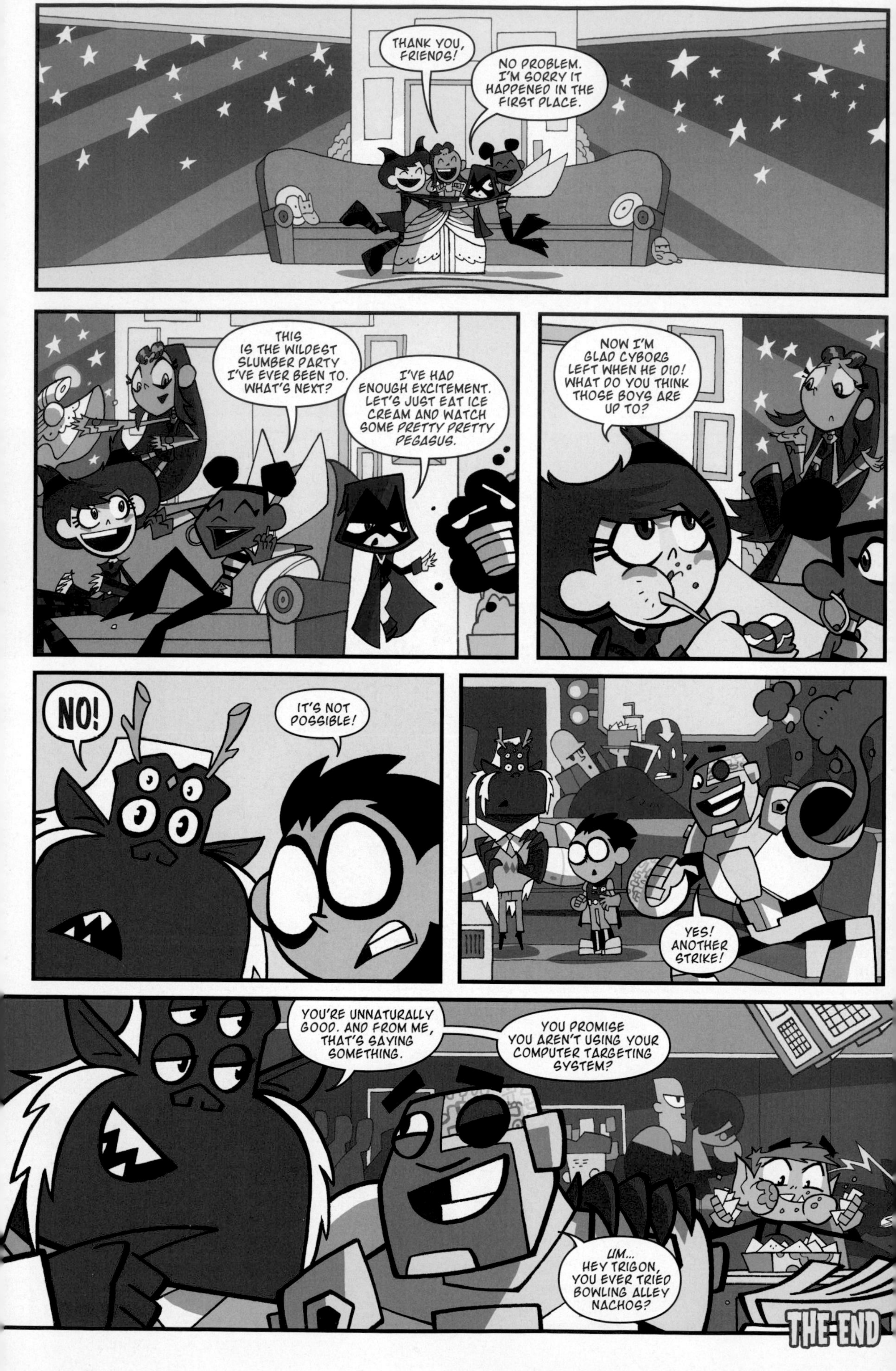
THANK YOU, FRIENDS!
NO PROBLEM. I'M SORRY IT HAPPENED IN THE FIRST PLACE.
THIS IS THE WILDEST SLUMBER PARTY I'VE EVER BEEN TO. WHAT'S NEXT?
I'VE HAD ENOUGH EXCITEMENT. LET'S JUST EAT ICE CREAM AND WATCH SOME PRETTY PRETTY PEGASUS.
NOW I'M GLAD CYBORG LEFT WHEN HE DID! WHAT DO YOU THINK THOSE BOYS ARE UP TO?
NO!
IT'S NOT POSSIBLE!
YES! ANOTHER STRIKE!
YOU'RE UNNATURALLY GOOD. AND FROM ME, THAT'S SAYING SOMETHING.
YOU PROMISE YOU AREN'T USING YOUR COMPUTER TARGETING SYSTEM?
UM... HEY TRIGON, YOU EVER TRIED BOWLING ALLEY NACHOS?
THE END